Thorns in Eden

&

The Everlasting Mountains

By

RITA GERLACH

Revised 2 in 1 Collection

Dedication

On the corner of Bentz and 2nd Streets across from the majestic stone Methodist church in the historic district of Frederick, Maryland, is a plot of ground where the remains of Revolutionary War patriots lay beneath green sod.

Their chiseled tombstones are buried with them, their names now unknown to those whose feet tread over them while visiting the War Memorial and the Ten Commandments Stone.

This book is dedicated to those brave patriots who fought for America's liberty, whose names are written in the Book of Life.

And…

To all those in need of courage in the face of danger, peace in the midst of trouble, comfort in a time of loss, and hope in moments of despair.

Be of good courage, and he shall strengthen your heart, all ye that hope in the Lord. Psalm 31:24 KJV

The Maryland Wilderness
1773

John Nash shoved back the brim of his hat and gazed up at the night sky to find the North Star hoping he would make it to the border before dawn. He urged his horse on and drew near a sycamore marked with three notches, its mottled bark bright in the moonlight where it had stood for a hundred years or more as a guide.

He touched the grooves and looked down the road to see the Monocacy. The river, called by the tribes *the river with many bends,* ran troubled and lapped against the deeply cut banks. Age-old trees shadowed the water with dark quivering forms.

The rider with him drew his horse alongside. "It's hard to believe three hours ago we were sitting in a corner of Mrs. Charlton's tavern in Fredericktown discussing over a pint of ale the trail we should take."

Nash nodded. "Less, talk. We are not out of danger yet."

"You don't mind me calling you Jack, do you?"

"Everyone else does. Now, please be quiet."

The man shifted in his saddle. "Right you are. Sorry. Not another word."

Nash moved his horse at an ease gait, aware the letters tucked into the lad's saddlebag would implicate men good and true if confiscated. Franklin wanted the allegiances of the Frederick County gentlemen who opposed English rule. Men like Thomas Johnson and John Hanson guaranteed the leaders in Philadelphia powder mills along the Monocacy and Antietam Rivers, as well as an iron furnace for cannon and gunlocks in the Catoctin Mountains. In addition to these, Frederick County would provide an arsenal, military prison, and the best musketmen in the Colonies.

They had gone a quarter mile when the horses flicked their ears. Nash's horse, Meteor, raised his head, snorted and pawed the ground. In the distance, lights trembled through the trees, and campfire smoke drifted in the breeze.

The courier sniffed the air. "British soldiers. I can smell their dirty uniforms a mile away. Why their foulness floats on the wind."

Nash put his hand against the hilt of his flintlock and steadied his horse with the other. "Unless you want them to see us, be quiet." He spoke in a firm whisper, then nodded for his charge to follow.

They turned their mounts in another direction. The horses stepped over the path's soft ground. A torch rounded the bend. The coats of two soldiers appeared red as garnets. In their white breeches and crossbelts, they stood out in the dark like marching phantoms. Moonlight struck the brass of their muskets.

Nash released a long breath. "God, help us." He halted his horse, and laid his pistol against his thigh. His eyes locked onto an officer on horseback.

"Halt! Who goes there?"

A soldier raised a musket. Another rushed forward and ordered them to dismount. A cold sweat broke out over Nash when a soldier stepped up to him and shoved the tip of his musket into Nash's ribs. He clenched his teeth, kicked the musket aside. The soldier stumbled back and his musket fired.

The officer's saber swung toward him, sliced through his sleeve, grazed his skin as if it were butter. Cold blue eyes met his in the moon's eerie glow. The sword swung high again. It arched toward Nash with a *whoosh*. He turned his horse and fired his pistol. The officer dropped his sword and slumped forward.

With no time to lose, Nash dug in his heels and galloped his horse past the officer. At the break of a ridge, he looked back. The courier shook from head to toe and followed him for his life.

CHAPTER 1

Ashburne House, Cornwall, England
September 1773

Rebecah Brent drew her legs beneath her and glanced over at the jittery servant sitting in the armchair next to the fire. She tried to appear unmoved by the storm's rage thinking it would calm Margery Holmes, but every time thunder boomed, her breath snatched and she gripped the letter harder in her hand.

"Oh, this storm…my poor nerves," Margery muttered. "Dear me…the wind…It seeps straight through the windows."

"I'm sorry, Margery. What did you say?"

Margery pulled her woolen shawl tighter across her shoulders and shivered. "The wind—it blows through the windows."

Rebecah folded the letter closed that had come earlier. "Ashburne is an old house. Drafts are to be expected."

Sighing, Margery stood and tidied the room though it was already neat. Everything was in its place, with a place for everything. Rebecah knew the woman's nerves were on edge and keeping busy gave her ease. But when lightning flashed, she jumped.

"Heavens!" Margery dropped a pillow on the floor, retrieved it and held it against her bosom.

Thunder shook the windowpanes. Wind whistled down the chimney. The room grew colder, the fire smaller. The old retainer set a log in the hearth, stirred the ash and embers until it caught. Flames grew. Wood crackled.

Orange light flickered over the bricks, over the floor. Now she would be warm. If Margery would light more candles and close the curtains the lightening would not overtake the darkness. It would appear less fierce with more light in the room. But candles were a luxury they could not afford to waste. She had to make do with the one on her bedside table.

The warm glow touched Rebecah's face and eased through the blanket over her lap. She glanced at the window. A flash and then darkness and a candle flame.

The storm frightened her, yet she hid her fear by opening her father's letter again. The words blurred as she listened to the wind and rain. Dread rippled through her. Perhaps she needed to read his missive again—search between the lines.

Time to settle down and enjoy his estate, he wrote. She knew what it meant. She would be married off to the highest bidder—to a man she did not love.

Is there such a thing as true love? What choices do I have other than Lanley?

Indeed, for no one else had asked for her hand.

How can I go against Papa's wishes? I hope he listens and allows me to explain.

After a second read, she set the letter on the table beside her. Rain streaked the windowpanes. For a moment, she fixed her eyes on a single drop. She watched it rivet down the glass, melt at the bottom. The mantle clock ticked on. The minutes dragged closer to the hour he said he would arrive.

By the hour strike, she stepped to the window, leaned against the jamb and searched the sky. A cold ebony vault, then an illumined violet cavern hung over Ashburne like a heavy hand.

The clatter of coach wheels rolling over the high road, mingled with thunder. Between the lightning flashes, she saw horses pounding their way toward the house. She leaned closer, watched the brass lanterns sputter. The coach slowed, pulled to a stop. The horses pawed the gravel, shook the rain from their manes.

"Margery, come look. My father is home."

She hurried away from the window, took Margery by the arm and drew her back. They stood side by side gazing below. The coach door opened. A man dressed in a black cloak stepped out. He turned back, reached inside to aid another—Sir Richard.

"My father is wearing the red cloak I made him."

"Aye, he is…That man is helping him up the stairs."

"It must be because of the wind."

"I'll go down, Miss Rebecah. You stay here."

Rebecah frowned. "I remember the rule. Whenever Papa arrives home I must wait to be called."

She sat on the side of her bed when Margery left, listened and waited. She gripped both arms as if cold air rushed over her. Then she crept to the door. Grasping the handle, she opened it, drew in a breath and peered out.

Huffing and puffing, Margery came up the staircase. Rebecah watched three men lag behind. Grave faces. Dripping wet cloaks. Muddy boots.

Before she saw her father's eyes she shut the door, though she wanted to rush out to him, throw her arms around his neck and kiss his cheek. But he would chastise her for any emotional greeting shown to him in front of others.

Margery turned back inside. Candlelight from the candle she held spread over her plump face. "Not a pleasant evening for a homecoming."

"Did he ask for me?"

Margery gave her a look of sympathy. "No."

It hurt. Perhaps he needed time. She handed Margery her brush, and the older woman glided it through Rebecah's long tresses.

"I didn't see Lanley with him. I'm relieved. I have not seen him in three years…I hope he stays away forever. He has as much appeal as an undertaker."

Margery twisted a lock and fastened it behind Rebecah's ear. "Your father desires you to speak well of the choice he's made."

"You know as well as I, Lanley does not love me."

"But his gifts and letters say he has an extreme fondness for you."

"Shall I mention his indecent morals and lack of charity? He has no faith in God."

"Would you rather be a missionary's wife living in some heathen country, than be wed to the lord of the manor?"

Rebecah laughed. "Can you imagine Lanley a missionary? The heat would cause him to swoon. The food would upset his delicate constitution. The natives would frighten him to death. In a week, he'd pack up and head back to England to his creature comforts."

"You paint a vivid picture, miss."

"I would marry a missionary for love."

"I cannot see you marrying such a man. Life would be too harsh for you living among the tribes."

"Perhaps I shall find myself such a man."

"Poor? Is that what you want?" Margery looked appalled.

"No. I wouldn't wish to starve. What I mean is I want a man with a noble heart."

Margery smirked. "It is not good for a young woman to be so wishful."

"I suppose you're right." Rebecah glanced over at her door. "When is Papa going to call me?" Anxious, she slipped on her shoes. "He must realize I am a grown woman now. Not a child."

With a touch of her hand, Margery stopped her from going on. "Go softly. He is unwell."

10

"Why did you not tell me?"

"He said I mustn't upset you."

While Margery spoke, Rebecah hurried out the door. She rushed down the corridor toward her father's bedchamber. Mucky boot prints led from the staircase right to the threshold. The door sat open, and she paused outside it.

"The infection has grown worse?" she heard her father say.

"It's very bad," an unfamiliar voice said. "What's the army getting for field surgeons these days? Village butchers, or Indian witch doctors? You would've been better off to have stayed in America, then to have made the sea voyage back to England and gotten into trouble. There must be at least one competent doctor in the King's army."

"It was my choice. England is home. My daughter is here." Her father's raspy voice distressed her. He did not sound the way she remembered, strong and disciplined.

"True. Nevertheless, it will cost you dearly, Sir Richard. The infection will spread."

A chill rippled over Rebecah's skin. Her heart sank to her soles. A pause followed, then, "In the name of heaven, what did they use for stitches—horsehair?"

"Leave me alone. Call my daughter."

Stepping through the door, Rebecah entered the room. Her father lay in the four-poster bed he once shared with her mother, pillows piled behind him, a counterpane covering him up to his chin.

With the utmost care a man in a tight gray wig, unraveled bloodstained bandages. She shuddered when she saw the infectious lesions invading her father's bicep. The shriveled arm streaked red and molting, shook at the physician's touch.

Beads of sweat glistened on Sir Richard's forehead. Rebecah wanted to save him, heal him, take away the pain. She went on her knees at the bedside and held her father's hand.

"Papa?"

11

The physician glanced at Rebecah over the rim of his spectacles. "Young woman, it is best you leave the room."

"He needs me, sir. I will stay."

In the past, Rebecah's father had always returned hale and hearty, blustering through the front door, barking out orders to servants, with his hounds leaping and baying around him. When she first read his letter saying he meant to come home, she thought he was in good health. But now to see him mortally wounded, she repented of her feelings, of thinking of herself, of what his homecoming meant for her.

His eyes were closed. Did he not hear her, feel her hand close over his? His face ashy, his breathing shallow, his movements stilled. The surgeon asked if he could speak with her outside in the hall.

"I did not want your father to overhear in case he woke."

Rebecah's throat tightened. "Is my father dying?"

"He's in danger." He removed his spectacles. "The bullet was removed carelessly in my opinion, a sloppy job, and the wound sutured with I know not what. Infection set in and inflamed the arm. It is amazing he lasted this long."

"Do you know what happened?"

"I've been asked not to divulge the details." He held out his hand. It had blood on it. "I'm Dr. Harvey, by the way."

"Forgive me for not shaking your hand, sir." She glanced at his hand and he withdrew.

"Oh, I beg your pardon." He placed it behind his back.

"If you remove the arm, will my father live?" she asked.

"He has a better chance. I've administered mercurial ointment, wrapped the arm in warm cloths soaked in vinegar, and bled him before we made the journey here. There has been no improvement."

"You mustn't let him die. He is all I have in the world. I lost my mother a few years ago. I'll do whatever you ask. Money is not an issue. I must go to him."

"I promise to do all I can. I'll bleed him again from a larger vein and draw out a substantial amount of blood. It will help purge the infection from his body."

"That you're willing to try, sir, gives me ease."

"Pray for your father. It's the best thing you can do for him."

Together they returned to Sir Richard's room. With each step she took, Rebecah made an anxious plea to God.

* * *

Night grew old and Sir Richard's fever grew more intense. Wind groaned against the house. Rain pelted the windows. A candle sputtered and his mouth moved in silent speech.

With his condition worsening, Dr. Harvey wished to go on with the procedure. He shook his head as he examined the wound.

"I cannot wait any longer, Miss Rebecah. Your father has passed into a stupor and will not feel it. If we wait any longer, I fear he will die."

The horror of losing her father gripped her. She lifted the candle from the table and moved closer. "I pray God will lead your hand, sir."

"Thank you. I'll do my best. Please have your servant bring in a bowl and pitcher of water."

Margery hurried out, her rapid footsteps tapping down the stairs. With dread, Rebecah watched Dr. Harvey apply a tourniquet. She bulked at the putrid smell coming from her father's arm. Listening to his labored breathing brought tears to her eyes. She wanted to cry, but managed to hold them back.

Dr. Harvey opened a leather box lined with red velvet. He lifted the felt cloth covering his surgical tools. The amputation saw, the curved knife. The instruments reflected the quiver of the hearth fire. Distraught, Rebecah scanned her eyes over them. A chill rippled up her spine, passed like ice water through her veins.

"Fill the bowl, if you please," Dr. Harvey told Margery. She poured water from the pitcher, and brought the bowl to the bedside.

"Hold the candle closer, please," Dr. Harvey said when she stepped back. "Hold him down, Ralph."

The assistant laid the weight of his body across Sir Richard's chest. Then Dr. Harvey bent his head and leveled his tool. Forced to be strong so not to be put out of the room, Rebecah fought the faint feeling in her head. She took in a breath, released it and drew in another. But nothing could calm the rapid beat of her heart.

Harvey looked over at her. "You may want to look away, Miss Rebecah. This is not for your eyes."

She turned her face, shut her eyes. The grate of the surgeon's saw cutting flesh, through muscle, then bone, pained her through and through. Her poor father did not deserve this. The sharp metallic scent of blood, the rancid smell of contagion, assaulted her, made her sick.

Tears pushed against her eyes. *How much longer? What if he wakes?*

Shivering, she closed her eyes and waited for it to be over.

The mantle clock ticked on. The fire in the hearth seethed. Her hand shook as she gripped the candlestick tighter. The clink of the surgeon's tools tossed into a tin pan brought some relief. But she was afraid to look, to see her father changed.

"Take it away, Ralph," she heard Dr. Harvey say.

While her heart lurched inside her breast, she listened to the creak of hinges, then the latch. Rebecah opened her eyes. Gore stained the sheets. Doctor Harvey dipped his hands into the bowl of water and washed. Rebecah shut her eyes when he wiped then in a towel and she saw the stains.

"I'll need to give Sir Richard laudanum as soon as he wakes. It will keep him calm. I've nowhere else to be, so I'll sit up the rest of the night with him. Have you a bed for my assistant?"

"My maid will show him to a room." She turned to Margery and gave her instructions. Dr. Harvey sat in a chair near the fire, and within minutes dozed off. Rebecah drew her wrap over her shoulders, set another log on the fire, and waited by her father's bedside.

Several hours later, a high wind shoved the rain southward, and dawn rose. Rebecah's father turned his head and gazed at her with a painful glint in his eyes.

She smiled at him. "Hello, Papa. I know I was supposed to wait, but I couldn't help it. I hope you're not disappointed in me."

"Never." He tried to rise. "No feeling in my arm, daughter. No feeling."

Barely could he speak the words. His voice raspy and low, gurgled from a dry throat. She gave him water, and he coughed. With trembling fingers, he shoved the glass away, reached over to touch his septic flesh, the cotton bandage, the stump. His face turned white, and he let out a ragged cry.

Tears sprang into Rebecah's eyes and she embraced him. "It's alright, Papa."

"That self-righteous Methodist took off my arm," he cried.

She tried to soothe him, touched his face. Dr. Harvey bolted from the chair, urged Sir Richard to be calm. Rebecah took the flask of laudanum from his hand and spooned it into her father's mouth. "It'll help, Papa."

She leaned forward and kissed his cheek. He looked at her and she realized he had lost the will to live. Such sadness and despair were in his eyes. Such fear.

"I'm no longer a whole man. What is left for me now? You should have married before I left. Then I would not be grieved you will be left alone."

Sir Richard reached for Rebecah's hand.

"You'll not die, Papa. We'll have good times together again. I learned to play backgammon while you were away. Remember you told me to learn so you could beat me?"

Fear seized her as his eyelids fluttered and closed. She spoke to him. She held his hand tight, pressed it against her cheek. Margery stepped closer and Rebecah turned to her. The look on her face broke Rebecah's self-control. She went into her arms and wept.

"Come, away. He's at peace and no longer in pain."

Rebecah looked into her father's face. Though he had been good to her, his reckless spirit had driven him into a military career. He had gambled away his inheritance, died a penniless, broken man, whose achievements were meager in the eyes of the world. Nevertheless, to his credit was the love he had for his daughter.

Wiping the tears from her eyes, she leaned over and kissed his forehead. She moved away from the bed to the window, opened the sash and felt the breeze, allowed it to quiver the curtains.

"I'm deeply sorry." Dr. Harvey touched her hand. "I tried to…"

"I do not blame you," Rebecah said. "There is no one to blame—except the man who did this, and my father for being so careless with his life."

CHAPTER 2

Near the Monocacy River in Maryland

John Nash drew in a lung-full of air and gazed at the foothills shadowing his land. Dogwoods, oaks, and maples shimmered in the light of an autumn sun.

He brushed back his hair and put on his slouch hat. "I hate to leave, Joab," he told the man standing beside him. "Watch over my land while I'm away."

Joab nodded. "I will, Mr. John. It sure is a pleasant place. The good Lord blessed you."

Joab, age sixty, once a slave, was now a freeman thanks to John Nash. His eyes had remained clear and sparkling in spite of the hard years he had lived. His hair, speckled with gray, receded above his forehead.

John Nash put his hand on Joab's shoulder. "You know, I believe one day you and your descendants will own land."

Joab shook his head. "I haven't any family that I know of."

"You have me." Nash smiled.

Old Joab chuckled. "Indeed I do. I'll stay with you until the day I die."

"Well, for now, while I'm away, think of this place as your own. You're master in my absence. Don't let Mrs.

Cottonwood bribe you into working for her while I'm gone."

Joab let out a quiet laugh. "I don't mind helping her when I can. She's a widow, and the good book says I'm supposed to help widows and orphans. Now don't it?"

"Yes, you're right. But she'll take advantage of you."

Tramping through the leaves, they reached the road that bordered his land. Nash wore his fringed hunting shirt and moccasin boots.

"Excuse me for asking, Mr. John, but what's those round your throat?"

"Indian beads given to me by Logan."

"The Indian chief of the Virginias?"

"Aye. I won the chief's favor after spending time in his village along the Yellow River."

"Must've been long time ago."

"Time enough, before I bought my land here. Logan was impressed when I wrestled his strongest warrior to the ground in a friendly match."

"I sure would've liked to have seen that."

Nash looked back over his shoulder. "I've not chosen a name for this place."

Joab scratched his head. "It'll come to you sooner or later."

"Got any suggestions?"

"Nash's Choice? Or how about River Bend?"

"Those are good. But I don't know. How about Laurel Hill?"

"Good as any, Mr. John. There's lots of mountain laurel growing in the hills."

"Laurel Hill it is. I'm glad that's settled."

The dwelling stood two stories, the window glass made in the Catoctin furnace. It had been hard work building the house, digging out stones from mountain and field, hauling them to the site, laying them with mortar. Neighbors from all over the county had come to raise the small barn.

18

From where he stood he smelled the sweet waters of the Monocacy and Potomac rivers. The currents flowed pure and crystal, teaming with bass and sunfish. Jeweled dragonflies hovered above muddy flats in hoards. Swallows wheeled above the water in search of insects, their black wings sharp and their underbellies yellow in the light of a ruby sunset.

They spoke of other things as they strode along. A stag and young doe sprang from the woods and leaped across the field. Nash watched them until they disappeared. The unexpected thought of living alone without a woman made him feel empty, incomplete.

Pulling down the brim of his hat, he walked beyond a hedge of evergreens. "It's going to be strange in England. I've been gone so long. But I must see my father. No king was ever easy to let part of his kingdom go. King George is no exception. My father does not like the King's politics, and if war comes, his views could bring him grief."

"He'll be glad to see you, Mr. John, especially if the Revolution lasts a long time."

As the last light of day disappeared over the mountains, Nash saw a whirl of dust round the bend. A horn blew from the coachman's trumpet and he held his hands high in the air for the coachman to see him. Nash's horse stiffened his ears, reared his head and whinnied.

Nash patted Meteor's neck. "Take care of him, Joab. Don't let him get into any clover."

"I won't, Mr. John. Nothing but straw and oats for him."

Nash handed the reins over, took hold of Joab's hand and wished him well. Then he climbed inside the coach packed with people heading for Annapolis.

Joab twisted his hat between his hands. "Mr. John, I ain't got much. So I was hoping…"

Leaning out the window, Nash smiled from one corner of his mouth. "I'd bring you back a gift? What could you want from that misty island, Joab?"

"A new pipe and it doesn't have to come from England. Bring one from Annapolis on your way home."

With a wink, Nash touched the brim of his hat. "You'll have your gift, my friend. Stay well."

The coachman snapped his whip and the horses carried on. A cloud of rust bellowed out from beneath hoof and wheel.

"Headed for England, are you?" a passenger asked.

"Yes, for a visit only, though I cannot say I'm looking forward to the voyage."

"By your clothes I'd say you were a settler in these parts. But to go to England says you might be loyal to the King."

"He lost my loyalty a long time ago. I'm going back to see my family. Revolution is coming and I may not have another chance."

"Aye, 'tis true," the man agreed. "So you plan to return?"

"I must. I have land here, and like every able-bodied patriot, I aim to protect it and win my liberty."

The man's wife, a woman slim and gray, set her hands over her lap. "You plan to bring back a wife? That is if you don't have one already."

"Marriage is the least thing on my mind, madam."

"Why not?"

Nash shrugged. "I haven't met a girl smart enough to lure me into those bonds any time soon—an English one I would disregard completely."

CHAPTER 3

Raising the coach shade, Rebecah looked back at the brick gables of Ashburne House. Closing her eyes, she searched for strength, for she grieved in innumerable ways and this was one more thing added to it. The father and mother she adored were gone, and Ashburne was now in the hands of her uncle.

Raindrops on the ivy sparkled in the evening light. Fog drifted into the woods where tall hemlocks imprisoned shadows. The dank scent of dusk gave way to autumn rising from the drenched earth.

Margery leaned forward. "You'll like Endfield. You've two cousins near your age there."

Twisting the fringe on one of her gloves, Rebecah sighed. "I'll miss home."

"For a time. Endfield is much closer to society. No doubt, there'll be parties and outings, and more than likely your aunt will have you stay a season in London."

"London is too far."

"True, but the journey is part of the experience."

The coach rolled by a row of poor tenant houses. Barefoot children played with a stick and an old rag made into a ball along the road. Rebecah slapped the roof of the coach. "I want to give them money."

Margery frowned and settled back. "If you give them a penny their father will waste it on drink."

The horses slowed and the coach eased to a halt. Rebecah climbed out.

"Oh, don't go near those children," Margery warned. "You'll catch something."

Ignoring her maid, Rebecah gathered her skirts and walked down the rutted road, her cloak flapping in the breeze. Holding close her hood, she called to the children whose expectant eyes grew fixed on the lady coming their way.

Rebecah handed them each a coin and looked into what she knew were sweet faces underneath the grime. "I saw a farmer down the road selling apples. Perhaps this is enough to buy some."

The children thanked her. Off they ran in the direction of the farmer.

Rebecah turned back. Margery glared out the coach window. "I caught nothing. No need to give me such a look."

Margery scooted back. "Hurry before the cold soaks through your shoes."

Settled in her seat, Rebecah pulled her gloves tighter. As the coach traveled on, she looked out at the countryside. Her thoughts changed now from admiring its beauty, to the plight of impoverished children. How many of them were orphans too?

After a pause, she reached over and patted Margery's hand. "Why are you angry with me? I did a good thing."

"You're too compulsive for a young woman. Your uncle will not tolerant you wasting money on beggars."

"It was mine to give."

"You'll not be allowed to ride bareback at Endfield, I would think. And your aunt will force you to wear shoes all the time."

Rebecah smiled at her opinionated servant. "Then I shall run away the first chance I get back to Ashburne."

Margery rolled her eyes. "Oh, don't think of it. You deserve better than what you've had."

"For instance?"

"Friends and the company of young gentlemen of quality for a start."

"I cannot bear to hear this sermon repeated."

Margery gasped. "Well, I try to find the right words hoping you'll agree."

"I cannot be fitted into a mold, Margery. I'll resist."

"No doubt Lanley will visit Endfield and want you to."

"He can *want* all day, and I'll not change."

"You must admire something in him."

"I haven't dwelled on him enough to know."

"He's witty and handsome, and dresses so well."

"I agree, he dresses very well, though a little too extravagant for my liking. However, I disagree on all other counts. His wit is dry, and he is not at all good looking."

"Beauty is in the eye of the beholder," countered Margery.

"I'll give him credit for his fine manners, but he is lethargic as a snail, Margery."

"You misinterpret a quiet disposition for lethargy, miss."

"He has been too lazy to visit Ashburne. It is not grand enough for him."

"Well, now that your uncle owns it, perhaps he'll restore it to its former beauty and Lanley will appreciate it more."

Rebecah changed the subject. "How far is Endfield?"

"We should arrive by nightfall," replied Margery. "I do hope they feed us. I'm starved for a heavy dinner."

"I'm hungry, too."

"That's a good sign. You've hardly eaten in days."

"I not dare ask for a meal when we arrive."

"Had your father taken you to Endfield often, you'd be more at ease."

"I think I was there twice in my life. I don't know my relations at all."

"There's more to family than father and daughter."

Rebecah nodded. "We were close, and I adored my mother. We were happy when she was living."

"It is not my place to say. But why he kept you from your cousins, I'll never understand."

"He called Uncle Samuel a scoundrel."

Yet he would tell Rebecah it was a virtue to think the best of people, to bless and not curse, to bend and not stiffen. His estranged relationship with his brother always baffled her though. A portrait hung in the hall at Ashburne of the two brothers as children. Their long brown curls made them look like a pair of cherubs instead of mischievous boys.

"Must've been a quarrel that parted them," Margery sighed. "The last time I saw of Samuel Brent was at your christening. What a handsome man. But his eyes were proud, unlike your father's."

"I too have wondered what caused the rift between them. Papa died without reconciling with his brother."

"A sad affair they made of it. Perhaps your uncle will make things right now that you're under his roof."

Rebecah's face remained turned to the window. The sky grew thick with clouds and rain fell in soft airy sheets.

Margery eased back and closed her eyes. Rebecah watched her with affection. How could she do without Margery? Surely, her uncle would allow her to stay.

They rounded a bend and through the gloom Rebecah saw the manor atop a hill.

"Ho, coachman!" A voice called out.

A man and boy stood to the side. The coach halted and she heard the man speaking to her driver. "The bridge is out. Move the coach off the road. You'll have to unhitch the horses and lead them."

The door swung open and a face appeared. "Good evening." He had a warm smile. "Your uncle left me instructions to meet you. The bridge over the stream is out and the wheels will get stuck. I'll have to carry you over."

Margery moved her charge back. "How are we to know you speak the truth and aren't a highwayman? Maybe you mean to rob us."

The man pointed to the house. "Is that not my master's house?"

Margery set her mouth. "I suppose it is."

"There's no question, is there?" He handed his son the lantern. "My name's Henry Carrow."

Taking Henry's hand, Margery climbed out first. She squealed when her shoes sunk into a puddle. Henry chuckled and led her to a dryer patch of ground.

"We'll have those toes of yours warming by a fire shortly."

Next, he lifted Rebecah into his arms. She pulled the edge of her hood close to her face against the rain. Margery held her skirts higher than propriety allowed.

"I'm not about to have my best petticoat ruined like my shoes…Oh, this wind is too much."

"Stay close behind me," Henry advised. "This large frame of mine makes a good wall against the wind."

Henry sloshed through ankle-deep puddles, stepped into tracks and grooves made by other coaches and horses. Afraid he might slip and fall, Rebecah gripped his shoulder tighter.

The stream flowed in a glassy ribbon of black. Its surface rippled with large stones and on each side tall grass swayed and bowed with the weight of the pelting wind. Henry told Margery to stay where she was. He stepped into the stream. The water whirled around his legs.

Rebecah put her face toward his shoulder.

"Don't fear, miss. I'll get you across safely."

Within minutes, he set her on the other side. He turned back. Then he lifted Margery and took her over. Safe now, he put the serving woman down. He went to lift Rebecah again.

"I don't mind walking," she told him. "I can slip my shoes off."

"And catch your death? I'll not be responsible if you do."

She pushed back the rim of her hood and looked ahead. "So this is Endfield House?"

"Aye, miss."

The trees were old and majestic. Rambling ivy clung to the stone facade. Candles sparkled in the lower windows, beautiful amber amid the gloom. The scent of cedar fires burning in the hearths blew through the chimneys. She could not wait to sit by one and get warm.

Henry carried her all the way to the front steps when the door opened. Candlelight lit the interior of the entryway. The cold stare of an old woman confronted Rebecah. Dressed in black, and wearing a lace cap, the woman stepped closer. She skimmed her eyes over the newcomer without a smile.

"I'm Mrs. March. Welcome to Endfield."

"Thank you." Rebecah drew back her hood and tried to smile. "I'm Rebecah Brent."

"I know who you are." March crossed her hands over her waist. "We were expecting you earlier. I suppose the roads delayed you."

The tone of voice, the chilly stare, caused Rebecah's heart to sink. The prospects of a happy life at Endfield faded. A discerning heart told her March was an unfeeling woman.

"Go back where you belong," March jerked her chin at Henry. "You don't belong in the house."

Rebecah frowned at her thorny prejudice, and waited for Henry to retaliate. Instead, he gave March a smart look and stepped out the door. A gust of wind whirled inside as he closed it, and Rebecah's thoughts turned once more to a fire and a soft bed.

Margery helped with her cloak. "Miss Rebecah is weary from her journey and chilled to the bone. Please show us to her room."

March stared down her nose. "This is your servant?"

"Yes. Margery has been in the family's service for decades."

"She's permitted to stay the night. Follow me." March proceeded up the staircase. "In the morning the coach will return her to Ashburne. Those are Sir Samuel's orders, and he's never questioned."

Rebecah had not expected this and paused on the staircase with Margery. "I will speak to my uncle."

March turned. "Do not hope to dissuade him."

Rebecah tasted the desire to put the old woman in her place. March was a servant, below her. She should be hers to command, not the other way around. Surely, her uncle would grant her this one request.

Margery reached over and touched Rebecah's hand to calm her. March proceeded up the stairs.

"Food shall be brought to your room. Afterward, I will show you to the library. Sir Samuel is due back within the hour and shall want to speak with you."

They followed March to a long gallery. Through the candlelight, Rebecah glanced at the paintings on the walls. Portraits of her male ancestors stared severe and dark. The painted flowers in the women's hands were blood red roses. In their eyes, Rebecah noticed longing stares. Were they speaking to her out of the past?

Tread bravely upon the path chosen for you.

Nearing one bedchamber, she heard the patter of feet. The door opened and a shaft of light crossed the floor near her. Wide blue eyes stared at her with happy curiosity.

"Are you Becah? I'm Hugh." The child announced his name with a proud lift of his chin.

Rebecah bent down. "Yes, I'm Rebecah."

"We are cousins?"

"Yes, and I hope we'll be friends."

27

"Only if you know how to play soldiers and will read to me. My sisters don't." He frowned a moment. "I know how to fish, too, and catch dragonflies."

"I'm impressed. You are young to know such things." She caressed Hugh's head, and he smiled.

"Where are your brothers and sisters?" He looked past her. "Where are your mother and father?"

"I haven't any brothers or sisters, and my parents are in Heaven."

He screwed up his face and fumbled with the doorknob. "I could be your brother."

"I would be pleased." Touched by his innocence, she kissed his cheek.

March's shadow fell over the boy like a dark cloud. She tapped the toe of her shoe on the hard floor. Hugh lost his smile and the bright gleam in his eyes vanished. Rebecah drew him close, wanting to protect him.

March glanced at her. A challenge flashed in her eyes. "Master Hugh, get to bed at once, before the rod lies upon you."

A curl fell over his teary eyes and he dashed it aside. "It is cold in my room."

"Have you that dog in there?"

Hugh meekly nodded.

"You know your father's rule. Send the beast out."

With a regretful swing of his hand, Hugh's forlorn greyhound trotted out the door and down the stairs. Rebecah saw the anger in the boy's eyes, sadness caused by more than the loss of his dog.

Crouching, she met his eyes with a warm smile. "Perhaps in the morning you and I can play catch with your dog."

At once, a proud gleam returned. "I've seen her catch rats."

"She is a good hunter?"

"Yes, and I know where there's a badger's den."

"I would like to see it."

28

Hugh squared his shoulders. "Someday I'll be master of Endfield, and have lots of dogs and they will go everywhere with me." He stepped away. The door clicked shut.

"The hour grows late." March moved on and Rebecah followed the gaunt figure down the long corridor. She took out her key ring and opened a door. After drawing the draperies shut, she left the bedchamber without a word.

"Lord, forgive me for judging her, but March hasn't a kind bone in her body." Margery drew off her shoes and set them in front of the fire.

"I do not fear her." Rebecah warmed her hands.

Margery unpacked with agitation. A pool of tears glazed her eyes and rolled down her cheeks. Grieved to see her troubled, Rebecah put her arms around her servant's shoulders. "Do not worry. I will speak to Uncle Samuel."

Margery shook her head. "Whatever he decides, we must accept."

Rebecah brushed a tear from Margery's cheek. "He will see my way."

The door drifted in, and blonde ringlets appeared. "Dear cousin. Welcome to Endfield. I'm Lavinia."

Lavinia's eyes were ocean-blue and her face looked like porcelain. Were they really cousins? The difference between them was striking.

She grasped Rebecah's hands. "You've no idea how glad I am you have come to us."

"You are kind to say so. But I feel like an intruder."

"You mustn't. We will be good friends."

"And your sister?"

"Dorene is a spoiled, vain creature."

"I met her once when we were children."

Lavinia pouted. "Is it not sad we were kept apart? I shall never understand why. Are you going downstairs as soon as my father arrives home?"

"I am." Rebecah reached over and took a bit of cake from the tray the maid brought in and tasted it.

Lavinia touched the lace on the edge of one of Rebecah's dresses. "Wear something else when you do. No one in the family is permitted to wear black or gray, except for March, only because it suits her, the old crow."

Margery spoke up. "Miss Rebecah has lost her father. No one mourns at Endfield?"

Lavinia frowned. "Of course we do."

Rebecah looked for something else to wear. "I had intended to shed my mourning clothes. Will these please him?" She held up the sleeves of two gowns.

Lavinia eyed the folds of silk. "Wear that one. I will see you in the morning. Sleep well."

When she had gone, Rebecah began to undress.

"First, I'm commanded to Endfield. Then I am told I no longer have a say in what happens to you, Margery. Next I'm told by my cousin what I can and cannot wear." She sighed. "I don't like it, and fear my independence will get me into trouble."

"Be obedient. Less trouble."

"I mean no disrespect. I'll grieve in my heart, silently all to myself."

"You don't mean to wear that dress, do you?" Margery scoffed at the dark blue silk Rebecah held against her.

"It is the best I have. First impressions, you know."

A knock fell upon the door.

Her uncle had summoned Rebecah downstairs.

CHAPTER 4

Rebecah waited alone in the library. The walls, covered in an unusual shade of green, were bare except for one painting of a rolling countryside. She admired the trees, the sun-streaked sky, and the shepherd with his flock of sheep. Birds circled above a willow and a lone steer stood beyond a split-rail fence.

The library was magnificent compared to her late father's. Purple velvet curtains hung over the windows. High-backed chairs and a Turkish carpet embraced near the hearth. The fire crackled and seethed, mingled with the tap of rain against the window.

On one wall were shelves filled with books. Rebecah's eyes skimmed over the meticulous rows. There were classics and a variety of rare volumes. She noted the books on Latin and Greek, the historian Josephus and Homer. Bound in leather were works of Shakespeare, Dryden, Swift, and Defoe. She would not lack for something to read.

She felt the heat of the fire caress her skin and she turned to it. Upon the rug lay the greyhound, whose sad eyes looked her way. The dog stood, stretched, and wagged its tail.

"Hello, girl." She ran her hand over the dog's sleek fur. It nuzzled closer, and then moved away. A shadow fell across the floor.

"Her name is Jess." Brent's smooth, refined voice startled her. "She's a good dog with a gentle nature."

He stood tall and broad shouldered, handsome. But his eyes were severe. He wore a coat of dark brown with matching breeches and hunting boots. An air of haughtiness marred his face. His dark hair, tied with a broad black ribbon, had gray at his temples.

"Uncle Samuel." She lowered her head and curtseyed.

"You had a tiresome journey, I hear."

"Yes, Uncle." She raised her eyes.

"Well, you may go to bed when we finish talking." He moved near the fire and poured himself a brandy. He took a swallow, and paused to study her face. "Come here, Rebecah. Let me look at how you've grown."

She did as he commanded. She noticed his hands were large, his fingers long, touched by fringes of lace from his cuffs. He took her chin in hand and turned her face from side to side. She did not like his touch.

"You favor your mother." His tone disturbed her. "She was graced with beauty and fire. Have you fire, Rebecah? Can you keep the jackals at bay?"

She looked away. "I don't understand your meaning."

"I speak of men. My daughters are lovely, but you are far superior in looks. Your voice is appealing, and I think the inner anger that rages within a man may be tamed by your soft inflection."

Rebecah lowered her eyes at his forward words.

"Your father was anxious for you to marry a rich man with a good family name. But that's all I can say Lanley has in his favor."

He motioned for her to sit, and she went to the chair across from him. She had hoped he would not bring this up.

He looked at the amber liquid in his glass. "Look how the light plays within this, how it moves with a twitch of my hand. Women are the same. Sweet, yet they can burn…I received a letter from Lanley yesterday. He'll pay

us a visit soon after his return to England. He's anxious to
see you again—anxious to marry."

"But I am not." She hoped he'd agree. But by the stern
expression on his face, her expectations were dashed.

Brent raised one eyebrow. "You think by waiting you
will find true love?"

"If there is such a thing, would it not be worth waiting
for?"

"What you seek does not exist." He sipped his brandy.
"You resent what I said about your mother?"

She saw pain in his eyes at the mention of her mother.
What had Sarah Brent meant to him? "Why should I
resent any compliment you pay her?"

"Why indeed?" He set his empty glass aside. "I'm sure
you know your father and I were not on the best of terms."

"Even so, blood is thicker than water."

Brent laughed. "What does it matter? Richard is dead."

Rebecah stared into the fire. Her uncle's words stirred
her grief. The image of her father's last moments rose in
her mind and she felt the sting of death again.

Her uncle called Jess over to him. He stroked the dog's
ears. "Now that my brother lies cold in his tomb beside his
wife, he thrusts you upon me."

Dread flooded Rebecah. So this is what her uncle
thought of her?

*He sees me as a burden. What have I done to deserve
it?*

Determined to endure this first meeting with her uncle,
she rallied her courage. "If I am a burden, Uncle, allow
me to return to Ashburne."

"That would be wrong. You are my niece." He moved
the ring on his left hand with his thumb. "What talents
have you?"

"I play the spinet, though ill I believe. I draw and ride
well."

"Your cousins enjoy riding. Your aunt did at one time.
But after a fall last summer, she shows no interest."

"When will I meet her?"

"I'm afraid she has retired with a headache." Jess nuzzled his hand and he slipped his finger beneath her collar and rubbed her neck. "You'll meet her in the morning."

"She shall meet me now, Samuel."

Lady Kathryn entered the room dressed in apricot colored silk. Her long hair fell across one shoulder. Light from the fire reflected upon her skin. The perfect oval of her face matched the large eyes of deepest brown and her well-formed lips. Rebecah felt the tenseness ease with her aunt near, especially when she stretched out her hands in welcome. They embraced and Lady Kathryn kissed her cheek.

"What a pity you have come to us under these circumstances, Rebecah. I'm sorry for your loss. Does your room please you?"

"Very much so. Thank you, Aunt."

"Good. If there is anything you need, you must tell me."

Rebecah paused to take in a long breath. Now was the time to speak about Margery. "There is one thing…"

"Yes?"

"I would like to retain Margery Holmes. Please don't send her back to Ashburne. She has been with me all my life."

A look of displeasure rose on her uncle's face. "Out of the question."

Lady Kathryn stepped forward. "Let her stay, at least until Rebecah grows accustomed to us."

He stood and his shadow fell over Lady Kathryn's face. "Richard may have indulged her, Kate. I cannot. Do our daughters have private servants? To have another would be a waste of money. Rebecah will make do with what we have."

"Perhaps Margery could assist our girls too, Samuel."

"We've enough servants."

34

"I'll be happy to pay the woman's wages."

"I'll not have my lady pay a servant out of her purse."

Wishing she had held her tongue, Rebecah clasped her hands together and lowered her eyes. Her uncle's lashing out at Lady Kathryn was her fault. "Forgive me. I spoke out of turn. I should go."

"You'll leave when I say," Brent told her.

Rebecah dropped her hands to her sides. She realized to let him see she feared him showed weakness. With her resolve growing stronger, she met her uncle's eyes. "Then we have more to discuss, Uncle?"

"No, the discussion is over."

"Samuel." Lady Kathryn took a step forward. "We could make this one allowance, for a short time. It isn't much to ask."

He stiffened and Jess whined. "The answer is no, Kate."

"My love, I have never questioned you before, but…"

"Do not start now." With a sigh he lowered himself into his chair and shut his eyes.

"I'm sorry," Rebecah said. "It was selfish of me. I should not have asked. You've done so much for me already. Please do not think me ungrateful."

"Well, at least you admit when you are wrong, Rebecah. I accept your apology."

She looked at him without reply. Out of duty and respect she'd obey him. It struck her. Samuel Brent had made up his mind not to love her. Eaten with bitterness, blind and hardhearted, would he ever change? She would have to endure living with him for a time, but he would not be a permanent part of her life.

Lady Kathryn squeezed her hand. "Go to bed now, Rebecah. Sleep well."

Rebecah leaned forward and kissed her aunt's cheek, then in a soft voice, "Good night, Uncle." Then she strode from the room.

Upstairs in her room, a fire blazed in the hearth and lit the room in a sepia glow. Her empty trunk sat on the floor near the bed. She closed the door and noticed the absence of a key.

"Is all well, miss?" Margery helped her unlace her bodice.

"I cannot talk about it, Margery. But I'm to lose you." She wiped the tears from off her cheek. Margery let out a heavy sigh.

The drapes were closed. She went to the nearest, pulled them back, and looked out. "The moon is behind the clouds."

Out on the road beyond the gates, a curious shape emerged, like a man on horseback with dark cloak and hat. Rebecah leaned nearer.

"What is it, miss?"

"I cannot see in the dark to know." Her imagination leapt within. Her saddened heart pounded.

Beside her now, Margery peered out the window. "It's the gate swinging on its hinges."

"I think you're right. Where will you sleep?"

"In the servant's quarters upstairs. Goodnight, miss."

After Margery left her, Rebecah stepped away from the window and slipped under the covers. She shut her eyes and hoped to drift off. It proved hard. To be in a strange place, in a bed not her own, made her lonely for home. She tried not to think of Ashburne, of Endfield, the loss of her father, and now Margery. But her mind would not let go.

She turned to prayer, not as a ritual, but an outpouring of her heart to her maker. She spoke to him until her lips could move no more, until the clock in the hall struck the quarter hour and she fell to sleep.

CHAPTER 5

A ship from the American Colonies loaded with tobacco, furs, and sassafras, quietly laid anchor. John Nash leaned against the rail, his memory stirring. Nothing had changed since the day he had left England.

In the distance, he could see the enormous bell tower and steeple of Saint Charles Church plunging into the sky. It seized Nash's heart like the churches back home. The clustered spires shot into the sky like giant spears, piercing silvery clouds, stretching toward Heaven.

Thinking about them caused him to feel homesick.

A seaman leaned over the rail. "As I recall there's a tavern a block away that serves good English ale. Will you not join us, Mr. Nash?"

Nash swung his bundle over his shoulder. "Thank you, Mr. Guthrie, but I must be on my way."

"Do it while you have the chance. When you sail back home, you'll not taste English ale for a long time."

"You may be right. But I prefer Boston beer."

He threw him a salute and walked away. A female voice hailed him. "You there. You in the strange clothes."

A coach and four waited on the street. A young woman poked her head outside the window and held down her wide-brimmed hat with a gloved hand. Her brown ringlets fell over her throat. Rice powder paled her face, and on her cheeks were two bright spots of rouge. Beside her mouth, the black patch she wore looked like a tiny mole.

Nash stopped and stepped up to the coach. His clothes were not as fashionable as the men passing him, but was he all that different? Perhaps it was the Indian beads about his neck she saw. She gazed at him breathless. "My companions and I see by your attire you're not from our country."

"I've come from the Colonies, ma'am."

Her eyes faltered and met his again. "Will you come with us to a gathering we are headed to? You'd bring us a great deal of attention. We'll pay you two guineas."

Nash stiffened. "I'm not for hire."

She looked baffled. "But two guineas."

"If you're anxious to part with your money, I suggest you give it to those poor wretches lingering on the street corner."

She followed the direction of his eyes. "Are they hungry you think?"

"I've no doubt they are."

"I wonder how it feels." She paused and one of her friends nudged her. "Oh, will you not reconsider?"

"Sorry. I must be on my way."

Unmoved by her further pleading and the overtures of her companions, Nash moved on. Outside the bustling city, he trudged his way to a road wide enough for a horse.

He had been away for five years and, with the war inevitable, he longed to see his parents while he had the chance. They lived in a country house, where in his mind's eye he saw them seated by the fire with their dog curled on the rug.

His father in his reckless youth traveled across the ocean to try his hand in Virginia. The only success he made was a son by Charlotte Easton, the daughter of a planter. They were married six years and in sequence their babies came and passed away in infancy. Being of a gentle fortitude, Charlotte died after birthing their son, causing Sir Rodney to return to England with him in his arms.

Devastated by the loss of his wife, Nash's father drowned himself in his grief and loneliness until he met Margaret Lacey, cousin to Kathryn Brent. Within six months they were wed, and their years together were happy. As a boy, Nash thrived beneath Lady Margaret's gentle but firm hand. She was the only mother he knew, and he loved her with tireless devotion.

When he reached the glades of his childhood home, he paused in the road to gaze at Standforth House. It had not changed. The same thatched roof, the square mullioned windows, oak door, and front garden, livened his memories. The dog sitting on the doorstep perked its ears and sniffed. Then her shaggy tail wagged and she raced down the lane toward him.

"Toby!" He patted and rubbed the dog's coat, while it licked his face. "Good old gal, I've missed you."

A man in work clothes came around the corner of the house carrying a hoe. Wispy tufts of hair sprouted from the old fellow's ears and chin, and on the tip of his long angular nose was a large brown mole. One eye was blind, the watery pupil white, just as Nash had remembered. He stood in his tracks and stared.

"Is Sir Rodney and his lady at home?" the younger Nash inquired.

"Maybe he is, maybe he ain't." The man stuck out his chin and cocked his noxious eye. "What you want with him? If it's money, forget it. If food, come round the back."

Nash stood. "I want nothing but to see my father."

The man squinted. "Sir Rodney's son is in America."

"Your eyesight has weakened since I left, Angus."

The man stepped closer. "Scratch me raw, young Jack, 'tis you. You're dressed like a heathen."

"These are what I'm accustomed to wearing. Buckskin breeches are comfortable."

"Buckskin? I recognize those beads you're wearing from the last war. Never thought I'd see the day when an Englishman would wear them. What's the world coming to?"

"*The Thirteen*, sir." With a brisk stride, Nash walked to the door. Angus trailed behind him.

His father was in the habit of rising early and retiring late. He would be in his study reading the Gazette and his Bible. A biscuit would be on a plate and a cup of tea to the side. Nash opened the doors and stepped in.

The moment they laid eyes on each other, Sir Rodney dropped his cup. The china handle broke against the saucer. He scrambled from his chair. His son smiled. The same blue eyes graced with dignified lines glowed with fatherly pride. Dressed in a buff coat and cream breeches, Sir Rodney smelled of milled soap.

He searched for his spectacles and with trembling fingers, shoved the wires over his ears. "Jack!"

Though his name upon the baptism records in Virginia called him one thing, his father gave him the name *Jack*, for he thought it endearing.

"On my word, you've come back to us. Bless God." His smile broke into joyful laughter. "Your days of wandering have brought you home impoverished?"

"Not at all, Father. I've done very well."

"I'm glad to hear it. We've missed you." He threw his arms around Nash's shoulders and embraced him.

"Are you better? Have you recovered from your fall?"

"My ribs are good as new." Sir Rodney tapped his left side with his palm. "I still have the horse that threw me."

"Where is Mother?"

"Upstairs. You've no idea how she has missed you." Sir Rodney walked his son to the door. "She has kept you in her prayers since the day you left."

"That answers many things. I'm sure her prayers saved my life on more than one occasion."

Sir Rodney drew back and frowned. "You had a few brushes with danger? You must tell me about them over supper."

The morning sun spread over the wall, as Nash ascended the stairs. The Persian runner in the hallway quieted his steps. He approached his stepmother's room, noticing nothing had changed; the pictures on the walls, the candles on brass hooks, the blue velvet draperies.

Her door sat ajar and he saw her seated by the window in her favorite chair. Still beautiful, even though the radiance of youth had faded, ruby light touched upon her cheek. She drew her shawl close and turned a page in her book.

"Hello, Mother."

Startled, Lady Margaret dropped her book and leapt from her chair. "Jack," she cried. "You've come home."

He rushed forward, took her in his arms. "There, Mother. Don't cry. What's the use when I'm here safe and sound?"

She touched his face. "I cannot help it."

"You look well. You are well, are you not?"

"I'm better now that I see you. Has your father seen you?"

"Yes."

"He has no consideration for my poor heart." She laid her hand across it. "It is pounding so hard it might have burst. He should have warned me."

"I brought you something." Nash drew the beads over his head. "Let me have your hand." He turned her palm over and placed the gift there.

She held up a strand of beads of an unusual shade of orange. The stones caught the light coming through the window.

"Oh, so beautiful. How did you come by them?"

"An award given to me by an Indian."

Surprised, she glanced at him. "An Indian, you say? Why these must be rare indeed."

"Chief Logan is a peacemaker in the Virginias, and my friend."

"These are too rich for me. I'm not deserving of them." She wiped her eyes.

He closed her hand over them. "If I ever see Chief Logan again, I shall tell him you wear them proudly."

"I shall treasure them always. You must be hungry and tired, and in need of a bath. And those clothes. Is this what the gentlemen wear in the Colonies?"

"Only those living in the frontier."

Sir Rodney entered the room and she held out her hand to him to see the necklace.

"Look at what Jack brought me, dear. Are they not fine?"

"You'll be the only woman in England to own anything like them."

Lady Margaret turned to her son. "Tell us what you need, Jack, and you shall have it. We shall have a feast tonight."

"You need not spoil me, Mother."

"We must celebrate your homecoming." Lady Margaret grabbed him by the arm and embraced him. Toby leapt and barked, and Nash felt his heart lift.

There was more merriment in that house that day, than there had been in more than a year.

* * *

Rebecah could have allowed Endfield to suffocate her. But she refused to give in to its bleak atmosphere. She had found a sister in Lavinia, and they spent all their time together. She loved Hugh, and took every opportunity to take him out of doors, to the woods, stream, and fields.

Every morning she opened wide her bedroom curtains to let the sun in.

The day of John Nash's arrival in England, she sat at the spinet in the music room tapping out a tune. It grew cloudy outside, and her music cut through the dry monotony like a sunny day. Outside the door, servants hesitated in their work to listen. The piece she played was difficult. Rebecah lifted her fingers away from the keys and stared at the sheet music wishing she were better.

She glanced over at Lavinia. Reclining on the couch, she twisted a ribbon between her fingers and sighed.

"Are you weary with my playing?"

"You're playing is fine. But I'm bored to tears."

"Is there something you'd rather do? My fingers are stiff."

Lavinia sat straight up. "Yes. Let us go for a ride. There is a patch of blue along the horizon."

Rebecah could not refuse an invitation to escape. She hurried off to change and joined Lavinia in the stable. Slipping the bridle over the horse's neck, she kicked off her shoes and put her foot into the stirrup, clicked her tongue and flicked the reins. The mare trotted out of the stable into the sunlight.

"Rebecah." Lavinia called. "You cannot ride without boots. What will my mother say?"

Rebecah glanced over her shoulder. "She will never know unless you tell her. I also prefer to go without a saddle. But for your sake I shall endure one."

Lavinia rolled her eyes. "I should hope so."

Far from the house, they paused to give the horses drink from a brook south of Endfield. Rebecah pulled her hair free from its fastenings, shook her head and allowed the curls to tumble over her shoulders. She loved the feel of the wind through it, how it crossed her neck. Beyond the hill, she saw the Carrow's farmhouse. Forests were above it and to the north open hills met the sky.

Lavinia brought her horse alongside Rebecah's. "Your life has been sheltered, Rebecah. I think I may envy you for it in some ways. You seem so…free."

"I wish you wouldn't say such things, Lavinia. There is no reason to envy me."

"You do not understand. The only goal my father has for my life is that I marry well."

"I understand perfectly. It was my father's goal as well. Who can blame them?"

"Perhaps your view would be different if you had known our male cousin. Your father kept you from everyone."

"John Nash sounds more like fiction than fact, and may disappoint you if you see him again."

"I do not think so."

"Are you in love with him?"

"Indeed, not. Do you remember last week the young man who spoke to me and offered to carry our packages to the coach?"

"The lawyer?"

"You don't approve?"

"Of course I do. But it's not a question of my approval, but your father's."

Lavinia frowned. "I know. He wants me to wed a man with a title and plenty of money."

"One should marry for love."

"He has not said he loves me. But I see it in his eyes."

"Then there is hope. There's an understanding between you."

"Do you know what would happen if I married David without my father's consent?"

"He would disown you?"

"I believe he would. But I love David so much, it hurts. Why do we torture ourselves with love?"

Rebecah raised her face to the sun as it broke through. "I'll be spared the agony, for who would love me?"

She snapped the reins and galloped her horse ahead of Lavinia's.

* * *

Soon the sun skimmed along the horizon. The sky grew misty, painted with purple and vermilion. At the door, March stepped into the fleeing light. Her sour expression deepened while she tapped the toe of her shoe against the flagstone.

"Where have you two been? Supper is over, and the master is indignant. No doubt you've been riding through the countryside like a pair of gypsies."

"It was invigorating." Lavinia stepped by the old woman into the light of the window.

"This arrived earlier." March handed Lavinia a letter.

She took the letter in hand. "Do not tell my father."

"What letters you receive are none of my business, Miss Lavinia. I do not run to Sir Samuel about everything that goes on in this house. I know my place."

While Rebecah removed her gloves, March approached. "A gentleman awaits you in the music room."

"His name?"

"Sir Cecil Lanley. In this house, we do not keep guests waiting."

Rebecah pulled her cloak off and handed it to March. Reluctant to see him, she walked unhurried down the hallway and paused outside the door. She searched for time. She needed to calm her nerves, rehearse what she would say to Lanley. Perhaps she should have told March to tell the snobbish suitor she was ill with a headache. But he would return. She had to get it over with.

Her fingertips touched the latch. She turned the handle. The door moved in enough for her to hear Lanley speaking. She stepped back, but kept the door ajar.

"I've anticipated seeing Rebecah again," she heard the drawn aristocratic voice declare. It still had a nasal tone. "I intend to settle in the country, a suitable place for a young wife. The diversions of London would leave her fatigued."

His words affronted her. Like her father and uncle, Lanley meant to isolate her in a lonely country house. When she heard his insipid plans, her mind rebelled. It should be her right to plan her life—not the right of others.

CHAPTER 6

Inside the sunlit room, Brent stood by the window. His hands were clasped behind him, while he considered the man chosen by his brother to wed his niece. His mind drifted back to a time long ago when he declared his affections to Sarah. He loved her to the point of obsession, but she bruised his masculine pride too many times. His love turned to dislike the day she married his brother.

When he received word of Sarah's death, the pain was bearable enough to conceal from his new wife Kathryn, but fierce. And when his brother died, Sarah's image came to live under his roof. He found it difficult to love Rebecah, and saw Lanley as a means to be rid of her.

But the idea of his money and future connection to the family restrained his feelings. Why Rebecah? Why not Dorene or Lavinia? Could he sway Lanley's choice?

"You're rich and could have any woman in England." His words caused Lanley to raise his head. "Why not one of my daughters? They both have beauty and handsome dowries, unlike Rebecah who has near to nothing."

"I haven't the need for more money," Lanley told him. "I wish to marry Rebecah because I'm besotted. It's much like choosing a thoroughbred, would you not say?"

Brent frowned at the comment. "It's in poor taste to liken women to horses. Besides, you wouldn't know a quality filly if you fell over one."

Lanley wobbled his head. "Sink me if you're not right." He bent forward. "I know absolutely nothing about them."

Repulsion burned in Brent's mind, for Lanley was indeed a bored, spoiled dandy, overdressed and overused.

"You think my daughters are not good enough for you? Why would you prefer a girl who is below them?"

"Lavinia and Dorene are rich prizes. But I've been in love with Rebecah for a long time, and promised to wed her."

"Yes, I know about *the promise.*"

"Would you ask me to break my word? Do you disapprove of my suit?"

"A man is only as good as his word, Lanley. You may do as you wish."

The door drifted in and Rebecah stepped inside. Lanley stared at her with his mouth gaping. Brent watched with cold interest the influence she had on him, how he twisted his handkerchief between his hands and shifted on his feet.

Rebecah curtsied. Brent told her to come inside and close the door.

"Lanley has traveled far to see you. You should apologize for keeping him waiting."

"I was out riding. However, I did not change from my riding habit, after I was told you were here."

Lanley dabbed his mouth. "With anticipation nagging at me, I admit the wait proved difficult." He smiled, his gums red, his teeth a creamy yellow.

Brent moved Rebecah to the center of the room. "Well, I'll leave you to renew your acquaintance."

Lanley bowed his head. "Thank you, sir. *Adieu.*"

* * *

Brent had left through a door leading to the study. Rebecah hoped he could not hear beyond its walls. Lanley approached her, picked up her hand. He raised it to his lips. They were cold as chiseled marble, unlike the liquid fire burning within his eyes. Slim and dark, they were set against a gaunt face made ghostly white from the rice powder he had applied. His hair lay hidden beneath a wig tied by a black silk ribbon.

"Do you like my new suit, Rebecah?"

"It's nice."

"I bought it in Holland." The scarlet color cast a rosy blush beneath Lanley's pointed chin.

"Look at the embroidery on my waistcoat, and these pure silver buttons."

She did not answer.

His silk stockings shimmered, and his squared-toed shoes, polished to a high sheen adorned with silver buckles, covered his large feet. Rebecah thought he looked ridiculous.

Lanley was the picture of wealth, a paragon of everything aristocratic. However, stripped bare, this outer veneer covered a man of flesh and bones, weak and lacking in spiritual depth and virtue. His god was his money, and he turned up his nose at the poor, something she despised.

Lanley gestured for Rebecah to sit.

"I prefer to stand."

"I thought my attire would impress you, help you see how prosperous I've become."

"Oh, you intend to stay long?"

Lanley let out a puff of air from his cheeks. "I'm back in England for good. My father passed on and I have an estate to run. Have you no kiss, no embrace for me? I hoped you would be glad to see me. Are you not glad?"

"I'm happy you are well. Did you have an enriching time in Europe?"

"I had a splendid time."

"The room is stuffy. I shall open a window."

Brushing aside the damask curtains, she turned the locks and pushed the windows free. The air rushed inside and quivered the cut holly on the table.

Lanley drew out his lace handkerchief and sneezed in it. "I wish you would close them. I easily catch cold."

She shut them wishing he would go away. She knew Lanley watched her, ravished the way twilight outlined her body. As if she could break, he put his hands upon her shoulders. She stiffened.

"I'll be patient. I realize we must get to know each other better. So, I promise to woo you until you surrender."

Rebecah moved away. This was not what she wanted. The idea of living with a man she did not love grew unbearable. They were worlds apart.

Lanley's brows pinched together. "Burn me raw, madam! Have I offended you?"

"I wish you wouldn't speak of marriage."

"It's not uncommon you should feel shy at first."

He drew her close, kissed her cheek.

"On my word," he breathed out. "How beautiful you are, how soft like a rose petal in June."

She turned out of his arms. "We should not be alone. Let me call Lady Kathryn and my cousins. Surely they would be glad to see you."

She went forward but he grabbed her hand. "I did not come here to see them. You remember the plans made for us by our fathers?"

"Yes, I remember. They were made at an age when I had no understanding of marriage. I had no say in it."

"My patience is running dry. I've made great efforts in wooing you, and you're cold to me." He looked away hurt and put the handkerchief against his lips.

"I don't mean to hurt you. But you refuse to listen. This is no trifling matter you speak of."

"Perhaps it is because we've not seen each other in so long."

"How can I be warm when I'm not in love with you?"

One corner of his mouth turned upward. "Gad, my dear. Love is found in novels and plays. We live in the real world."

"Then you understand." Of a sudden, she felt hopeful, thinking she had made progress, that he had the maturity to see the difference.

He yawned. "I understand."

"Then you agree with what I'm saying?"

"I see. You do not love me, and therefore would not naturally show affectionate toward me. In time things will change."

She was baffled. He was unsteady as a rotting fence. The first strong wind and down he would go. "Other ladies would be flattered by your proposal, and there are plenty looking for a husband like you. You should not but your hopes in me alone."

Lanley played with the lace on his cuff. "Gentlemen pay for those women whose names are unspoken in good society. As for the rest—aristocratic prudes."

Rebecah shook her head. "You've given me one more reason not to desire you for a husband."

Rigid with insult, Lanley narrowed his eyes. "I see your game. You intend to play hard to get."

Rebecah wanted to hurry away. He grabbed her hands, forced her into a chair and dropped to one knee beside it. She drew back, snatched her hands away and hid them behind her. He pled with such awkward vigor she thought she would go mad.

Again, she told him she did not love him, and it would be unfair to both of them to live together as husband and wife. "You deserve love as well." She tried to explain, but he only grew more sullen. "I would make you unhappy."

"Is there another you've given your love to? Would you dare throw me over for someone less deserving?"

"There is no other."

"Then there's hope." Lanley breathed out. "I'll write you a poem tonight. It will be my best yet." His visage changed instantly, and his cheeks under rouge, brightened his flesh.

"No, please. I do not want your poems..."

"Cut me down to my bare bones, Rebecah. I shall not give up. I know you'll have me yet." He bowed low, with his hand over his heart. Then he turned and walked out.

Rebecah sank back in the chair. The tramping of horses and the turning of coach wheels passed down the drive. A moment later, the door opened and her uncle stepped inside.

"Lanley left sooner than I expected. When I asked him to stay for dinner, he turned me down. He looked distraught, and I know it is your fault. What did you say to him?"

A chill raced through her. "I cannot give him the happiness he seeks."

"You will agree to this marriage. If you don't, I shall throw you out into the streets like the poor wretch you are."

He leaned over and she smelled brandy on his breath. "You're so much like your mother. The next time Lanley pays you a visit, you will be gracious and attentive. Better still you will pen him a letter accepting his proposal."

Rebecah stood and rushed for the door, but he stopped her by grabbing her arm and whirling her around to meet him. She gasped. The way his eyes looked at her made her tremble.

"You will do as I say," he commanded.

"Throw me out. But I cannot love Lanley."

"I don't care if you love him."

A sob escaped her lips. He flung her away and she steadied herself against the wall. "Why do you treat me so cruel? I'm your own flesh and blood."

"Do you think I care? Think of it to beg, to be hungry and cold, and to be in ragged clothes. Is that what you want?" He spread his hands out to her. "Choose."

Lifting her eyes to look into his, Rebecah mustered her courage. "I'll never go hungry or be cold."

The door opened and in stepped Lady Kathryn. "What are you doing, Samuel?" Her ladyship put her arm around Rebecah. "Why is Rebecah crying? Where is Lanley?"

"I don't answer to you, Kate." His violent temper blazed through his eyes. He went toward the door and left the room.

"Come, Rebecah." Lady Kathryn held out her hand. "Forgive him for his unfeeling ways. He means well."

The room darkened. March came to light the candles. Rebecah walked out into the shadowy passageway and up the long staircase.

In her room, she gazed at the moon flowing through the window. It stood above the inky treetops full and yellow and bright.

She blew out her candle and sat alone in the dark. Though her heart ached, a sudden sense all would go well filled her. Yet she knew she must go through the fire to reach what she desired most.

CHAPTER 7

From his boyhood window, Nash also looked out at the moon. Ribbons of clouds floated over the orb thin as gauze. The night sky was spangled with stars, and the breeze rustled through the trees he climbed as a boy. Now he yearned for his mountains, where the wind rushed wilder, filled with the scent of earth and forest.

He turned to Sir Rodney. "I'm homesick."

"In such a short time, Jack?"

"Yes, Father. I miss my land." Nash ran his hands through his hair, gathered and fastened it in the back with a new black ribbon.

"Ah, I cannot blame you for feeling as you do. I remember Virginia."

Sir Rodney looked away. Reflection, after long years and life had moved on, caused his smile to fade. "In Virginia, I buried the mother who bore you. She was young and frail. I should have done more for her and saved her somehow."

"You cannot live that way, Father, wondering what you should have done. You must live for today, not yesterday. She would want you to."

"You're right, but you are also too young to understand the pain that comes from the death of a wife. I pray you never do…Do you plan to return to Maryland soon?"

"Not until I've settled some business and made sure you and Mother are well taken care of."

Sir Rodney patted Nash's shoulder. "Don't worry yourself over us, Jack. As long as my mares keep producing healthy foals, the Nash's will stay in the black."

A feminine voice called them to supper. Lady Margaret set a bountiful table. A bowl of nuts and fruits sat in the middle and amber light flickered from the candles.

"I want you to be happy, Jack. Does anything lack? Is it in order?"

"A feast, Mother." He kissed her cheek, and sat in the chair beside her. "Not a thing lacks."

"Shall we give thanks?" Sir Rodney reached for their hands. Heads were bowed in thanksgiving for much had been given.

His father poured wine into the glasses, save for his lady's. "There's but one thing lacking."

One corner of Nash's mouth curved into a smile, and the dimple on his left cheek deepened, for he knew where this would lead. "And what is that, Father?"

"A wife, my son." Sir Rodney raised his glass. "Whoever she is, wherever she may be, I toast her." He drank his wine and then placed a thick slice of beef on his son's plate.

Nash shook his head with a short laugh. "My heart remains unattached, sir. It shall remain that way for a long time, I believe." He sliced his meat and raised it to his mouth. "This is good, Mother."

Lady Margaret patted her husband's hand. "Let him eat, Rodney. Perhaps a full belly and a good night's rest will soften him to the idea."

"You're right, Margaret."

"I tried to follow in your footsteps," Nash said to his father.

Sir Rodney winked. "Not too closely I hope."

"Some men would have squandered their money on ale and petticoats. I used it to buy land and build a house."

"We knew from your letters you purchased land. Now you've built a house, Jack? Well done."

"Five hundred acres, fields of wheat, a good horse, and a house is all I need."

"You're alone?"

"I've the company of a freed slave named Joab. He helps me with the farming. I'll not enslave men."

"I could not take on farming, nor own slaves. So I tried my hand at business in Williamsburg."

Lady Margaret looked concerned. "Are you far in the wilderness?"

Nash smiled. "I'm close to Fredericktown. My friends are mostly farmers and councilmen, except for Joab and Black Hawk."

"I must say I'm distressed over slavery and the way the Indians have been treated and forced off their lands."

The younger Nash found her empathy something new. He realized she had been transformed. An inner peace emanated from her eyes. She told him she had been converted through the preaching of John Wesley, and although she witnessed injustices done in the name of God and Church, she had adored the Savior from her childhood, and understood the ways of men were not always the ways of God.

"John Wesley says it is wrong what has been done to the Indians," she went on. "I heard him speak of his journey to Georgia. He and his companions spent the whole night in a snowstorm with nothing to shield them but their clothes and the trees."

"They should have had a better guide. A backwoodsman would have known how to make a shelter."

"I suppose. While on his return to England, a terrible storm rose on the sea. He thought he was about to die, but lashed to the posts where Arab Christians singing praises. Mr. Wesley marveled at the scene, they being ready to die and singing no less, and he fearing for his life. It changed him forever."

"Are there God-fearing people living in Maryland, Jack?" asked Sir Rodney. "It would be a solace to your mother if that were so."

"Yes, Father." Nash smiled, thinking of various people he knew.

"You see, Margaret. That should please you."

"I know the wilderness of America is not so uncivilized," Lady Margaret replied. "I've read books on the subject."

"You would like the house, Mother. Though it is not as grand as an English manor, it's built of mountain stone for strength. No wind or rain could ever knock it down. And the land is beautiful with lush forests. The rivers and streams teem with fish the length of my arm."

"It sounds enchanting." She reached over to fill his plate with pie.

After supper, Nash sat on the floor in front of the fire. Toby curled beside him and put her head on his lap.

Lady Margaret set her needlework down. "Rodney."

He drew his pipe out from between his teeth and looked at her.

"I have little chance to change any man's mind except your own from time to time. Yet it would please me if I could change our son's."

Nash poked the fire. "About going back to Maryland, you mean."

"You should find a wife while here in England."

Nash laughed. "I have no time for a wife."

Lady Margaret looked discouraged. "A good wife would complete your life. Your father and I would rest easy if we knew you were settled and happy."

"I shall be married to the Continental Army soon."

Lady Margaret sighed. "An army of rebels?"

"Patriots, Mother."

"I admired your conviction. But things like wives and children make a more pleasant topic of conversation."

Sir Rodney groaned with humor, and then smiled over at his wife. "She intends to drive her point home, my son." Lady Margaret patted her husband's hand. "Jack might consider the young ladies at Endfield, don't you think?" This pricked his interest strangely. "There were children at Endfield last I knew."

"Children grow up, Jack. We've received an invitation to Endfield from my cousin Kathryn. Say you will come."

"For you, I will."

"My cousin's niece Rebecah is at Endfield, and we've heard she is a beauty and of a good nature."

"Richard Brent's daughter?"

"Yes. He is dead. Infection. They say it went to his heart."

"So sad," Lady Margaret said. "Jack, you might like Rebecah. I hear she is sweet and has an adventurous streak."

Leaning back, Nash smiled. "Sweetness does not make it in the wilderness, Mother…"

"But one can make a success of it if one is adventurous. I imagine it takes daring to settle in the American frontier." She stacked a few of the books left around. "But I'll say no more. Forgive me if I've meddled."

Sir Rodney cleared his throat. "We must also remember, my good wife, Rebecah is practically betrothed to Sir Cecil Lanley. He owns more land than anyone the Brents know. The man reeks of money."

"The man is a libertine."

She kissed her husband's cheek and said goodnight. Nash sat alone with his father.

"Brent died of infection you say?"

Sir Rodney took out a pouch of tobacco. "His reward was a bullet. How it came about I don't know."

Nash paused momentarily. "As I understand it, Brent accused certain men of treason, Thomas Johnson being one of them."

"And who may he be?" Sir Rodney lit his clay pipe.

"He owns Richfield, the most prosperous plantation in the county. Johnson is an outspoken advocate of independence, and is destined to be our first elected governor."

Sir Rodney blew blue smoke into circles above his head and looked at his son. "Brent was a zealot. I hope you did not run into him while he was in Maryland."

Nash looked away. "I did, but only once." He stood and grew quiet. He walked to the window and gazed out at the moon. Clouds hung near the edge of its face.

"Americans are sick of the British bulling them. If you only knew the things done in the name of King George…"

"I'm afraid I've been isolated from such news."

Nash turned. "Forgive me if I've offended you."

"I respect your views. We've always been able to talk freely with each other. The world grows cold with each passing year, so we must remain close, and hold each other to a higher standard."

Nash crossed the floor and sat in front of his father. He leaned forward with his arms across his knees and felt quite sober looking into the face of the man who had taught him everything he knew.

"Will I shame you if I call myself a patriot? Will you disown me if I turn against the King and fight?"

Sir Rodney drew the stem of his pipe out from between his teeth. "You could never bring me shame. Now, we must speak together in the gravest of confidences, for I must tell you what I'm involved in to help your *Glorious Cause*."

CHAPTER 8

The following Sunday, a high wind blew cold and strong. It drove wispy slate clouds across the whole of Cornwall. Woodlands were vaporous, the moors misty. Trees blackened with winter. Roads plagued rider and coachman with potholes and deep muddy ruts.

The church stood on a plot of grass off the road. The Nashs arrived moments before the service got underway, as the bell rung and people passed through the door. Upon entering, John Nash glanced up at the gallery. Crude wooden benches were packed with common folk, whereas the best pews below were reserved for the upper class.

Seats were supplied for Lady Margaret and Sir Rodney. The pews were crowded and so Nash offered his to a lady and stood beneath one of the windows. Airy sunlight dusted through the mullioned glass, mellowed the wood and stone of the building.

The minister stepped out and all stood to sing a hymn. Nash caught Lavinia's eyes. He could hardly believe it. Her face still held the same girlish gleam he remembered. She gave him a brilliant smile. But when she leaned toward the girl beside her, he could not help but switch his gaze.

He saw a rose among thistles, a pearl amid beads of clay. To her right sat three elder women, dressed in dreary gray and old lace, shallow of cheek and eye. The young woman raised her hand and brushed aside a curl near her eye, beneath a wide-brimmed hat decorated with a broad dark pink ribbon. He watched her as she fixed her eyes on the minister. Then she glanced at her prayer book. The sweep of her lashes, the softness of her eyelids, the graceful way she moved captivated him. He felt his heart move, and it made him uncomfortable.

He turned his eyes away, but his mind traveled back to her. He wondered if she were Rebecah Brent. If so, how could such a flower spring from a thorny brier like Sir Richard? He advised himself to take care of his thoughts, for beauty was skin deep, and who knew what lay beneath her pretty shell?

She looked back at the minister and Nash saw how she tried to focus on the sermon. The elderly clergyman paused, drew out a handkerchief and wiped his brow.

"Let us rejoice." He motioned the congregation to rise.

A hymn filled the church. Lavinia's voice was distinct, but lost in the sweeter voice of her companion. Between the crackling tones of the older women, the girl sang like a nightingale. She glanced over at him and their eyes met for the first time. A gentleman stood behind her, cleared his throat, and shot Nash a warning. His look was not one of jealousy or indignation, but a proclamation of ownership. And when her wrapped slipped below her shoulders, he lifted it back with a proud grin.

The service concluded, Lavinia hurried from her seat and made her way through the crowd. "Jack," she called, ignoring disapproving stares. "Oh, I'm so happy to see you, I can barely speak."

He kissed her hand. "You've grown. I imagine you've a swarm of beaus by now."

"A few," she said as they exited the church. "When did you arrive?"

"A few days ago."

"How exciting. You must tell me all about it."

Nash looked through the crowd. Where had Lavinia's friend gone?

"Have you returned for good?" she asked.

"I'm here for a visit only."

She pouted and looped her arm through his. "Oh, that is disappointing."

"I've acquired land and must return."

"Have you found a wife? Pray tell me. Is she here with you?"

He smiled. "I've no wife, Lavinia."

"Well, I suppose in a way I'm pleased. I want you to meet my cousin. She's over there with Sir Cecil Lanley. He plans to marry her. Father has been very insistent upon the match."

Rebecah stood beside the churchyard fence. That popinjay with her hovered about like a love-struck schoolboy. She moved away, averted her eyes as he spoke. Lanley held her hand against his lips, and she drew it back.

"They don't seem suitable."

"I agree. Ever since the day she arrived at Endfield, I've thought how perfect she would be for you, Jack."

Were all the women bent on marrying him off to the woman of their choosing? He wanted to be left alone.

"I'm not looking for a wife, Lavinia. Do not try to push us together. It would only complicate my life and hers."

She sighed. "I suppose if there's a Revolution you will be fighting and…oh, I understand how things would be. But meet her at least."

"Not today."

"Come on, Jack." Lavinia tugged on his arm.

She hurried him along, calling out to Rebecah. Lanley turned and looked at Nash and Lavinia. He bowed his head. Nash returned the gesture, thinking how childish this whole thing was.

"Rebecah, Sir Cecil. May I introduce Mr. John Nash, Sir Rodney's son from America?"

Lanley stepped forward. "America? What is the name of your estate?"

"Laurel Hill, Sir Cecil."

"It's where exactly?" Lanley lifted his hand and waved a handkerchief in front of his nose. Nash thought he looked absurd.

"In Maryland, near the Potomac and Monocacy rivers."

Lanley pursed his lips. "I'm unacquainted with those places. You are a settler in the Colonies?"

"If you prefer to call me that, yes."

"I assume you live in, what is it they call them, a log cabin?"

A corner of Nash's mouth twitched. "Not exactly." Disliking the way Lanley treated him, Nash decided not to describe his house. *Let him wonder.* He could tell by the look in Lanley's eyes it would drive him crazy not knowing.

Rebecah raised her eyes. The mention of a faraway land captured her attention.

"The Monocacy flows into the Potomac, does it not?" she asked. "And the Potomac separates Maryland and the Virginias, flows from the mountains in the west, and pours into the Chesapeake. Am I correct?"

Impressed by her knowledge, Nash smiled. "Yes, on all points."

"My father had an atlas in our library. I would sit for hours looking at it. I…we would love to hear about your life there."

"Are you extending an invitation?" he dared to inquire.

Lavinia bounced on her heels. "Yes, Jack. You must come to Endfield. Tell us everything."

With one brow raised, Lanley moved closer Rebecah. He posed a question, Nash knew, meant to affront.

"Will you take up arms against England when this wretched war begins? Or have you returned to stay?"

Lavinia pouted. "Must we discuss politics?"

Lanley drew back his shoulders. "Why not, Miss Lavinia? Revolution is the main topic of discussion these days."

"Let us hope our differences are resolved without the shedding of blood," Nash replied.

Lanley narrowed his eyes. "If the shedding of blood means England will keep what is rightful hers, then so be it. The Americans will be on the receiving end."

A muscle in Nash's cheek jerked. He wished he could silence Lanley's sarcastic mouth. But for the sake of the ladies, as well as his parents, and that he stood on church grounds, he gave Lanley a steely glare instead.

Lavinia set her hand against her head. "Sir Cecil, will you be so kind to escort me to our coach. I'm feeling a little faint."

Under Nash's shadow, Lanley put Lavinia's arm through his. He hesitated a moment, then turned and walked off.

Rebecah moved from the fence onto the gravel path leading to the Brent coach. "Pay no attention to Sir Cecil. He speaks his mind without thinking first."

"And you're engaged to such a man?"

"It wouldn't be appropriate for me to discuss my situation with you, Mr. Nash. We just met."

"Forgive me. I spoke out of turn."

"No harm done." They walked on through the gate, trailing behind Lanley and Lavinia. "I'm glad my uncle is not here today."

"May I ask why?"

"A discussion with him over politics is more insufferable than can be imagined."

"I may call at Endfield sometime as long as Lanley isn't there. I don't think I could abide a conversation with him again."

A light laugh passed through her coral lips. "You would have to ignore him as one disregards a spoiled child."

When she reached the coach, she paused in front of the horses. She ran her hand down one mare's nose. "Are all rebels like you?"

"I don't know what you mean, Miss Brent."

"There's an air of bravery about you, yet you are restrained. You could have argued back, but you didn't."

"There was no point."

The coachman broke in. "Lady Kathryn wishes to hurry home, miss."

Rebecah lifted her skirts, as a footman open the door and helped her inside. Nash lingered back as Lanley strutted past.

Lavinia poked out her head. "See mother, I told you John Nash was here."

Lady Kathryn leaned forward and placed one gloved hand on the sill of the coach window. "I never doubted my daughter, Jack. Your parents are overjoyed to have you home. I'm happy as well."

He bowed to her. Little had she changed, but for a few lines about her eyes. She spoke in the same refined voice he remembered.

"Have you any reason to refuse an invitation if it comes from me?"

"None that I can think of, my lady."

"Then we shall look forward to seeing you."

The coachman cracked his whip. Rebecah's eyes caught his as the coach rolled away. Besieged, he held them fast. Stepping away, he put his hat back on.

What have I just committed myself to?

CHAPTER 9

Evening fell and candles glowed in the windows of Endfield. Torches swayed along the drive brightening the stone facade. The moon hung in a vast sea of stars.

Guests were arriving. In the courtyard, footmen in lavish livery helped ladies exit their coaches. In the center directing activity stood Henry Carrow, his shadow spreading across the lawn in the torchlight.

"Who do you see, Lavinia?" Rebecah clasped a bracelet to her wrist.

Lavinia looked out the upstairs window. "Sir Rodney and Lady Margaret have arrived with their son."

Lavinia turned and drew Rebecah over. She gazed at Nash with a quickening heart. The wonderful sensation confused her and she squeezed the lace of the curtain within her hand. He waited at the foot of the stairs, his hat tucked beneath his arm, dressed in dark blue. He looked up. A gradual smile eased over his mouth.

"You have a new admirer, Rebecah," Lavinia sighed.

Rebecah turned away. "He is not my *admirer*."

"Ah, but he is. Just how you will get rid of Lanley, I don't know."

"You need not worry about me. You've your own set of problems."

"I'm not worried. David and I are meant to be together." She moved away from the window. "Do you not like John Nash?"

"I hardly know him."

Lavinia looked aghast. "You make me want to scream."

She pulled on Rebecah's shoulders. Rebecah gave her a look of resignation. "Yes, I like him. He is…"

"Dashing? Handsome?"

"Yes."

"Rugged and mysterious?"

"Yes, that too. When he looks at me, I feel…Oh, I cannot find the words."

"I knew it. You're in love." Lavinia whirled Rebecah around.

"I'm not. Falling in love takes time."

"You don't believe in love at first sight?"

"No."

A burst of laughter rose from downstairs. "We must hurry; else we'll miss most of the fun."

Dorene entered the room. She paused at the mirror. "Make him wait, Rebecah. It keeps a man interested."

"I don't need your advice, Dorene."

"What a pity. For I do think he shall be put off by the color of your gown." Dorene stood back, snapped open her fan and brushed the white ostrich feathers across her chin. "It darkens your skin and heightens the rust in your hair."

Rebecah refused to look at Dorene. Agitated she pulled on her silk stockings. She had been at Rebecah from the day she arrived. Rebecah had tolerated her.

"The heart is everything. Beauty fades. Silks turn to rags."

If Dorene's eyes were daggers, they would have drawn blood. Raising her head, she glided over to the door in a huff. The maid hurried to open it. Dorene left the room.

Lavinia sat beside Rebecah. "Dorene doesn't know what she's talking about. Your gown is lovely."

Rebecah stood and looked at the mauve silk in the mirror. "I should despise it."

"Why? You look beautiful."

"I don't wish to look beautiful tonight. Lanley."

"Forget him. Your betrothal is not etched in stone."

Despite Lavinia's encouragement, Brent's words came back. Since that day in his study, she prayed for a way to escape. The thought of being wedded to Lanley, made her feel as though she were dying inside.   .

"If only you knew the threats your father has made, and how difficult he has made things."

"I know better than you think." Lavinia headed for the door. "Tonight you need not worry about my father or Lanley. Jack is here."

* * *

Nash felt out of his element with the new clothes and the scent of milled soap upon his skin. And then there was Rebecah. He had seen her four times, in the village or passing on the road, since they had first met. Their encounters had been brief, always in the presence of others. Conversation had been limited to the fine day, or the wellbeing of their loved ones. When he saw her standing in the window, his heart pounded. Then she moved away and he bounded up the stairs and stepped inside the house.

Lavinia and Rebecah emerged from upstairs and his eyes lifted to see her, to watch the way she walked down the runner toward the stairs.

"Is that your cousin?" A girl dressed in blue damask, whose powdered face and black patch made her look more like a harlequin than a young woman, moved beside Dorene at the foot of the staircase.

He slipped back, so not to be seen, listened, and watched how she vied for attention. *Dorene has not changed at all.*

Another girl in the cluster tapped her fan. "I caught a glimpse of her in the market. I thought no great thing of her."

"I've seen her in church," spoke a third. "The men cannot keep their eyes from wandering her way."

"Is it true Sir Cecil Lanley has asked for her hand?" probed the girl with the patch.

"Yes, and someday my cousin will get all she deserves." Dorene proceeded into the ballroom with her clutch of friends. Nash breathed a sigh of relief she did not see him. A moment with the prideful Dorene surrounded by gawking females would vex him.

Samuel Brent walked by, stopped and turned.

"Sir Samuel." Nash bowed. "How are you, sir?"

Brent looked him over with scrutiny. "I'm always in excellent condition. Come to Endfield with your parents, have you? Rodney told me you intend to sell your land and are seeking a buyer. Why?"

"I've settled in America, and can use the money." Nash took a step back to let a lady and her gentleman pass.

"So, have you become a traitor to king and country?" Brent leaned forward. "Are you one of those *Sons of Liberty* we hear about?"

Nash made no reply. Why get into a debate?

"You are aware I'm in favor of hanging traitors." Brent smiled in quick greeting to his guests. "We've enough loyal Englishmen in the Colonies to squash a rebellion."

"Yet they should not underestimate the patriots' fervor."

Brent frowned. Lady Kathryn drew beside him. Nash kissed the hand she held out to him.

Rebecah was coming down the stairs. Brent's face flushed and Nash saw something dreadful snapped in his mind.

Lady Kathryn touched his arm. "What is it, my love?"

"You don't see it, do you? She is the image of her mother."

"Slightly, Samuel." Lady Kathryn opened her fan.

"You will excuse me." Pain and anger glazed Brent's eyes. "I'm not good at parties."

His wife looked disappointed. "It would be discourteous, Samuel."

"I don't care, Kate. This is my house and I shall do as I please." He took his wife by the elbow and led her down the hall. Nash heard the door click shut over the din of people.

Brent's reaction to his niece troubled Nash. Was he over protective, or was there something else concerning the past that caused this slight?

He walked toward her. She gave him a hint of a smile. "I heard the roads were filled with fog. I hope the journey was not too unpleasant."

"The hard ride was worth it now that I've seen you."

"There's Lavinia, and David Harcourt. Perhaps you haven't spoken to them and should?"

"I'm beginning to think you don't like me, Miss Brent. Is it so difficult for you to accept a compliment?"

"How am I to know you are sincere?"

"You must take my word for it. Perhaps it's a matter of the two of us becoming better acquainted."

A roll of laughter and a voice drawn and high pitched, drew their attention. When Lanley entered, heads turned. Dorene took his arm and led him inside. Ladies fluttered and clustered around him like bees drawn to honey. Tapping his silver snuffbox, he bobbed his head to search the crowd.

When Lanley started toward her, Rebecah looked at Nash with entreaty. "Take me into the other room before…"

"Lud, my dear!" Lanley quickened his pace and stopped in front of her. He sighed, gazed at her starry-eyed.

"Have I passed on to Paradise? Are you an angel in disguise?"

"Your flattery isn't necessary," she replied.

Nash scowled at the way Lanley gawked. He saw beneath that smooth veneer of politeness, how he kissed Rebecah's hands with ashen lips, thin and drawn beneath a long angular nose, a libertine. She withdrew and joined Lavinia.

"Your manner is too free," Nash commented.

Lanley smirked. "What is that you say?"

"Kissing a lady's hand once is enough. More is impolite and licentious."

"You challenge my manners?"

"Some might say you are a womanizer."

Lanley poked his chin up at Nash. "I take liberties with the lady due to the fact she is to be my wife…someday."

"She does not seem to like your *liberties*."

"Yes she does…"

"Ask her."

Lanley's face burned scarlet. "Our method of wooing is obviously above the crudities of frontiersmen."

Amused, Nash grinned. "I'm in no need of instruction in that art."

A swaying beauty passed them, and Nash's eyes shifted. Dorene smiled seductive and moved on.

"Do you know Dorene Brent?" Nash asked.

"I know her well." A lustful gaze glazed Lanley's eyes as he watched her glide away.

"You play the field while you've an understanding with another woman?"

Lanley laughed. "The field is exactly what a man should play before the bonds of matrimony hold him forever. I've the best of both worlds, as long as I play wisely."

Disgusted, Nash set his mouth and turned to leave. "Will you be returning any time soon to that untamed country of yours?"

Dorene reappeared. "You can never go back. I'll not allow it." She stood close to him. "Life has been so dull since you left. I have missed your free spirit, your recklessness. Will you not kiss my hand?"

Nash leaned over. The kiss was formal, cold.

"Allow a true English gentleman to do that, Dorene," Lanley said. He brushed his lips over the top of her hand, and Nash walked off. He needed fresh air.

If I could only leave.

He found Rebecah out on the balcony, her hands firm upon the railing, her head down. He moved beside her, looked out at the night sky.

"Are you alright?"

She nodded. "I suppose."

"Lanley embarrasses you, doesn't he?"

"Often. I'd rather not be here."

A pause followed. Then Nash said, "I would rather be sitting on my porch watching the sun sink behind the mountains, or hunting with Black Hawk my Indian brother."

"You have an Indian brother?"

"In Indian fashion, I do. He is the best of men, a skilled marksman and hunter."

"It sounds wonderful where you live."

"Perhaps you should consider the Colonies for yourself."

He turned and leaned against the rail. Torches and a bonfire out on the lawn warmed the air. Reflections of the flames danced against the house.

"It takes courage to leave home for a strange land and settle there," she said.

He adored the way the moonlight changed the color of her eyes. "Your voice is alluring." A cackle of laughter caused him to pause. "Unlike those."

"My uncle says my voice is too bold for a girl."

"Your uncle is wrong."

He walked on with her into the shadows, beneath the bough of ivy hanging over the porch. The plucking of a violin drew people out on the lawn.

"It's the Carrows and the others." Rebecah waved to them.

Henry and Jane danced a country reel near the bonfire. Coachmen and footmen, laborers and servants, clapped their hands and stomped their feet in time with the music. Such a striking contrast to what went on inside.

Nash took Rebecah down the stairs and across the lawn. Joining the country folk, he swung her around, holding her hands and smiling with her.

CHAPTER 10

After the guests departed, the family gathered in the drawing room. The door flung open and Samuel Brent entered. His neckcloth hung loose about his throat. His hair lay loose from its binding. The cuffs of his shirt were stained with wine.

"Over the last few months something has troubled my father." Lavinia spoke quietly, leaning in her chair toward Nash. "He refuses to speak of it, even to my mother. I've stood by and watched his shifting moods of depression and anger, his thirst for wine, his brooding."

"Perhaps he is ill and should see a physician."

"I believe his heart is troubled. Rebecah thinks she is the cause."

Nash frowned. "What could she have done?" He glanced over at her. "She is an angel. It's all in your father's mind."

Brent slammed the door. "The food is half-eaten and wine spilled on the new carpet."

Lady Kathryn looked at her hand of cards. "What is left the servants will eat. And they will clean the carpet."

"A waste of money," Brent shouted. Everyone froze and stared at him.

Lady Kathryn stood with genteel grace and touched his hand. "Do not speak so, my love."

"There will be no more parties at Endfield." He stumbled away from her.

"You are jesting, Papa," Dorene said.

"I'm the master of this house and what I say is law." He tossed himself into a chair and covered his eyes with his hand. "Hugh has been screaming for you, Kate, and given me a headache."

"March said he was sleeping soundly a moment ago," Kathryn said.

"You rely too much on March to do what you should as a mother. Go silence him before I take a rod to the boy."

Lavinia rose from her chair. "Let me go, Mother."

Lady Kathryn agreed. "He will mind you, Lavinia."

Lavinia walked out, avoiding her father's path.

Brent put his hand on Sir Rodney's shoulder. "Rodney, come with me to the study. Let us drink like we did in the old days and remember real living before we took wives."

"Thank you for the offer, Samuel. But I had enough wine tonight. I would be happy to have some strong black tea though, and talk over old times."

Brent laughed. "Your Methodist wife must think it a sin? And I can see you do not approve of my behavior. You find it brash. By heavens, have you been converted too?"

"I'll not judge you, my friend."

"Ah, but you should. I am a poor example to my son. Though I admit my wife makes up for the shame my daughters and niece bring me."

Nash saw Rebecah's eyes lift.

"Surely that is not true, that you are ashamed of them."

"You of all men should understand, Rodney. When the war starts, your son will take up arms against us. It's enough to make any English father cower in shame."

Brent's words caused Nash to stiffen. He saw the sad expression in his father's face and tightened his fists at his sides. He drew in his boots and stood. "My father isn't swift to judge a man, even his son."

Brent looked Nash in the eye. "It is his love for you that covers a multitude of sins, I suppose."

"His love, in spite of my failings, is more than I deserve."

Brent's eyes narrowed. "I agree. At your age, I knew my place and my duty."

"I can assure you, I know mine."

Brent clenched his jaw. He turned away and drew Rebecah from her seat.

"Do you disapprove of me, Rebecah?"

She stepped back.

"Say something!" Brent stumbled toward Rebecah.

"You condemn us without reason, Uncle. Yes, I disapprove."

"I did not have to take you in, and I don't have to keep you."

Nash hurried forward to move her away from Brent's abuse. Brent raised his hand. Too late to dodge the blow, Rebecah tumbled to the floor. Lady Kathryn let out a cry. Nash grabbed Brent by the breast of his coat and dared to hit him, but Sir Rodney caught him by the arm.

"No, Jack," he implored. "It will make no difference."

He shook the drunken Brent. "He is a coward to have struck her." He flung Brent into a chair.

Brent's face looked wretched, the whites of his eyes heavy and bloodshot. He spoke not a word, only stared forward. Then he covered his face in his hands.

"Forgive me, Rebecah. I did not mean to hurt you."

He held out his hand to her. Tears drifted down her face and a red mark stood out on her cheek.

Nash pressed his mouth together and tried to restrain his anger. He watched her go from her aunt's arms to standing in front of Brent. He could not believe what he saw.

"You must sleep, Uncle." Rebecah spoke softly. "In the morning you'll feel better."

Nash shook his head. Baffled she had not lashed back at this madman, he wondered how she could forgive him. It caused him to pause at the secret he hid from her, hoping someday, when he could explain, she would be as forgiving toward him.

Brent stood. His face looked drained and gaunt. He turned and stepped from the room with Lady Kathryn's arms around him. Rebecah held out her hands to Nash and he took them. His were strong and rough, and the tender grip with which he held her made him hope she felt safer.

Before letting her go, he touched her fingers to his lips. She then left with Lady Margaret. Dorene followed for there was nothing else to do. That night clouds passed over Endfield and left behind a cold mist in the empty darkness.

CHAPTER 11

Upstairs in one of the guestrooms, Nash tried to sleep. He had a troubled mind. He missed home, his own bed in his own room, the chirp of crickets in the tall grass and the tree frogs in the forest.

He stood by the window and watched the moon and stars until the clock on the mantle chimed the half-hour. Night deepened into dark purple, and the logs in the fire turned to ash. Outside, the air was still and cold and he heard an owl hoot in the distance.

Pulling off his boots, he lay down with his hands behind his head and stared at the ceiling. His thoughts were cluttered, restless. He closed his eyes and whispered a prayer in the dark as the candle at his bedside gutted.

He heard his door open, close, saw a womanly figure etched in moonlight come toward him in the dark. Her hair fell forward. She touched his face.

He looked into her eyes. Greedy, unrestrained passion showed deep within them, unlike Rebecah's, whose eyes were tender and beautiful.

"Everyone is asleep. You want me, Jack?"

Dorene!

He shoved her away, got up. "Get out!"

She twisted a strand of hair between her fingers. "When was the last time you were with a woman?"

He reached to pull her up, but she moved back. "Go to your room, or I'll throw you out."

Arrogant disbelief covered Dorene's face. She pressed her lips together and lay back against the pillows. "I shall not leave."

"You will, I say." He took her by the arm and hauled her up. "It may come as a blow to your enormous conceit, Dorene, but I don't want you. I never will. What you have to give, I do not want. Understand?"

Pulling away from him, she shook her head. "No, I don't understand. Would you rather have Rebecah than me?" She grabbed a pillow and threw it at him. "Christian! Rogue! Yankee traitor!"

He laughed. "Call me what you will. Nothing will change my mind."

Throwing her arms around his neck, she pulled herself against him. "Why must God have his way, Jack? Why can we not do what we want? Forget your morals for one night."

He pried her arms free. "How clear must I be? If you wish my bed, you are welcomed to it. I'll find somewhere else to sleep."

"I hate you! You'll regret your insistence on following some ancient moral code."

With nothing else close by to throw, Dorene tore the bedclothes apart, scattering the pillows, beating the bed with her fists. Nash ignored her and went out into the dark corridor.

Shadows swept to and fro through the gallery of windows. He turned and without warning bumped into Rebecah. She looked up at him with a start.

"I'm sorry if I frightened you."

"No harm done. I should go back to my room."

"You've been crying."

"It's nothing."

Footsteps passed down the corridor and he moved her back. He saw Dorene slip out of his room. Thankfully, she went the other way.

"It looks like someone else cannot sleep." Rebecah turned to go. She had seen Dorene.

Nash stopped her. "Dorene is the reason I left my room."

"I want to believe you…I know what she is like…"

"I had nothing to do with her."

He placed his hands on her shoulder. "Rebecah, you're unhappy. Is it possible, I could change that?"

Her lips parted. She hesitated, looked into his eyes. "Yes."

He would have brushed his lips over hers, but she stepped back and hurried away.

* * *

Sir Rodney and his lady woke early to the song of a mockingbird singing in a willow tree. The day begun cloudy, with streams of sunlight piercing through misty veils. After he dressed, Sir Rodney jerked the bell-pull three times. He wanted to be done with breakfast and head home. The night before had left a bad taste in his mouth.

Lady Margaret ran a brush through her hair, long and soft, tinted with silvery gray. "Did you notice the way he looked at her?"

Sir Rodney yawned and stretched his arms. "You mean Jack?"

Her ladyship turned and set the brush down. "Whom else would I be speaking of? Little escapes me when it comes to our son. Oh, I need my tea."

"Our son is a man, and makes his own decisions. Let us hope they're the right ones." Sir Rodney sat on the edge of the bed and pulled on his shoes.

"There are times when one is blind to what is right. Or one may resist."

80

"You know matchmaking can lead to disaster, Margaret. We must leave him alone."

She stood and kissed his cheek. "It's true we should not interfere. But if he asks our advice we should give it."

"I'm proud of Jack. He did what was proper as a man, to stand for her against a bully."

"Yes, it is sad the way Samuel behaved and how he treated Rebecah."

"I tell you this, after last night I'm anxious to leave Endfield." He tightened the sash of his robe with a jerk. "And never come back."

"I cannot say as much. I promised Kathryn I would return next week to look at her garden plans. Also, her dressmaker will be expected, and I should like to see a few fabric swatches and patterns. But not for me, mind you. A few ladies are not faring well in our fellowship and are in need of new clothes."

Sir Rodney squeezed her waist. "Love, gardens, and clothes…I will have coffee and the London Gazette if they have it."

She lowered herself upon his knee and wrapped her arms around his neck. "That you, an Englishman, would drink anything other than tea is astonishing."

"I like coffee," he smiled.

"Drink it in private."

"Why?"

"Some might think you sympathize with the Americans."

"Let them. I can stand up to scrutiny."

She brushed his lips with her finger. "I think your boldness attracted me to you, and your good looks and the way you kissed."

"On my soul," he breathed. "You still light a fire in me." He kissed her once more, only this time upon the lips and with more passion.

* * *

From a white porcelain basin, Nash splashed his face with cold water, dried off with a towel, and paused. This foreign pang refused to leave. It burned in him like fire, pounded him like a tempestuous sea. He mulled over what to do. Should he follow the demands of logic, or the dictates of his heart? Could he fulfill both his duty to his country and love an English woman?

He put his face in his hands. What he considered doing now would change everything. Tensions were mounting in America. The country poised for war. He knew he should leave England soon, or risk being trapped there. But he was torn. He did not want to leave Rebecah. He loved her.

A coach pulled up at the front doors. From the window, he watched Brent walk toward it dressed in dreary gray. Inside the ban of his tricorn hat, a red tag showed his loyalty to English sovereignty. His cloak wrapped around his body as he climbed in. The footman adjusted the step, closed the door, and climbed to his seat. With a crack of the whip, the horses jerked forward and the coach rolled away.

He felt a sense of relief for Rebecah the tyrant was gone.

An hour later, the Nash's coach waited for them on the drive. After they had boarded, and it rolled away, he looked back to see her standing outside the front door, hand raised, her hair unbound and lifting in the breeze.

For the next week, he paced, wrote letters, and counted the days when he would see her again.

CHAPTER 12

The cottage Henry Carrow lived in with his wife Jane and two boys stood off a beaten path south of the manor. He worked the land for the Brent's for two decades and thought to himself it was really his, not the haughty gentry's. He sat smoking a clay pipe by the kitchen fire. Jane wiped her forearm across her brow, smudged flour over her freckled face while she kneaded dough for the day's bread.

Henry watched her with vested interest.

Jane looked over at him as she pushed the dough. "Is it not time you get to work, my love?"

"How can I, my darlin' girl?" He drew on his pipe and blew circles into the air. "It looks like rain."

"If it's a piece of pie you want, go on eat it. I'll not slap the hand that feeds me."

Henry reached over and drew the pie closer. Pulling a large hunk out of the plate, he leveled it to his mouth, closed his eyes, and took a bite. Jane smiled. She was an attractive woman, not much older than Kathryn Brent. Her face was round and smooth, her eyes deep brown beneath slim auburn brows the same color as her hair.

She tossed the dough it into a greased wooden bowl and laid a piece of cheesecloth over it. Soon it would rise and the cottage would fill with the smell of baking.

Jane ran her hands across her apron when her oldest son Harry came into the kitchen. He was nine years of age, strong in body, with dark hair and eyes. His arms were loaded down with wood for the fire. His younger brother Christopher, age six, followed behind him with the kindling.

"We saw a man walking up the hill toward the house," said Harry. "Do you know him, Papa? He's coming from the manor."

Henry rose from his chair. "Well let's see who the man might be."

"I know him," announced Christopher with a chipper. "It's Mr. John from America. He has a flintlock pistol, Da. I bet he's got a knife too, and fought plenty of Indians and low Frenchmen with it."

"More likely it'll be Redcoats soon enough, my lad."

Jane threw her hands to her hips. "Such talk, the lot of you. If the gentleman is coming to see us, don't pester him with such things as fighting Indians and low Frenchmen. Nor make mention of Redcoats. You mind me."

Off the boys scampered while their father watched John Nash walk up the hill. "I wonder why he's coming' here, Janie."

"Lord knows, my dear. Be sure to offer him some of that pie before you gobble it all down."

From his doorway, Henry waved. Nash lifted his hat. "The lad's got a strong stride, my pet. I imagine living in the frontier makes a man that way."

Jane came alongside her husband. "Don't be angry with me for saying so, my love, but I've never seen a handsomer man. It's a wonder the girls aren't pining away for such a face."

"You can count on it, Janie."

* * *

The first thing John Nash noticed about the Carrow's cottage was how the thatched roof turned golden brown in the sun—a warm comfortable dwelling, unlike Endfield.

He pondered how Henry kept the farm, how Brent need not lift a finger. If the Carrows lived in *The Thirteen* they could own land and keep the profits. Yet, Nash knew first hand that was easier said than done. In the frontier there was much to worry about—famine, fever, drought, and Indian raids. Only the stoutest of souls settled there.

He knew, too, there were prying eyes at the manor. Deciding not to fight the feelings he had for her, Nash slipped Rebecah a note by way of the chambermaid.

Once inside, he sat by the fire in Jane's kitchen. A few moments later, Rebecah stepped through the door. Her eyes met his. Wispy curls touched her cheeks. She pushed back the hood of her cloak and his heart pounded.

"How many loaves have you baked today, Jane? I smelled the bread coming up the path."

"Five in all, miss. I'll send some up to the house if you think they'd want some."

Rebecah put her hand on the oak table. "I'm sure they would, as long as you have enough."

"Oh, there's plenty. I'm sending a loaf home with you too, Mr. Nash."

"Thank you, Mrs. Carrow." He smiled. "I leave in the morning on business in the north. We'll have it with our supper tonight."

Rebecah drew in a breath. "For how long, Mr. Nash?"

He stood. "Miss Brent. Would you walk with me?"

She agreed and they took the bridle path. "I received your note. The chambermaid promised not to tell anyone where I've gone."

"It's a shame we have to meet in secret."

"Only because my uncle would not approve."

Spears of sunshine streamed through the branches of the trees and dappled the path with light. It was not much different from the woods at Laurel Hill. He described them for her, the tranquil Catoctin Mountains, the teaming forests, the rivers cutting deep into the valley pouring into the Potomac.

"It sounds like the Garden of Eden."

"To me it is. To others it is overrun with thistle and thorns."

"My father wrote to me about the Colonies. He never described things like you."

"Perhaps he was too busy with military affairs to have noticed."

"Will you be returning soon?"

"Yes, in a few months I think."

"But war may come, and you are Sir Rodney's only son."

"My father will support whatever I choose to do."

They walked on.

"Sometimes I wish I had been born a boy."

He laughed. "Why?"

"I could do what you've done. For English girls, our lives are planned out for us."

"You speak of marriage. You have a choice."

"There are consequences no matter what I decide."

"I wouldn't wish Lanley on you for the world." He kicked a stone and sent it rolling down the path into the dry leaves. "Why would you agree to marry him? You don't love Lanley, and he has nothing to offer except his estate. I refuse to believe you are the kind to want a man for his money."

She looked at him with those beautiful eyes of hers. His heart told him to fight, to claim her before she'd slip through his fingers into the arms of another man.

"Love is a luxury, Mr. Nash. Better to marry for wealth, I've been told. Better to marry a title than a good man who has none. Now you tell me, you're going away and…"

They stared at each another. Her lips parted, while her eyes glistened from the sunlight, and a single tear formed in the corner and caught upon her lashes.

Nash's heart slammed against his chest, and desperation rose. "You could leave this place." He stood close and the breeze blew the hem of her cloak around his boots.

He stopped. "Don't marry him, Rebecah."

"I don't want to."

"Promise me you won't do it."

He reached for her, kissed her long and soft as the ruby sun slipped above the treetops.

CHAPTER 13

Lady Kathryn's sitting room fell silent when Rebecah walked through the door. Her hands trembled as she removed her gloves. Her face felt flushed and joy pulsed through her veins. Never had she felt so happy. Nash declared his love, and she could hardly concentrate. Her mind whirled wondering if he would next propose.

Please ask me. I'll go away with you and love you forever.

America. Yes, she would go there to begin a new life with the man she loved, and nothing on earth could stop them.

"Rebecah?" Lady Kathryn sat a swatch of blue silk on her lap. "Where have you been?"

"Out walking, Aunt."

"I grew concerned. It is rather cold out. Are you well?"

"I am." A smile trembled over Rebecah's lips.

Her ladyship turned her attention back to the petite dolls that modeled the latest fashions. "This is a fine silk, don't you think?"

"Yes, It's very nice, Aunt Kathryn."

"It makes for a lovely bridal gown. Do you agree?"

"Yes, Aunt. But I hope you are not thinking of me."

Lady Margaret reached for Rebecah's hand and drew her down beside her. "Mrs. Rigby. Haven't you anything else? Say, some light wool or broadcloth?"

An elegantly dressed woman in a wide-brimmed hat cocked her head to one side, which caused her head of heavily powdered ringlets to sweep over the white lace edging of her bodice. Upon her cheek, she wore a black patch, an odd thing, thought Rebecah, to wear this time of day. Rice powder and rouge made up the rest of her face.

"These are the latest fashions, my lady." Mrs. Rigby widened her eyes. "Londoners are paying top dollar."

Lady Kathryn sighed. "Expense is no matter."

Rebecah listened to the conversation and then looked over at Lady Margaret. The tone of her voice was soft yet firm, and the way she carried herself was so unlike other genteel women. She graciously voiced strong opinions on matters of politics and religion, yet with temperance. Her charity was renowned, though she herself never spoke of it. Rebecah felt the sudden impulse to know her better. She wondered, too, what Lady Margaret would say if she knew her son had confessed his love for her.

"Why waste money on such extravagance? One does not need a silk or brogue for every day of the week."

Mrs. Rigby leaned forward. "Because of your status, my lady, it is a necessity." She chose a chocolate from a box on the table and popped it into her mouth.

Lady Margaret looked over at Rigby and smiled. "I don't care much for status, nor for fancy silk gowns. I'll buy twenty yards of this gray broadcloth."

"For charity no doubt." Mrs. Rigby smiled, her cheek puffed out with more chocolate. "But perhaps this blue would be a bit more cheery?"

"Yes, perhaps." Lady Margaret studied it. "I'll take twenty yards of that also."

Rebecah stepped forward. "It's a lovely color, my lady. Like the sky in winter."

Lady Kathryn looked at her niece confused. "What has come over you, Rebecah? No offense, Margaret, but the color is dull."

Lady Margaret leaned toward Rebecah, while Lady Kathryn finalized her transaction with Mrs. Rigby. "Has my son gone home?"

"Yes, my lady."

"It's alright, Rebecah. I know how he feels about you."

"He told you?"

"Yes, last night. I assure you his feelings are true and honorable."

Lady Kathryn handed Rigby back a doll and bid her good day. Once she was out of the room, Lady Kathryn spoke.

"A letter came to me a little while ago from Sir Cecil. He requests you go to Ashburne and get the house in order. You are to make a list of all repairs and changes that must be done, and a list of all the furnishings. You may leave tomorrow."

So Lanley thought this would cinch an engagement? She would go, yes. Escape, yes. Change anything, make lists, never. And above all, she would refuse Lanley.

Lavinia entered the room.

"This is as good a time as any," said Lady Kathryn. "I would not dream of having Dorene go with you. She'd get up to no good, I'm sure. Lavinia can go with you."

Lavinia shook her head. "No, Mother. I'm not feeling well. I came to tell you, I think I am coming down with something."

"Well, then go to bed."

"May I have some broth in my room?"

"Yes, of course, my dear." Lavinia leaned down to kiss her mother's cheek, but Lady Kathryn held up her hand. "It would not be wise, Lavinia."

Hugh's hound scampered into the room. A rope dangled from her middle. "Mama!" A curl fell over Hugh's eyes and he brushed it away. "I had Jess pull my wagon. It's my chariot of fire, and she's my steed. But I'm tired of it now."

90

"I imagine you are worn out, my darling." Lady Kathryn ran her fingers through his hair.

"Come upstairs and play soldiers, Becah." He turned to her. "I'll be the Yankee, like John Nash, and you can be the Redcoat. Lavinia can be an Indian."

Lavinia moaned. "We did that yesterday."

Rebecah looked into his sweet face and a pain seized her. She gathered the child into her arms and hugged him. A shadow then fell across the floor.

March stood erect by the sitting room door. "It is bedtime for Master Hugh."

Lady Kathryn kissed Hugh's cheek. "Be good, my darling. Do as you are told, and do not forget to say your prayers."

Hugh sauntered off, his dog trailing behind him. And while Lady Kathryn's eyes were upon her young son as he left the room, Lady Margaret reached over and touched Rebecah's hand.

"I'll be sure he knows where you have gone."

CHAPTER 14

Snow drifted across the land, frosting the hedges and fieldstone walls, settling in the niches of Ashburne. A rider set on a fine chestnut gelding marked his destination by the light burning in the distance. The flame swayed and sparkled inside a brass lantern hanging from a pole beyond the door. His coming there was unknown to Rebecah as she sat near the fire, upon the looped rug that had been there before she was born.

The wood seethed and crackled. She stretched her hands out to warm them. Nothing had changed in the years she had lived there—the same furnishings, the same books, the same painting over the mantle of a foxhunt.

Margery stepped inside and handed down a mug of hot beef broth. "Here's something to take away the chill."

"Thank you, Margery. I've missed your broths—and Ashburne." Rebecah took it in both hands. The clay mug felt warm.

"It's been lonely since you went to live at Endfield."

"I'm sorry you're here alone."

"You do understand why I've taken another position, don't you?"

Rebecah sipped the broth. "I would do the same if I were you."

"It's a good house and Hampshire is a lovely part of England. The gentleman is one of those Parliament men, and his wife is a godly woman to be sure, firm with her children. I think I shall be happy there."

Rebecah thought about this new turn in Margery's life. "You're happiest with people to care for. As for Ashburne, I shall not see it again."

Margery brows shot up. "Why not?"

"Life is leading me somewhere else, somewhere far away."

"God will have to get Samuel Brent out of the way for you to have any freedom at all." Margery frowned and dusted off the table next to her with her apron.

"I'm not frightened of him." Rebecah reached for the servant's wrinkled hands. "Do you know Sir Rodney Nash's son?"

"The one who left England to live in Maryland?"

"Yes. Promise you will be silent. Promise, Margery."

"I haven't any right to speak a word of what you've said. But a Colonist is not the man for you. It means you going to that heathen country and living a poor life and…"

"I'll go away with him, rich or poor."

"It's just a fancy…"

"I assure you it is not. And he is not a poor man. He owns land and is prosperous and respected."

"But the Colonies? Such dangers are there. Why just the other day in the market a soldier told the crowd how Indians kill white women by the dozens or capture them for wives. They take the slave women too."

Rebecah sighed. "I would not believe everything you hear."

Appearing dismayed, Margery shook her head. "Are you that much in love?"

"I believe I am."

"Are those his letters that have been arriving for the last three weeks?"

"They are."

"Well, for a man to write so often to a lady either means he is in love with her, or after her money."

"I have little in the way of money."

"Yes but whoever marries you inherits Ashburne."

Rebecah knew Nash did not care about some crumbling estate house in England or any money it might bring. The way he talked about his Eden made her love him more.

Someone lifted the heavy iron knocker and let it fall.

"Who could it be at this hour?" Margery complained. "A beggar, no doubt. I shall not answer."

Rebecah dashed from the room. She pulled back the bolt and opened the door. A gust of wind forced itself inside, and Margery moved Rebecah back with her hand and held the candle high. Quivering light fell upon a man in a black cloak and hat. Flecks of snow lay on his shoulders and in his hair. He took a step forward and pulled off his hat, revealing a handsome face.

"Would you be so kind as to give shelter to a traveler?" He addressed Margery, but his eyes turned to Rebecah. She wanted to run to him, throw her arms around his neck.

Margery protested. "I will not! We are but two women here alone. I'll not have a strange man under this roof. Go to the barn. There's hay a plenty to keep you warm and oats for your horse."

"Let the gentleman in, Margery. He is a friend."

Margery did as her mistress ordered, and he stepped over the threshold. She closed and bolted the door. Nash took off his cloak, shook the snow from it, and handed it over.

"I shall not sleep sound in my bed tonight," Margery tossed it over her arm. "Unless you're loyal to His Majesty King George and swear to do right by two women."

Nash inclined his head and smiled. "The King will not lose sleep over my politics tonight, and neither should you, madam. As far as doing right by you and the lady, you've nothing to fear from me."

Margery huffed her way over to the fire and put his cloak across the back of a chair to dry. "Well then, you'll not mind knowing I keep a pistol under my pillow and that the floors of this old house creak."

"Margery, this is John Nash—Sir Rodney's son."

"Is he? Well, it ain't proper you should come here at this hour, sir. Tongues will wag."

"Only if you do the wagging." Rebecah turned her toward the door. "Now, go to the kitchen and bring back a plate of food for Mr. Nash. He looks hungry."

Margery toddled off, mumbling under her breath.

"I did not give you fair warning. Forgive me." Nash sat in a chair near the fire. "It was growing dark and the snow deepens."

"It's alright. Standforth is still a distance, and you needed shelter."

"Truly that is the reason I stopped."

Rebecah lowered to the carpet. He noticed her feet were bare and was quick to point out how lovely they were in the glow of the fire, how her hair fell in thick waves over one shoulder, and how her skin glowed in the firelight.

"Were you able to finish your business in the north?"

"Yes, I'm free of it. I stayed three days with a man of my father's acquaintance. I'm more than convinced I've done the right thing after talking with him, plus I had plenty of time to think. And you, I could not get out of my mind, day or night."

Margery brought in a tray. "Here's a meal for you, sir, with good English ale. I daresay it will taste better than any Mr. Adams could offer."

"Thank you," Nash said. "If I see Mr. Adams, I'll tell him you said so."

Rebecah smiled and watched him while he ate the stew. He paused and gazed back at her.

"Aren't you going to have any? It's good."

"I've had mine." She leaned against the chair behind her. He continued gazing at her, the corners of his mouth turning into a smile. After one more mouthful, he put the spoon down and drank his ale.

"She's wrong. American ale is better." He dug back into the stew. "So, does Brent still plan to marry you off to Lanley?"

"Yes."

"You will stay in England and I'll go home to Laurel Hill, unless you've decided differently."

"I've decided long ago not to marry him, if that is what you mean."

Taking her hands in hers, he knelt. "Rebecah, marry me."

"Marry you?"

"Yes," he said, his eyes shining.

"I am not an easy person to live with."

"Nor am I."

"I am sullen and quiet. I read constantly, and I'm not always a lady. Some say I speak my mind too boldly, and I should be more reserved."

"What you mean to say is you think deeply about things and settle your mind by being alone. And your hands are the loveliest I've seen. Your hair is beautiful, and you should wear it like that all the time. You're self-educated and like to ride bareback. You have opinions worth hearing, and have a lively spirit."

She lowered her eyes.

"You are everything I admire—all I want."

They were silent a moment, the fire the only sound in the room. He kept her hands within his.

She laid her head against his chest. "Last night, I dreamed you left. I woke with the most awful feeling I would never see you again."

Nash took her in his arms and his lips touched hers. She closed her eyes. "Oh, I feel as if I'm floating," she said with quickened breath. "And my heart, it pounds so."

"Then come away with me. We can leave tomorrow. I'll take you to Standforth first, to tell my father and Lady Margaret. They'll keep our secret until we have gone."

She leaned against him, rested her head on his shoulder. The fire crackled and seethed. Wind whispered. They talked long into the night, of their plans, their dreams, until the hall clock struck out midnight and they fell asleep in each other's arms.

* * *

Morn approached. The house felt cold, but the coziness of it remained. Together they breakfasted on warm scones and tea. Before they were through, Margery burst into the room.

"There's a rider making his way to the house. It looks like Henry Carrow."

Rebecah hurried to the window and looked outside. The sky was heavy with clouds, the land heavy in snow. After a moment, she recognized Henry and the horse he rode.

Cold air rushed inside the house when Margery opened the door. Henry climbed off his horse. He looked exhausted, frozen from the journey. Hastily dressed, his shirt poked through the top of his coat. His woolen scarf was tied in a knot at his throat and his hat sat awry on his head. His boots were his field boots.

Rebecah drew him inside. "Henry. What is it? Is something the matter?"

"I came as fast as I could." Henry breathed hard. "You're needed back at Endfield." He glanced over at Nash standing in the doorway of the sitting room. "Hello, Mr. John. Didn't know you'd be here."

"Margery, get Henry something warm to drink," Rebecah said. "Henry, Mr. Nash was caught in the snow."

Henry shook his head. "The wind were fierce, weren't it? I'm glad the snow didn't come too deep, else I don't think I would have made it here."

"Come sit by the fire," she urged. "What has happened at Endfield? Tell me."

In front of the fire, Henry put out his hands and rubbed them vigorously. "Her ladyship and Miss Lavinia are sick. The fever, that's what's got them and some folks in the village. The doctor says he's quarantining the whole place and the bordering farms."

Dread stole inside Rebecah. "And my uncle? Has he remained in London?"

"Aye," Henry frowned, drinking Margery's hot broth. "I suppose he'll be coming home. Lady Kathryn called for me and told me to find you. She wants you with her."

"Then we must go," Rebecah said urgently.

"I'll saddle your horse for you." Henry set his mug down and left. He looked over at Nash worried. "Mr. John, word is this thing has spread as far as Standforth. Your parents are at risk."

Nash looked startled. "Then I must leave immediately." He picked up his hat and cloak, reached for Rebecah's hand and held it. "I'll ride with you to the border of Endfield to be sure you and Henry arrive safe. Send me word as soon as you can. And when this is over…"

She leaned up and kissed his cheek. "I know, Jack."

They left Ashburne and headed across the stark land beneath the misty sky. At Endfield's gate, behind the hedge of trees, Nash leaned over in the saddle, put his arm around Rebecah and kissed her goodbye. Then he pulled down his hat against the wind, turned his horse and galloped off.

What he could not know was the feeling of dread that stabbed her while she watched him race up the hillside and disappear over it.

CHAPTER 15

The moment Rebecah entered through the front door, March came down the stairs with a washbowl and a towel. Dark circles were under the woman's eyes.

"Thank God you're back."

"How are they?"

"Lady Kathryn is sleeping, but will want to see you. The doctor said if they make it through the night, they would recover. But thus far it has been a terrible struggle."

Rebecah hurried to take off her cloak and gloves. "I shall sit with Lady Kathryn."

Dorene stood motionless six steps up, her hand on the banister. Her dark eyes bore down on Rebecah.

"Hugh is safe, Dorene, and you?"

"What do you care? I know what you've been up to. And you'll never know how much I hate you for it."

Rebecah, troubled by her cousin's words, went to pass her. "Why must you be so jealous of me?"

"You give me good cause to be."

"Perhaps when this is over we should talk. This is hardly the time to discuss our differences. Go and rest."

"How dare you tell me what to do? You give me cause, I say."

"I don't know what you mean."

Dorene grabbed Rebecah by the arm. "You do!"

Rebecah jerked herself free. "I do not. Now, let me pass."

"So you can run to my mother? You've always been so crafty with her. She has taken your side too many times. But now she's too sick to protect you."

"I'll not stand here and argue," Rebecah told her with force. Pulling her arm away, she moved on. Dorene followed.

"Father will be back soon, if he thinks it's urgent enough to pull away from business." Dorene shoved her hair away from her face and gripped the stair rail. "I expect he will be interested to know you went to Ashburne."

"Why should he care? Ashburne is my home."

Dorene laughed under her breath. "I looked out the upstairs window and saw a man with you at the gate. I saw him embrace you and then ride off. It was Jack."

"He was on his way to Standforth."

"Was he escorting you from Ashburne?"

"He helped me here."

"From Ashburne?"

"That is all I shall tell you."

"You had Henry."

"The roads were treacherous."

"I'm going to tell my father you were with Jack. You've stood in my way for too long."

"Your imagination is too strong and misdirected, Dorene. Do not let it lead you too far astray."

"It shall lead me to ruining you."

Lady Kathryn called from down the corridor. Upon entering, Rebecah rushed to her aunt's bedside. Dorene remained in the doorway. Rebecah knew Dorene was afraid she would catch the sickness if she entered. She covered her mouth with a handkerchief, waited a moment to see if her mother wanted her, and then left.

Lady Kathryn's hand felt hot. Fever ravished her body. Red blotches covered her skin. Her breathing labored and her lungs were congested. She looked thin, pale as her bed sheets. The quick smile she once gave, looked lined and forlorn, her lips white and cracked. Rebecah held a glass of water to her ladyship's lips and tried to get her to drink. She only had enough strength to wet them.

Rebecah had listened to a horse galloping down the drive toward the house. She hoped it were her uncle. March walked inside Lady Kathryn's room with a letter.

"Word has come from Sir Samuel. He wishes you, Dorene, and Master Hugh to leave Endfield immediately. The three of you will be safer in London, away from the sickness."

Rebecah looked over at March. "I cannot leave."

"Sir Samuel does not want his grief compounded."

"Since Dorene and Hugh have stayed out of the sickrooms they should go. I'll stay."

"You'll have to answer to your uncle why you disobeyed his orders."

Lady Kathryn coughed violently, and Rebecah turned to her.

"I'll keep it in mind, Mrs. March. Now, please bring the water inside. I shall need clean bed sheets. Burn the others. Lady Kathryn will need bathing and a clean shift to wear. We must do the same for Lavinia."

"If you think it will ease their suffering I will do as you say."

The lady, Rebecah believed to be the most beautiful among her family, had grown frail as a plucked rose, her bright eyes dull, her hair disheveled about her drenched body. Kathryn Brent uttered incoherently as she fell deeper into the grip of fever. Breathing grew more difficult as the minutes went by.

Rebecah heard the commotion outside the room. Hugh called for his mother, pleaded he not be sent away. It cut deep within her he could not see her. Jess howled. She heard Dorene scold her brother.

Wondering if she had made the right choice, she went to the window and saw the footman strap a trunk to the back of the coach, while the coachman held the door open for Dorene. As soon as the door shut, the coachman climbed back to his perch, cracked his whip, and the coach rumbled away. Jess ran after it and stopped at the gates.

"Samuel?" Kathryn searched a void. "Are you here?"

Rebecah turned. "He is on his way." She stroked Lady Kathryn's hair, and hoped it were true. "Rest easy. March has sent him word you are ill, and I've no doubt he is close by."

Lady Kathryn grabbed Rebecah's hand. "Pray for me. I'm afraid."

"It will be alright."

"Lavinia?"

"March is with her."

Kathryn Brent drifted off. March entered the room. She would sit with her awhile if Rebecah would go to Lavinia. She ran her hands over her eyes, and left her aunt in March's care.

For over an hour, Rebecah soothed Lavinia's head with a cool cloth, brushed out her hair, and assured her she would recover quicker if she tried to drink the broth March left on the table beside the bed. But in the other room, Kathryn Brent grew worse, and March called for her.

The light coming through the windows of the house grew dim. Twilight came and the house grew colder. Stressful hours dragged with the howling wind, and a slow wet snowfall brushed the windowpanes. Rebecah's eyes grew heavy and she fell to sleep with her head nestled in her arm. Her hand held tight to Lady Kathryn's, just as she had held her father's hand the night he died.

When dawn broke, Rebecah opened her eyes. Ruby clouds stretched across the sky beyond the enormous window in the bedchamber. She looked over into her aunt's quiet face. Kathryn breathed out slowly. Her hand slipped down along the bedclothes. The long night of the soul had ended. Like a candle flame it vanished and left a trace of its vapor to linger a moment. Rebecah stared at her aunt's face and trembled.

"I'm glad I was with you," she whispered. She wept, desperate with grief and hating death.

Samuel Brent arrived too late to console his wife in her final hour. He would not go into Lavinia's room, for like Dorene, he fear he would catch the fever. With a heavy gait, he stepped inside the bedchamber. Rebecah stood behind him with March. He stopped at the edge of the bed, gazed at his dead wife, the glow of a candle alighting upon her face. He fell forward with a cry and gathered up his lady's lifeless body in his arms.

"Kate, my dear Kate," he wept.

Rebecah could not fight the tears, and she knew to leave him alone. She turned and walked down the corridor, numb with sorrow.

* * *

Brent sent a courier to London ordering the return of his daughter and son. A private service was held at Endfield on Tuesday. The body of Kathryn Brent was borne from the house to the Brent mausoleum overlooking green fields. Old trees shadowed one side, and a pond mirrored the sky of swift moving clouds.

A funeral drum marked the procession. With each repetitious beat, Rebecah felt her heart break a little more. Lady Margaret walked beside her, while John Nash walked in the rear with his father. She turned her head and looked at him. She could not smile today.

The minister opened his prayer book. "We are but dust," he read.

103

Rebecah felt her heart lurch.

"And to dust we shall return."

Her eyes filled. The finality struck her. Where could she find the comfort in such words?

Lady Margaret grabbed her hand and held it. "All is not lost. All is not forgotten. The day shall come when God shall wipe away all our tears. There shall be no more death, or mourning, or crying, or pain. For the old order of things shall pass."

The wrought iron gate was shut and the mourners moved away. Rebecah looked back to see her uncle standing alone in front of the tomb. She went in a different direction from the others, down the grassy hill toward Merry Marsh Church.

Dim daylight made its way through the windows. She collapsed in the last pew, buried her face in her arms. Then other hands touched hers, warm and firm, manly and comforting. He moved them away from her face and she looked up. Nash pulled Rebecah into his arms.

"I'm sorry. I liked Lady Kathryn."

"I do not know how the others will do without her. I cannot believe she is gone."

"She remains in your heart and in your memories. You must hold on to what she gave you."

"I will."

"Let us wait a few days before I come for you. You are needed here."

She moved from his shoulder and gazed at him. His face and eyes expressed with such varied emotions, of sadness and grief, of tenderness and love.

Footsteps came behind them. Sir Rodney, hat in hand, looked embarrassed to have interrupted. "I apologize, but Samuel wishes us gone. He wants no one at the house."

Nash stood and placed his hat on his head. "I understand, Father."

Then he took Rebecah's hand to lead her home.

David Harcourt lingered outside on the lawn. They said a few words, and then Nash mounted his horse and rode off.

"It must be hard for you, Rebecah. Sir Samuel should have allowed the Nashs to stay," David said.

"He seldom thinks of comforting others. He's in his own grief."

David took a step forward. "How is Lavinia? Is she going to recover?"

"Her fever broke last night. Come inside."

Not a sound could be heard in the house. March took David's hat and cloak, and he waited in the foyer. Rebecah felt the loss of control, and rather than be embarrassed by a burst of tears, she hurried up the stairs.

In her room, she rummaged through her clothes, tossing onto her bed what she would take. She felt panicked to leave, wanting Nash more than ever.

Someone cleared their throat and she looked up. David stood in the doorway turning his hat between his hands.

"I'm worried about you."

She turned back to her clothes. "I'll be fine. But I appreciate your concern."

"You are leaving Endfield?"

"I cannot stay any longer."

"You are going away with John Nash?"

She wondered how he knew. "You will not say anything, will you, David? It's so important you do not."

"Of course I won't. In fact, I'll do whatever I can to help. I want Lavinia to come away with me as well. So you see we both know what you're feeling."

Rebecah laid a dress in her valise. "She loves you, you know."

He glanced down the hallway. "Can I see her?"

She went to him. "I'll find a way."

He followed her by way of one of the servants' stairs. Lavinia had been moved to another room on the upper floor, away from the rest of the family. Dark paneled walls and old Turkish runners heightened its venerable atmosphere. After a quiet knock, Rebecah opened Lavinia's door and went inside.

"How are you feeling?'

"Better. But I missed mother's funeral."

"You've been too ill. She would understand."

"I cannot believe she's gone. My heart breaks, Rebecah."

Moved with compassion for her cousin, Rebecah drew Lavinia into her arms to comfort her. "Someone is here to cheer you up."

Dashing tears away, Lavinia moved back. "Who? I look frightful."

"David. He's waiting outside the door."

Lavinia sighed. "David?"

"To think he cares so much to ride all the way from Plymouth in the cold, risking life and limb sneaking in here, just to inquire after your health. How many men do you know would go so far?"

"John Nash is the only other one I can think of." Lavinia smiled. "David loves me, doesn't he?"

"I am convinced he does. You should see him. Surely you cannot turn him away now."

Rebecah opened the door and allowed David in. She waited on the threshold, watched him bend over and kiss Lavinia's hand. In whispers he spoke tenderly, stroked her cheek.

David looked over at Rebecah. "She is getting better, don't you think?"

"Lavinia is strong, and your visit has made her happy."

"We want to marry with or without Sir Samuel's approval. As soon as she is strong enough, we are going to Greta Green. My practice is prosperous now and I can provide well for her. Can I count on you to keep our secret?"

"Yes, David. All I want for Lavinia is for her to be happy."

"Thank you, Rebecah. We shall not forget it."

* * *

The following day, Samuel Brent looked from his window at a hired coach outside on his drive. The coachman put Hugh inside, then shooed Jess away with a kick of his boot.

Hastily clad in a winter cloak, Rebecah rushed to the boy, as the coachman mounted his seat and dragged the reins through his hands. Brent observed her closely. She hugged Hugh, kissed his head, and then Hugh kissed his cousin's cheek. She held his small hands, and Brent could tell she was speaking to him.

He wondered what she was saying.

His face grew rigid. How could she defy him? But then, the sudden memory of having once loved and lost, and having married not loving, whipped through his mind like a tempest. The reality of it for Rebecah pounded at the door of his locked heart. For a moment, he wondered if he were wrong. Was he dooming her to an unhappy life with Lanley? Gathering his will, he tossed the idea aside. In time he learned to love Kathryn and she him. So, it would be the same for Rebecah and his daughters.

He balled his fist and knocked it against the windowsill. A vow trembled on his lips. He would not allow her to see John Nash again. He would banish him from stepping anywhere near Endfield.

Endeavoring not to listen to the pounding in his head, he gripped his hands together until the knuckles turned white. *It is not possible she cares so much for a traitor. She must know the truth. She will learn to hate him.*

The coachman cracked his whip and the horses lunged forward. Brent frowned hard and turned away. A moment and he heard Rebecah's footsteps outside the door. She paused a moment and then went on. He knew she and the others were hurt he had sent Hugh away and wanted to tell him so. But of course they could not. He wouldn't hear of it. His pride steeled him and he swallowed a large glass of port wine.

"I had to do it." He tossed down the glass. "The boy is in need of an education. A governess would spoil him. It's the right thing to do."

Hugh, like most boys, grew inquisitive and bright. A cast of the old philosophies and old conventions, Brent failed to see it. After all, his father had sent him away to school when he was a lad. Rarely had he seen his father more than twice a year. Attention and affection softens a boy and will make him grow up to be a weak man. Strength came from firmness, aloofness, and reserve.

As much as he tried to justify his actions, Brent knew he had flaws in his reasoning. His beliefs were broken and his soul empty. He stared in the mirror hanging over the settee. His haggard face frightened him. Left alone without his wife terrified him.

A painful revelation flooded his mind. His family was torn without Kathryn, and his own son a stranger. What legacy had he left his heir? His daughters would marry as would his niece, and then he'd be abandoned to live out a lonely existence in his large house with its aging furniture and dusty old books and carpets.

He sank into a chair in front of the fire, and covered his face within his hands.

"Oh, God, help me."

CHAPTER 16

Rain lingered over the countryside for a week. Fog entwined both day and night. Previous snows melted and rivers and streams swelled. Roads were muddy and full of ruts and holes. Rooks crackled in the trees and the drenched earth smelled of mold and trodden leaf.

Rebecah stood out on her balcony in the early morning light. She watched clouds part to the north, giving way to a blanket of blue. She breathed deep the crystal air. Hope beat in her heart. Soon she would be with the one she loved and leave this place. But why hadn't she received his letters?

She looked back inside her room to see her valise sitting near the door. A sudden sense of dread seized her. Perhaps they had been intercepted.

She tightened a loose ribbon hanging from her bodice. Then she went downstairs. Quietly she approached the study. Her uncle sat in an armchair by the fire, as he had done each day since his wife had passed, in the dark with the drapes closed. He took no care in his appearance. His beard was days old and his hair hung limp against his neck and shoulders.

She hoped to speak to him…or simply listen. Feeling sorry for her uncle, she wondered if it would help.

"It's extraordinary this letter arrived," she heard March say. "The courier insisted he give it to Miss Rebecah."

"A secret correspondence?"

"I snatched it out of his hand."

"You've never taking such liberties before, March. I'll trust your intuition this time."

Brent tore the letter open. Rebecah stepped back, feeling her heart beat harder. The letter had to be from Jack. About to burst into the room, in hopes of getting the letter before her uncle could read it, she halted with her hand on the door when Sir Samuel spoke.

"How dare him," he stormed. "That turncoat intends to meet my niece tomorrow at dusk. Well, he shall find himself alone. I tell you now, March, if he so much as darkens my door to see her, slam the door in his face."

"Yes, Sir Samuel."

Rebecah's hands clenched to see him tear the pages to pieces and throw them in the fire.

"Where is Rebecah? I want to speak to her."

Hearing footsteps, Rebecah backed away. March opened the door wide. A flash of sunlight came through the window and revealed the widow's gaunt face, expressionless mouth, and sad eyes. What, or who, had made the old woman so bitter, so old and stern, so sad, was a mystery.

"Miss Rebecah, Sir Samuel bids you come in."

The library was warm with a fire. Brent motioned to Rebecah to close the door and come inside. Struck by the worn condition of his eyes, she felt compassion for his loss, though he showed her none.

She sat opposite him, avoiding his stare. Then, rallying her strength against him, she raised her eyes and fixed them upon his.

"It has occurred to me perhaps this time of grief for the family has lead you to think your marriage to Lanley will somehow be delayed."

"There should be an allowance, Uncle, for the time of mourning."

"I'm aware of the custom. But there will be no delay. You can look forward to your wedding at the end of the month, after the bans are read."

She felt the blood rush from her face. "But I'm not ready to marry. It's too soon."

"We've discussed this before. I think you want to argue for other reasons. What are they?"

"For one, I do not love him."

"A poor excuse these days. Tell me the rest."

"I have no other reason other than what I've told you. It should be enough."

"Strike me deaf, Rebecah! I'm too tired to argue." He covered his brow with one hand in an anxious gesture. "You will marry Lanley. By law, you are constrained to be submissive. You are not an independent being."

"You cannot force me to wed him."

"Oh, I cannot, you say? Shall I pack you off and send you to Lanley's aunts?" Brent rubbed salt into the wound.

"No, Uncle. Lavinia needs me."

"She is recovering and has Dorene and March to look after her. You can hardly use her as an excuse, now can you?"

"Perhaps the suit should have been Dorene's, not mine."

"It would have been if not for your father's agreement. The truth is you're blinded by your love for another man."

Rebecah lifted her eyes away from his. "Is it wrong?"

"You are letting your emotions rule you."

She placed her hand against her chest and grew cold at his heartless words, words that frightened her like a dagger caressing her skin. She felt the throb of her heart increase against her palm.

"Lanley is a gentleman of means, that is true. But money does not guarantee happiness. I am thinking of him as well. Must he have a wife who does not love him?"

"Lanley hasn't a care whether you love him or not."

"Send me anyway but not to Lanley…"

"Have you failed to see your duty?"

"I have a duty to my heart and to God, sir."

"Then you are a fool. Would you defy what your father commanded on his deathbed?"

"I do not love him, Uncle Samuel."

"Love is unimportant."

"It is everything."

"You argue now, but soon you will see the sense of it."

"I would be living a lie if I did."

"You will be obedient!"

"At least give me more time." Rebecah looked at him with a plea. She hoped her eyes cut him deep.

"I learned you visited Ashburne. Your aunt consented?"

"Yes. She sent me to put the house in order."

"And did you?" She did not answer. "Nash followed you there. Do not deny it. Dorene said you admitted it."

"He did not follow me. He was on his way to Standforth and the snow prevented him from going on. He took shelter at Ashburne. Nothing happened."

"Too much happened between you."

"Do not condemn me for something I have not done."

"Lanley will hear none of this, I assure you. It would bring shame to us."

"Shame will come if I marry a man I despise."

She glanced at the fireplace, at the bits of Nash's letter turning to ash. Would her uncle confess to her what he had done?

Brent clenched his teeth. He stood and lifted her by the shoulders. She let out a cry. "You will wish you never laid eyes on John Nash. He is responsible for your father's death." He shook her violently. "Do you hear?"

"It's a lie!" Rebecah threw back her head. Tears filled her eyes.

"It's the truth and I can prove it."

"No, you're trying to turn me against him."

Squeezing her arm, he pulled her over to the table in the corner of the room. "Read it."

Upon the glossy finish, beside a gilt candlestick, lay a letter with a broken red wax seal. She picked it up and opened it. Immediately she recognized her father's handwriting.

My Brother,

Though we have been estranged these years, a separation I regret, you remain my only brother. Who then can I send my beloved daughter to, save you? Therefore, I bequeath the guardianship of Rebecah into your hands. I've left her no fortune. I pray you forgive me. An arrangement has been made for her to wed Lanley. This is my last request.

Shield her from any contact with John Nash if he should dare to tread upon English soil again and invade our family with his traitorous person. While in Maryland, I had a confrontation with two men. John Nash was one of them. I do testify he shot me, an act done out of a heart rebellious to a divinely appointed Empire, and treason toward His Royal Majesty the King. The confrontation had been heated, and in the confusion surrounding us, we met eye to eye. I ask that what I believe is the truth, be held in secret for the sake of the family's reputation, and the grief it could bring to Rodney Nash, a man I've always admired.

For the sake of my daughter, she must never befriend this man, for certainly in the normal course of this life she may encounter him.

I remain your brother,
Richard Brent

Rebecah gasped. A long shuddering moan escaped her lips. The room grew narrow and dark, the air stifling. Cruel, gray horror shadowed her face as if she stretched out her hand and touched the side of a brier.

Her eyes were wide and tearless, her face pale. The reality of it seized and tore, rippled through her in a surge of pain to break her. Something died within; a thing once beautiful shattered and turned ugly. Love crumbled away, like a rose once dewy and soft, succulent with life, pressed, then turned to dust.

"He robbed you of your father," Brent said. "He courted your emotions with such passionate vigor. How could he have been so kind, and yet hide the truth?"

Rebecah stood in the glare of sunlight coming through the window. Her eyes remained fixed on the letter in her hand. If only she could close her ears and cause the words on the page to fade.

"How did you come by this letter?" she asked, in a voice sad and quiet as the wind brushing against the windowpanes.

"Margery Holmes sent it to me. I read it the day I buried my lady. It was found among a stack of Richard's papers."

"Had Margery read it?" Rebecah asked.

"Of course not."

"Are there others?"

"Should there be?"

"I just thought…"

"Richard had no reason to lie."

"No."

"You don't understand what it took for me to hold back when Nash stood in my presence at my lady's burial. I did it for Rodney, for he has been a good friend to me, and his wife is my lady's cousin. Bad blood is what Rodney got for marrying a colonist before Margaret. I could have Nash arrested and hung."

She shot him a glance of desperation. "No, for their sakes!"

She hurried over to the fire and threw the letter into the flames. It caught and the fire consumed it. Then she regretted what she had done.

Brent's eyes widened. His face stiffened. "Do you know what you've done? You've destroyed the evidence."

She got to her feet. Her legs felt like lead as she went up the stairs. Once in her room, she shut the door and turned the key in the lock.

She looked around the room and listened. How she hated the stark quiet.

With tears streaming down her face and her breath coming up in short gasps, she stretched herself across the bed, folded her arms under her face and wept. Her heart broke. Her hopes and dreams of lasting love shattered.

CHAPTER 17

Rebecah threw on her gray riding frock and wool cloak and headed out to the stable desperate for open spaces. It would do no good crying in her room. She would ride out to Merry Marsh, sit in the sanctuary of the church and watch the sunbeams come through the stained glass windows.

The scent of fresh hay filled the stable. Star snorted and shook his golden mane. Tears of grief rose in Rebecah's eyes and she leaned her head against the horse's broad neck. She'd been ill all night, sleepless, trying to accept the fact Nash was not the man she thought him to be. She wanted what she felt for him removed, replaced with cold repulsion. Perhaps then, it would not hurt so much.

Nightmares haunted her during the night. Lanley's face stood inches from hers, his hot breath touching her skin. 'Let us cinch the marriage,' he urged. 'I must touch you. I must.' And he would reach toward her.

In her dream, Nash stood in her doorway with his back turned, while Lanley spoke his words of lust. He would walk out, fading into a fog. She'd hear a pistol fire and her father's voice calling.

The intolerable night ended and a new sun prevailed on her to escape the house and face what promised to be an unbearable day. She waited impatiently, watching the groom saddle her horse. Once he was finished, she waved him off and he left for other duties.

A frisky border collie waved its tail, brushed against her, and whined for a caress. Rebecah patted the dog. "Hello. Where did you come from?"

"She's mine."

When she looked up to see Nash, a sharp pain raced through her.

"Come, Toby. I hope she didn't frighten you. She followed me."

He leaned against the stable door. She could not help but notice the new suit of clothes he wore. She sensed the brown coat and knee-high riding boots were meant to impress her. He looked hurt, disappointed, and moved toward her.

"It would ease my mind if I knew you were delayed."

What could she say? She stared at him, her heart thumping. She had to keep her guard up no matter how smooth he spoke, no matter how handsome he looked.

"I waited an hour."

"I don't need to explain," she told him, looking away.

"Yes, you must. Is it because of Lady Kathryn? You are grieving for her?"

She hung her head. "Death is never easy to bear. The sting lingers for a long time, sometimes the rest of your life. You wish somehow to avenge it. But you cannot, can you? You can never punish what brought it enough."

"What is wrong, my love?"

She knew by his tone, cold dread was rising.

"You must go and never come back."

He shook his head. "I don't understand. Why are you saying this?"

"Ask no more questions of me. Let us part here and now."

"Part? We love each other."

"You must accept what I asked of you."

"What, that everything has turned to dust and ashes, over and done, without any explanation?" He reached for her and when she moved, he grabbed her by the hand and pulled her against him. "What has happened? Tell me."

"Let me go." She twisted, but his grasp was firm.

"You know I love you and would not do anything to hurt you."

At an inconvenient time, Lanley walked through the stable doors. Or was it? It was bitter, heartless humor. He appeared washed of color with the gray of day pouring down upon him. He gave Rebecah a smile, a short bow.

"My dear." He took a step forward. "I hoped to find you alone, so we might go riding together. I've come all this way, you see."

Rebecah moved away from Nash. "And so you have, Cecil." She forced a smile, calling him by his first name for the first time.

A slow breath slipped from Lanley's lips. A look of surprise lifted his brows. "Then you'd be glad to accompany me?"

"The groom saddled me a horse. I meant to ride alone."

"Oh, you cannot do that. A woman ride alone? It's unheard of. I see Mr. Nash is here."

"He was just leaving." Lifting her skirts, she walked past him.

"Rebecah, where are you going? Come back at once."

She wanted to turn on her heels and lash back. Instead, she kept walking. To stay another moment would be unbearable—she did not want Nash to see the tears in her eyes.

* * *

Dumbfounded, Lanley stared after Rebecah. "I say, Nash. Females are moody creatures."

118

"Yes they are." Nash, too, stared after her, but with thunder pulsing through his veins.

"What are your intentions?" Lanley asked, lifting his nose higher.

Nash gave no reply. He hurried past Lanley to go after her. Toby followed at his heels, and he turned and ordered her back. He saw Rebecah walk up the hill. The woods were heavy with the gray sky, and the ground wet from melting snow. He followed her into them and his boots sunk into layers of rotting leaves.

"Rebecah!"

"Go away," she called back. "I don't wish to speak to you."

He could tell she was crying.

"Stop, my love. Tell me why."

She turned, her eyes misty. "If you follow me, I'll scream."

"I haven't a care if you do."

She walked on.

He went after her.

"What has turned you against me?" he asked. "Why do you want me to leave and never come back? Do you think I can? Do you think I can throw away what I feel and forget you?"

She tumbled. Nash hurried to her. Although he was angry, he saw beauty in her face and grew weak. His heart hammered. "Are you hurt?"

"Go away." She moved and moaned.

"You're hurt. I'll take you back and have March send for the doctor." He went to lift her.

She shoved his hands away. "No. I don't want your help."

"Be still!"

"Don't order me!"

"I will. You're being foolish."

"Yes! I'm very foolish. If you had told me everything from the beginning concerning the quarrel you had with

119

my father, I would not have gotten involved with you. But no, you concealed the truth from me."

His chest tightened. "Rebecah, let me explain."

"No. Lies always grow into worse things."

"And now you hate me?"

"I cannot love you."

"You will not hear me out?"

"At the moment I find it hard to do."

Lanley came staggering through the trees. "She is injured badly?"

"A twisted ankle," Nash said.

"Dear me, I cannot lift her. You'll have to do it," he said looking at Nash.

Nash frowned. *Of course he had to show up.*

Though she protested, he lifted her in his arms and carried her through the woods with Lanley high stepping alongside. He took her to the house. March stood by the window, and saw them coming up the gravel drive. She hurried and opened the door.

It was explained in brief, as Nash lowered Rebecah to a couch. He looked at her a moment, then turned and left. If he had been alone with her, he could have done and said more. But with Lanley and March there, it was impossible.

He went to get his horse with his heart broken and bleeding. A shadow fell by the stable door and in stepped Dorene. Her hood, lined with rabbit fur, brushed against her cheeks.

With a proud lift of her head, she moved closer. "I thought you would be here."

"I cannot stay." His manner was cold, and he reached for the reins.

"Don't go, Jack. I can see she hurt you. It makes me angry, you know."

When she took off her cloak and let it fall to the floor, a carnal sensation shot through him. He did not want it to, but he was hurt and vulnerable.

She leaned back, her hair falling over her throat as she ran her finger along a post. "I'll miss devotions today I think."

"I doubt if they would do you any good, Dorene. But perhaps you should try."

She caught him in a moment of weakness. The intoxicating sweetness of previous days when he and Rebecah confessed their love for each other had been poured into a bitter cup. Dorene touched his face. Her fingers were soft and warm. Raising herself up, she brushed her lips against his. He gave no response.

"What is wrong, Jack? Don't you like to be kissed? Come. The hay is soft and warm."

"No, Dorene." Roughly, he put her back from him.

"I do care for you. I always have." She put her hand against the curve of his jaw. "Again I ask you. Don't you like being kissed? Is it not comforting when you're heartbroken?"

With her fair speech and seductive gestures, Dorene caused the want to yield build in him. With flattering words dripping like a honeycomb, she meant to break him. Her timing had been precise, to catch him in a moment of weakness. He lived the moment in twilight, in the dark night of the soul, and it was to her advantage.

Dorene tossed her head back. "You're not crushed. You've been rescued. It's better for you to be free than bound. Don't you agree?"

"If I went further with you, I'd be like a bird hastening to the snare."

She laid her hand against his arm and her smile faded. "It's not true what you say."

"Isn't it?"

"Solace yourself with my kind of love."

"How, when I don't love you and you are not my wife?"

"Oh, please!" She stomped her foot. "Must love always be the issue? Why not enjoy the pleasures without the chains?"

He put the reins over his horse's head. "I want neither pleasures nor chains. I'm leaving. Most likely you and this Brent bunch will never see me again." He put his foot into the stirrup and swung into the saddle.

"Expending yourself in a revolution will not help you forget."

"Perhaps not." He dragged the reins through his hands and steadied the horse.

"I'll never forgive you for this, Jack. You've been cold to me. While you're away, I'll make life miserable for Rebecah, just to get back at you. I'll tell her how you kissed me a moment ago."

"Ever the liar." He frowned. "But what does it matter now what you tell her?"

He nudged the sides of his horse and it moved out the stable doors. His dog ran ahead. He followed the high road with vinegar in his heart. He wrestled against the pain clawing at his soul, tried to suppress it as cold wind hit his face. He mulled over Rebecah's words again and again, and soon felt sorry for her. She was hurt.

His heart sank deeper, as his horse galloped on. Could he blame her for being hurt? Yes, he had met up with her father while escorting a patriot to the Pennsylvania boarder. Yes, they engaged, and he fired his gun. But whether it was his bullet that caused his death, he questioned. Regretting he had withheld the event from her, he wondered who had told her, and in what manner was it revealed.

Who then was his accuser?

* * *

Rebecah managed to get upstairs to her room after refusing Lanley's feeble attempt to help her. Her body ached, but she did not care. Her heart ached more.

"Do you believe this slander?"

Lavinia pushed the door closed and leaned against it. Rebecah could see how troubled she was by the frown on her face.

"How can it be true, Rebecah? How could Jack be held responsible for your father's death?"

"They confronted each other in Maryland…"

"I heard from my father about the letter and its contents. It doesn't add up."

Frustrated Lavinia took Nash's side, Rebecah turned away. "My father would never lie about a thing like this. When he came home he was dying. I saw the wound…I saw… heard them remove his arm."

"We should make inquiry to the physician."

"What good would it do? The only thing he can tell you is my father's arm became gangrene, and he removed it. But it did not save his life." Then she recalled Dr. Harvey's words.

I've been asked not to divulge the details.

What were these details? If only he had revealed them to her.

Lavinia sat next to Rebecah. "There was a man in the village five years ago who cut off his finger and died of an infection in less than a week. There must be more to this than what you've been told. How could he have lingered so long, crossing the ocean with a wound like that and then traveling home? You must think, Rebecah."

Rebecah made no reply.

"I'm sorry you're hurt," Lavinia went on. "But you must listen to sense."

"I don't wish to speak of it anymore."

"Oh shame, cousin. Are we God that we should condemn Jack? He must be heard out. Speak to him again and let him explain. How else will you know the truth unless you seek it?"

Rebecah's eyes filled with bitter tears. "Say no more, Lavinia. What is my pain compared to yours?"

"Your pain is greater."

Rebecah looked at her cousin. The room had grown dark. Outside the sky thickened with clouds and sleet fell. She listened to it pricking against her window.

"I still love him. And that is the greatest burden of all."

CHAPTER 18

For Nash the journey to Standforth grew agonizing. He rode for miles, blind and brooding, watching the sky grow thick and heavy with clouds. He mulled over the events of the day, tried to recall each thing she said, each look, each action.

He tightened his grip on the reins, stressed and baffled by the accusation laid upon him. He caused the death of Sir Richard Brent?

Impossible. But she blames me.

His mind drifted back to the day of the skirmish. Could a bullet wound fester so long before it would kill a man? *No.*

In a fair wind, it would take weeks to cross the ocean. Surely the British field surgeons would have cared for Sir Richard and gotten him well before making such a journey.

Perhaps the infection returned, and I am the cause.

His mind wrestled back and forth in a flood of questions. Then the guilt settled deeper. If he had caused this…"

How can she ever forgive me?

He crossed the windswept countryside, rode into the valley and edged his horse over a narrow cobblestone bridge. Beneath it, water flowed amid crusts of ice. A candle burned in a lantern beside the door and he sighed, his heart heavy.

Nash looked into the deepening sky. *What shall I tell them?*

Angus met him in the courtyard. Nash dismounted, handed him the reins and entered the house. Upon the table lay his letter to his parents explaining his departure. A moment and he stared at it, then snatched it up in his fist and crumbled it. A fire blazed in the hearth. He strode to it, threw the pages into the flames, watched them burn away to ash.

He waited for his heartbeat to calm, heard movement outside, the whinny of horses, and his stepmother's delightful laughter.

Margaret Nash came through the front door flushed and lively. She slipped off her cloak and laid it aside. She was plainly dressed, her frock a soft brown wool.

"What a beautiful day. You should see the sky, John." She sat by the fire and pulled off her riding boots. "Your father will be in directly. You know how he is about the horses."

Nash walked over to the door, stood on the threshold and looked back at her. In a few days he would leave and he wanted to remember her like this. Lady Margaret glanced at him with a worried smile. He saw, by her changed expression, she marked the fatigue in his face and the melancholy in his eyes.

She pulled the cord for her servant and ordered food brought. "Come and sit, Jack."

Nash ran his hand over the smooth polished wood of her table. He had no appetite. Food was no longer important—neither drink or material things.

"What is wrong? You were in some kind of scuffle?" She looked at him for an answer.

"It was an equal match." He tried the beef. Tonight it was tasteless in his mouth.

"You must be careful while in England, Jack. People are talking. The King's men are on guard every moment for dissenters and sympathizers."

"Let them watch me. I don't care." He shoved the plate aside. "I shall go in rags and pledge everything I own, even my life for *The Glorious Cause*."

She reached over and touched his hand. "You know war is the least thing I want for you. What will your father say?"

"That I'm a man and have a right."

She drew away her hand from his. "I'm meddling."

"No, Mother. I realize how much it troubles you."

"We might talk of something else. Did you hurt the man?"

"I was not in a fight with a man, but a woman. Hurt her? Indeed I hurt her."

Lady Margaret's mouth fell open. "What woman?"

"Rebecah. We quarreled and she broke it off. It was not meant to be."

"You're hurt as well."

"I'll get over it. It's my own fault for getting involved. I should have known better."

"Whatever happened between you and Rebecah can be mended." She tried to be encouraging. "Lovers do quarrel, and they make up."

He looked at her with sad, uncertain eyes and leaned on the table. "Can God change the heart of a person? Can he help me forget?"

"He makes every attempt to help us."

"Perhaps I'm just a blind fool."

"No, Jack. You're not that."

"Will it grieve you when I leave again?"

"Of course. I'll miss you deeply."

"Father should sell Standforth and come with me."

"Someday. But not yet."

"I understand."

127

"When you left home for America, my heart was heavy as lead and I grieved for your going. I worried and prayed. When at last you had come home and you told us of your success, I was put at ease."

"I hope you will remain at ease. I'm returning without a wife, which I can tell you regret."

The front door slammed. With his face flushed from the cold, Sir Rodney strode into the room.

"Ah, Jack, you're back. Good. Did you know my lady is a better judge of horses than any man in the county? The gentry are asking for her opinion on horses."

Nash smiled. "I was thinking of her better judgment."

Sir Rodney nudged him on the shoulder. "It's a shame you did not stay and go with us, being a brisk day and the countryside so pleasant. How has the day passed for you?"

"I'll leave you men to talk." Lady Margaret gathered up a book she had left on the settee and exited the room.

The troubled son put another log on the fire, and for a time they sat quietly looking at the flames build.

"What ails you, Jack?" asked Sir Rodney.

Nash faced his ever-patient father. "Rebecah has rejected me. She heard about the altercation I had with Richard Brent."

"Surely she understands the circumstances."

"She blames me for his death."

"Ridiculous. I cannot see how."

"Nor can I, unless…"

"What are you thinking?"

"He could have recovered, and then the infection reoccurred."

"After so long?"

"I do not know." Nash ran his hands over his face.

"This must be Samuel Brent's doing."

"I don't know who accused me…"

"Well, someone filled her ear. It had to be him. He wants her to wed that namby-pamby Lanley. Oh, he has gone too far this time. Is Rebecah blind?"

"I'm the blind one."

Sir Rodney shook his head. "There is more to this than meets the eye. I'll go to Samuel and speak to him in your defense—in front of Rebecah."

"I don't think that would be a good idea."

"I know Samuel well enough to know, he would not hesitate to have you arrested. Perhaps there's no time to clear you."

"I agree, Father."

Sir Rodney leaned forward. "As much as I hate this, you must leave, my son."

"Cowards run."

"Do it for our sakes, your stepmother's and mine."

Nash paused to think, then nodded. "I'll go first thing in the morning." He took hold of his father's arm. "But promise me this. You will come as soon as the fighting is over. Let us be a family again. Let me take care of you and your lady in your old age."

Sir Rodney hesitated a moment. Then he threw his arms around his son.

* * *

Before dawn, before swallows dipped and banked across the sky, Nash embraced his father and slipped into his stepmother's room to wake her. Her hair peeked out of her nightcap and she looked at him with startled eyes. He kissed her cheek and spoke tenderly. A moment later, he climbed into the saddle of his horse and looked back at the house he had grown up in one last time. Sir Rodney stood with his arm around his tearful wife at the front door, and raised his hand in farewell. Nash lifted his hat and spurred his horse. His heart was pained to leave them, and he steeled himself with a struggle.

The roads were clear, but he took a different route over the hills and open fields. When Endfield came into view, he reined in his horse and looked at it from the top of the hill. A new day had risen over the horizon, and the birds had begun to sing. His heart beat in his breast and he struck up his courage.

March's mouth gaped when she opened the door. "You're not welcomed here." She went to close it, but he brushed by her without saying a word.

He walked through the house, down the hall to the breakfast room expecting the family to be there. March hurried at his heels. "Stop, Mr. Nash. You mustn't go in there."

She may be right. I may be a fool for doing this. But I must have the last word.

The first face he saw when he walked in was Rebecah's. His eyes met hers, and she froze. Disbelief shadowed her face. Her uncle stood with an oath.

Dorene set her napkin down. "Jack. Have you come to grovel? You see, Rebecah. He has come to beg for your forgiveness."

"I've come to say my peace. A man has the right to face his accusers." He looked at Brent. "Throw me out, but let me defend myself before you do."

"How did you get in here?" Brent stormed.

"I tried to stop him," said March. "But he forced his way inside."

Brent moved from the table. "You may leave, March. I'll handle this." She obeyed and closed the door. The room remained silent except for the crackling of the fire.

"Hello, Jack," Lavinia said quietly and with sadness. "I'm glad you came if no one else is. I imagine you're leaving for America and we shall not see you again."

"Be silent, Lavinia!" Brent commanded.

"No, Father. I believe you're wrong about Jack."

"Be silent, I say!"

Humiliation swept over Lavinia's face, and she stared back at her plate. Rebecah reached over and gripped her hand. He wondered if this were a sign of empathy. Had time given her the chance to reconsider her rejection of him? Did she now realize what he had been accused of was folly?

"Say what you want, and be done with it." Brent shoved back his chair. "It won't change anything."

"I can assure you," said Nash, stiff with conviction, "I have one vow to keep and that is to leave and never return. Of that I'm certain you're relieved."

"More than you realize."

"My father and his lady have done nothing against you or you against them. I wouldn't want this to break their ties with the Brents."

"I do not intend to break ties with them. I do intend to have you arrested."

"What proof have you?"

"I shall acquire witnesses to my brother's story."

"It's true I met Sir Richard on the road going north. There was a confrontation." He went on describing that night in Maryland, how it was dark, how he and his companion were confronted by Redcoats, and the threats made by the officer on horseback. He told them all he knew. Yet in Brent's eyes he saw an unwillingness to believe anything he said.

"But I question whether my bullet was the thing that brought on the infection that killed him. How could he have survived as long as he did?"

"You admit to firing your pistol at him?"

"I do."

"There you see, Rebecah?"

Nash stepped forward, hat in hand, gazing at her. "You once loved me. Through an accusation your feelings for me have been destroyed. Had I been questioned fairly and heard out, perhaps our love would have been spared."

"It was my father that accused you." She spoke with such bitterness that her hands trembled. "I read his letter."

"Rebecah, forgive me. Believe me. I did not mean to hurt anyone. I may not have caused this. Let us make inquiries together to discover the truth…"

"I can take no more." She stood and rushed out of the room. Brent looked pleased at this, and a smug grin spread across his face.

"Once more you've upset my household. Leave a once. You'll pay the consequences soon enough."

Knowing there was no more he could do, Nash put on his hat and strode out. He caught a glimpse of Rebecah. He picked up his pace. She turned to face him, her back to the wall. The light from the window touched her face, etched the tips of her hair.

He took her in his arms. "Please tell me, I'll not be forced to live without you."

"Accepted it as I have."

"You're asking me to forget everything between us. You want to throw away our love based on an assumption."

"I have a duty to my father."

He brought her closer, his lips within inches of hers. "Rebecah, we love each other. What we feel cannot die as easy as you say. Let us find the truth about your father together. And if indeed I am the cause, I beg you forgive me. But I assure you there's more to this than what you've been led to believe. Please…"

Breathing hard and trembling, she raised her eyes. There were tears in them, and it cut him to the quick.

"It hurts too much. And I cannot bear it. Now let me go."

Pained he drew back, pressed his lips together to stifle the aching in his soul. He looked at her one last time, and walked out with thunder pounding through his veins.

CHAPTER 19

When night grew old and the clock in the hallway struck midnight, Lavinia and Rebecah stole down the servants' stairway in the dark. Never before had the wood creaked so loudly. Softly now they stepped. Once down, they made their way out a side door toward the grove of trees beyond Endfield's gate.

A pair of horses stood beneath the trees. David stepped forward, called to Lavinia, and lifting her gown, she rushed into his arms.

"You're so brave to leave," Rebecah told them.

"It would not have come to this if Sir Samuel had given us his consent," David said.

"You will come see us, won't you?" Lavinia asked.

"Yes, of course I will."

They embraced, bound by the selfsame search for tender love. But one held fast that treasure, while the other had tossed it away as if, instead of choice gold, it had been rust and tin. If only things had been different, she and Nash would have run away together too. She wondered if her father's letter had saved her or ruined her life. Time would tell.

"We must hurry." David helped Lavinia onto her horse. He looked at Rebecah and sighed. "My thanks, Rebecah. You took a risk." He leaned over, kissed her cheek, and climbed into the saddle.

Turning the horses out onto the road, they rode off and vanished in the gloom. Rebecah stood alone, listening to the hoof beats fade. Silence followed, then the wind rose and whispered through the trees. She gripped her arms together oppressed by the shrouding darkness. The wind blew back her hair from off her face. It stung her eyes until tears welled.

"I know you are everywhere, God," she whispered. Tears fell down her cheeks and she shook with broken emotion and a beating heart. "You are even in this dark place, where it seems there's no escape, where love seems a fantastic dream and I'm lost and now without a friend."

She tasted the salt of her tears on her lips. Then she walked on but not back to the house. She wanted to lose herself in the fields, lose herself there in the wind and cold, under the beckoning sky. But fear seized her, and she turned and ran back to Endfield.

She envisioned her beloved an ocean away, dressed in buckskins, a hunting shirt and leather leggings, moccasin boots laced to his knees, his hair tied back in a leather strip, an Indian standing beside him with folded arms. In the background she saw smoke and fire. She heard the blast of flintlocks, muskets, and the screams of men.

Then in a moment he was gone, gone with the drumbeat of battle, and the cold winds of war.

CHAPTER 20

March 1774

It was not the most beautiful months for a wedding. The hills were thick with frost, fields brown and muddy. Rivers and streams swelled, rushed, and murmured. Skies by day remained gray and nights were long and cold.

Outside Rebecah's window, hungry sparrows ate the breadcrumbs she left on the sill. They pranced, chirped, and fought for the morsels with beating wings. Sitting on the side of her bed, she stared at them, then at the gown hanging from the armoire. It was not what she had dreamed of wearing on her wedding day.

She had imagined a gown done in lace and apricot silk, trimmed in pearls. This gown was somber ecru linen, trimmed at the neck and sleeves with satin piping, laced in the back.

But it was not only the gown that made her sorry. It was the fact she was marrying a man she did not love. Yet she was going through with it. It was what her father wanted, what her uncle now demanded.

Seizing upon the chance that Nash was far from her, Brent expedited the arrangement. There was money in it for him and the freedom of an unwanted burden.

Lanley was more than pleased to change his plans. Rebecah's dowry was minimal, but he did not care. He was filthy rich. He had two country manors and a townhouse in London.

She tried to love Lanley. It was impossible. But she had come to esteem him at least. He indulged her with presents and love letters. He made promises she knew he would never keep, but they were pretty to hear.

She went to the fireside. As the flames warmed her, she thought of the night she and Nash were together at Ashburne. She loved him, but buried her feelings deep into an unforgiving heart.

* * *

John Nash stood at the rail of a ship with a heavy heart unaware it was Rebecah Brent's wedding day. He looked out upon a shining sea and brilliant blue sky. The smell of saltwater was strong. The roar of the sea crashed against the ship's haul and could not compare to the roaring in his soul. He gripped the timber of the ship, and looked west to a different world where an uncertain future awaited him.

He pressed his hand against his breast. Inside his coat pocket was the small leather-bound Bible his father had given him before his departure. Sir Rodney inscribed a dedication.

To my son, John Alexander Nash.

Herein find your courage and strength. Let God be your fortress and high tower, and an ever-present help in times of trouble.

Your loving father,
Sir Rodney Nash
In the year of our Lord, 1774

He missed him already, wished he could be half the man his father was. With the news he had heard from crewmen, he knew he would need more courage and strength than he could ever imagine.

The firebrands of revolution smoldered in France. The wheels of religious intolerance ground slowly and finely in Europe. The British lion and the American eagle stood eye to eye, one to preserve its power and dominion, the other to break free of what had become cruel and unjust dominance. Church bells tolled in Philadelphia, and children were starving in Boston. And out in the frontier and Indian War had begun.

Tucking the Bible back into his coat, he looked back toward the east. England and he had separated for good.

* * *

After a soft knock on Rebecah's door, March stepped inside and announced Lady Margaret wished a word. The slim, but stately lady, entered with a sweep of her skirts. Her face looked rosy and young, with sad, searching eyes. Rebecah curtsied and greeted her warmly.

Her ladyship's expression showed a strange pity, not joy for a bride to be. She held out her hands.

"Forgive me for coming to the house. We were meant for the church, but I could not stay away. I wish to speak with you before you go downstairs. I know we have time."

"I am always happy to see you," Rebecah said. "Especially today.

"Yes, your wedding day." Lady Margaret slipped off her gloves and set them aside. "How pale you look. Where is the bright bloom of a young woman in love?"

"I was not aware there should be a physical change, one way or the other," Rebecah replied. "I'm as I've always been."

"I don't agree. May I have my say?"

"I suppose you've come to advise me on the duties of a good wife." A smile struggled over Rebecah's lips.

"As your elder I could demand your ear. But I shall not impose on you in that way. I'll speak if you're willing to listen."

"Of course I'll listen, out of my esteem for you."

Lady Margaret frowned. "I suppose that shall be enough. But I hope your heart is willing."

"If I implied otherwise, excuse me for it. I sense you are troubled."

"I am."

"I hope I'm not the cause."

Lady Margaret clasped her hands together. "I'm grieved. My heart is pained for what you are about to do."

"Dispel your misgivings. Lanley will make a good husband."

"In name only. See sense."

"There's no better blood in England. I shall not lack for anything."

"He may be willing to provide dutifully toward you, but have you no regrets?"

"I do, but not with the decision I've made."

"You are not in love with him."

"I admit I am not."

"Do you no longer believe love is a prelude to marriage? The heart is what binds a man and woman together, not a title or wealth. Must you throw away your life?"

"My father made me swear before he died I would marry Lanley. I cannot go back on my word."

"You were once willing to do just that. Or have you forgotten?"

Lady Margaret stepped to the window to look out at the empty scene toward the woods. "You must forgive me for being so bold with my words."

"It's a quality I admire in you, my lady."

Lady Margaret hung her head. "I would have preferred you had called me mother."

Rebecah sighed. "I would have, if…"

Her ladyship turned sharply. "Please tell me what happened. Tell me or I shall fall apart. What did he do to make you despise him?"

"I don't hate him. But we cannot be together."

"I'm not blind, Rebecah. Jack was deeply in love with you."

Rebecah stared into the fire. *He loved me, yes, but not enough to tell me the truth.*

"What we shared was a brief infatuation."

Lady Margaret shook her head. "I don't believe it. You still love him."

"There are unhappy moments in life and one must accept them."

"Yes, and you are placing yourself into one by marrying Lanley." She paced away from the window, along the carpet the met the door. "I should not have come to you at all."

Rebecah knew Lady Margaret was right, but refused to admit it. She could not bring herself to tell her ladyship what had transpired. Already she was hurt by his leaving. To add injury to an open wound Rebecah could not do.

Lady Margaret took her by the shoulders. "I think you are making a grave mistake. Please reconsider. Please think."

Rebecah tried to give her a reassuring smile. "I have done both."

"Then you are going through with it?"

"Yes."

Lady Margaret shrugged. "Well, I am only too glad Jack is not here to witness it. He left, you know, for his friends and property."

Rebecah glanced at her with a start. "He is gone?"

"Yes, and I doubt he will ever return. I pray it makes him happy. But I doubt it. Not until he meets a woman who will love him unconditionally."

Rebecah lowered her eyes. *He is gone. I'll never see him again.*

"I pray he knows God's forgiveness," said Lady Margaret. "I wish he had yours."

"I cannot give it. My life now must go on with Lanley."

Lady Margaret snatched up her gloves. "Then take your path, Rebecah. I'll always be here for you if you should need me. I hope Lanley makes you happy. But try to see the course of unforgiveness is a lonely one. The end results of its achievements may bring more disappointment than you may imagine."

The maid entered to help Rebecah dress. Lady Margaret left to join her patient husband in the coach.

Inwardly, Rebecah grieved their meeting had ended so badly.

* * *

Lavinia could not stay away. Words had to be spoken, and so she and David traveled back to Endfield to see Rebecah married and try to make amends with Brent. The house buzzed with activity. Tables were being set, maids rushed about. Lanley's aunts were directing everything for the wedding feast, and complaining like a flock of geese.

"Your cook hasn't brought up the cake," they said. "How can we conduct a reception without the cake?" Brent walked away from their cackling.

Lavinia waited at the front door watching the scene within. "Father?" she called.

Abruptly Brent turned, and when he saw his wayward daughter, he looked at her stern and cold.

140

"Father, David and I are married. We've come to make amends and attend Rebecah's wedding." She held both hands out. "Give us your blessing and say you love me still."

Brent paused. He sighed. "You're not welcomed in this house. You will not see your sister or Hugh. No one is to speak to you again."

"Father, please!" Lavinia continued pleading with him, but he turned his back and walked away, leaving her in tears. David put his arm around his wife and led her back down the steps outside.

Despite her father's rejection, they would head for the church, fearing the worse was about to befall Rebecah.

* * *

An hour later, the Brents' coach came to a stop in front of the village church. Rebecah felt the deepest sense of foreboding course through her when she saw the cold stone facade and the black clad minister standing beside his church door.

With eyes moist with quick sensation, she looked beyond the hand extended to her to see people passing inside. Then her resolve weakened. Taking in a deep breath, she fought to regain it. She gripped a fold in her gown, and with her arm in her uncle's, she crossed the threshold.

At the altar, Lanley turned to see her. His expression appeared as one of gentlemanly arrogance. He wore a white silk coat and a silver-shot waistcoat, with breeches of blue brocade and white silk stockings. His scanty hair lay hidden beneath a fashionable wig, the buckles of his shoes silver, and an exquisite ruby sparkled on his finger. Lace tumbled in soft cascades over his hands.

Lanley looked boorish, effeminate to the girl approaching him. His receding chin quivered under a drooping lower lip. He fanned his nose with a lavender scented handkerchief. A moment more and their eyes made contact. Rebecah hesitated and busied her hands with the nosegay of holly she held. She felt her skin grow cold and she shivered. She wondered if Lanley could see in her eyes a fearful apprehension.

She saw passion rise in his eyes. She knew then her effect on him was overwhelming. He was experiencing carnal love, the desire for something kept from him, the kind that grips a worldly man furiously if allowed. He could not remove his lustful eyes from her.

Soon her hand lay sedate in his. Before her mind's eye, she saw herself lavished with gifts, flowers, and well wishes. Dinner was to be given with wine and dancing. Then Lanley would carry her off to his Georgian manor, a chilly house with enormous rooms and elaborate furnishings. There, weary and exhausted, she'd sit in an armchair beside a fire. Nearby would be a bowl of fruit, a bottle of wine, two glasses, and a candle. The fire would bathe the room amber. Its trembling light would set her skin to a velvety rose, her hair an irresistible bronze cascade. But her silken beauty would not dismiss the frightened glaze of her eyes. She was to be Lanley's, his to possess and enjoy as he wished.

In her vision, she saw Lanley watching her. Pulling her from the chair, he wrapped her in his arms. He kissed her. Her lips delighted him, but would not yield. She stiffened as he explored the curves of her body. She pleaded, but he did not stop.

She opened her eyes and met reality in the face. Terrified, her heart cried within. She remembered the vows made by the man who adored her, the warmth of his embrace, the gentle way he kissed her, loved her. Then she recalled his hurt and pleading eyes.

What am I doing! Wake, Rebecah, before it is too late!

142

She was startled back by the voice of the minister. "Will you repeat the words?" he asked in a whisper, noticing her fearful look. He stared at her with concern.

Lanley took her arm. "The vows, Rebecah. Say them."

She glanced at the minister then at Lanley. "The vows? No...I cannot."

Lanley squeezed her hand. "Rebecah?"

"Forgive me, Cecil."

He caught her as she fell and laid her upon the floor, a look of disappointment and bewilderment bursting upon his strained face. Brent quickly rose from his seat and rushed forward. The witnesses gasped.

"She is dead," uttered Lanley with wide eyes.

"Have you not seen a woman swoon, Lanley," said Brent irritated. "Get her up."

"Here is Lady Margaret," Lanley fanned his face with his handkerchief. "She will help."

Her ladyship knelt beside Rebecah. She pillowed her head on her lap and unfastened the lace at her throat. "We must take her back to Endfield."

"Is she ill, my lady?" asked Lanley on a note of fear.

"Indeed, she is." She looked over at Brent, then back at Lanley. "It appears the wedding is delayed."

CHAPTER 21

Frederick County, Maryland, Early Summer

After a long bone-shaking coach ride from Annapolis, Nash alighted at the same spot he had left months before. It was late in the afternoon on a Sunday. He walked down a hillside toward the river and home, on a trail scarce the size of a bridle path. Far in the distance, he heard church bells ringing in Fredericktown.

Returning to Laurel Hill was the foremost thing on his mind, though now and again the face of a girl clouded his goal. He failed to ignore his love for her, yet believed he had been foolish to assume she felt as he did. It annoyed him like the vines hanging over the road. With a quick jerk of his arm, he pushed them out of the way.

He welcomed the rush of cool air and breathed in until his lungs were full. Spring had come and mountain laurel budded along with the dogwoods and hardwood trees of the forests.

He climbed another hill, and from it he could see the tip of a church steeple piercing the horizon. Fredericktown seemed too remote to be rocked with the tumult of the world. Its fine houses of brick and stone sheltered godly folk of neighborly dispositions. Timber whitewashed houses and log cabins gleamed in the sunshine, where children played in grassy yards and housewives hung their

144

washing and churned butter. And like today, the bells of the clustered spires were heard for miles across the valley.

Nash had not slacked his pace. The road turned and there stood a row of evergreens twenty feet high. Passing slowly beneath their shadowy limbs he crossed onto his land. All this would make his memories of England fade he hoped. His heartbreak would be soothed and soon he would be over Rebecah.

He strode across an open field where he had felled trees. It was time to plant wheat. He imagined it knee-deep, rippling in the breeze like waves of the sea. Farther down a slope, he came to a creek shadowed by locust trees. Water sparkled blue as the sky above. He spotted his house now, and sprinted toward it.

Strange, but not a soul came out to greet him. He thought Joab would have been sitting out on the porch. He walked through the door.

"Joab!" he called.

He scowled at the dust that lay everywhere. Joab always kept the house clean—until now. A sinking feeling moved through him. What if something had happened to his old friend?

He went to the old man's room next to the kitchen. A patchwork quilt lay neatly over the bed, a tic pillow at the head. He searched the floor beneath it. No shoes. But there were some clothes in the closet. The kitchen larder was empty, save for a bit of flour and sugar.

Perplexed, Nash laid his pistols on the table in the front room and drew off his hat. He sat in front of the cold hearth and rubbed one of the barrels with a cloth to polish it. He hated the solitude. If things had been different, Rebecah would be with him tonight, and he would not be polishing pistols.

Tomorrow he would ride to town and make inquiry as to Joab's whereabouts.

The sun dipped lower, and he lit a candle. Pulling from his writing desk paper and quill, he penned the events of his voyage and journey home to his father. The words flowed at first and then lessened. He lifted the quill in a weary gesture and put it back into the inkwell.

His thoughts were too cluttered to continue. Besides the likelihood of his father receiving a letter was small. It would cost him to send it out from the Chesapeake. Suspicions were running high. The British were searching anything going out of the country.

Instead, he opened his Bible and found a blue ribbon marking a place in The Song of Songs. It was her ribbon, one he had gently taken from her hair while he kissed her. She had smiled and looked into his eyes, willing to bestow such a token of affection. He held it between his fingers and read the verse it marked until his eyes grew weary from the dull light.

Darkness had fallen and the moon shone through his windows. Outside an owl hooted. Though it sounded like the great horned bird, he could tell it came from human lips. He placed the ribbon back in its place, then picked up one of his pistols and pulled the hammer back.

He walked to the window and looked out from the edge. In the moonlight, he saw an Indian standing at the foot of his porch. Over one shoulder hung a bearskin fastened to a leather thong, the teeth hanging down the Indian's breast. Poised in his large hand was a bow.

He stood silent and tall, in beaded moccasins, with eagle feathers in his hair—Black Hawk, his friend and brother.

Two seasons ago, Nash had been tracking a buck he had shot, when coming through the woods he stumbled upon the lone Indian. Startled by Nash's sudden appearance, Black Hawk pressed himself against a tree. He stood rigid, proud, at his full height, his thick arms folded and his head raised unafraid. He stared back at Nash through valiant eyes, shaking with the fever that ravished his body.

Taking a step forward in a useless effort to plunge his knife into the breast of the white man, Black Hawk fell. Nash remained standing with his flintlock musket aimed in the direction of the fallen warrior. His body glistened with sweat, smearing the black war paint crisscrossing his limbs and face. Across his eyes, the black band lined in red remained unmarred. His raven hair, long and cropped short at the top, was dressed with feathers.

That day the warrior rambled incoherently. Nash, being the man he was, raised him to his feet and led him back through the forest. He nursed the Indian back to health, and Black Hawk said he would have killed Nash if he had been able. But now he owed him his life and his view of one white man changed.

Moonlight trembled over the feathers in his hair, upon the beads around his throat, upon knife and tomahawk. "I knew when the season of blossoms had come, and the bucks cry in the forests, my brother would return."

"You are welcomed, my brother," said Nash, as he came out the door. "Come inside. We will talk, if indeed you will sit in the house of a white man."

"You're my friend. We will speak as brothers in your house."

Black Hawk sat on the floor. "My brother is well?"

"As well to be expected. It was a long journey, and I missed home. You carry your weapons to visit me, Black Hawk. Has anything changed?"

"Not between you and I, my brother. But since my brother left, the woods have been full of noise. The jay has not been silent for many moons. Deer have been swift to hide in the deep places. The woods are dark, my brother. Rivers beyond the mountains run red."

Nash stared curiously at the Indian and frowned. "Trouble and darkness are everywhere. So shall it be until the end of time."

Black Hawk nodded. "The end of time will come when the Great One will take our bones from the earth and make us live again." He balled his fist and swept it downward, then upward as he spoke. "The bones of my people will not always be in the dust. We will not always mourn."

"I believe this too. Why do the rivers run red?"

"There is war. The whites have killed our people."

"The Indian does not accuse without a cause. He despises a lying tongue."

"This is so, my brother. But we too are men and act unjustly. The Indian has killed and burned men's houses. The whites have killed and burned our villages. The Indian has hated as the white man has hated. Our blood is the same color."

"So we are alike. None is different."

Nash thrust his boots on his table and leaned back in his chair. "But there are those who are evil men. Logan is a good man. Jefferson is a good man. But I've heard of Daniel Greathouse and the evil thoughts he has toward your people and the murders he and his men have done. Few believe it, but I know them to be true and not wild tales."

"My brother's spirit moans like the wind. I've not seen my brother sad in the face. England was not good to my brother?"

"My time there for the most part was well spent. But I was not wise, for I failed to guard my heart."

"Perhaps, my brother's heart is stronger for it. Now you understand when the warrior is not vigilant trouble comes. Now you are wary like the wolf."

"You are wise, Black Hawk. I'm glad you're my friend." He handed the Indian more venison jerky.

"Will your god give you power to heal your wound?"

"He has done so."

"He gave me the power to take this bear. His skin is a gift to you." Black Hawk untied the tong and swung the skin over his shoulder, then spread it out on the floor. "The fur is good, my brother."

Nash touched the bearskin. "It's too rich a prize to give me. But I thank you for it."

He knew not to refuse a gift from an Indian. It would be a great insult, and he thought of what Black Hawk went through to get it. "You took it with your knife, I see. You rival Logan in your hunting skills."

Black Hawk gently smiled at the compliment.

"Have you heard how the British makes war against us?"

"It is in the wind."

A low growl came from outside. Black Hawk rose and went to the door. "I tamed a cub."

Nash looked out and saw an animal rolling on the ground. "A mountain lion?"

"He is a kitten, my brother."

"How did you capture him?"

"The wild thorn growing in the mountains caught him. After I freed him, I brought him here to my brother's house. The dark-faced man was frightened of him and got his gun. But I would not let him shoot him. When he saw the cub would do no harm, he dressed his wounds with oil and I with the herbs in my pouch."

Nash smiled. "He will no doubt protect you."

"When you bring your maiden into your house, he will frighten the wolf from her door."

Nash frowned. "I've no maiden."

Black Hawk shrugged. "It is time I go."

"Sleep here if you wish."

"It is the roof. I cannot sleep beneath it on such a night. I will sleep in the woods beyond the house and look at the stars." Black Hawk walked into the grass and stood beside his cub. "Logan sits before his lodge. He is troubled. If my brother comes to the village, he will smoke the peace pipe with you to show his love. He asks that you come."

He watched the lithe warrior disappear into the darkness. For some time, Nash stood alone on his porch. Black Hawk's words troubled him. Would he ever love again as deeply as he had with Rebecah? Some would call him crazy to think it ever was love in such a short time. But he knew what he felt, that it ran as deep waters within his soul.

He then ran his hands through the length of his hair, and reentered his house.

* * *

The following day, Nash headed into town. The sun was brilliant, the day hot. The shrill song of a red-winged black bird filled the air, the cicadas twilled in the dusty trees.

Mrs. Charlton's tavern stood on the southwest corner of Market Street. He heard laughter from within and walked up to the open door. Pausing a moment, he stood across the threshold and watched the revelry inside. Tobacco smoke filled the room with a blue haze. A serving girl stepped between rough-hewn tables, laying down mugs frothing with ale.

A gray-headed older man leaped from his chair. No one knew Tobias Johnston's age, not even he, but most people believed he was the oldest gent in those parts. His dull gray eyes fastened on Nash. Wiping his hand across a bristly face, the old man's eyes brightened and he raised his arms over his head with a, "Yee haw! There stands Jack at the door, lads!"

Heads turned. Men sprang to their feet and cheered. A tumult of greetings followed. Backwoodsmen, farmers, and local businessmen hurried out of their seats and threw brotherly arms around Nash.

"We see England didn't swallow ya up, Jack!" A round of laughter followed.

"You've returned to the frontier in one piece, bless God. We were worried you'd not come back."

With a wink and a smile, Tobias raised his mug in a toast and drank it dry, the ale dripping along his beard.

Nash soaked in the warm greeting and smiled. "No one missed this place more than I. It's good to be home."

He could hardly be heard over the excited murmur of the men. Meg, the serving girl, put down a plate piled high with meat pie. Nash went to pay her and she pushed his hand back. He stood and thanked her with a kiss. The men cheered "Hurrah!"

Meg's cheeks turned red and she hurried away.

Soon enough he got an earful of news. "We're all mad as hornets, Jack. You'd not believe the measures they took to rescue the East India Company."

"Aye, they were facin' bankruptcy. Those Parliament men put a tax on tea."

"Yes I heard. It isn't right." Nash sat in the middle of the bench. "But you men don't drink tea, do you?"

"No but our wives do." A toothless man seated across from him slapped the table and roared with laughter.

Tobias blinked. "Well those patriots up in Boston gave them a real nice tea party in the harbor lettin' them know what they think of their tax."

In a more serious tone, the men talked about the angry southern Regulators, the disputes that brewed between Whigs and Tories, how debates rose to a fevered pitch at local town meetings. Marylanders remained in the thick, while crops prospered and the tobacco trade increased.

"Don't think, Jack, that it's been nothing but peace and plenty around here. That's not all that's been on our minds." Andrew Clarke surrounded his mug with callused hands, and his angry eyes looked at Nash.

Nash set down his mug of ale. "What has happened to make you so livid, Andy?"

"The British are bribing the Indians with the promise of guns and food." Clarke leaned forward. "We've had Indians attacking innocent folk west of here and their heading down this way. We'll be fighting two wars. Word has it some of the chiefs want to kill every white east of the Allegheny."

While he spoke, the tavern door opened and through it stepped a dark figure of a man. Jean François LaRoux tossed a dozen or more otter and beaver pelts onto the counter. He looked at the tavern keeper with a cruel twitching of his lips, his bronze face hard as clay, his eyes black pools.

"I'd have no dealings with the likes of him, Jack," said Tobias.

"It's LaRoux, isn't it? I've heard of this man."

"Aye, who hasn't?"

LaRoux was a man without boundaries, without an allegiance, or a nation of his own. He was his own ruler and refused to believe a higher authority existed. He did as he wished, took what he wanted, and went were he liked.

Tobias wiped a trickle of sweat off his temple.

"The man makes you uneasy. Why fear him? He blows into town with his furs and leaves."

Picking up his pelts, LaRoux stalked out of the tavern. The tension in the room went with him.

Clarke scooted forward. "Word has it there was a massacre near the Ohio. Maybe LaRoux was involved. That's why the Indians are on the warpath."

Deeply troubled by this news, Nash shoved his plate aside. "What have you heard?"

Tobias clenched his mug. "Nine of Logan's family was murdered including his wife and his sister who was with child, and Shikellimus."

Nash's heart trembled. "Logan's father? Mellana and Koonay?"

"Aye. You don't want to hear what they did to Koonay. Only the wickedest of men could have done what they did."

A chill ran through Nash. He knew these people, had known the warmth of their hospitality and their peaceful ways. He had heard Shikellimus speak to the elders, words so wise men were left in awe and reflective. Chief Logan was a man of peace. But with his heart and spirit broken, he would revenge his people.

"Shikellimus was a peaceful man." Nash frowned, the news unbelievable to him. "Mellana and Koonay were among the gentlest women. Why would anyone want to hurt them?"

"The blame has been put on Michael Cresap." Clarke's mouth twisted. "He may have held the Indians in some contempt, but to butcher women and children and an old man? Cresap is a wiser man I believe."

"They should have been left alone." Nash lifted his eyes and looked around the room. "Can any of us blame Logan for wanting revenge? He loved his family as much as any man. How many of us could stand such a loss as his?"

Grim silence followed his words. Then, among the men at his table, others spoke what they knew as well as their minds.

"Some of Cresap's men have straggled back across the border and have spread the news of the massacres."

"Aye, and Lord Dunmore appointed Cresap as major-general of militia."

"And wants a thousand savages to serve under him in the event of rebellion."

"Cresap would never fight for the British once Revolution is declared."

"He's a traitor and a coward!"

"He's been wrongly accused, Andy. It's Greathouse that's the guilty one."

"Logan and Cornstalk won't join forces with Cresap, either way. Dunmore is out of his mind."

"Dunmore is crazed alright. He's promised twelve pounds sterling for every rebel scalp taken by the Indians."

"We'll have to wait and see how God sorts this out. The killing of women and children will incur His wrath."

Nash's blood boiled. The more the men talked, the more enraged he grew. He could not help but picture the fear in Mellana's eyes, hear Koonay's screams, and Shikellimus's pleas for mercy. And the children—oh, what they must have suffered. And Koonay's unborn child—

Now settlers were reaping what wicked men had sewn.

Nash stood, his fist clenched. "So Dunmore sprung his trap. By this, he started a war that will turn the Six Nations against us. If it is treason to make a stand, then I'm guilty. We must resist these bullies who say they have a divine right to govern us."

The room roared with cheers.

"We are with you, Jack!"

"Liberty or death!"

Nash's speech was heated and the men listened intently. It was now a life for a life, and many scalps now decorated an Indian's belt. That night, the black horse ran through the wilderness and made its way down the banks of the Potomac, across the mountains into the westward frontier.

Tossing the waiting girl a coin to pay for his ale, he picked up his hat. "I'm looking for Joab. Do any of you know what he's been up to?"

"He didn't run off, Jack," Tobias answered.

"I wouldn't think so. But he isn't at Laurel Hill."

"Mrs. Cottonwood has him. She figured he'd be idle out there at Laurel Hill and so asked him to work for her until you'd come back. We heard she promised to pay him for his labor, seein' he's a free man."

"Did she now? Well, I'll make sure she does." Nash put on his hat and stepped out the door.

* * *

After making a round of visits to friends, all of which greeted him home with the warmest of welcomes, Nash made his way to the Cottonwood house moments before sundown. Shadowy silhouettes pranced like marionettes behind the white muslin curtains of an upstairs window. Bounding up the stairs, he knocked upon the black oaken door and waited.

When it opened, Mrs. Cottonwood raised her arms and let out a shriek. She howled so loud, Nash feared she would rouse the neighbors. But they were accustomed to her screeching, for she performed it whenever company arrived.

'Beware, Mrs. Cottonwood', they warned. 'You're like the boy that cried wolf.'

She was a widow in her middle years, her hair steel gray in tight curls about a face that resembled a full moon.

"Bless my soul! 'Tis you, Mr. Nash! Come home have you?" Her voice sounded like she was stricken with a nasal cold. "And so far a journey. I did not expect to see you. My, the night is a balmy one, and how the stars do shine. Do come inside."

With her mobcap on her head, and her tiny almond-shaped eyes blinking, she snatched Nash by the sleeve and pulled him in. Hurriedly, and with a catch of her breath, she shut the door.

"I've come for Joab, ma'am." Nash turned his hat in his hands, anxious to get this over with.

"Oh, I see." Pausing a moment, she wiped her nose with a handkerchief. "I figured as much."

Nash smiled politely. "I'm sorry, but this is not a social call." He followed her into the parlor. "I've only been home a day."

"A day, Mr. Nash?" She turned on her heels and leaned toward him. "And weary to the bone from your journey, I imagine. And you've brought no wife home with you from England?"

"As you see, I am empty handed."

She laughed. "It would be better if you found a nice girl from here, like my Drusilla." With a heave, Mrs. Cottonwood sat in her best chair. "Do be seated, sir."

"Forgive me, but I cannot stay. Where is Joab?"

"He has been a great help to me. I shall compensate you for his time."

"There's no need, Mrs. Cottonwood. Joab is a free man. Compensate him."

"Yes, I forgot. Since my husband passed on the work, well you know. A woman cannot do such tasks. The girls spend their time doing needlework and practicing music, as girls should. Good breeding is so important." She sniffed.

"Of course."

"I hope you're not angry with me, Mr. Nash. I may have spared you a lot of bother."

"How so, ma'am?" He grew irritated by the wait and shifted on his feet.

"Joab might have left the county," Mrs. Cottonwood explained.

"I arrive home and my house is a shambles. If he had stayed, I doubt I would have found it so."

"I'm sorry to hear your house is not up to your expectations. There was nothing for him to do out there alone. You know what they say?"

"No, Mrs. Cottonwood, I do not."

She squared her shoulders, bobbing her head like a hen. "An idle mind is the devil's workshop. I think that applies to idle bodies as well. Wouldn't you agree?"

"I would, Mrs. Cottonwood. But Joab is neither idle in body or mind."

"He willingly accepted my offer."

"It was his to make."

"Then you should not be bothered."

"You must forgive me. Now if you do not mind, I would like to see him. It's late and I have a ways to go."

Bustling from her chair, she went to the open doorway. "Joab!" she called, in a singsong voice. "Mr. Nash is come home. He wishes to see you."

In haste Joab appeared. The degree of his imprisonment at the Cottonwood home was more than Nash expected. Joab's attire consisted of a black waistcoat, beige breeches, polished shoes and buckles, and a white cravat. When he entered the room and saw his friend, he broke into a wide smile.

"Mr. John!" Jubilant, Joab put out his hand and they shook. "I'm sure glad you're home!"

"You've put on a few pounds." Nash smacked Joab on the side.

"Mrs. Cottonwood has a good cook, Mr. John. I'm afraid she's spoiled me—the cook I mean."

"You plan to continue your employment here?"

"Well, it was a temporary thing, until you was to come back."

"Go get your belongings, my friend, if you wish to come home."

"I'll be right back." Joab swiftly left the room.

"Leave the good clothes, Joab," Mrs. Cottonwood called after him. She turned to Nash. "Such things cost a pretty penny these days, Mr. Nash. If I get another man to help, I shall need them."

Mrs. Cottonwood followed the pair to the front door. With a cautious glance, she scanned the neighborhood to see if anyone watched. "Shall we see you in church on Sunday?" she asked.

Nash nodded his reply and lifted his hat.

"My Drusilla is near sixteen now. I expect you'll see her there and perhaps pay us a call later."

In an upper story of the house, curtains over a front window were pulled back. Out popped the heads of the Cottonwood girls. Nash lifted his eyes. The three younger, Lila, Penelope, and Felicia, were fair-haired and skinny, the marks of adolescence showing on their faces. Drusilla, the eldest, was clear of skin and bonny, with brown hair to her waist.

Nash walked out into the street. No one could compete with Rebecah. If he were to give his affections to a girl like Drusilla, it would be half-hearted. He pushed back his hat with a sigh and looked over at Joab striding beside him.

"Those clothes suit you much better."

"More comfortable, that's for sure." Joab slapped on his hat.

"Please, tell me nothing has happened to Meteor, that you stabled him in town."

"I did, Mr. John," Joab answered. "Mrs. Cottonwood let me keep him here. He's around the corner."

The moment Nash stepped inside the cramped stable Meteor lifted his head and nickered. While he patted the horse's neck and spoke to him, Meteor nudged against Nash.

"He's sure pleased to see you, Mr. John."

"I'm pleased to see him. Thanks for taking good care of him, my friend."

"As if he were my own chil', Mr. John," Joab replied with a big smile. "I love that horse."

"You wish to ride him?"

"No, sir. He and I are good together walkin'."

Nash climbed into the saddle and walked Meteor alongside Joab. Market Street was quiet, candles in the windows, a few folks sitting in their rockers on front porches.

He felt the coolness of night sink in and tried not to think of war. But his heart spoke a painful verse, and he considered the girl he loved.

He imagined she most likely was married to Lanley by now. If Lanley had been a man half worthy of her, he would have been happy for Rebecah. But for her to be that conceited blue blood's wife made his mouth twitch with anger. Memories were hard to shake and he tried to suppress the pain that gripped him.

"Tell me what you did while I was away, Joab." He looked down from atop his horse, wanting to divert his thoughts. "Perhaps you've a few stories to tell?"

For the next mile, Joab spoke of the Indian and mountain cat, of the storms that had come over the hills, and of Mrs. Cottonwood and her girls.

"You're a free man, Joab. Why did you go there?"

"I've a hard time sayin' no to folks needing' help." Joab walked on with a whistle, with his hands in his pockets.

They came to a bend in the road, an open place where moonlight bathed the land misty blue. Joab moved closer and touched the side of Nash's horse.

"Over there's where they found a man dead few weeks ago beneath the pines. He'd been robbed. Scalped too. Whoever done it left him sitting against that tree with his hands and feet hangin' limp as rags. Nobody ever found out who the man was. He's buried up there on the hill in Mount Olivet." Joab stood stone-still. "What's that?" He laid a hand upon Nash's boot and gripped it until his hand shook.

"Let go, Joab. It's nothing but shadows and the wind moving through the trees."

"It's the dead man's ghost."

Nash leaned down. "Dead men cannot walk, Joab."

He nudged Meteor with his knees, and the horse stepped forward. It whinnied and halted again. A twig snapped. The sound echoed through the woods. Nash made out a dark form moving toward them and drew his pistol. Slowly he pulled back the hammer. Shadows of swaying trees and flickering moonlight danced upon a man. Cautiously he stepped forward with his hand on his knife.

"A shot from your pistol might be swift. A thrown knife can be just as fatal."

Nash's horse shifted under him and he steadied him with a touch. "I've no reservations as to whether or not I should shoot if you pull your knife from your belt. If it's money you seek, seeing you lay in wait for a passerby, I've none to give. If it is my horse, men hang for less."

Raising his hand, LaRoux pointed his finger. "You're John Nash. You're a friend of Logan and an Indian called Black Hawk. You treat them as your brothers."

"I treat any man well who has well within him."

LaRoux twitched his mouth. "Little good is found in the heart of the Indian."

"You speak against your own people." Nash set his pistol against his thigh, while keeping his eyes fixed on LaRoux.

LaRoux stiffened. "I'm French. The blood of nobles runs through my veins."

"A Frenchman is deemed worse than any renegade Indian in these parts. People haven't forgotten the last war. Dark memories haunt some minds."

"A troubled mind is what they deserve," seethed LaRoux through clenched teeth.

LaRoux drew closer to Nash's restless horse. Nash raised his pistol.

"Stand aside!"

"Of course. The path here is too crowded."

Swift as a deer, LaRoux plunged into the forest. A horned owl glided from the broad limb of an oak. Its body and outstretched wings floated like a black kite as it screeched.

"We best hurry home, Mr. John," said Joab.

"Here climb up."

Nash pulled Joab up behind him. Soon they were free of the dark woods, entering upon a field brightened by moonlight. Purple clouds hung low above dark hills in translucent veils. Stars stood out bright and fiery to show the way home.

After a short distance, Nash turned in his saddle and looked back. The forest was level. Branches bobbed in the breeze. In a bloodcurdling cry, Jean LaRoux cursed white man, soldier, and Indian, including the man he just reckoned to his list of enemies. In revelry and violence his voice rose, fell, and went deathly silent.

CHAPTER 22

Rebecah closed the book she had been reading.

"Lady Margaret is downstairs wanting to see you." March held out to her another letter, one sealed in scarlet wax. "It is her wish you read this first."

Curious, Rebecah took it in hand, held it near the candlelight, and broke the scarlet seal. Her heart lurched when she saw it was from John Nash.

Dear Rebecah,

I've enclosed the lock of hair you bestowed upon me. It is no longer mine to possess. Yet the memory of it is mine, of its softness and color, and how the light played within it when I first kissed you. In time, such a remembrance will fade, just as I shall fade from your mind as quickly as I did from your heart. I pray you shall be happy in life.

Your Servant,
John A Nash

She ran her finger over the lock of hair and laid it back inside the letter. The thought of him so far away hurt. Now she must face Lady Margaret. There was no telling what she would say. When she stepped inside the room, her ladyship looked at Rebecah with a quick and friendly smile, and held her hands out for her to take.

"I'm so glad to see you. Samuel does not know I'm here. No matter. I would have come with or without his approval. I tried to come twice, but twice he told me I could not see you. A wretch of a man is he…Have you been crying?"

Rebecah wiped her eyes. "I'm composed now. Shall I have March bring tea?"

"The letter made you sad? I'm sorry I gave it to you. But it would've been wrong of me to have kept it."

"How were you to know what he would say, my lady?"

"His words would not have hurt you so deeply if you did not care."

An inner aching surged. Windswept were her hopes and dreams. It was yet too painful to speak of him. She gestured for Lady Margaret to sit. Lady Margaret looked over the room, her mild eyes showing worry. A plate of untouched food sat on a table near Rebecah's window.

"You've hardly touched your breakfast. And your bed looks as if no one has slept in it for days."

"No one has."

Her ladyship looked surprised. "Where have you slept?"

"Over in the window seat."

"That is not healthy, Rebecah."

"I have blankets." A mound of warm flaxen-colored wool lay on the seat.

"Why do you sit there, sleep there?"

"I like to look at the moon and stars. I end up falling asleep."

"March tells me Samuel has ordered you to stay in your room."

Rebecah nodded. "He has."

"That is nonsense. Such a rule is ridiculous. What is there for you to do all day long?"

"Read. Write letters."

Her ladyship set her lips tight. "I've brought some other news...from your cousin."

Thrilled, Rebecah looked at Lady Margaret. "Uncle Samuel has disowned her and forbidden her to come to Endfield. I've written, but I believe all my letters have been intercepted."

"I know they have. March told me that too."

"How is Lavinia?"

"She sends her love and is well and happy as you would hope. She is with child."

Joy filled Rebecah. "How wonderful for her and David. Too bad my uncle is so bitter."

"Ah, yes, bitterness. It keeps one from many things."

"How is David?"

"His practice is prospering. He too sends his well wishes. Lavinia asked me to give you this."

Rebecah pressed the letter to her heart. "I'm grateful. Thank you."

"It is the least I could do. Your cousin would be upset to see how you've been treated.

"Indeed it would grieve her. She is helpless to do anything about it."

"But you are not."

"I shall not stay here forever."

"I'm glad to hear it. But you will be cut off too."

"Foolish as it may seem, I do not care."

"You must pray for strength, Rebecah, for surely you are in despair. It does no good to bury what you feel. If you do, it will rob you of any happiness you might have. If you love him, forgive him. Then go on for your own good."

Rebecah shook her head. "You make it sound so easy."

"I never meant to imply it was."

Rebecah stood and looked at the courtyard through the window. "Has Sir Rodney come with you?"

164

"I'm afraid not. He is away on some kind of venture and will not step foot in the house. He is angry."

She saw a hawk circle above the southern line of trees, and one of the farm cats pounced across the grass. She desired to go beyond the gates, to see other people and do other things. To get away from Endfield forever was what she wanted.

"Men always seem to be away."

Lady Margaret rose and stood beside her. "Do you wish to be away, to leave Endfield?"

"Yes, more than anything."

"Come live at Standforth. You can come and go as you please. See whomever you wish."

Rebecah turned to Lady Margaret with wide opened eyes. "You want me to live with you after breaking off with your son?"

"Yes. Collect your things. Waste no time."

"But your reputation, my lady? Is it not true there has been talk of me, about what happened with Lanley?"

"I don't care what people say," Lady Margaret replied. "Do not think so long on this, else you'll change your mind and disappoint me greatly."

Rebecah threw her arms around Lady Margaret's neck and hugged her. "Thank you. I will come for a time, until I feel strong enough to go."

"On my word, Rebecah, go where?"

"To Lavinia. I could stay with her until the baby comes. Then I'll apply for a governess position."

Lady Margaret looked astonished indeed. "There's no need for you to do that."

"I need to make my own way in the world."

She stepped away, but before she reached her armoire, the door swung open and her uncle appeared in the doorway in his muddy riding clothes. Lady Margaret stood with a lift of her face, undaunted by his stern demeanor. Rebecah moved next to her.

"Ah, Samuel." Lady Margaret gave him a proud look. "You're back."

Brent looked at the women suspiciously. "Business is none concluded, Margaret. War comes, and with war there is profit to be made."

"I assume if His Majesty sends his troop and fleet to the Colonies, your stock in the iron mine shall not suffer for it. It should bring a good profit I should think." She swept forward, her skirts making a soft rustle along the floor.

"You're too outspoken for your gender, Margaret, and wiser in business than most men." For a quick moment, Brent stared at Lady Margaret. "What a beautiful woman you are for your mature years," he was bold to say.

"It isn't often I receive a compliment from you. But I'll forgo accepting it."

He shrugged. "Why?"

"Strong drink inflames your emotions and makes a mockery of a man."

"So, what has brought you to Endfield?" he said ignoring her comment. "March said you were up here."

"Rebecah is coming to live with me." She looked him straight in the eye. More and more Rebecah grew to admire Lady Margaret's courage. "Do you understand what I'm saying, Samuel?"

He swung around to meet Rebecah. "Is this true?"

"It is." She spoke with an air of respect, but not lacking confidence.

"She is of age, Samuel." Lady Margaret stepped forward. "You must yield your desire to control her. What you've done is outrageous and cruel. These are not the Middle Ages when men kept women under lock and key."

He threw out his arms. "I don't care if she goes. It's one less burden for me, one less mouth to feed. You've ruined your reputation, Rebecah. You'll never be able to show yourself in society. You've shocked the world by throwing off Lanley."

166

"Hardly the world, Uncle."

Brent frowned. "I've endured glances and whispers everywhere I've gone. With you leaving, perhaps people will think the better of me for it. Soon they will forget."

"Perhaps, but I will not."

His mouth fell open. "I took you under my roof when you were orphaned. The least you can do is thank me."

"You took her in out of duty, not love, Samuel," Lady Margaret said.

He looked at her troubled, and Rebecah saw he was broken and lonely without Lady Kathryn.

"It's good to let her go."

"Do not instruct me, Margaret."

"Lanley was not for her and you're disappointed. But she must live her life and be the only one accountable for it."

He slammed his fist on the table. "When have I not thought of what was best for her?"

Margaret frowned. "Hardly ever, I'm sure. Sometimes we demand what we think is best for the young without considering their feelings or the outcome."

He stiffened, unable to usurp the truth of her reproof. "She will regret not having Lanley when she has no money."

"She must find her own path and not follow the one you wish her to tread." Lady Margaret matched his words as well as his emotion.

"And what about your stepson? Shall you sway her mind concerning him?"

"He is innocent and you know it."

"The fact he shot a British officer, is enough," he stormed. "Whether or not it did Richard any injury to bring on his death, I admit I don't know. Yet he deserves some kind of punishment."

Rebecah's limbs trembled. He did not know? He now confessed his uncertainty after accusing Jack, after tearing them from each other?

"You succeeded in that, Samuel."

Brent raised his hand to his forehead. "It gives me a headache to think about it, madam."

"You deserve more than a headache. You were not compassionate toward Rebecah, or toward Lavinia your own daughter. It is coldhearted to force a woman to wed where she does not love, and then to separate her from the man she does by some unfounded accusation. For shame."

When Rebecah took a step toward him, a burst of sunlight streamed through the window. She stood in the shower of it, her cheeks burning and her eyes set without fear upon her uncle.

"Wish me well, Uncle Samuel. I've nothing else to say, except I pray you fare well in life."

She held out her hand. He looked at it and turned away.

"Forget you ever had a family at Endfield." He moved his hands behind his back and faced the window, so not to look at her. "You've chosen to be rebellious and disobedient, shirking your duty to marry where you should. You're an unfaithful daughter to the wishes of your father."

Rebecah's heart sank. Lady Margaret took her by the hand and she left the shadow of that dark and dismal house. Stark in black, her face bewildered and sad, March stood in an upper story window with her hand raised in farewell. Rebecah returned the gesture as the coachman cracked his whip above the horse's ears.

CHAPTER 23

Plymouth brimmed with ships loaded with riches brought in from the far reaches of the Empire. The air smelled of tea and spices from the Orient, tobacco and cotton from the southern Colonies, exotic fruits and sugarcane from the islands. Along the narrow streets, merchants hawked their wares, mingled busy housewives and servants. Shopkeepers opened their shops in hopes of a brisk day of business. Gentlemen huddled at a street corner to buy a newspaper describing America's latest treason.

A sooty palm pushed through the window. "Please, milady, a coin. Please." A woman ran alongside the coach through mud and horse dung. Stringy black hair fell out from beneath a dingy mobcap. Over her shoulders lay a tattered wool shawl. Her eyes were glazed with hopelessness.

Lady Margaret ordered the driver to stop. She feared the coach wheels might do harm. "Have you no work?"

"No, milady."

Tears flooded the woman's sunken eyes. Behind the dirty face may have been youth and possibly beauty. But the green eyes were lonely and desperate.

"You're speaking the truth and not lying in order to get money?" Lady Margaret said.

The beggar woman's eyes widened. "I'm not lying, milady. No one will hire a beggar. My husband left me— went to sea and has never come back. I lost the babe I carried and I've been sick ever since."

"In heart as well as body, I imagine. Get to a doctor, you understand? This should take care of it." Lady Margaret placed two coins in the tattered woman's hand. "When you've recovered, go to the Methodists meeting here, and tell them Lady Margaret Nash sent you."

"I wish to help as well." Rebecah handed the woman the last coin she had in her reticule. "Please do as Lady Margaret has told you."

The woman nodded and the coach moved on.

Lady Margaret eased back against the cushion. "I wish I could help them all. But, we shall have the poor with us always, so said the Lord Jesus."

Rebecah looked out at the crowded street. Deep down, she was angry with the world, angry with John Nash, angry with Samuel Brent, angry with her dead father. She looked over at the woman who had taken her under her wing and wished she could be more like her.

The road lay dappled with sunshine. Along the wayside were houses of black beams and plasterwork. Some were red brick with varnished doorways, thatched roofs and high gables.

Soon the coach halted and they were in front of Lavinia's house—a modest dwelling compared to Endfield. Rebecah admired the stone graced with ivy, the sun streaked windows, and boughs of wisteria over the door. It was a warm and inviting home.

After the coachman alighted from his seat and stretched his legs, he helped the ladies out. Rebecah noticed a black horse tethered to a post. It looked over at her and blew out its nostrils.

"It seems another guest has arrived." Rebecah walked with Lady Margaret over the flagstones. Her hand held down her hat against the breeze. "Will we be intruding?"

"Intruding? Not at all. We are expected."

The door swung wide and Lavinia hurried out with her hands stretched forward. "Rebecah! Oh, Rebecah, you've come!"

A whirl of laugher followed their embrace. The coach rolled away, and the ladies entered the foyer.

Lavinia kissed Lady Margaret's cheek. "I'm so glad to see you both. Was your journey tolerable?"

"As tolerable as may be."

"Please, come inside and lay aside your hats. I shall have tea brought in." She summoned her maid, a petite girl of sixteen, with hair and eyes as brown as the wood floor she stood on.

In the sitting room, Rebecah untied her blue hat strings and laid the hat upon a chair. The room was comfortably decorated and the walls were painted a soft yellow. It had a large bay window facing the garden and a white marble fireplace.

Lady Margaret stood by the door. "Do you have a room where I might lie down a while?"

"We've a comfortable room upstairs." Lavinia looked concerned. "Are you alright, my lady?"

"The journey was long and I'm weary. A rest will do me good."

Lady Margaret left with Lavinia's serving girl, and the two cousins sat alone in the yellow room. They drank cold tea and Lavinia indulged in the scones and cream.

"Did you know I shall have a Christmas baby? I hardly know where to begin. We've so much to talk about."

Rebecah smiled. "How wonderful, Lavinia. I'm so happy for you and David."

"I was saddened to hear how father treated you. I don't understand him."

"Do you remember the last time we spoke to each other?"

"How can I forget? If it were not for you, I may have lost my courage."

"Your courage has never been lacking, cousin."

"Thank you for saying so. I did the right thing. But it has broken my heart my father has disowned me."

"He will come around in time. Perhaps when the baby is born and he learns he has a grandchild his heart will change."

"I pray for him every night," Lavinia said.

"I try. Sometimes it is hard."

Lavinia set her teacup aside. "I'm glad you did not go through with it with Lanley. I hoped you would not marry him out of a broken heart. He would have made you very unhappy."

"Yes, I believe he would have, and I him. Lanley has forgiven me, I think. For him there are other choices."

"Lanley is a good man at heart."

"Indeed that is so."

"But Jack is a better man."

Rebecah stared at the floor, stung at the mention of his name. "It would not be a good idea for us to discuss John Nash."

"Still, I'm troubled by the change in you, cousin. Would it bother you if I told you what I plan to name my baby?"

The sparkle returned to Rebecah's eyes. Speaking of the baby would be a better topic.

"Not in the least. I want to hear."

"Tell me it will not anger you."

"Why would it?"

"You may not like it. So you must understand my reasons. If it's a boy, he will be called David John. The first name is after his father of course and the middle name John after John Nash. You know I was close to him growing up. He was like a brother to me—still is."

"And what if you have a girl?"

"Kathryn for my mother. Grace for David's grandmother. Do you know she is still living? She is ninety and two. We visit her once a month."

"It is kind of you."

"I adore her. We want our baby to bring her joy in the time she has left. It's so important people have joy in their old age."

"That is true."

"I wish you joy, cousin."

"I have all the joy I need seeing you again."

"What are your plans, now that you're not married and have left Endfield?"

Rebecah put the rest of her cake on the china plate. "I plan to find a position as a governess."

Lavinia's eyes enlarged. "Well, at least you don't desire to be a teacher sequestered away into spinsterhood. A wealthy family with a fine house is much better. But now that you are with me for a time, perhaps your ambition will change."

"I know what you're leading to, Lavinia."

"I cannot help it, cousin. I can see you're still in love with Jack."

"Perhaps you are seeing what you only wish to see. Perhaps you are wrong."

"Can you deny your feelings?"

Rebecah sighed. "I don't love him enough to ruin my life and betray the memory of my father."

"He was good to you and loved you."

"He loved me enough to lie?"

"Lie? I see no lie. He told you the truth as he knows it to be. Do you think from the time of their meeting, to the time of your father's departure for England, then the voyage home, he would have survived as long as he did?"

Rebecah clasped her hands. "Why would my father warn his brother to keep Jack away from me if there wasn't a good reason?"

Lavinia took Rebecah by the shoulders. "I know I said it before and it bears repeating. Write to Sir Richard's physician."

Sweeping her skirts forward, Rebecah stood. "I don't know what to believe or what to do."

"Then talk to me, Rebecah. I'll listen, and perhaps together we can find answers."

Her eyes resigned to the tears she fought. They pooled, slid down her cheeks. She brushed them away and hardened herself against them.

"You're right. We loved each other, but I couldn't have gone through with marrying him."

"Why not?"

"Don't you see? It would've been the worst way to begin. I pushed the matter of love to the back of my mind and have hurt myself by doing so. What happened showed me what kind of woman I am." She turned back with her fists at her sides. "I'm suspicious, bitter, and unforgiving."

"You're none of those things," Lavinia said.

"It's true. I've grown to hate myself for what I feel. And the words in that letter? I've mulled over them time and time again. I thought about what you and Lady Margaret said. How could my father have survived such an infection for weeks and weeks? I need to find Dr. Harvey. "

Lavinia went to her cousin with an embrace. "It's alright. You must have a cry. You're safe here."

"I shall die loving him. He thinks I hate him and now his love for me is dead and he is gone. Oh, how he must despise me."

"Somehow it must be mended."

Rebecah pushed back her hair and wiped her eyes dry. "I'm glad I came to you. I shall find a great deal of healing in your house."

"A heavy burden was given you. You carried it as best you can. Now you must let God carry it for you."

CHAPTER 24

Shortly after daybreak, Nash woke to a growl beneath his window. He rose, looked into the violet haze of dawn, and saw Black Hawk standing there with his arms folded across his chest, his face lifted proudly. Nash raised his hand, and went to dress.

When he opened the door, the cub rolled in the grass. "Your cub is your shadow, my brother. He too is hungry."

Black Hawk frowned. "I have not come to beg. I never hunger for I am a great hunter. I have given a turkey to the dark-faced man."

"Not an easy catch in these woods. Joab and I are grateful. You must feast with us."

Black Hawk glanced up at the window. For a moment his eyes looked as though they admired the glass panes, then his brow rumpled.

"I do not understand why the white man sleeps in a high place with walls all around and a roof above him. The ground is softer and surer."

Nash too looked up. "I see what you mean. Well, I shall be sleeping under the stars tonight and the forest will wall me in."

He went to the troth on the side of the house and doused himself with rainwater. Black Hawk watched the white man's ways, and Nash saw him turn his eyes toward the towering hills. He pointed to a steep smooth mountain.

"Upon that ridge I met Logan's messenger. Logan asks for you. He sits within his lodge where he has had a dream. He fears it and does not eat meat for a long season. Logan has laid aside the peace pipe."

Nash wiped his face with his hands. Massacre disrupted his quiet and peaceful soul.

"I know why he has done this, Black Hawk. I have heard about his father, wife, and sister. Even the most peaceful of men would desire revenge."

Black Hawk crouched to hold his cub. "It is true, Logan is restless and angry. You must come and speak to him, before the war drums beat louder."

It was hard to leave Laurel Hill, but he had to. His horse pawed the grass, shook its head, and tossed its great black mane into the wind as he pulled up onto his back.

Black Hawk ran his hand down Meteor's neck. "He is wild and his eyes blaze with fire."

"That's why I chose him. I'll let you ride him during our journey, Black Hawk. I can tell you like him."

"I need no horse, my brother." It was true, for his feet were fleet as a buck's.

Turning in the saddle, Nash called back to the old man who stood near the doorpost of the house. "Only the Lord knows how long I'll be gone, Joab. If you need help of any kind, Mr. Boyd is the man to see."

Joab nodded and wiped his sweaty brow. "I ain't goin' to Mrs. Cottonwood's no matter how much she begs. I'm stayin' right here. Godspeed, Mr. John."

Nash smiled at his friend and slipped his musket into the leather holster on his saddle. Then he rode off toward the forest. The Indian walked alongside him.

With the sun burning above the horizon, Nash and Black Hawk traveled along the banks of a stream, down to the Potomac. A great swell of mountains loomed above, the tops round and smooth as river stone.

Upon the slopes grew oaks and locust trees, sycamores and maples. Hanging from limbs were stocky vines. Airy ferns covered the forest floor competing with moss and lichen. Poised at the water's edge leaned willows. They swayed above the mirror of the current, while in the distance deer came to drink in shallow pools.

Nash followed Black Hawk into the water and they crossed a shoal where it flowed knee-deep. Small islands, formed from ancient rock, dotted the river. Cranes and blue herons stood upon them.

From there they traveled through rough forests. A sense of awe overwhelmed Nash as he passed under the leafy canopy above him. Deer dashed and leaped. Bird calls echoed.

At night they camped near the water's edge, broiled fish over the open fire, slept under the stars. Before sunset, on the third day of their journey, they came to a precipice of limestone. Nash dismounted, and with Black Hawk moved to the edge and looked into a canyon of trees to a rushing stream littered with rocks. Black Hawk pointed at a band of Cayuga warriors passing through the trees. When they had gone, they carried on, going into the deeper cover of the forests until they reached the Allegheny Passage and traveled across the Youghiogheny River.

When they reached Logan's camp, a dog ran alongside Meteor's flanks and barked. The horse sidestepped and snorted. Nash loosened the reins and went to climb down from the saddle.

Black Hawk forbade him. He walked into the center of the village, was met by a dozen or more braves dressed in deer hide loincloths and beaded moccasins. Their chests were bare, gleaming in the sunshine from the bear fat rubbed upon their skin. Scarlet cords held their hair in tails and feathers adorned them. Circled around their biceps were copper bands and war paint riveted down their bronzed skin.

Black Hawk spoke. Savage eyes turned upon the white man. Nash felt the beat of his heart quicken and pound against his chest. A warrior stepped forward wearing the mask of the wolf. Clenching his teeth, he spoke a harsh word that could not be stripped of its bloodthirsty intent. He threw back his head and shook his fist.

Black Hawk stood in front of his white brother's horse. In an instant a breathless hush fell. Tense like the loll before a storm, it struck the anxious heart of John Nash as his palms grew slick.

"Hear my brother's words." Black Hawk raised his arms. The warriors listened with stern faces. "Talgayeeta has sent for him."

Their leader shook his head. "Lies. He is of the same mind as Cresap. He will die, as will all white men for the deaths of Talgayeeta's family."

"My ears do not hear your words, Angry Bear, that I'm to die," Nash said. "My ears hear the weeping of your women for Logan's children, for Shikellimus his noble father, for his sister Koonay, and his beloved wife Mellana. Logan has sent for me and I've come."

"Lies! You come from Cresap. You come to kill our chief and our people."

"Logan is my friend," Nash told him, sliding off his saddle. "You will dishonor your slain by killing me. Will you will betray Logan in this way?"

Black Hawk moved beside Nash. "He speaks the truth. Honor your slain."

The Indians stared at Black Hawk.

"He is my brother," cried Black Hawk, with marked authority. "He saved my life. Talgayeeta smoked the peace pipe with him. Will you, when you sit in his lodge answer when he asks where his friend is? Brothers of a war chief, are you fools or men? Will you strike the war post?"

"The war post has been struck." Angry Bear threw his fierce look at Black Hawk and drew his hunting knife. "He must die."

178

Black Hawk shook his head, forbidding him to continue. "Because of the paleness of his skin you would send him to his death? Your words are not wise, my brother. They are mixed with bitter water."

Nash steeled himself and approached the throng, fixing his eyes on Angry Bear. "Go tell your chief I've come. Ask him if he demands of me my life this day. See what he will answer."

The Indian sneered. "I will go to him as you ask. But stay clear of my knife, white man."

The warriors fell back as Angry Bear turned. He headed into the forest, slipped into the shadows and was gone. A moment passed until Angry Bear was seen again coming through the trees. Chief Logan, known as Talgayeeta, appeared behind the warrior. He wore soft doeskin leggings and moccasins. Four white-tipped eagle feathers thrust through his scalplock quivered in the breeze. A row of beads hung around his neck, and upon his youthful forearms were bands of beaten silver.

Logan's face was scarred and lined with sadness. For a moment, no words were exchanged. Logan stared up into the canopy of leaves. Then he lowered his eyes and stood on a rise of ground in front of Nash.

Nash made the sign of brotherhood. "It has been a long season since last we spoke, and by the cinders on your brow you mourn for the dead. I too mourn for them."

Logan held out his hand. Nash took it. Relieved by the gesture, and with pity in his heart, he met the eyes of this noblest of men, a peacemaker bereft of his loved ones.

"Sit with me, for we must speak." Logan turned and stepped through the doorway of his lodge. "Black Hawk must come to."

Together they sat upon soft, fine skins. A squaw brought them smoked fish and corn cakes. A mockingbird sang in a tree outside the door, and Nash felt a sense of dread fleet through the air.

Logan handed the calumet to Nash and blew blue smoke into the air. Lines on his face deepened into crevices and the shadow of his eyes into dark pools clear and determined.

"For many moons I've not seen you."

"I was in England."

"I dreamed you had forgotten your Indian brothers. It brought me much sadness."

"I had not forgotten."

"Why did you go to England?"

"To see my father and his wife."

"I remember now. They are well?"

"Yes. I gave my stepmother your string of beads."

"She did not reject them?"

"No, she sends her thanks."

Logan pitched his brows. "Your father and his lady are noble people. But some whites in my country are not."

"You speak the truth, brave chief."

"There is liberty in truth."

"Yes, and suffering in war."

"You understand this?"

"I do, for Dunmore, Cresap, and Greathouse all declared war upon you and the Five Nations."

Logan balled his fist. "Their hands are stained with the blood of those they have murdered. This blood stains the land and cannot be washed away by the rains. I have great anger in my heart. Once I loved my white brothers, so much my countrymen said, 'Logan is the friend of the whites', whenever they saw me. If a white man entered my lodge, I gave him meat. If ever he came cold and naked, I clothed him. If he were wounded, I dressed his wounds. Such was my love for them."

"I'm a witness to your love," Nash said grieved.

"The moon, once white and full of peace, is now a moon of blood. I vowed for peace, but now I seek vengeance. Do you see women about my lodge? Do you hear the laughter of children? Have you spoken to my noble father, to my wife, and sister?"

A tear fell from the corner of Logan's eye, slid down his cheek, touched the quivering hard lips.

Nash's heart ached. "I've heard of their fate. My heart is crushed within me."

"When I found them, great anger swelled in my spirit. I found my wife Mellana in the dirt, her face covered in blood, her beautiful eyes no longer looking at me with joy. I saw fear in them and cried out. In my love for her, I gathered her in my arms and when I touched her lips, I found them cold."

Shaking with emotion, Logan drew in a long breath. Sweat beaded on Nash's forehead. He glanced at Black Hawk. His eyes were intent, his mouth tightly pressed.

"I cut free the body of my sister," Logan went on, speaking slowly as if he were reliving the event. "They had torn her clothes from her young body—hung her from a pole with her feet above the ground. They cut open her belly—killed the child she carried. My father lay dead near his lodging."

"And Koonay's husband?"

"John Gibson was not there. He has wept bitter tears over Koonay and his unborn son. His daughter lived and is with him. He is of the same heart as I. He went to find Cresap—to kill him."

The atmosphere was storm and stress. Nash knew what it meant for the settlers surrounding the dominion of such a powerful man. Blood, tears, and sorrow would plague the land alongside revolution.

The squaw reentered and placed a jug of fresh water before Logan. She whispered a word to him, yet he did not reply, nor did his dull eyes leave their fixed place upon the ground. Food lay cold within the wooden bowls, and the feathers on the calumet fluttered.

Logan looked at Nash. "You must leave me in the morning. You are safe here among my people for the night. When you return, tell your people hailstones will not beat me to the ground. Pleasant words will not quench the fire burning in my heart. Peace is no longer upon my lips."

"I'll do as you ask." Nash took in a breath to calm the anxiety moving through his body.

Chief Logan rose slowly to his feet and made a promise. "My word to all warriors is they are not to harm you or anyone within your house. You were adopted into my family. If they harm you, they harm me."

"You have my thanks."

Then from around Logan's neck, he drew off his beads. "These are the sign you are our son and brother. Wear them so you may show any warrior you are beloved among my people."

Nash nearly wept. He took them in hand, drew them over his head and looked into Logan's eyes. "Thank you, my father, my brother."

Logan called his sentry. Then he grasped Nash's arm. "I wanted to see your face one more time before I join my fathers in death. We shall not see each other again."

Nash squeezed Chief Logan's hand and thought how many lives could have been spared if men had not hated with such wickedness.

* * *

Nash lay on a fur mat in a lodge kept for guests. The moon rose high and he thought of the girl he left in England. His heart longed for her and he hoped he would soon forget. He must invest his thoughts in other things, but while the stars burned softly, while the breeze whispered through the trees, when loneliness was most apt to fill a man, he lost the battle of forgetting. She was ever with him, especially now.

Sleep eluded him, so he rose with a groan and walked out into the cool night. The fire that once blazed in the center of the village burned low in a heap of glowing red coals. He raised his hand to the Indian sentry who sat beside it with a musket over his arm, then passed on into the forest.

The moon poured through the breaks in the trees. Crickets and tree frogs murmured. Nash stared hard at the stars and the tranquility amazed him. It dominated forest and sky, and he wished he could take it in his fists and hold it, feel that sense of peace that passes all understanding. His heart grew heavy and he walked to the edge of the river where he sank to his knees, his hands upon them and his head lowered.

"God," he breathed. "It seems you've given me a commission. I take it, but I need your help…all of us will. Father, hallowed be Thy name. Thy kingdom come. Thy will be done. Forgive us…as we forgive…Lead us not into temptation…deliver us from evil…"

He raised his hands to meet his face where anguish caused him to tremble. Wind rose and blew on the other side of the river and rustled through the trees. It crossed, and the pines surrounding Nash freed their dry needles. They fell to earth where ancient layers of the same lay rotting. He listened to the sound they made as they fell, stared at the steeps of pines, while a voice rose in his being that reassured him of his safety.

He stood and remained there until the moon sunk beneath the hedge across the river. The memory of his time in England came back. He could still feel her touch, hear her voice as if she stood beside him.

Closing his eyes, he breathed out in an effort to return to the present, which was not a good place to be.

CHAPTER 25

The realities of such dangers were unknown to the girl who had lived all her life sheltered in the English countryside. She had never seen an Indian dressed in fringed leggings and bright beads, his face painted for war, his belt laced with the scalps of his enemies. She had not drank from a clear mountain stream, walked through an all engulfing forest, felt dwarfed by towering hills and trees, nor experienced both the joys and horrors of wilderness life.

Today Rebecah sat in Lavinia's garden watching insects play over the marigolds. Worker bees moved from blossom to blossom, their legs heavy with bright golden pollen.

"The London papers say war is certain with the Colonies." Lavinia sat in a white wrought iron chair and set her teacup on the saucer.

"David said, John Adams and Benjamin Franklin were slandered for their tough stand on independence, and Patrick Henry's orations could cause riots in London. All loyal Englishmen should agree the King's army is invincible. David says America's revolution will fail in a matter of weeks." She leaned back against the chair and sighed. "The worst of it, traitors could either be hung or sent to prison.

Rebecah wondered what Nash's fate would be. She admitted to herself she cared what awaited him. She listened to Lavinia drone on. *Prison, execution,* these words seized her heart.

Lavinia groaned. "Rebecah, you haven't heard a word I've said."

"I'm sorry, Lavinia. I don't know what to say."

"Doesn't the news worry you?"

She swallowed. "No, I've had other things on my mind." But it wasn't true. She was worried—terribly worried.

"I'm anxious for Jack. He will be in the thick of it, I believe. We must pray for him."

"It is not in me to hate him, you know."

"You love him, don't you?"

"I have tried not to."

"Have you forgiven him?"

"If ever God does a thing for me, I pray He spares his life, for I fear something terrible has come upon him…something far worse than my not having forgiven him."

Lavinia's lips parted and concern covered her face. "Oh, Rebecah. That is a knowing that comes from deep within. I shall fear for him more than ever."

The coach, meant to take the ladies on a day's outing, rolled down the gravel drive toward the house, and upon hearing it, Rebecah rose with Lavinia and went inside. Lady Margaret had fetched her hat and was adjusting the ribbon beneath her chin.

Together they boarded, with Lavinia seated beside her ladyship. Dressed in pale blue and cream lace, Rebecah's wide-brimmed hat shadowed her eyes. She pulled her hair over her right shoulder and leaned back against the seat.

When they reached their destination, she looked from the window to a field where people gathered. The field belonged to a rich man who loved his Bible and honored the men that preached it. He had leant it that day to John

185

Wesley, along with a wagon Wesley used for a platform. Having never seen so many people gathered in one place, Rebecah watched the crowd with a sense of excitement. Most were farmers and herdsmen, among them well-to-do ladies, shopkeepers, weavers, and blacksmiths. Children nestled against their mothers' arms, and there were lame and sick folk.

The coachman opened the door and led Lady Margaret out, then handed Rebecah down. She stepped onto the thick carpet of field grass and looked over the shoulders of the people to see a man who could be heard from afar. His voice was pastoral, robust, smooth and convincing. He held a well-worn Bible in his hands. Its pages fluttered in the breeze. People huddled together and drew closer to hear the words Wesley spoke.

John Wesley wore a black coat with an upright collar and narrow white stock. His hair was clean and cut above his shoulders. Rebecah thought his face, his eyes, were kind.

"How unlike others who stand in lofty pulpits, my lady," Rebecah commented. "And his voice. Is it not comforting?"

"Indeed it is, as it should be from a man of God. Let us draw closer."

They walked into the crowd and stopped to listen a few yards away from the wagon. Two clergy of the established church stood nearby. One had his arms folded across his chest, a look of irritation on his blanched face. The other stood with his fists clenched at his sides and his head lifted high.

Wesley raised his hand, bidding all come near and listen. A hush fell over the crowd. The sun stood halfway behind a cloud and beams of light filtered down through the heavens onto the land.

"Blessed are the poor in spirit," Wesley said, "for theirs is the kingdom of heaven. Hear what Luke's gospel says. But love your enemies, and do good…and lend hoping for nothing again, and ye shall be the children of the Highest, for he is kind unto the unthankful and to the evil."

Rebecah fixed her eyes on Wesley while he spoke. The words pierced her like a dagger. Tears swelled in her eyes and she felt convicted.

"Be ye therefore merciful, as your father also is merciful. Judge not and ye shall not be judged. Condemn not, and ye shall not be condemned. Forgive, and ye shall be forgiven. Oh, people of God, you are most blessed when you forgive your brother. If you've aught against any, go to him and be reconciled to your brother. Forgive those who have trespassed against you, else ye be given to the tormentors."

Her hand went to her mouth and she looked down with her vision blurred.

"All our trespasses and sins are forgiven us if we forgive and as we forgive others." Wesley stretched out his hand. "This is of the utmost importance. Our blessed Lord is so jealous lest at any time we should let it slip out of our thoughts, that he not only inserts this in the Lord's Prayer, but presently after repeats it twice over. If any malice or bitterness, if any taint of unkindness or anger remain, if we do not clearly, fully and from the heart forgive all men their trespasses, we so far cut short the forgiveness of our own."

A gray-haired man staggered forward. His brown coat was faded and torn, his shoes worn and old, his hat full of holes. He drew it off as he looked up at Wesley, trembled and fell to his knees.

"Help me, Brother Wesley!" he cried. "I've been a wicked, unforgiving man. My wife and child died because of my neglect. God, have mercy on me!"

He gripped his hands together until the knuckles turned white. Then he pressed them to his teeth and wept. The crowd was silent, motionless, waiting to see what Wesley would do. The preacher stepped down. He laid his hands on the man's shoulders, brought his head closer.

187

Astonished, Rebecah saw Wesley's lips move and his eyes close tight as he prayed. Others went on their knees. The penitent man dragged his hands over his eyes. Presently, he rose to his feet as Wesley lifted him up to face him.

"Repent of your sin," Wesley told him. The man bowed his head. Others poured forward.

"Pray for me also, sir!" they cried. "Help me, Brother Wesley. What must I do to be forgiven?"

The crowd pressed upon the women. Rebecah drew Lady Margaret up close beside her. For a moment, she stood stark still. Then she rushed forward. Her limbs felt like water as she moved through the crowd and approached Wesley.

"Please. I've found it hard to forgive someone," she said upon reaching Wesley. "Would you help me?"

He nodded and took her hand in his. It felt warm, his grip strong and gentle. Without asking any questions, he prayed for her. She closed her eyes and the words flowed into her soul. Her lips moved and she found herself praying with him.

Something broke at that moment. Love breathed again. It was as if she had been in a dark room. Now, the windows were thrown open and the light flooded that dark place, and dispelled the lonely gloom.

* * *

That same moment in a forest far from England, John Nash walked alongside his Indian brother. The sun drew near to setting along the western hilltops, the lowland still bright in the waning light. Mountaintops turned inky black against a clear magenta sky.

Nash paused and looked up. "There's a color we shall soon see plenty of." The hue deepened, and his heart grew heavy along with his tired body.

The Potomac scented the breeze as they hiked along the banks. Swallows darted above rapids and dove for insects near the surface. Cascades were tinted pink from the setting sun.

Black Hawk bent down. Nash did the same and looked through the trees to the other side. Elms mingled with a hedge of willows along an inlet of shallow water. The sun poured over a pool bright green with algae. Standing on the bank stood five whitetail deer. Wind blew from upstream, and the stag threw up his head and sniffed the air, stomped one hoof, and sprang away. His does followed and vanished into the sanctuary of the woods.

"What frightened them off?" Nash whispered.

He kept his eyes fixed on the distant shore. Behind a thick row of cattails moved warriors painted with streaks of black, their faces and chests striped with yellow. Eagle feathers dressed their dark hair, and their leggings were adorned with scalplocks. Through their belts gleamed knives, and upon their backs were quivers full of arrows and a bow. Out from the shadows and into the glare of light they stepped over rocks that littered the river. The leader paused, glanced about, then stooped to drink.

Nash's breath hurried. "Now we know."

"They will go." Black Hawk waited beside him. "They have not seen us."

They watched the Indians slip into the forest.

Troubled by what he had seen, Nash stood and brought his horse deeper into the woods at the foot of a towering limestone cliff. A stream sang over the rock ledges and he cupped his hand and drank. The cold water tasted sweet on his tongue, and soothed his throat. Yet the bitterness of Logan's War remained.

As they moved on, sunlight streamed through the trees, and Nash felt it graze across his shoulders. The old hunting trail twisted and turned, dipped and rose as Nash rode Meteor along it, Black Hawk keeping pace. A mile down river they splashed across Catoctin Creek. Black Hawk stopped and pointed at the sky. Nash looked up. Vultures circled above the trees and it was an ominous site to behold, for where vultures flew, death was certain.

Farther along they saw smoke rising above the trees, and so Nash dug his heels into Meteor and climbed the slopes. Black Hawk ran ahead, and soon they came into a glade of tall grass. The smoldering remains of a cabin arrested Nash's senses, struck fear into his heart for the souls within it. He reined in his horse and slid off. He and Black Hawk drew near, saw the bodies of a man and woman lying side by side. They'd been scalped, their limbs mutilated by tomahawks.

Black Hawk outlined a moccasin footprint with his finger. "The prints are fresh."

Nash turned away, his heart lurching. Meteor whinnied, ears pricked back straight as arrows. Nash turned.

"Black Hawk! Hurry!"

No sooner did he shout than the whistle of an arrow sliced through the air. His leg surged in pain. He gripped his thigh, fell back. He clenched his teeth, moaned in agony. Blood oozed hot between his fingers. He struggled to his knees. A warrior rushed toward him, tomahawk raised. Nash lifted his musket to his shoulder and shot him dead.

Black Hawk drew his knife. An Indian threw himself forward, swung his tomahawk. Black Hawk leapt back. Nash feared for his friend's life, and pulled the plug from his powder horn, making haste to reload.

Black Hawk yelped, and then plunged his blade into the bare chest of the painted brave.

* * *

With Nash slumped over the saddle, Black Hawk led Meteor up a steep hill, over moss and lichen, leaves and twigs, until they reached level ground. Sweat covered Nash's face, and his hair hung limp and wet against his neck. His hands trembled as he gripped his leg. Dizzy with pain, he looked out at the line of trees below and saw the river. The surface churned and foamed and swallows swooped above the peaks.

Black Hawk helped Nash dismount. He set him on the ground, his back against a tree. He took out his knife and cut away Nash's bloody legging.

"The arrow has not gone deep, my brother, across the surface of a muscle. I will break it and pull it out."

"We must hurry. They're right at our heels."

Black Hawk pushed Nash back. "No, my brother, the storm has not yet come. Your God has given us a moon to see by. We will travel by night until we reach the valley."

"Pull the arrow out." Nash clenched his teeth.

"My brother must not shout." Black Hawk set a firm hand on Nash's shoulder. "If others are near, they will hear, as will the wolves."

A ravenous howl crossed the river. Soon the pack would prow and move to the other side by the lure of blood. Black Hawk pressed his hand against Nash's chest to hold him down. Nash moaned and sank back. Feeling nauseous, he opened his eyes and saw the trees sway, then his vision blurred.

Black Hawk reached around and broke the arrowhead off the shaft. Then he put his hand around the shaft where it met Nash's flesh and pulled. Nash stifled a cry and twisted against the pain as he drew the shaft free.

"My brother's courage is strong."

"Not strong enough." Nash groaned.

From his medicine pouch, Black Hawk took out herbs.

191

"What is that?" Nash asked.

"Bloodroot. It will keep your wound pure and end the bleeding." He laid the herb over the wound and bound it with a strip of cloth torn from Nash's shirt.

"My brother is a great warrior."

Nash's smile twitched. "Even though my heart is racing like a buck's?"

A smile lifted Black Hawk's mouth, and he helped Nash up and mount his horse. Black Hawk pulled the horse along and glanced back at his friend.

"He makes my feet like hinds' feet, and sets me upon my high places." Nash's face grimaced and slumped forward in the saddle. "He teaches my hands to war, so that a bow of steel is broken by my arms."

The cub, which had followed at a distance, stood on a limestone shelf above. Black Hawk spoke a blessing to it in his Indian tongue. The cub narrowed its eyes, stood and walked off into the forest.

"I shall not see him again," Black Hawk said.

By moonlight, they traveled the mountain trail until coming into lower hills and vales. Mountain springs murmured and ran clear. Lush grass and moss cushioned the travelers.

An hour later, they reached the top of a cliff. The moon rode high and flooded the forest. Nash looked down upon the sleepy valley. Flickers of light beamed in the town.

On clear summer nights, when the sun touched its fiery rim along the horizon, the clustered spires of Fredericktown's churches appeared incandescent as amber glass. In the cool and colorful autumn, the valley turned golden brown and crimson. In winter it turned gray, the mountains stretching heavenward against pale skies filled with clouds, the town looking like a red and white patchwork quilt.

What right did any man have to disrupt the peace of such a place? To Nash whatever bloody strife boiled elsewhere between patriot and loyalist, Indian and settler, could stay far away. But tyranny had crept into the frontier like a slow moving sludge. Heavy burdens had been bestowed upon the people. It was not only the shackles of stamp acts and three pence payments on tea that encumbered the lowly folk. The iron heel of dominance struck and bruised the souls of men, from Boston to Baltimore, down the Eastern Shore to Annapolis and up along the Potomac into the far reaches of the frontier.

Black Hawk paused beside him. "I will go to the town with you, then to the mountains. There I will seek the path I must take."

"I'll pray you find it, Black Hawk."

The throbbing in his leg caused his lungs to heave. Yet his mind turned to the town nestled in the valley.

CHAPTER 26

The Belgian clock on the mantelpiece struck out the hour. The whirl of carriage wheels could be heard coming to a halt in front of the house. Closing the book she'd been reading, Rebecah stood and peered out the window. David's partner, Edward Deberton, had arrived.

Drawing back the curtain, she watched him step out of the carriage. How funereal he looked in his all black attire. His Grecian nose gave him the look of a much older man, and his eyes were dark brown and forlorn. He was a prosperous respected lawyer, and what he called a misfortune, others called a privileged bachelor's life.

Dropping the curtain back in place, she returned to the book she'd been reading, *The Vicar of Wakefield* the story of a benevolent clergyman and his large family facing devastating circumstances.

How sad it was for Arabella Wilmont and George Primrose, the vicar's eldest son, that a sudden revelation of poverty prevented their wedding. Arabella's father and the vicar, who at the last moment discovered his misfortunate and felt it only honest he should reveal the news to all, both insisted the match unsuitable.

Rebecah knew how painful lost love felt.

Thinking it would serve as a distraction, she attempted to finish the last paragraph in the chapter she was reading, when she heard voices out in the hall. It would be rude not to speak to Mr. Deberton and so she set the book aside once more and stepped out into the foyer.

Morning sun poured through the windows, cast a golden glow throughout that touched her face. If no one had noticed a change in her, she felt it. Her heart was light as a butterfly's wing. Her eyes sparkled like sunshine on oceanic waters. At last her smile had returned.

When she entered the sitting room, eyes turned. "Mr. Deberton, you remember my cousin Rebecah Brent?" Lavinia drew Rebecah beside her.

"I do indeed. How are you, Miss Brent?"

"Very well, thank you."

"Rebecah is visiting us with Lady Margaret Nash."

Deberton drew off his spectacles with long nimble fingers and tucked them away. "Yes, David informed me of that fact."

David put his hands behind him. "I've asked Edward here because we have something to discuss with you."

She smiled. "Business? What could you want to discuss with me?"

Deberton fixed his eyes on Rebecah. "A woman's intuitiveness brings prudence to business affairs."

"How so, sir, seeing we are forbidden to have a profession of our own?"

"You participate in ways you are not aware of, dear lady. More men have been advised by a look, a gesture, a sweep of the lashes."

"Or led astray by them."

Lavinia was startled by Rebecah's comment. She reached for Rebecah's hand and made her sit beside her on the settee. "Rebecah," she whispered. "You dare to cross propriety?"

"Your cousin meant no impropriety, Mrs. Harcourt," said Deberton. "I completely agree with her. 'But she considereth a field and buyeth it.' Is that not how the scripture goes?"

"Yes, Mr. Deberton," Rebecah answered.

He nodded his approval. "Well, may we disclose the nature of our business?"

"Please do."

Rebecah pushed a stray lock away from her cheek and tucked it behind her ear. Perhaps the action was more from nerves, for the anticipation had built and she wondered what this business meant for her.

"Rebecah, I know your feelings toward Mr. Nash haven't been favorable ones," David said.

She frowned. "So this *business* concerns him?"

"It does. Bear with us."

"I'm not sure I want to."

"Please understand it is not my intention or Mr. Deberton's to stir up your feelings. We will not tread were we should not."

She raised her eyes, wistful at the mention of the man she still loved. "Forgive me for sounding harsh. I'll listen."

"Mr. Nash has left you a sum of seven hundred pounds."

Deberton leaned forward. "We want to advise that you accept it in good faith. Do not allow it to collect cobwebs."

She stared at the floor in disbelief. "I fail to understand. Mr. Nash should have known I would not accept it. What about his mother? What about Sir Rodney?"

"They are well provided for through their own means, and through Mr. Nash."

"But how, David? John Nash is not a rich man."

"He is wealthier than believed. He sold his land up north, a large estate of good farmland. He came to us with his wishes. He did not want you to have the money until he had gone, and only if you did not marry Lanley. He hoped it would get you away from Endfield."

She pressed her fingers against her temples. "I've done that on my own."

"Nevertheless the money is yours and…"

"Did he think I would not survive without his help?"

"He did. However…"

"Oh, David, you should have advised him differently."

"He was very firm, and nothing would have changed his mind. You see, he was afraid if you did not marry Lanley, Sir Samuel would cast you out and you would be impoverished."

Lavinia reached over and squeezed Rebecah's hand. "And you know my father would have done it."

"Yes, March told me she had overheard his plans to send me away. I knew he would eventually."

"I am not surprised. Look how he has disowned me. Do you think he would treat you any better?"

"How can I accept it, Lavinia? I would feel kept." She lowered her head. "You should know the reasons."

"Whatever they are, Miss Brent, do not feel obligated to take the money," said Deberton.

"I disagree," David said in a raised voice.

"I have heard of his behavior, David. It is up to Miss Brent what to do. We must allow her time to think this over."

David shifted on his feet. "The likelihood of seeing Mr. Nash again is slim, Rebecah. He is in America. You are in England. Perhaps, this is his way of saying how sorry he is, and if you do not wish to use it to live on, you could give it to a charity."

Settled by his suggestion, she engaged his gaze. "Your advice is well taken. But I must have time to think about it. I do have that option, do I not?"

"Of course you do." Deberton stood and pulled at the bottom edge of his waistcoat. "We will not speak of it again until you're ready. So for the moment, will you accompany me into the garden? Let us see what flowers have bloomed."

* * *

When the evening's light descended and bathed the land in a ruddy glow, a special dinner was prepared, for in the morning Lady Margaret and Rebecah were to leave for Standforth. Rebecah waited in the dining room with the others. Mr. Deberton was late. When he entered, he stopped short by the door, bowed to Lady Margaret and Lavinia, then looked over at Rebecah and inclined his head to her.

She was dressed in a gown of silk linen. He complemented her on the color. "Such a soothing shade of blue, Miss Brent. It heightens your complexion."

Tiny pearls were in her hair, hair that cascaded down her throat and shoulders in ringlets. He pulled out a chair for her, and his hand lightly touched her back, his fingertips brushing over her locks.

As the ladies talked among themselves before the food was brought in, Deberton sat next to David.

"There sits an angel," Rebecah heard him whisper. "I'm indebted to you."

From the corner of her eyes, she saw David look at him curious. "How so?"

"For bringing me and the lady together."

"You imply we meant to match you up? Edward, it was just business that needed to be taken care of, if it was taken care of at all. You should not have delayed her."

"She should not be pressured into taking money from a man who is neither her relation nor her friend."

David curled his lip in a smile. She looked away, but heard him say, "She still loves him, I believe."

She shut her eyes, knowing it were true, resigned to it so much so that her heart ached. She made no reply to the conversation between the two men. She unfolded her napkin and laid it on her lap, hoping Mr. Deberton would give more attention to the food than to her. She did not dislike him, just his growing attraction to her. Time and time again, he strove to impress her with his dry wit, his educational credits, and his knowledge of worldly things.

He talked about his distaste for politics and religion. The law was all that mattered.

"I so appreciate a good meal in the company of beautiful ladies." Deberton smiled.

Lady Margaret inclined her head. "I'm sure you would appreciate a hearty meal with or without our company. But we thank you for your compliment."

"You assumption is correct, my lady. But the absence of a soft hand and a sweet voice would make for a very dull evening."

David tasted the soup and set the spoon down. "I never knew you felt that way, Edward. You should have been a poet."

"A bachelor's life is a lonely one, my friend, and it brings out the bard in a man. At least I've a good cook in my house."

Everyone laughed at his comment, except Rebecah. She moved the spoon back and forth in her bowl. She had no appetite.

"Rebecah is lost in thought tonight, Mr. Deberton." Lady Margaret looked kindly on her charge. "You must excuse her."

Deberton looked embarrassed. "Mine is but dull conversation, my lady. I'm sorry if I've bored you, Miss Brent."

She glanced at him with a slight smile. "I was listening, Mr. Deberton. You were saying something about London?"

"I was saying the poor houses are overflowing. As a last resort, people have fled to the Colonies. Once they get there they find they must endure more suffering."

"Do you find fault in leaving?" She spoke with soft care and challenged him with grace. She did not want to show her private feelings for his comment.

Deberton drank his wine. "I cannot say I do. But I've mixed feelings."

"Many do, Edward. That's the problem." David leaned back in his chair. "No one can make up their minds one way or the other, whether over love or marriage, politics or religion. We have Tories on one side of the fence and Whigs on the other waiting to duke it out."

Deberton mashed a boiled potato with his fork. "If we go to war, then we shall be fighting the lowest of England's castaways. The majority are or were indentured servants and from lower class families. Sons and daughters of Liberty they call themselves. Patriots. It's folly and will quickly end."

Lady Margaret looked into the flame of the candle nearest her. "I have a stepson in America, Mr. Deberton."

Deberton shifted in his seat. "My apology, my lady. I had forgotten."

"Jack is content as a landed gentleman and is prospering. His father and I are quite proud of him. He told us the land is beautiful there."

"So I've heard." Deberton smiled, trying to smooth over his words. He tuned to Rebecah. "I hope you never go to America, Miss Brent. It's a dangerous place for a woman."

"Danger exists everywhere, sir."

"But it's a wilderness. Life is hard there, so I hear."

"Life is hard no matter where you live, Mr. Deberton."

When the meal concluded, the ladies left for the drawing room, leaving the men to their cigars and port. The evening past quietly. Rebecah read aloud by the fireside, Lavinia dozing in the chair across from her, and Lady Margaret listening. Soon the clock in the hall counted out midnight and everyone retired for the night.

Rebecah lay wide-awake. Drawing her arms over her head, she studied the patterns on the ceiling, shadows of dark hues moving in gentle unison from the willow tree outside. A full moon glowed bright that night. Its light dusted the room.

"If I do not speak now, I don't know what I shall do." Deberton held his hands out to her. "I'm in love with you."

She moved back.

"I've loved you from the moment I first saw you. Be my wife. Allow me to prove my devotion to your happiness."

"Please, sir, try to understand. This isn't right. You must move away from the door and let me out."

His face flushed. "I did not mean to keep you. I was too hasty. I spoke too soon." He was sincere, and the pain of rejection showed in his face. She did not want to hurt him, but what could she do?

"I forgive you."

"But I do not regret it, Rebecah. I'm here before you, your humble servant to command."

"You're not my servant, nor will I order you to do anything—except one thing."

"What is it?"

"Open the door please. Let us part as friends."

He nodded, and did as she asked.

Rebecah felt sorry for him that he could not master the temptation to plead. He was like an abandoned puppy rooting at her hand for a touch of affection.

Bewildered, she set the candlestick down on the bedside table. "Oh, God, I want to be with Jack. Please, make a way, and help me to be brave."

CHAPTER 27

Rarely did people bolt their doors in Fredericktown. After suppertime, it was customary to sit on the porch with friends and family. Men smoked long-stemmed bowl pipes, talked of horses, agriculture, and politics. Women tucked their children in bed beneath downy patchwork quilts as the last glow of sunset faded over the Catoctin Mountains. Dusk swept across the floor of the valley and evening stars brightened.

When night fell, a dream-like peace fell with it, bringing the choir of frogs, the symphony of crickets. Soon lanterns were lit and men headed for the tavern to hear the latest news.

That night, when Black Hawk strode down Market Street leading a horse with a wounded man slumped in the saddle, women retreated indoors.

A candle glowed in a lower window of the Boyd House. Black Hawk looped Meteor's reins through the iron ring near the street and helped Nash down. Holding him up by one arm, he pounded with the fist of the other on the door. It swung open.

Archibald Boyd, the town clerk, gasped and went to shut the door. Black Hawk leaned in. Nash glanced up with a slight smile.

"Evening, Mr. Boyd."

Boyd's brows shot up in surprise. "John Nash!"

"I'm sorry to disturb you. The hour is late."

Boyd glanced at Black Hawk and Nash caught the fear in his eyes.

"Not to worry, Mr. Boyd. Black Hawk is my friend."

"He's a savage."

"Indeed to some, Mr. Boyd. But to me, he is my salvation. May Black Hawk bring me inside? It's urgent."

Boyd gasped at the blood-soaked bandage around Nash's leg. "Come inside quickly. Billy, come quick, my boy."

A youth came into the light. Together he and Boyd took Nash from Black Hawk's arm and led him upstairs. Black Hawk remained on the porch, arms folded and head lifted high.

A moment later Boyd returned. He put his hand on the boy's shoulder. "Fetch the doctor. Tell him Mr. John Nash of Laurel Hill is injured and he must come straight away."

Off the boy dashed, down the stairs and into the street.

Mr. Boyd turned to Black Hawk. "He will be cared for. You may go around the back of the house. I'll have my cook bring you food and drink."

Black Hawk nodded. Meteor shook his mane and snorted.

"Is that Nash's horse or your own?" asked Boyd, as they moved Nash inside.

Black Hawk glanced back. "If he were mine, he would have no saddle."

"If this wound kills me, he is yours, Black Hawk," Nash managed to say as they took him up the staircase. Mr. Boyd opened a door to a small bedroom. "Bring him in. Set him on the bed carefully."

Nash flinched. "I don't mean to intrude, Mr. Boyd. I only meant to come with news on my way home."

"Well, let the doctor be the judge of whether you can travel tonight."

"We've left Meteor in the street."

"When Billy returns I'll have him brush him down and give him oats."

Boyd gestured to Black Hawk to step from the room with him. Black Hawk followed him down the corridor. "You need not worry about anything here, Black Hawk. You can return to your village."

Black Hawk shrugged. "I've no village."

Boyd lifted his chin. "How is it you and he became such close friends?"

"My brother saved my life."

Boyd's eyes softened. "I see. Not even among whites have I found such a loyal friend as you, Black Hawk. Thank you for bringing him safely to town."

Black Hawk nodded. Then he stepped outside to the path buried in darkness alongside the house. In the rear, a lantern hung near a back door. A wary serving woman handed him a bowl of stew through the window. He thanked her in his language and saw her swallow.

"Put da bowl on da porch when you're done. But if you want more, tap on da window."

"It is enough."

Black Hawk sat on the stoop. The woman shut the window.

* * *

Upstairs in the Boyd house, Dr. Cole examined Nash's wound. "Your Indian friend did a good a job. You shouldn't have too much trouble, some pain now and then. But otherwise keep the wound clean to prevent infection and you will be fine."

"How long before I'm on my feet?"

"That depends. Weeks most likely. Don't rush it. You should stay here until you completely recover."

"I'll go home after I speak to the men of the town. There's trouble out in the frontier headed our way."

The doctor straightened up.

Boyd leaned in. "You believe the settlers in our county are at risk, Jack?"

"I've seen it with my own eyes."

His leg felt numb around the wound and he set his hand on his thigh. The gentle pressure of his fingers pressing into the muscle above it eased the pain somehow.

After the wound was washed and dressed, Dr. Cole gave instructions to Mr. Boyd and his daughter Theresa. She stood within the doorway, a look of worry covering her fair face. After her father and the doctor had gone, she moved to the window and opened the shutters wide.

"Several people have gathered across the street, Mr. Nash. News spreads fast."

"They saw Black Hawk coming into town with me. More than likely that has their curiosity at a frenzy."

A voice called up to the window from the street. "Miss Boyd, how's our Jack?" It was Tobias.

Nash lifted a corner of his mouth. "Tell him I'm in good hands and to spread the word the men are to meet at the tavern in the morning."

She leaned out the window to convey the message. Then she removed the candle from the casement and drew the muslin curtains closed. She tucked in the fresh bed linens. "You must lie still and go to sleep. Try not to think about things for now."

Nash closed his eyes. A moment more and he fell fast asleep. The medicine the doctor administered proved strong.

* * *

For a long while Theresa sat near the window, her hand cupped her chin as Nash slept. She studied his face. His eyelids were smooth and sleek, with dark lashes. The curve of his mouth inviting for kisses. She thought he was handsome, but she had no attraction to him other than a friendly admiration.

Nash turned his head and talked aloud in his sleep. "Rebecah."

Theresa smiled, realizing there was a woman in his life. She knew of no one in Fredericktown with that name. Whoever Rebecah was, she had no idea the man who apparently loved her lay wounded in an upstairs room of the Boyd house, out in the frontier. She had no idea he dreamed of her, spoke her name as sweet as honey from his lips.

Tears moistened Theresa's eyes. She wished a man would whisper her name in his sleep. She had pretty looks, blonde, slim, and misty-eyed. However she was not beautiful and lacked the graces of genteel ladies. She had not come to the revelation it did not matter.

The room grew darker as the candle melted. The breeze blew through the open window against her face and she stepped over to it to draw the curtains. Looking down she saw Black Hawk. She gulped at the sight of him. He walked forward, stopped beneath the window and looked up. An oak grew alongside the house and he climbed it.

Most women would have fallen back into the room and shut the window. But Theresa figured she had nothing to fear. He was John Nash's friend. When Black Hawk reached the windowsill, she met his eyes and saw something in them she had never seen in any other man. He was admiring her.

"What is it you want?" she said in a stammering whisper. "You must go away."

Pulling himself up, Black Hawk put his hand on the sill. "My brother is well?"

"Yes. He is sleeping. Go away."

Amusement danced in his eyes. "It is good a woman cares for him. I am at ease now."

Theresa scrutinized Black Hawk. His face looked bronzed in the moonlight, friendly. She noticed the bands surrounding his forearms and the feathers fastened in the locks of his hair.

"Your hair is the color of the elms in harvest time," he said smiling.

Theresa's heart leaped at his words. "Go away!"

"I will go." Black Hawk climbed down. "Tell my brother I've gone to the mountains."

Lithe, Black Hawk dropped from the tree. In a moment, he disappeared into the night. Theresa watched for a long while from the window, while John Nash slept and the moon skimmed the horizon.

* * *

Nash woke early as dawn crept over the hills. He pulled himself up on his elbows and looked at his wound. A fresh bandage had been applied. He had a raging appetite and thirst. He had not eaten in days.

He set his teeth and groaned as he tried to get out of bed. It was no use, so he fell back against the pillows. He lay there wondering for a moment why he had met with such misfortune. The breeze flowed through the window. Cool and fresh, it touched his face. He was thankful to be alive.

The door swung open.

"I've brought some food, Mr. Nash. You must be starved. When was the last time you had a home cooked meal?"

He thought of Standforth and Lady Margaret. She been the only mother he'd known, and although she had not given birth to him, she worried over him. He recalled the first night home and the bounty she had set, how good it was to be with her and his father. Feeling a little guilty over leaving them, he looked over at Theresa Boyd with a sad smile.

"Home cooked? Months ago. My mother set a fine table."

"Then you must eat as much as you can in order to regain your strength. I'm sure she would insist upon it."

Theresa put extra pillows behind him and helped him up. Nash felt a little foolish that he needed help and tried to swallow his pride.

"The doctor says you were lucky. The arrow missed an artery. Thank God, otherwise you would have bled to death. You may need some help walking for a while."

"How long have I slept?"

"Twelve hours." She poured tea into a china cup, handed it to him. "Hilda made those eggs special for you. She will be upset if you don't eat them."

He ate while Theresa explained all the doctor had done.

"I hope I've not been a burden to you and your father." She smiled. "No."

"Well, I won't impose on you any longer. I'm grateful for the help you and Mr. Boyd gave me. I don't know if I could have made it back to Laurel Hill."

"Dr. Cole is very good, don't you think."

"I've always thought so."

He saw her glance at the window, her face contemplative.

"I met your friend Black Hawk. He climbed the tree outside the window, paid me a compliment about my hair."

"You were not afraid of him?"

"I had no reason to be, since he is your friend."

"He is admirable." He drank the last of the tea, thankful but anticipating Joab's strong coffee.

Theresa shifted in her chair. "If you don't mind, who is Rebecah?" Her eyes held a glow of curiosity, and Nash handed her back the tray.

"How do you know that name?"

"You talked in your sleep."

"Oh? What did I say?"

"You called out to her."

Yes, and he had dreamt of her all night.

"Should I send her word?" Theresa asked. "I can write a letter for you and have it sent this very day."

"That won't be necessary." His heart felt heavy.

Theresa looked disappointed. She went to the door. "If she is someone dear to you, she should know you've been hurt."

"You're kind to offer your help, Miss Boyd. But unfortunately, I'm not dear to her."

Her eyes gazed at him sorrowfully. "Let me know if you change your mind." She turned out the room and shut the door.

Nash reached for his buckskins, and tried to think how he would address the men of the town without causing a major panic. Yet his thoughts were crowded, disrupted by the mention of Rebecah.

Slipping into his hunting shirt was easy. Putting the buckskin trousers on was painful for his leg. He must be careful not to force the bandage open if he meant to keep it. He positioned one hand on the table beside the bed and pulled himself up, standing on his good leg. Determined not to let it get the best of him, he tried to walk.

With his hand guiding his leg, he limped forward. A knock on the door, and Joab came inside the room. Looking worried, he rushed over to Nash and put his arm around his shoulder to help him.

"I've been worried sick, Mr. John."

"I'll be alright, Joab."

"You should be in bed and not runnin' around."

"We'll be home later, and you can fuss at me then. I need to speak to Mr. Boyd."

Being the town clerk, Boyd was dressed for the day. He waited at the bottom of the staircase, hat in hand.

"Are you well enough to be up, Jack?"

"Yes. Forgive me for barging in on you last night. You were the first person to come to mind to go to."

"I've sent word to all the Committee of Observation members that we are to meet at the tavern to hear your news."

"Do you have a cane I could lean on? It's embarrassing, but I cannot use Joab as a crutch."

Boyd reached behind the door and handed him the only one he owned. "I daresay you won't be dancing with the ladies of the town for a time."

Nash smiled. "I was never a good dancer anyway."

"How did this happen?"

"A Shawnee arrow. If it had not been for Black Hawk, I don't think I would have made it. He knew what to do for my wound, and knows the trails better than any white man."

"He has gone into the mountains."

"I knew he would."

"You saw warriors this far to the east?"

"A band painted for war. We came upon a farm...they'd burned it, killed and scalped the couple living there."

Mr. Boyd's eyes widened. "God help us."

"I pray He will."

They passed out the door down into the street. John Nash's heart sunk to see the people moving along it going about their day in this peaceful town still untouched by Logan's War. Mothers holding their children's hands paused as the men crossed the street and headed for Mrs. Carlton's Tavern. Soon a crowd of townsmen followed Nash, grave-faced and silent as they filed inside.

CHAPTER 28

Later that night, in the tavern on the corner of Market and Court Streets, men huddled together discussing the grim news brought to them earlier in the day. There were no rounds of ale, for the atmosphere was of a solemn nature.

"He was carryin' Nash over his shoulder because he'd been shot straight through the leg, I tell you," one man with a great beard and thick spectacles said.

"I heard it was an arrow that got him," said Tobias. "But nothin' takes Nash down easy, you know. He reminds me of a fellow I knew under General Braddock's command. Been shot in both legs and lived to tell about it. Now that was a war, the French and Indians, and the General was a great man."

Andrew Clarke had been listening to the entire buzz for the last twenty minutes. He was silent until he could stand it no more. He stood, knocking his chair backward and leaning his hands upon the table. His face twitched with anger.

"He was shot alright." He lifted his mug, took a swallow, and wiped his mouth with his shirtsleeve. "I'll put down my last coin it was an Indian that done it. A renegade on the warpath."

"Calm down, Andy." Tobias patted him on the shoulder.

"Aye, and I heard it were an Indian that saved Nash's life by bringing him here," said Sam Evans the town blacksmith.

"I saw him comin' into town with Nash. Bold as brass was he, and noble an Indian as I ever saw," said the tavern maid Meg as she set down the mugs.

"Set your heart to pacin', did he, Meg?" laughed Tobias, followed by the others. Meg shook her curls and nudged him on the shoulder.

Evans downed his cider. "Let's be happy Nash weren't killed."

Clarke slumped in his chair. "We better face the facts. You were at the meeting, Tobias. You heard what Nash said."

Tobias looked grim. "Aye, I heard. Nash sat there still as a post, not movin' a muscle, not showin' any pain as he told us the news. But you could see the worry in his eyes."

"Keep your muskets oiled," Clarke said to the men. "Now we got two wars to fight, one with the British, the other with the Indians. Cresap better not show his face around here for what he's brought on us. Too bad John Gibson didn't shoot him dead when he found him in that cabin."

Sam Evans leaned over the table. "There's no proof Cresap done anything. Who we gonna believe, an Indian chief or one of our own. I say we wait and hear Cresap's side of the story."

"The Committee is mustering a militia to protect the settlers," said Clarke. "I'm staying, and I'm sending my wife and baby girl to Baltimore to stay with her aunt until the whole thing blows over. I'll not see them murdered and scalped."

"It'd be wise if we thought of our kin," said the bearded man.

"Some of the women won't go," said Sam. "They're as much attached to the land as their menfolk. I doubt Indians will come as far as the town though."

216

"Well the militia will keep the hordes of hell away."

"What's a handful of men against a whole nation of braves?" said Clarke.

Creaking on rusty hinges, the tavern door swung open. In stepped a man who dared show his face in Fredericktown. Heads turned and eyes watched this loathsome creature of the backwoods walk up to the tavern keeper. He demanded whiskey, and when he was told it was dry, his face twitched red with anger.

Andrew Clarke did not take his eyes off the man's arrogant face. He remembered how LaRoux looked at Nash with unfounded hatred the last time he was in the tavern.

"Well, well." Clarke stood. "What do you want in our town, LaRoux? Come to flaunt any new scalps?"

LaRoux turned at Clarke and put his dirty hand over the hilt of his knife.

"Been to the Potomac, you French mongrel?"

LaRoux took an abrupt step forward. Tobias reached up and grabbed Clarke by the sleeve. "Let him go, Andy. He's not worth it."

Shaking his arm free, Clarke moved around the table and faced LaRoux. Fire flared in his eyes, fire and hate. Unmoved, Clarke met him stare for stare with equal hatred.

"Logan's family was murdered by a band of butchers. It's bringing every Indian down on our heads from the Ohio to the Hudson."

LaRoux leaned back against the counter and crossed his arms. "I heard about it. What's that got to do with me?"

"We'd all like to know. Logan rallied with Chief Cornstalk. The six nations are at war with us and are out to kill every man, woman and child that has white skin."

"Let them have their warpath." LaRoux glared and turned away.

Clarke clenched his fists, as all eyes watched. "You wouldn't have anything to do with the family killed near the river. Because if you did, there isn't a rope too short or too long in Fredericktown for your neck."

LaRoux's eyes blazed. He drew his knife and lunged at Clarke. The men in the tavern sprung out of their seats. Clarke fastened his hand around LaRoux's wrist. LaRoux twisted and slammed his fist into Clarke's side. Clarke gasped. Bounding from his chair, Tobias came between the two men and pushed LaRoux back. The blacksmith and innkeeper threw their hands forward to keep the men apart

"If any killing happens, LaRoux, you're to blame and you'll hang from Smith's oak by sunrise!" Tobias warned. "Put your knife away and get out of here before we haul you off."

"No man will take me,"

"John Murphy was the last man hung back in forty-nine. You want to be next, LaRoux? Cause if you are, we'll see to it for attempted murder."

LaRoux clenched his teeth and broke free. He sprang at Tobias. A tangled mass of men reached for the old man, for Clarke whose wrist was bleeding, others for LaRoux. A man drew his pistol and shot it into the rafters hoping to end the fight. Yet the knife gleamed in the air and descended into a feeble breast.

A chilling cry pierced the shouting. Everyone froze. Tobias fell to the floor. LaRoux burst from the throng. Like a rabid animal, he ran from the tavern and disappeared into the blackness. Men ran out into the street, but LaRoux was nowhere in sight.

"We'll go after him!" Cursing, Clarke started out the door of the tavern.

"He's gone, Andy. We won't find him now." Sam Evans pulled him back by the shoulders with his great hands.

Clarke blinked his eyes against the darkness then hurried back. He knelt beside Tobias. The old man lay shaken on the edge of death.

"I'm not ready to die." Blood was in his mouth, and forming in the corners of his lips.

Mrs. Carlton tore the edge of her petticoat and pressed the cloth against the wound. She was a middle-aged widow, with hair streaked silver, robust and as good at business as any man in town. "He'll never step foot in my establishment again, Tobias. I'll guarantee you that, my dear."

Tobias looked up into her eyes. "I can't believe he got me."

"Now you lie still and don't talk anymore. Some lads have gone for the doctor. He'll have you fixed up in no time."

Meg was crying.

"Quiet, Meg. You'll only make things worse."

Tobias choked. "Turn away, Meg, so you don't see me die."

Andrew Clarke tightened his grip. "You're not gonna die. You're made of cast iron."

"I did well though."

"Aye. Didn't know you had it in you. Every lad in the county will talk for years how Tobias Johnston fought the French-Shawnee bravely—another tale to add to the ones from the last war."

Tobias blinked his glazed eyes. "A legend is it?" He withered in pain, and settled back against Clarke's arm with a look that said he was afraid.

"Hold on, my friend."

Sam Evans stood at the door watching for the doctor. "He's coming up the road. I see his horse."

"I shouldn't have started it with LaRoux. Look what I've done." Clarke moved his head back and forth.

Tobias gripped his arm. "Ain't your fault, Andy."

"You saved my life, you old fool." Clarke held him harder. "You hold on."

Dr. Cole rushed inside the tavern and knelt beside Tobias. He lifted the bloodstained cloth and a look of dread spread over his face.

A light smile crossed Tobias's mouth. "Tell them to bury me under the sycamore next to my dear Jenny, up at Mount Olivet in the peaceful hills. You keep my musket and powder horn, Andy."

A slow breath slipped from his lips. Then the light within them faded. Tobias closed his eyes and died in Andrew Clarke's arms.

CHAPTER 29

The ruins of a church were in darkness. Moonlight broke through the clouds, bathed the ancient stones in variegated hues of blue and purple, flowed through glassless windows. No one was certain of its history. But legend had it Queen Elizabeth had once made a secret rendezvous there with the man she loved. Torched by the Parliamentary Army, its walls stood as a testimony against the pride of man and a memorial to those who had worshiped there.

Rodney Nash slid off his horse and pushed aside a low branch that hindered his view. He looked up. Stars flickered against the cold black sky. He entered the place that had once held the church door. The breeze blew against him in a single breath.

A tall figure of a man stepped out of the shadows to meet him. The look in Laban Huet's eyes touched a part of Sir Rodney most men of his time ignored—a lost and stricken gaze that spoke of poverty and struggle.

Long cries in the wilderness concerning the plight of the poor had fallen on deaf ears. The rich and powerful said the poorhouse, debtors' prisons, diseased streets, and country shacks were enough. Some went so far as to support the kidnapping and transportation of the penniless to the Colonies, no matter what age or gender.

Yet there were charitable men like Sir Rodney, who made the poor one of his causes. His soul stirred while looking at Laban. The fellow clutched a tattered hat with dirty and callused hands, and even in the gloom, Sir Rodney could see beneath his well-worn coat bony shoulders.

"We must be quick, Sir Rodney. The sun will be up soon."

Sir Rodney put his hand on Laban's shoulder. "Do not fear. No one has seen us. Do you have what I asked for?"

Laban nodded and handed Sir Rodney a packet.

"You've earned your wage. Here."

Laban looked at the coins in Sir Rodney's hand. He frowned. "No, Sir Rodney, this is more than we agreed."

"You've worked hard for me, Laban. We've known each other many a year. Take it and say no more." Sir Rodney reached out and took Laban's hand. He then slapped the coins in his gritty palm.

"I'll be taking what we agreed on, sir. The rest is charity, and I'll not be takin' charity."

"Ah, 'tis your pride speaking, man. Accept it, so your children will have more on the table to eat. "

Laban raised a somber face and acquiesced. "Thank you, sir. But just this once."

Sir Rodney pushed back the tip of his hat. "How many children do you have besides the two?"

Laban shifted on his feet. "I've four in the ground. Two were gone at birth, the others from the fever when they were babies."

"Death will reap its due reward in the Judgment. I'm sorry, Laban." Sir Rodney pulled his black cloak over him and went to his horse. "Does your wife know what you're doing?"

"She thinks I'm doing work up at Standforth. She asked me if I'm doing something I shouldn't, because she's afraid I'd go to prison if I were."

Sir Rodney climbed into the saddle and looked at Laban with a reassuring smile. "Tell her not to worry."

Laban frowned. "But what we're doing', sir, is it considered smuggling? Peyton, he's a smuggler, right?"

"You let me worry about Mr. Peyton, Laban. You need not discuss what you do for me with anyone. Besides, you've only been my courier, and know nothing of my business. Now, it's time you headed home to your good wife and little children."

Stepping back through the portal, Sir Rodney drew his horse out onto the road, nodded to Laban, and rode off toward Standforth.

* * *

Laban waited several minutes after he could no longer hear Sir Rodney's horse. Then he scanned the stretch of grass before him to the road and the woods beyond. It seemed safe to go, and so he trudged back home with money in his pocket.

He'd have his wife go to market in the morning, buy a fat goose and flour for bread. A happy smile lifted his otherwise unhappy mouth. He picked up his pace with a little skip in his stride and made his way down the road toward his house.

The wind pitched the branches of the trees. He paused at the top of the hill, looked at the cottage where his wife and children were sound asleep. A candle burned in the window, and he headed down the slope thinking how pleased his wife would be to see the coins he had earned.

When he opened the door, he drew off his hat. He placed his foot on the first step of the staircase. He heard movement, turned and strode from the tiny hallway into the little parlor. There he found his wife in tears, his children huddled in her skirts, and soldiers waiting inside.

* * *

Not long after sunrise, Sir Rodney sat in his study penning a letter. If something were to happen to him, he wanted his wife to know the depths of how he felt about her. He dipped his quill in the inkwell, hesitated, and then set it down to rub his eyes. Toby lay on the braided rug in front of the fire looking at him.

"I must choose my words with care, old girl. For if they're the last words I ever write to her, they must be lasting."

Setting his hands on the sides of his face, he looked out the window. The hills were dotted with sheep. The sky above the horizon looked pale. In his memory, he saw his son at play as a boy. He heard him whistle to his dog, race across the field without a care in the world. Sir Rodney's heart ached with missing him.

Lady Margaret entered the room. "Good morn, my love."

He made no reply.

"Are you feeling alright, Rodney?"

Sir Rodney raised his head and looked up. "I fair well, Margaret."

"I'm glad to hear it. What a glorious day."

"Indeed, yet I think it shall rain. Where is Rebecah? Is she up?"

"She is. I've asked her to arrange a vase of flowers for our breakfast table."

"I'm not very hungry."

"You must have breakfast, my love." She moved over to the window. "How can you work in here with it being so stuffy?"

"Margaret." He held out his hand and she came to him. He wrapped his arms around her waist. It was still pleasing.

"What is it, Rodney?" She ran her fingers through the front of his hair. "Is something troubling you. You miss Jack?"

"We must talk."

"I'm listening, my dear."

He touched her face. Then he dropped his hand. "You've found a great deal of peace in your faith, haven't you?"

"I've found assurance. I wish you would come to a meeting with me. But I'll not harp on you, for that would be wrong."

"I love you, God knows." He snatched up her hand, squeezed her fingers, pressing them against his lips.

She looked at him troubled. "Something is wrong. I can see it in your face."

"I should have told you long ago. But I felt it best to keep you out of it. I've never wanted you to worry. But now I feel I must tell you. I've been involved in a business that is against the King's law."

Her mouth fell open and her hand trembled in his. "What do you mean?"

"I believe in America's cause. I believe our son has the right to be free."

"So do I, my dear."

"Then you'll understand. I'm involved in sending goods and money by way of privateers. They take what they can to the patriots."

Anxious tears filled her eyes. "Why must you tell me this?"

"So you will know what to do if I'm found out." He took her hands and squeezed them. "My will is drawn up. Mr. Harcourt has the original copy."

"Rodney…"

"Also," and he opened a drawer to his desk, "I've money for Rebecah's passage. You must promise you will try to convince her to leave England and go to our son.

The key will be kept in the vase over there on the mantelpiece."

She stared at him, then at the contents in the drawer. "Yes, my husband. You know I'll do whatever you ask. But God forgive us if we are meddling where we should not."

He pulled her close against him. "Do not weep, my love. Perhaps I'm over dramatizing things. Perhaps nothing will happen and life will go on like always."

She lifted her head from off his shoulder and gave him a grave look. "If you stop what you've been doing, then no harm will come."

"I promise to be careful for your sake."

Outside an unbroken rhythm of horses came up the drive.

"Someone has come."

"Let us hope it is some of your friends." He stood with her. "I'm in need of assurance. Perhaps I shall join your group, Margaret, if they will have me."

He moved to the window where he had a clear view of the front drive. Leaves on the trees were twisting in the breeze. Some fell from the willows and floated to the ground.

Rodney Nash thought his heart would stop when he saw Laban Huet being pulled by a lengthy rope held by a mounted soldier in glittering scarlet. Laban's wife and children were staggering behind him.

Lady Margaret drew up beside Sir Rodney. He heard her gasp, her breath hurried so much so she could not speak.

Lottie Huet's forlorn eyes turned to them. She stretched out her hands. She cried out, ran toward the house. A soldier grabbed her. She fought back and fell. The children rushed to her. She pulled them into her arms.

"God, help us," Sir Rodney uttered in a heavy breath. "On my life, they have Laban Huet."

CHAPTER 30

LaRoux was a hunted man, and enjoyed it with a morbid kind of pleasure. After murdering Tobias Johnston, he joined his band of thieves. The Indians among them had no attachments to Logan, no allegiance to Cornstalk or Blue Jacket, no loyalties to any tribe.

The day Tobias was eulogized a blanket of blue sky hung above the earth. Not a dry eye sat among the mourners in Saint John's Church. The sun beat on the dome and the cross of the steeple, and slipped through the windows like a heavenly veil. The town had gone silent, except for Mrs. Cottonwood's dog Caesar, a fox terrier. It ran up and down Market Street chasing squirrels and barking at anything that moved.

Old Tobias's last request would be granted. After the service, a fife and drum preceded the crowd. A pine box sat in a wagon pulled by two of Sam Evan's black horses. Townsfolk walked toward the giant sycamore that stood in the center of Mount Olivet Cemetery and gathered around.

Six men bore the box on their shoulders. Andrew Clarke first to the right and opposite him was Captain John Nash who walked with a slight limp without the pain showing on his face. He kept to the steady slow pace. The men strained against the weight as they lowered Tobias's body into the ground. Then he stood back a pace and watched with angry eyes the dirt shoveled into the hapless grave. He wrestled with the idea God had called Tobias home this way. He could not accept it. Something born of darkness had done this. The sting of death twisted and turned in his heart like a knife. He felt his chest tighten. Grief demanded tears, but he fought them back.

For a moment, he glanced away and saw a man with red hair and pronounced features swat a fly away from his face. His eyes were large, round, and pale blue. A mantle of highland plaid draped over his right shoulder. The man shut his eyes, bowed his head as the priest read from the prayer book.

Nash had not seen this man before. He watched him. With the confidence of a prophet, the Scotsman came forward and stood over Tobias Johnston's grave. Everyone's' eyes were upon him. He lifted his face to the sun along with a deep resonant voice.

"Vengeance is mine. I will repay, says the Lord!"

Nash felt his heart lurch. The scripture reminded him, God did not approve of this murderous act. Payment would be inevitable. The crowd stood silent a moment. Then everyone walked away.

Nash stayed behind, holding his tricorn hat between his hands and leaning up against the tree. The Scotsman stared at the red mound of earth, a single tear in the corner of one eye.

"You knew him?" he asked.

The Scot nodded. "Aye. He was a relative, a cousin on my dear mother's side. She was English ya see. I sailed all the way from Scotland to see him. He sent me word saying I should come live with him and start a new life. I learned of his death upon my arrival."

"I'm sorry you were too late."

"So am I. I've made an oath if I find this LaRoux fellow I'll haul him by the scruff of his dirty neck to the jail in town and have him pay for his crime."

"We all feel the same as you."

Maldowney thrust his large hand out to Nash. "Robert Maldowney is my name."

"I'm honored." Nash shook Maldowney's hand. "I'm Captain John Nash. My friends call me Jack."

Staring at the grave, Nash picked up a handful of earth. He squeezed it tight in his hand, then let it fall. "Rest in peace, Tobias. I've no doubt we shall meet again."

Maldowney sighed. "Aye."

Lifting his hat to his head, Nash stepped away. "Well then, Robert Maldowney. Will you join me for a mug of ale and a good meal? I would enjoy your company."

Together they walked on across the grass. Meteor munched tender blades and shook his withers beside a brown horse with black mane and tail. Nash cursed the limp in his leg, wondering if he slowed the sturdy highlander's pace.

"Tell me, where in Scotland do you hale from?"

"I was born into a poor life near Loch Maree, in the Highlands. I'm son to a chieftain, though I don't lay much brag to it."

Nash ran his hand down Meteor's nose. "Why not? To a Scot a chieftain is higher than King George."

Maldowney laughed. "Aye, and a wit saner too. But I serve neither, unless it is as one brother to another."

"Your meaning?"

Maldowney held out his hand. "To love my neighbor as myself 'tis hard at times, especially when it comes to the British soldiery. Yet I try best I can."

Nash smiled at his comment. "You're a wayfarer?"

"Of sorts. I'm a man bent on preaching to the poor and outcast whenever, wherever I can." I'm heart in hand with Wesley as well as the Protestants. I listen to them all."

"You're an ordained minister."

"No, just a humble disciple of Christ."

Nash climbed onto Meteor's back. The horse shifted beneath him. "Well, you're welcomed in my house. I could use some conversation on the subject."

229

"Thank you. The last man I spoke the Gospel to pelted me with stones."

"Were you badly hurt?"

"The Lord blessed me with a large frame and I took them easy. But see here, one gave me a scar," and he pointed to a place above his left brow. "It proves I'm flesh and blood. Keeps me in my place."

Nash nudged his horse with his knees and it stepped forward. "Logan has turned against us, and with good reason. Some settlers in our county have been killed by war parties. So I would suggest you go no farther west, unless you plan to lose your scalp."

Maldowney looked at Nash and nodded. "I'll heed your advice. I'm acquainted with the ways of savages." They passed along the road under a canopy of trees.

"How?" Nash asked, curious to hear how a highlander so far from his homeland met up with Indians.

"I was travelin' and stumbled into a village. I was greeted warmly and the people gathered around me. For an hour, I stood upon a log and preached to them the Kingdom."

"Did they listen?"

"Some. Others stared right through me. When I ended my sermon, they led me to the center of the village. There I was put face to face with the most vicious Indian. A leather strap was tied to each of us upon the wrist, and I was given a tomahawk and told to fight. Are you acquainted with that ritual, Mr. Nash?"

One corner of Nash's mouth curved into a smile. "Indeed I am, among others. Thank God, I'm here today to say so."

"You've had some close shaves, I take it."

"Yes, within an inch of my life."

Maldowney kicked a stone from the path to the woods. "I'm afraid of very little. But when I looked into the eyes of that warrior and saw he meant to kill me, my heart plunged to my boots and my blood turned to ice water in my veins."

"What did you do?"

"Only what could be done."

"You killed him."

"I let him live."

There was a sparkle in Maldowney's eyes, a kind of pride that he did not take the Indian's life. It meant the warrior was now indebted to him, and no doubt he had won the respect of the village. It caused him to think of Black Hawk, wonder if he had found his path, and if he'd see him again.

Maldowney went on. "I could have killed him easy. Instead, I snapped the leather throng that bound us together and threw my body against him, knocking him to the ground. For a moment, I held the tomahawk at his throat. The villagers carried on something fierce, cryin' and shoutin' until I thought I'd go deaf. I stood, and when they tried to hold me, I threw them off like Samson. I left that village and went on, they thinking' I was something special. That brave knows he owes me his life."

Nash felt a great deal of admiration for this man. "You were delivered."

Maldowney gazed up at the sky. "Hmm, clouds are gathering and it looks like rain. Are you a believer, Captain Nash? Are ye born again?"

"I would say I am."

"You're English by your accent. Had you ever heard John Wesley preach?"

"No, but he converted my stepmother. She attempted to persuade me into attending a meeting, but I was distracted."

Maldowney winked his eye. "Ah, a lady."

Nash smiled. "How did you guess?"

"What else causes a man to think of nothing else?"

Nash slid the reins through his hands. "What else indeed? That's my place over there. Come. We shall have a huge supper."

* * *

When Rebecah heard hurried steps outside in the hall, she went to see what was going on. Sir Rodney stumbled over the runner past her and rushed to the front door. He threw it open and went outside. His dog carried on at the strangers on horseback, snarling and barking until Angus took Toby by the collar and put her inside the house.

Lady Margaret stood in the doorway with Rebecah beside her. Soldiers, Laban, his wife and children, were out on the lawn. "Rodney, do something to stop them."

Rebecah clutched her trembling hand. Sir Rodney met a man in uniform.

"Good day to you, Sir Rodney. My apology, my men have trampled over my lady's flowerbed. May we go inside? I've some questions to ask."

Sir Rodney drew back his shoulders. "Why is that man being dragged like a common criminal? He's done nothing wrong."

Captain Neil Donley stood erect and raised his bows. Not a speck of dirt or grim on his cream-colored breeches. His powdered wig hadn't a hair out of place. He drew from his pocket his handkerchief and wiped his nose.

"That, sir, has been proven otherwise. He confessed to his crime. Now, tell me what you know about it."

Sir Rodney sharpened his eyes. "Laban Huet would never soil his hands in the affairs of criminals. He works for me, here at Standforth, as a laborer."

Donley raised one brow. "So he has told us. I suppose he had you duped as well."

Sir Rodney stiffened. "He is neither a liar nor a cheat."

232

"Then you agree with what I said."

"That isn't what I meant, Captain."

"Did you hear of the sea battle that occurred last night outside these shores?" Donley asked, inspecting the ground he walked over.

"I had not heard of such," Sir Rodney answered.

"An American privateer escaped out to sea with tattered sails and smoke billowing from her stern. It's unlikely they shall reach America now. We know certain men have been supplying these ships. We believe you're one of those men. You've been followed from time to time."

Sir Rodney's face turned white. His hands shook and he gripped them behind his back so Donley would not notice. Dread coursed through Rebecah, knowing by the look on his face he was somehow involved.

"If I confess to you of my dealings, do you swear you'll let this man go?"

Donley turned to face him. "Choose for him, sir. Prison or death."

Sir Rodney threw his shoulders back. "Very well, you have my confession. I've been supplying American privateers, but in a manner I do not see as treasonous."

Lady Margaret gasped, and Rebecah put her arms around her.

"Your son is a colonial, is he not?"

"You have no reason to mention him. He has nothing to do with this."

"Some are saying he is a traitor. But gossip can be unkind. Now, if you please, one of my men will escort you to a horse."

An armed soldier stomped forward. Lady Margaret rushed to her husband and he drew her into his arms. "I'm sorry, Margaret."

Rebecah faced the insipid captain. "You are supposed to be a keeper of the King's peace."

Donley turned and looked back at her.

"Why must you harass good Englishmen and frighten English women and children?"

The King's men moved forward. Donley waved them back, not once removing his eyes from Rebecah's face. Sir Rodney's eyes pleaded for her not to say another word.

"How can you, being a servant to the Crown and a defender of its subjects, question one of England's knights with such disrespect?"

A round of howls followed, but she thought nothing of it and went on.

"Is this the way you were trained, to be a bully and churl? My father was in His Majesty's service. I know what is expected."

Captain Donley's expression was one of surprise and shock. Rebecah met his stare, seeing he admired her boldness as well as her looks. His eyes told her everything—that he liked the way her hair fell over her shoulders, that her face enticed him to the point his temperature rose.

"If I had known such a flower graced this," and he swept his hand toward the house, "den of defiance, I would have found a way to spare you this grief."

She narrowed her eyes at his impertinence. "How dare you speak to me thus? I'm Rebecah Brent. My father was Sir Richard Brent of Ashburne, my uncle Sir Samuel Brent of Endfield."

"I know Sir Samuel."

"Then send one of your men to him, and let us see what he has to say about this. He will not stand by while a soldier bullies his relatives and those that serve us. I demand you release Sir Rodney and Laban at once."

Never had she thought to use her uncle's name for leverage. But now it was a necessary weight and she hoped it would convince Donley to let Sir Rodney go.

Donley laughed at her demand. "Sir Samuel was the one to inform us."

Her body stiffened at his words. "What? That cannot be."

"He had seen an American ship in the harbor and grew suspicious. Is he not law abiding, ma'am, and loyal to England?"

"My uncle would never accuse Sir Rodney."

"Indeed, ma'am. He had no idea his own relation was involved with that ship. No doubt he will be grieved when he hears of it."

Sir Rodney was taken away and mounted on a dark brown horse.

"You must listen!" she stormed.

"You need not beg, ma'am." Donley drew closer. She saw in his eyes insincerity. "I shall do what I can."

Her eyes narrowed. "Do what is right and release them both. You've no proof of anything."

"I most certainly do."

"Sir Rodney is loyal to the King. As for Laban, he is a simple man and penniless. Think of his wife and children. Surely he can do no harm to any one, especially the Crown."

"I must do my duty. You mustn't think me heartless."

"Oh, but I do."

Affronted, Donley ordered the soldiers to move forward and mounted his horse. Lottie hurried to Laban, and when she had thrown her arms around him, she was shoved away. Rebecah helped her up from the ground. She held her in her arms and tried to comfort her. Lottie pleaded and begged them not to take her husband. Tears stained her face and her frightened children snatched at her skirts. Lady Margaret wept on her doorstep. Angus stood with his teeth and fists clenched.

Donley turned his horse around and looked back at Rebecah. He gave an order. A soldier stepped forward and threw a rope over the thick limb of a birch tree. Two soldiers turned and raised their muskets to keep the others from coming forward. Laban struggled and cried for mercy. Lottie screamed as they put the noose over her husband's neck.

It was an unbelievable sight—Laban hoisted up in the tallest tree at Standforth. Lady Margaret, Rebecah, and Angus were stunned into silence, trembling and looking on with wide, horrified eyes. In tears, the women watched him die. Lottie pleaded, raked her fingers through her hair and tore at her clothes. She fell forward, dug her fingers into the grass. Her children were weeping.

Lady Margaret gathered Lottie and the children into her arms and held them fast. Rebecah stood speechless and shaking. Her eyes wide, and brimming with tears, she watched Sir Rodney hang his head in despair. Then she heard him swear an oath, but what kind she could not make out. Donley sneered and walked his horse toward Rebecah. Eyes brimming, she clutched the folds of her dress.

His horse stopped in front of her and he waited, looking as though he anticipated her to lash out at him.

"The King's law must be upheld. Lawbreakers must be made an example so others will not follow in their footsteps."

Her chest heaving with despair, she glanced at Laban's body swinging from the rope. Her stomach lurched and every inch of her went cold as a soldier brought him down.

Gripping her hands together, she stepped forward and looked Donley in the eyes. "God has seen what you've done this day. You've hung a man without a trial. I hope you are prepared to reap the consequences in this life and the one to come."

Donley leaned over the saddle. "You are mistaken, madam. I have my reward from my king. By obeying him, I've obeyed God."

Rebecah's face burned with anger. Donley turned his horse and trotted back to his troops, who were heading down the dusty road with Sir Rodney as prisoner.

That night at the Boyd House, miles and miles across sea and land, from the darkened forlorn house at Standforth, Theresa Boyd rubbed her eyes and closed the book she had been reading. Setting her hands in her lap, she stared out the window. She was deep in thought.

The glass in the window glazed. The moon's silvery light frosted it. She could not stop thinking of Black Hawk. She pictured his face and remembered the way he climbed the tree. She recalled his voice and poetic words. She thought about his loyalty to Captain Nash. Would she see him again? Was it wrong for her to think of a man who was not of her race, considered a heathen savage? As these questions turned in her mind, a prayer stumbled from her lips. The words were mixed, jumbled; yet she knew God understood.

"You don't see as other men see. Men look on the outward appearance, but you, oh Lord, look on the heart." She sighed and set her book on the table beside her.

She started when the grandfather clock downstairs chimed out the quarter hour. Taking her candlestick in hand, she went downstairs barefoot and wide-eyed to the front door. Yes, the bolt was in its slot for the first time she could remember. Next the windows. The shutters were latched. Moonbeams slithered through the narrow cracks in the wood. A mouse dashed across the wainscoting.

Theresa's heart raced and fear stole up within her. She shivered. Which path would her brave Indian prince choose? He seemed strong, yet gentle, his eyes dark, yet tender when he looked at her from the high branch. Wanting to wake from a futile dream, she shook her head and a lock of her hair fell over her eyes. She brushed it away and commanded herself not to think of him.

"What would my father say?" she whispered to the gray mouse perched on the window ledge.

* * *

At Laurel Hill, night had fallen and rain tapped against the windows. Maldowney stretched out in front of the log fire. He folded his hands over his chest and snored. His belly was full of salmagundi and ale. Nash sat in a chair near the fire with his boots up cleaning his pistol when he heard a whistle come from outside. He set the pistol down and went to the door. Looking out into the darkness, he saw Black Hawk standing alone below the porch. He was shadowed, except for his face when he lifted it to meet the moonlight. Nash motioned to him to come inside.

When Black Hawk stepped over the threshold, he put his hand over Nash's shoulder. "You are well, my brother?"

"Yes, but left with a limp." Nash poured another mug of cider, then handed Black Hawk a bowl of what was left of the salmagundi. He looked over at Robert Maldowney sleeping. "I've made a friend, Black Hawk. No doubt he shall be yours as well."

Black Hawk turned. "Who is he?"

"A Scot who says he will see men's souls saved. We've had a long talk, and he knows what happened to me, and to Tobias. He said I should be circumspect and keep my weapons clean and loaded."

Black Hawk sat on the floor before the fire to eat. His silence said more than words. It meant he agreed.

"I'm glad you're back," Nash told him. "Eat, then rest. In the morning tell me of your time in the wilderness."

Black Hawk looked up with a mouthful. He swallowed and held up his hand. "I must speak something."

Nash stretched his arms and yawned. "I'm tired, brother. But speak."

"You find rest in your dreams? Is the English woman in them?"

Nash frowned. "She dominates my dreams, and I wake hating the day."

"You must stay alive for her."

"If anything I must stay alive for my own good." Nash shrugged off Black Hawk's prophetic words. The mention of Rebecah pricked his heart.

"The ways of the white man are strange to me." Stretching out and leaning on his elbow, Black Hawk looked at the dead coals in the hearth. "Perhaps she will do what this man teaches and forgive you. It is hard for a warrior to do, but not for a squaw. A warrior never forgets and vengeance is his way. But a squaw can bury a hatchet and forget where it lay."

As he spoke, Maldowney woke. He turned onto his side, unalarmed by the presence of an Indian, for he saw and heard Nash speaking to him as an equal.

"It is hard for any man, white or red. For his heart seeks his own pleasure, and he takes a vengeful path when his mind is worldly."

Nash put his hand to his chin and looked out the window into the night. Perhaps he had given up too easily. Perhaps if he had stayed longer she would have believed him.

There was softness about her he had not known in any other woman, a gentleness that melted his soul. He doubted he would ever find a woman like her even if he searched the entire world.

He grew thoughtful and silent. Rebecah was not what he wanted to dwell on. He tried to forget, but something always reminded him of her. When the wind blew hard, he thought of her unbound hair blowing off her shoulders. When he stood by the river, he thought of the brook where they had stood together listening to the sound the water made rippling over the stones. The wildflowers he once ignored reminded him of the way she smelled. The leaves were the color of her eyes.

"I saw men in the woods near the two rivers today," Black Hawk said. "One was both Indian and white."

"LaRoux." Nash's eyes narrowed. How could he not hate the man that had murdered his friend? "It will be a good day when he is captured, Black Hawk. He is an evil man."

"I should have bounded from the trees, fought his men and dragged him back here to you."

"It's never wise to throw oneself into a pack of wolves. You know that."

Black Hawk grunted. "I followed them until the trail was lost. Blood was on the trail."

"Perhaps LaRoux is wounded and it will be his end." Nash frowned hard.

"Don't you worry, Jack. LaRoux will reap what he has sown." Maldowney laid back, his arms behind his head. "All in good time."

Black Hawk nodded and went out the door. Joab had long gone to his bed, and Maldowney snored contently. As a crescent moon descended along the horizon, Nash left his guests and went upstairs.

For most men, a memory of love lost fades with time. It becomes a scar instead of a bleeding wound. But for Nash, her memory prevailed. He looked over at the cold pillow next to his, imagined she could have warmed it if circumstances had not forced them apart. He would have loved her, protected her, provided well for her. He would have laid his life down for her a thousand fold.

He heard the flutter of wings outside his window. A pair of mourning doves alighted on the sill and cooed. They huddled together, bathed in moonlight, tucking their beaks inside their wings for the night. He watched them while shadows lengthened.

"Rebecah." He gripped the sides of the window until his hands shook.

An hour before sunrise, Rebecah sat in the window seat of her room. She clasped her hands about her knees, her head raised and pressed against the cool blue damask curtains, as she prayed for Sir Rodney, Lady Margaret, for Lottie and her children.

Her mind went over what had happened between her and Jack. Her breath came quick and painful. Her heart ached for him. She knew how angry and heartbroken he would be if he knew what had happened to his father. If only he had been here, he might have prevented the whole horrible event.

Lady Margaret's room was next to hers and she heard her crying through the wall. She pulled on her robe, stepped out into the hallway, knocked, and went in. Lady Margaret sat up; her eyes even in the weak candlelight were swollen and red, still moist with tears. She let out a little cry and stretched out her arms to Rebecah. Rebecah went to her and held her as she wept.

After a long desperate night had past, and the sun rose when the clock chimed out six, Lady Margaret and Rebecah dressed. Rebecah ran a brush through Lady Margaret's hair, watched her in the mirror. She stared forward, her brow turned down, as she sat motionless. The maid had been turned away when she brought in a tray of breakfast. By eight, they took horse toward Endfield with Angus as their guide.

CHAPTER 31

Rebecah nudged her horse on with a click of her tongue. Lady Margaret rode silent beside her the entire way. The hills were laced with patches of fog and the sky was gray as slate. No wind blew. She saw Henry Carrow trudging down a hillside with a hoe over his right shoulder, whistling as he went with his dog pacing beside him. He looked up and she raised her hand.

Henry waved back and picked up his step. With a flick of the reins, Rebecah's horse started at a canter. When she reached Henry, she smiled, masking the inner anxiety she felt.

With gritty hands, Henry pulled off his hat. His sparse hair lay flat against his head. He shoved it away from his eyes.

"Are you well, Henry?" Rebecah looked out from the brim of her hat. "How are Jane and the boys?"

Henry bowed short. "They're in fine health. Thank you, miss."

Angus and Lady Margaret caught up. She gave Henry a forced smile. She looked tired as tired could be, and her eyes were red and swollen. Henry gave her a quick bow, but said not a word. His startled face showed enough concern, Rebecah knew, and she drew his attention away from Lady Margaret.

"We've come to see my uncle, Henry. Have you heard the news?"

"Aye, I have. If there's anything I can do, I'll do it with a stout heart." Henry doffed his hat and bowed to Lady Margaret.

"Thank you, Henry." Lady Margaret nodded. "You are kind to offer."

"The master isn't home. He's gone and won't be back for a long time. He's hardly at Endfield anymore."

Rebecah felt deeply disappointed. She glanced over at Lady Margaret. "We will find another way. I shall write to him at once."

Henry took a step forward, hat in hand. "My wife and I will pray for Sir Rodney, my lady. It would be easier if your stepson were here."

Lady Margaret's eyes filled up and she looked away. "If ever there were a time when he should be home it should be now," she replied. "But I'm being selfish to think so. His life would have been in danger too, and then I would have had more to grieve over."

"And I with you, my lady." Rebecah fixed her eyes on the hill where Endfield stood and remembered all that had happened behind those windows. "Let us return to Standforth. Angus, once we are home, you're to go into the village and make inquiries as to where the army took Sir Rodney."

Angus turned his horse back, and as Rebecah and Lady Margaret did the same, Henry called out. "I think it was a miracle I saw you coming. My Jane and Miss Dorene are having a terrible squabble up at the cottage. I didn't know what to do, except maybe get March. If the master knew what they were arguing over, he'd have Miss Dorene sent away. Perhaps you could help. It's a woman's matter they be fighting about."

* * *

243

Jane Carrow dropped her wooden spoon the moment Rebecah and Lady Margaret stepped though her cottage door. It was as if the sun broke in on a darkened room. Jane picked up the spoon. She then curtsied to her ladyship.

Henry brought Lady Margaret a chair. Removing her gloves, she lowered into it. Still Rebecah could see the pain in her eyes, which she managed to conceal from the others.

How tender a person is Lady Margaret to allow this interruption in her mission.

"We cannot stay long," she said. "I thank you for the pause and a cup of tea if you have it."

"I do, my lady." Jane hurried with cup and saucer.

Rebecah preferred to stand. Pulling her ribbon free from beneath her chin, she removed her hat and set it on Jane's oak table. She turned to her cousin. Dorene stood by the window, her face heated by either the sun or shame, her arms hugging her waist. Her eyes were fixed on the swept floor, her lower lip between her teeth. Rebecah sensed her cousin was in trouble.

Jane talked about her boys and the neighbors down the road who just had their seventh baby. "Babies are fine and a blessing from the Lord. Do you not think, my lady?" Jane poured tea into a plain china cup.

"If it had not been for Rodney and my stepson, I would have been a lonely woman."

Clearly, Lady Margaret fought back tears. Rebecah drew beside her, set her hand on her shoulder.

"We share in your sadness, my lady," said Jane. "What is to be done?"

Lady Margaret lowered her eyes. "I don't know, Jane. We shall soon find out."

Dorene put her hand to her forehead.

"Are you ill, Dorene?" Rebecah asked.

Dorene raised her face. Rebecah noticed her cheeks were flushed, looked plumper than usual.

244

"I must be going home. I'll ask someone else to help me from now on, Jane, seeing you refuse. One of the scullery maids should do." Her voice was smooth, yet tainted with anger. Her dark eyes blinked to hold back fear.

Jane threw her hands over her hips. "I refused, my girl, because what you ask me to do is wrong. You go right ahead and try to make trouble for me with the master. It won't get you far because he'll find out why, and I'll be the one to tell him."

Dorene thrust out her hand. "I forbid you to speak!"

"Of this I must, Dorene Brent."

"No, be silent, Jane!"

"You go right ahead and try to stop me."

"You dare speak to me this way?"

"I do. Henry and I are willing to help in the right way, and so will your cousin and Lady Margaret if you let us."

"Don't say another word, Jane!" Dorene covered her ears with her hands. "You've no right to judge me. I'll do what I wish to do, and no one will stop me."

"What is wrong?" Rebecah moved around the table to her cousin, distressed by her outburst. Now she knew for certain Dorene faced some kind of grave misfortune. Shame and fear ebbed over her face, shone in her worried eyes. Gone were the haughty and proud expressions Rebecah was used to seeing.

"We've urgent business, Dorene," said Lady Margaret. "As you know, Sir Rodney has been arrested. I must go to him. For once swallow your pride and speak now if you need help. I've a spare room at Standforth if you should need a refuge."

Dorene jerked away. "You have no idea what is wrong."

"It is obvious."

Rebecah touched her hand. Surprisingly her cousin did not pull away. "Tell us what has happened. What trouble are you in?"

245

"I know you must hate me, Rebecah, for having wished you and Jack parted."

"You are wrong. I do not hate you. But you've behaved badly."

"Only because I wanted love so much. I wanted Jack, and I was jealous of you. But then, after you refused Lanley, he wanted me. He wooed me with soft words, words of love, promises of marriage. Now I'm left to face the consequences alone."

Dorene burst into tears and reached for the back of a chair. Quick to reach her, Rebecah drew her into her arms. Her wayward cousin laid her head upon her shoulder and wept. Distressed, Rebecah looked over at Lady Margaret.

"Take Miss Dorene to one of your rooms, Henry."

"Yes, my lady." Immediately Henry lifted Dorene who was too weak to resist.

"And Jane, bring some salts. You need not tell us why you and Miss Dorene argued. It would be apparent to any woman she is with child."

* * *

The Carrow's bedroom was furnished with the bare necessities, much in conflict with Dorene's taste. The bed was small and boxed with cedar. Down quilts covered the straw-filled mattress. Creamy muslin curtains banked the open windows. Upon the sill, Jane had placed a jar of wildflowers. Sunlight sparkled upon the glass, the water within it reflecting on the wall.

Rebecah freed the strings of Dorene's bodice, enabling her to breathe easier. Beneath her nose, she waved the salts and Dorene opened her eyes.

"Are you feeling better?" Rebecah asked. Dorene nodded. "Here drink this." She handed her a cup and Dorene tasted the homemade gooseberry wine.

"Now, talk to me without assuming what I might think? You're in trouble and I want to help."

"You want to help me?"

"Yes."

"Good." Dorene sat up on her elbows. "I want to see Mab Penhurvy."

Rebecah drew back. "The woman that lives outside the village in the woods?"

"I must go to her. Will you take me? I cannot go myself. I'm too afraid."

"I've heard of her, what she does in secret. Dorene, you cannot do this."

"You said you would help." Dorene fumed tearfully.

"I did and I will. But I'll not help you destroy your unborn child."

Dorene shoved Rebecah away and got up. "You don't understand a thing."

"I understand very well." Rebecah argued, her tone growing angry. "Life is worth saving, even when it's inconvenient."

Dorene's face stiffened. "I don't understand such things like you. Will you now preach at me? Will you tell me how God must condemn me for what I've done and what I'm wanting to do?" Defiant, she tossed her head and swung around to meet Rebecah. "Well go on, say it. I'm bound for Hell."

"Be quiet," Rebecah demanded. "We will work this out. What you carry inside you is a part of you. Do not reject the child in your womb. For all you know, that child could be your saving grace, the one who will love you all your life."

For a moment, Dorene's angry stare softened. She turned and stared out the window. Rebecah drew up beside her. Jane's boys were playing in the yard. Dorene reached for Rebecah's hand. Her reserve broke as they watched the boys roll on the grass.

247

"My father will cast me out," she said slowly. "I do not want to be like him."

"Think of what your mother would tell you."

Dorene turned to Rebecah. "Oh, how I wish she were here."

"You have people around you that care. Perhaps if you tell me what happened, it would make you feel better."

Dorene wiped her face dry. "Father was away on business. I was bored alone at Endfield. Lanley's visit was unexpected, but I was glad to see him. We supped together, talked long into the night, and then the conversation turned to romance. I ordered March not to disturb us. When I knew she had gone to her chamber, I took him by the hand and led him to my room. He stayed with me all night."

"So this is Lanley's child you carry?"

Dorene nodded. "I did not mean it to happen."

"You must tell him."

Dorene looked at her with wide eyes. "I cannot, Rebecah. He would deny everything and reject me. If word gets around, I'll be unwelcome in all good society. Lanley will not have me, and my father will send me away."

"I believe Lanley is an honorable man."

"He will reject me, I tell you. Do you know what happens to women like me? Your name is dragged through the mud. You become an embarrassment to the family, left to live out a life as an old maid. And the names people call you."

"It doesn't have to be that way. You must tell Lanley."

Dorene shook her head back and forth. "No. No."

"He will marry you quietly. Besides, he has always wanted an heir."

"That is true." Dorene's eyes flashed at the idea. "But I am afraid."

"You cannot let fear prevent you. You must think of the child instead of yourself. You've been selfish, Dorene. The child should be entitled to his father and his fortune."

Dorene looked at her with a shake of her head. "Why couldn't I have been more like you, Rebecah? Lanley wanted you. I feel I was an outlet for his pain of losing you. Second best. He will not have me. Not like this."

"You will not know until you try."

"You are so sure."

"I cannot say, but it is the right thing to do."

"I was wrong to meddle in your affairs. If I had not, you would have run off with Jack and married him. Lanley would have chosen me in the long run, perhaps."

"Perhaps he has chosen you now."

Dorene's expression softened. "I'm sorry, Rebecah, for coming between you and Jack."

"I try not to think of John Nash and what could have been." But it was hard and she felt the pain of losing him snatch at her heart.

Dorene leaned her head against Rebecah's shoulder. "I thought you would have hated me. You must forgive me for the wicked things I've said and done."

Rebecah stood. She walked over to the window and opened it wider. "I'm leaving today with Lady Margaret. We are going to Sir Rodney."

Dorene shot her a worried glance. "Oh, my trouble has delayed you. Here I'm crying over my situation, while Lady Margaret sits in Jane's parlor agonizing over her husband."

Rebecah's skirts whispered across the floor. Sunlight poured through the window and she felt its warmth. "I shall tell you now what must be done, and for once in your life you will listen to sense. You're going to have a baby. You need Lanley. It would be wrong not to tell him."

"He will despise me."

"I know him well enough to believe he would not."

"You're so sure, Rebecah?'

"To reject you would cause a scandal and I think he has had enough for one year. Let me speak to him."

"You would do this after the way I've treated you?"

A soft smile lifted Rebecah's mouth. "If I were in your shoes, I would accept any help offered to me. Promise you will not do anything until you've heard from him."

"Alright...I'll wait." Dorene rose and gripping her hands looked into Rebecah's eyes. "Thank you. Whatever happens, whatever he may decide, I will cherish this child."

Rebecah threw her arms around Dorene and embraced her.

* * *

Across the ocean, a bank of heavy thunderclouds rose over the mountains to the west. Nash waited beside his horse marveling how the peace of the natural world could exist alongside the terrors and cruel punishments of mankind. His heart grew heavy, so much so he wanted to shout aloud and wake the world from the dark slumber blinding the true mission of man.

It was beyond comprehension what had happened at the George Folke farm. He could never describe what horrors he and the others had seen there. Unmistakably warring Indians had committed the gruesome deeds.

Nash and his men had been on patrol when they saw smoke rising above the line of trees at the base of the mountain. He dismounted beside the smoldering cabin. The porch had burned, but the shell of the cabin remained, for its foundation was made of stone.

He and the others stepped inside. The stone fireplace jutted skyward through the rafters, blackened and stripped. Nash picked up the remains of a quilt. He turned the red and white patchwork over and saw the blood upon it. A doll lay broken beneath it. Dropping the quilt back in place, he stood and stomped outside.

The pigpen stood at the edge of the forest beneath the shade of the trees. The swine within it grunted and wiggled their noses between the slates in the stall. Mud and mire covered their tough skin.

"They burned everything but that." He strode off. Maldowney dashed ahead. When he reached the pen, he stopped short, stiffened, and spun around. "Stay back!" he shouted.

Nash hurried forward. "Robert! What is it?"

Maldowney wiped his mouth with his sleeve and held his arm out to prevent Nash from looking. Nash shoved his arm away and looked over the stile. The man within him tore and the want for revenge exploded. Folke, his wife and children, had been murdered, their bodies hacked and thrown to the pigs for fodder. Bits of bloodstained clothing soaked up the mud among broken bone.

Slamming his fist into one of the stiles, he let out a cry. Then he drew out his flintlock pistol and shot one of the pigs. He reloaded and shot another. His men stood stark still watching him reload, looking on with compassion and dismay.

Then Maldowney set his large hand over Nash's. "Stop, Jack. 'Tis not the fault of these creatures."

Slowly, Nash lowered his weapon. The men gathered around, and one by one they followed Robert Maldowney's lead and went down on bended knee. Nash stared at the ground with his jaw clenched, while his friend prayed.

He rubbed his eyes as if to wipe away the memory of the massacre. With his hand over his hunting knife, he headed for his horse.

"Black Hawk." The Indian raised his face. His eyes were proud and Nash saw in them warrior courage. "Can you track the men that did this?"

"Can the wolf find the wounded bear, my brother?"

Nash nodded. "You're that wolf. You tell me."

Black Hawk looked up at the hills and pointed. "They are above that line of elms, above the cleft in the rocks."

"You lead, Black Hawk." He climbed into the saddle and dragged the reins through his hands. "When we catch them, we will be walking into a hornet's nest."

Nash could see it troubled the Scot to see him full of vengeance. "No murder shall I do, Jack. Israel stood against the armies of the Philistines and the prophets blessed them before they went into battle. And so, I do the same. Let us try to capture these men and bring them to trial."

Nash shrugged. "They'll hardly give themselves the chance, Robert. For when they meet with us, they will try to kill us."

CHAPTER 32

Shadows lengthened across the forest. The air grew cool, and pockets of mist rose through the trees to the heights of the mountains. The sky turned hard blue to the south, granite to the north.

Nash watched Black Hawk steal silently through the trees. The feathers in his hair blended with the darker shades of the woods. He bent low, stopped and raised his hand. And when Nash lifted his in reply, the Indian prince stepped forward and halted in front of him.

Nash's heart had been pounding, for what Black Hawk had found he was anxious to know. Beads of sweat rippled down his temple and he wiped them away. "What can you tell us, my brother?"

Black Hawk pointed to a place in the hills where two mountains met. Mist lay thick and deep within the crevice. "Twenty shots from where the arrow flies. From the bridge in the rock, I've seen them."

With a creased brow, Nash stared up the hillside from where Black Hawk had come. The woods were thick and the undergrowth heavy. How any man could trek through it without making a single sound seemed impossible.

Taking up the reins of his horse, he turned to his men. "We have to leave the horses behind. One neigh, a hoof breaking a twig, will give us away."

"Over there are hemlocks." Andrew Clarke jerked his head in that direction.

Nash went on. When they reached the grove, he pulled Meteor inside, rubbed his nose, and tethered him there alongside Clarke's horse. He stepped away with the others, Black Hawk in the lead. They mounted the hill to a deer trail swept clear of leaves.

Halfway, a covey of quail erupted from the ground, took flight and scattered. Nash saw Black Hawk squeeze the hilt of his tomahawk. The men instantly crouched behind the brush. He locked his eyes on the ridge. Had the enemy found them instead?

He glanced over at Clarke, saw his hands tighten around his musket. He heard Maldowney suck in a quick breath. A whisper of wind rustled the leaves in warning. The sun slid behind a cloud. The forest shifted from shadowy daylight to grim twilight.

His heart raced and he steeled himself for the battle.

Over the crest of the hill a warrior stood. He threw his arms into the air with a blood-curdling cry. His war whoop echoed through the woods. Nash lifted his musket and took aim.

Five more warriors poured over the hill and ran toward them. A tomahawk whirled within inches of Nash's head, struck a tree behind him. Clarke fired his musket. Blood spilled out along an Indian's chest and he fell.

Nash took aim and fired. The bullet splintered a tree and passed into an Indian's heart. He glanced to his left. Maldowney threw himself upon a warrior that wrestled with Black Hawk. With his great hands, he pulled the man up, squeezed the knife from his hand, swung him around and shook him like a rag doll. Bending him like a reed, he then tossed him into the woods. The others turned, scrambled up the hill and over the top. One turned whose face Nash knew.

LaRoux!

Black Hawk sheathed his knife. "I did not need help."

Maldowney heaved a breath. "Perhaps not, my friend. But you're welcomed just the same."

Andrew Clarke curled up on the ground and moaned. Nash set him up against a tree and looked at the wound on his arm. "You'll be alright, Andy. Try not to move."

An aching grew in his mind as he looked at his bleeding friend. A strange desire to see the warring end surged through his veins like quicksilver. He untied the scarf around Clarke's throat and tied it around his arm. Nash looked up at Maldowney.

"Help me get him on his horse."

The two men held Clarke's arms over their shoulders and guided him back down the hill. Clarke's horse snorted as they helped him mount.

Meteor pranced with wide eyes until his master's hand calmed him. Nash noticed the blood on his hands when he drew the reins over the horse's head. He walked to a stream beside the path and washed the blood away.

CHAPTER 33

David's shadow fell across the threshold when he opened the door and stepped inside the sitting room. Rebecah looked over at him. Marriage had changed the man. He looked healthier, happier, deeply in love with her cousin, overjoyed with the baby they were going to have. It made her smile, gave her hope that true love could last.

"Mr. Deberton has arrived," he said.

With a quick turn, Lady Margaret moved from the window to a seat beside Rebecah.

"Has he news about my husband?"

She twisted a handkerchief between her hands, her expression drawn and anxious.

"Yes, and it would be best if I let him tell you, my lady. He's taking off his coat and gloves and will be in directly."

"Perhaps it will be good news," Rebecah said to Lady Margaret when she lowered her eyes. "Anything else, David?"

"Lanley is at his manor house. Word has it he will only be there one more day."

Rebecah bit her lower lip. She hadn't much time to speak to him on Dorene's behalf. "I wonder why he's leaving."

"Perhaps he is bored with the solitude of the country. But there is more news."

Deberton appeared in the doorway. David turned. "Ah, here is Edward. I was giving the ladies the word on Lanley."

"It's the least important thing I've to tell." Deberton drew off his hat and set it on the side table. He was dressed in drab brown from his waistcoat to his wool leggings. His hair hung slightly loose from its brown satin ribbon. No doubt, Rebecah imagined, his untidy appearance was due to the windy day.

Lady Margaret put her hand in Rebecah's and leaned forward on the couch. The mere grip showed how anxious she was to hear the news. Rebecah's fingers could feel the rapid pulse on her ladyship's wrist, and hoped the news would comfort her somehow. The blockades preventing her from seeing Sir Rodney had grown unbearable.

Deberton lowered into the chair across from the ladies. "Be at ease, my lady. Tomorrow you will see your husband."

Lady Margaret, overjoyed by the news, turned to stifle her tears.

"His sentence will be lenient according to the judge. The Court promises to be merciful."

"What might his sentence be, Mr. Deberton?" she asked.

"It's hard to say with any real certainty, my lady. He may remain in prison a good many years. But at least he will live."

Margaret Nash could not help but begin to cry. Rebecah drew her in her arms. She thought of the heartbreak love brings when the ones you're devoted to suffer. How hard, how frustrating it is to lack the ability to remove misery. At least Lady Margaret had her faith to lean upon, and so Rebecah prayed not only for mercy for Sir Rodney, but for Lady Margaret to bear her burden through the strength of her Savior.

"Thank you, Mr. Deberton, for all your efforts." Rebecah gave him a grateful smile.

"It does not end here, Miss Rebecah. We will defend him with all our strength."

Lady Margaret wiped her eyes. "I do not know how to thank you—and you as well, David. What my husband did is considered treason by some. Most would not dare to defend him."

"The way I see it, what father would not send support to his son when so far away? We shall use that as our platform."

Deberton stood and lifted his hat from the table. "Miss Rebecah." She looked up at him. "I insist you allow me to escort you to Rosewood. David tells me it is urgent you see Sir Cecil. My carriage is outside."

Rebecah looked over at Lady Margaret, worried to leave her.

"Go on, Rebecah. I shall be fine with David and Lavinia to look after me."

She stood and kissed Lady Margaret's cheek. Then she fetched her cloak and left out the front door with Mr. Deberton keeping step behind her.

* * *

A meticulous boxwood garden lined the front drive at Rosewood. Rebecah explained the urgency of this meeting to Mr. Deberton. He explained, "By law, Lanley is not obligated to the lady. But if he is an honorable person, he will own up to his actions and do right by her."

"I think he is, Mr. Deberton."

"Well, that's yet to be seen. You do realize you are treading in deep waters confronting a man like Lanley, who you spurned, who is now enriching his career in politics. A bastard child could ruin it for him."

"Nevertheless, I am confident he will hear me out." Yet she was unsure of his feelings toward her. Was he bitter and angry still? Uncertainty had to be ignored.

Amber flames flickered in the streetlamps, spread over the sidewalks and white stone facades of the manor houses. People were in the street, some hurrying, others strolling at leisure. A rider steadied his horse as Deberton's coach passed by.

The coach slowed and halted. He knew then they had arrived. The moments he shared with Rebecah were about to be interrupted. He stepped out and held his hand out to her. Then he guided her onto the sidewalk.

"We will not be long," Mr. Deberton said to the driver. "Keep the horses steady, and do not go off anywhere. I know you've a liking for that public house we passed."

The driver shrugged his shoulders with disappointment and eased back in his seat.

Rebecah, dressed in a lilac-blue gown, looked more beautiful to him than ever before. Her hair hung free down her back in lengthy waves and curls, and he wished he could run his fingers through it. Her hat, trimmed in blue ribbon, shadowed her eyes, and the sight of her cheek caused his heart to grip. He knew she would never have him. He knew she loved another. Yet, here she was with him, under the streetlights and climbing moon.

He drew his eyes away from her, and pulled the bell hanging outside beside the large oak door.

Rebecah drew in a breath. "I've been calm up until this moment. I worry what Lanley will say to me after all this time. Do you think he will refuse to see me?"

Mr. Deberton touched her elbow. "Do not worry. I'll see to it that doesn't happen."

The door creaked open and a servant appeared. "We wish to see Sir Cecil Lanley," Mr. Deberton said, taking the lead. "Is he at home?"

The well-dressed servant in a white wig and scarlet coat placed his hand on the door ready to close it. "He is engaged with dinner guests."

Rebecah stepped forward. "May we wait, please? It is urgent I speak with him. He and I are acquainted."

The servant looked into her face. His expression told Rebecah he fancied she was another of Lanley's ladies. Not wanting to anger his master, he said, "Yes, madam. You may wait. Who may I say is calling?"

"Tell him a friend he has not seen in a long while."

* * *

Lanley's butler showed them to a sitting room lit with candles. Rebecah looked up at its high ornate ceiling, remembering how her father hoped this would have been her house. Unimpressed by its lavish rosewood richness, she was glad it was not hers. Indications were Lanley had gained the whole world. But his mortal life, like all men, was fleeting, passing like the chaff in the fields. Here one moment, gone the next, and the corruptible riches left behind to decay and rust.

The door closed and she was left alone with Mr. Deberton. Together they listened to the servant's self-important footsteps go down a lengthy hallway. Rebecah removed her gloves and looked over at a portrait of Lanley's father. He stared at her with what she thought was anger. A flow-blue vase graced the table where she laid her hat aside. There were no flowers in the room, no books.

A moment later, they heard voices. Laughter followed and voices again. By the sound of Lanley's footsteps, she could tell he was irritated, having been torn away from his guests.

There was no turning back. The servant opened the door for his master and stood aside for him to enter. There stood Lanley, his head high with one hand poised on his hip. His hair was powdered, like she had last seen him. His eyes enlarged when he met her eyes. He glanced but a moment at Deberton.

Who the devil is he? The question shown in Lanley's eyes and did not escape Rebecah. Lanley had grown older, but none the wiser. A few wrinkles creased near his eyes and he had put on flesh. He took in a breath and stepped over to her. She smiled and held out her hand.

"Please tell me I am welcomed, Cecil."

He bent forward and kissed her hand. "I thought I had forgotten your hands, madam. But here you are in all your softness and rose scent, your memory rushing upon me like an angry storm."

She drew her hand out of his. A sincere smile played on her lips. "I hope you've forgiven me for the pain I caused you."

He stood straight. "Oh. Well, I have, my dear. But seeing you again, brings back bittersweet memories."

"Be happy I was not a dishonest woman. For if I had been, I would have married you without loving you and spent all your money."

This made him laugh. "You have a point there, Rebecah. We are still friends at least. But that Nash fellow. How I loathed him."

She lowered her eyes. How she missed the only man that meant what he said when he told her he loved her. It was her fault to have lost him.

"Yes, I know. But that too is over, as you probably heard." She returned her gaze. "I'm glad you are no longer hurt by me, Cecil."

"Hurt? Gads, my dear, I'm too much a man for that." He laughed again.

"What arrogance," Deberton said beneath his breath.

"Who is this gentleman?" Lanley asked with a swift turn. "An uncle perhaps?" The comment made Deberton set his lips. He bowed just the same to Lanley.

Rebecah took his arm and moved him forward. "May I present Edward Deberton? He is David's partner in the law."

"I don't understand. Why have you come with Rebecah? If it's a legal matter, I cannot imagine what. My servant said your business was urgent."

"Frankly it does not concern me, sir. I should take my leave to my coach outside and wait for Miss Brent. I accompanied her to ensure her safety."

"Hmm." Lanley sucked in his cheeks and sat in a chair.

Deberton excused himself, put on his hat, and walked out. Lanley looked over at Rebecah.

"You're more ravishing than ever. What have you been doing to yourself? How your hair catches the light."

She sat opposite him. "I'm still the same."

"No, you've changed. I can see it in your eyes." He leaned forward toward her.

"I'm at peace. I found redemption."

"You found religion?"

She shook her head. "No, Cecil. I found the faith I needed to carry on—and to forgive."

"Have you come to tell me you've changed your mind? If you have, I would take you back in an instant." He leaned back into the cushions. "Even though you are too strong-willed for me."

"Cecil, there is no need to flatter."

"But it's true. You're more beautiful, more enticing..."

Rebecah wished he would stop complimenting her. "I must talk to you. It's important. My visit here is serious."

"I promise to listen if you kiss me."

She moved away from Lanley and stood in front of the mullioned window. The golden light fell upon her and edged her hair. Outside the door, a wave of laughter came from the guests.

Lanley smoothed the cuffs on his sleeve. "They wait for me. Join us."

"I've interrupted. Thank you, but I cannot stay."

"Your diversion is welcomed, my dear. It has dawned on me you've never been inside my house. Do you like it?"

She picked up her gloves. "It is a fine house, indeed. But I see by the clock on the mantle I have taken too much of your time. I must talk to you, Cecil, seriously."

"I'm listening, my dear."

She looked straight into his eyes. "It concerns Dorene. I am here on her behalf, for she is afraid to speak to you."

He gave a short laugh. "Why on earth would she be afraid of me? I've done nothing to merit that. So be quick to tell me all, dear lady, else I'll lose the willingness to listen."

"She is not well, Cecil, and needs you."

"Me? Not well you say? Why the last time I saw her she was in perfect health, the picture of it."

"That was before she returned to Endfield."

"Does she need a physician? I shall send mine to Endfield at my own expense."

Rebecah sensed he suspected more.

"Cecil, listen to me." She touched his hand. "It concerns you. You must promise to do right by her before I say anything more. You will not deny the truth, nor shirk your duty."

He frowned, looked worried. "I'm a man of my word, Rebecah. Give me my medicine. I can take it."

"Dorene is carrying your child," she said.

He blinked his eyes. "She is what?"

"She is with child—your child. You understand?"

He raised his hand to his forehead and looked as though he would faint. "What a mess I've made—all for one night of pleasure."

"Tell me you will not reject her or abandon this child. You know what her father will do, and the rest of society."

He babbled on about his position, his fortune, and his reputation. Rebecah had the urge to shake him and make him see what he must do. Why did he have to whimper?

"Is this not what you've wanted all along—have a son, an heir? Now it has happened."

He looked at her, his eyes red along the rims. "You're right, Rebecah. I must do my duty. I'll go to her, take her to my country house until the child is born."

"You might consider marrying her."

"Marriage? Ah, Rebecah, I'm not yet over you, I think." He looked with longing into her face.

"You will never have me, Cecil. We will always be friends though. Here is your chance for a wife and family. It would be the right thing to do."

The door swung open and one of Lanley's guests peeked inside. "Come, Lanley. Time slips away." The gentleman hesitated when his eyes rested upon the woman who had drawn his host away. He bowed with a smile. "Forgive me. I see I've interrupted." He turned to go.

Lanley pulled his friend inside. "Dr. Tulane, may I present Miss Rebecah Brent?"

"Ah, I recognize the name."

A weak smile tugged at Lanley's mouth. "Alec attended me while I was ailing over you, Rebecah."

"I see," she said.

"After a week of bleeding and dozes of tonics, I was back on my feet."

"No offense," Dr. Turlane said, "but I was incredulous as to why a man would throw himself into a sickbed over a woman, at least until now. You're as fair as he described."

Turlane was a short man, no more than an inch taller than Rebecah. His boyish face was flushed, and he had a strong jaw and wide shoulders. His hazel eyes sparkled, yet the lines beside them hinted as to his age.

"I met the gentleman you came with outside in the hall. Deberton, I know slightly. If you should ever need a physician, Miss Brent, don't hesitate to send for me."

For a moment, Rebecah paused. Then she said, "Dr. Turlane, would you be willing to visit a prisoner?"

"If it is of some importance to you, certainly. Who is it you wish me to see?"

"Sir Rodney Nash. He is there unjustly, sir. His wife, Lady Margaret, is so distressed. I worry for her too. We plan to visit him tomorrow."

"I shall be happy to attend with you," Turlane said.

Lanley pulled the cork from the blue bottle of smelling salts and waved it in front of his nose. "I heard of Sir Rodney's misfortune, Rebecah. I'll see what can be done. And Turlane, I'll pay all expenses for Sir Rodney's care."

Rebecah smiled at Lanley. "That is kind of you, Cecil."

He took hold of her hands and held her fingers firmly. "And I will do the right thing by Dorene too. I do have feelings for her. Turlane here has no idea what we are talking about." Lanley turned to the good doctor. "I'm to have an heir, Turlane. You will attend my forthcoming wife?"

"I promised I would always be the physician to the Lanleys," he said, bowing his head.

Rebecah put on her hat and gloves to leave. "I may not ever see you again, Cecil. I will write and see how Dorene and the baby are. You will let me know about Sir Rodney too, won't you?"

Lanley looked shocked. His mouth fell open. This was too much news for one day. "Of course, Rebecah."

"Goodbye, Cecil." She held his hands tighter. He raised hers to his lips with forlorn eyes and kissed them.

Then, lifting her skirts, she headed for the door. "Good day, Dr. Turlane. Until tomorrow."

She found Mr. Deberton leaning against the coach waiting for her. Glancing back at the manor, she saw Lanley standing at the window. He raised his hand, and she threw him a smile. And when the coach rolled away, she told Deberton of Lanley's promise, how she hoped he would keep it.

CHAPTER 34

On a gray and stormy morn, Rebecah sat beside Lady Margaret in Dr. Turlane's carriage. It swayed over the road, and in the distance, Rebecah saw the gloomy walls of the prison. She looked at Dr. Turlane. The bumpy ride had not kept him from falling asleep. Lady Margaret held her prayer book open on her lap.

Turning her eyes back to the scene outside, Rebecah thought about the year that had transpired. She thought of the man she loved. Had he not been the center of those days, the object of first love and heartbreak? She pictured his face, and wondered what he was doing at this exact moment. How long would it take him to receive the letter Lady Margaret sent? Word was correspondence was becoming impossible.

When she stepped from the carriage and looked at the prison walls a shiver ran up her spine. She drew Lady Margaret's arm through hers and followed Dr. Turlane through the gate. Ahead of them, the jailer thrust a key from a ring of many into the door's keyhole. His fingers in the dim light were black with soot and his hands calloused.

He pushed the door in. Stepping through it, a terrible stench hit them. The jailer stopped and let out a string of coughs.

"Are you ill, man?" Dr. Turlane held the ladies back. "Have you seen a doctor about that cough?"

"No, sir," the man replied with a slur. "It's the air in here. Bad air, ya see. Bad, bad air." He shrugged and moved on. "This way. Watch ya step."

With sorrowful eyes, Rebecah looked at the faces of the prisoners behind bars. They sat in the gloom, heads low— broken, bent people, some repentant of their deeds, some not. Dirty hands reached between the bars. Some asked for money and bread. It had been a long time since they had seen a clean face or heard the rustle of silk.

Rebecah leaned closer to Dr. Turlane and whispered, "So many are sick. Can nothing be done to ease their suffering?"

"You needn't look at them." Turlane pulled her ladyship away with Rebecah.

"I wonder what King George would think if he visited this place?"

"He'd never come here." Turlane placed his handkerchief over his nose.

"Watch your step, ladies," cried the gaoler. "For there goes a rat!"

Lady Margaret cried out and buried her face against Dr. Turlane's shoulder. The gaoler cursed the hairy rodent and kicked it with the toe of his shoddy shoe. It squeaked and scurried off through a crack in the wall.

Lady Margaret murmured. "How long can a man last in here? Oh, my poor Rodney."

"I'll be glad when some of these scamps meet their maker. Five are to hang next Tuesday." The gaoler put his hand around his throat, bulged his eyes and pretended to choke. Lady Margaret gasped.

Rebecah held on to Lady Margaret. "Executions are hardly something to make fun of," she scolded.

The gaoler leaned forward, showing a row of blackened teeth. "Makes ya uneasy, don't it?"

Turlane stepped up to him. "Be silent and lead us to Sir Rodney."

Swinging around, the gaoler moved on, paused outside a door and peered through the bars of the small square window in it. "You got company, Sir Rodney—your wife and two others to see you."

Rebecah took note of how kind the gaoler spoke to Sir Rodney as he shoved the key into the lock. Perhaps his standing afforded him a little more respect than the other inmates.

"They have treated him kindly, I think," she whispered to her ladyship.

The rattle of chains came from within, and when the gaoler shoved the door open, Rodney Nash hurried forward. He looked pale, his face scruffy with a day's old beard and his clothes dirty.

"My love! My lady!"

Tears brimmed in his eyes. Lady Margaret fell into his arms. Their hands held fast together. He kissed her.

"Margaret, I'm so happy to see you. Ah, but for you to have come to such a place."

"Are you well, my love?" Lady Margaret caressed his cheek. "Are they feeding you enough?"

The gaoler stepped beside her. "I've seen to it Sir Rodney gets the best of everything, milady. For a few coins my wife can bring him something hardy of her own cookery every day."

Lady Margaret looked over at him with a smile that spoke of desperation. "I'll pay whatever you ask."

The gaoler bowed and stepped out.

"I never thought to see you again, Rodney," Lady Margaret said.

"Nor I you."

"You can thank Rebecah. She persuaded David there was a way. Upon her urging he pressured the judges."

Sir Rodney's eyes turned upon her and he held out his hand. "I would call you daughter, Rebecah."

She went to him. He kissed her cheek as a father would. He looked over at Dr. Turlane. "I see you've brought a gentleman with you."

"The name is Turlane, sir. Dr. Alec Turlane." And he bowed low.

"He has come to see if you are in good health," Rebecah told him.

"I'm in fair health, I believe."

Turlane nodded. "Yes, Sir Rodney. You appear to be so. May I?" and he held out his hand to take hold of Sir Rodney's wrist. He timed his pulse, looked into his eyes and mouth, felt his throat, and put his ear to his chest.

"Shall I live another day?"

Turlane smiled lightly. "Indeed you shall, sir."

"Then could you both excuse us? My wife and I are given so short a time."

"Certainly. Come, Miss Brent." Turlane held out his arm, and together they stepped from the cell into the corridor.

Out of the hearing of the others, Rebecah turned to Turlane. He leaned against the wall, and dug at the floor with the heel of his shoe.

"He is not well, is he?"

"His pulse is weak. I shall do everything possible to keep him alive."

She lowered her head. Her eyes filled and she blinked the tears away. Turlane picked up her hand and squeezed it.

"It's complicated, is it not?"

Rebecah nodded. "It is, sir. It all seems so unjust."

* * *

The gaoler was kind enough to give the couple one quarter of an hour together. Sir Rodney then asked for

270

Rebecah. Five minutes would due. Standing outside the grim cell, beneath smoky torches, Rebecah waited while the couple said their goodbyes.

"Before I go," Lady Margaret said, "I must give you these. Now, promise you'll wear them, and you will care for your health. I've included two books."

Sir Rodney took the bundle from her hands and opened it. In it were woolen stockings, a clean shirt, and knit cap. "I love you, Margaret. Pray for me."

Rebecah's heart ached seeing the way Lady Margaret touched his cheek.

"Times up, milady," the gaoler said, wiping his nose across his sleeve.

Reluctant arms slipped apart. Lady Margaret paused at the cell door. Then, with her hands folded at her breast, she turned and left.

Inside his cell, Rebecah looked at Sir Rodney with searching eyes. He held out his hand and she took it. He asked her to sit on the bench beside him.

"She loves you, you know."

"I've broken her heart," Sir Rodney said. "It seems we men in the Nash line have an unintentional way of doing that."

Rebecah shook her head. "Lady Margaret does not feel that way."

"Thank you for saying so, Rebecah." He squeezed her hand. "And I cannot tell you how pleased I am you are with her. I've something to ask you. Our time is short, so I must speak quickly."

Rebecah gripped his hands harder. "I'm listening."

"First, tell me what your feelings are for my son."

"I love him. I believe he told me the truth."

"If there were a way, would you go to him?"

"Only if I knew he would have me."

"I know he would."

"Tell me what I must do."

"At Standforth I have left instructions. A sum of gold is laid aside—a portion for your journey to Jack. The rest you must give to him. He will know what it is for."

Rebecah got to her feet. "For the rebels?"

Sir Rodney nodded.

Her mind reeled with what he was asking. A moment she paced the room.

He got to his feet. "Do not decide now. Think on it, and send me word through Margaret. You'll be in my prayers."

Rebecah kissed his cheek. "I will give you my answer now by thanking you."

"Time to go, miss," the gaoler said, poking his head through the doorway.

Outside the light of day was fading. The sky hung gray now, thick and forbidding, pressing and silent. The howls of the prisoners ceased to echo in Rebecah's ears, and her lungs took in the pure air.

Dr. Turlane climbed inside the coach with Lady Margaret. He leaned his head out the window. Rebecah stood a few yards off.

"Come inside the coach, Miss Brent," he called. "A chill of rain is in the air and we must be on our way."

She did not move or turn to him. Instead, she lifted her face to the wind.

"In a moment," she answered. "Let me breathe in the air a while longer."

The Everlasting Mountains

He stood, and measured the earth: he beheld, and drove asunder the nations; and the everlasting mountains were scattered. . .
Habakkuk 3:6

CHAPTER 1

Annapolis, Maryland

Rebecah's heart trembled as she gazed up at the stark white sails of the ship that had brought her across the Atlantic to the King's colony of Maryland. Canvas billowed in the salty breeze, shook with the gusts and softened. Clouds mellowed to dark hues of blue and purple. Seagulls flew above the water. In chorus, they screeched and glided against the sky now magenta along the horizon. Wings of white tipped with gray spread wide and lifted in the wind. She watched them work against the breeze. Impatience seized her. Awe filled her.

Her hands felt moist as she held to the sides of the boat. The oarsmen pulled against the current. Her fingertips touched the water. It rippled cold against her skin. She could not see beyond the trees, beyond the town nestled along the shore, to a wilderness where the man she loved dwelled, but she tried to imagine it in her mind.

Dusk fell. Shadows deepened. The air grew crisp. She glanced back to see *The Rearguard* anchored in the Bay, a merchantman with luck enough to make it out to sea under the cover of night.

When the dinghy glided to a halt along the wharf, a sailor jumped out onto the planks and coiled a rope over a piling. One by one, the passengers were handed up. At last, Rebecah stood on solid ground, her valise in hand. The breeze felt cool against her skin, smelled of saltwater.

Holding her bag tighter, she walked on determining which way she should go. She wore a homespun dress the color of gingerroot. Splinters from a plank roughened the hem and she inched it up with a quiet moan. A dove-gray cloak chased away the cool evening air. The hood covered her hair.

Her stomach growled, and her back ached from weeks of sleeping on a cot in the passengers' quarters. She grew to hate the sea. The memory of rations, of being tossed about, the weeks of seeing nothing but water and sky made her head spin. But now, the thought of soap and water and a warm bed with clean white sheets sounded heavenly.

She stood beside a fish stand. The owner spoke to her and Rebecah turned. A middle-aged woman with button eyes and a bit of whisker on her chin gave her a broad smile.

"The White Swan Inn is where you should go."

"It is a good inn?"

"Has the best rooms, good food, and a fair price."

Returning the smile, Rebecah thanked the woman. She handed her a pence for her troubles and looked in the direction she pointed out. At least people were helpful in the Colonies. That much encouraged her. Getting to Fredericktown would be easy with good people to travel with and a friendly colonial to drive the coach.

Annapolis seemed similar to the towns back home. A barking dog, a merchant hawking his wares, wagon wheels lumbering over the street were familiar sights and sounds.

She gathered up her skirts and quickly crossed the street, careful not to step where the horses had been. On the corner stood a red brick building. Chimneys were on each side, and a lawn surrounded the foundation. The sign read *The White Swan*. Upon it, a painted trumpeter swan skimmed over blue water, and evergreen boughs and pinecones made a halo.

Before she could make it to the door, a crowd gathered. She craned her neck to see what they were looking at. A long coil of human tragedy came trudging up the street. Each soul bore iron bands and chains upon wrist and ankle. Compassion, sadness, and utter dismay seized her. How could one man own another? How could they enslave another human being, shackle and command them against their will? How could their conscience be clear before God?

"What a shame." A man reached for the door to open it for her. He was an elderly gentleman, dressed in black clerical garb. His silver hair hung to the shoulders, and his gray eyes sparkled beneath wispy brows. He motioned for her to step inside.

"I had not expected…"

"To see such a spectacle?"

"Indeed, sir."

"As troubling as it may seem, you must put it from your mind. There is naught you or I can do for those poor wretches except pray for them."

Troubled, she paused to look around the inn. Tables were polished, with candles in glass domes upon them. A huge hearth hugged the center of a western wall, and above it hung a painting of a marshland with geese in flight.

"My name is Filmore, Reverend Allen Filmore." He glanced at her valise. "You're newly arrived to our country?"

"Yes. My name is Rebecah Brent, of Ashburne House, England. Do you know it?"

"I'm afraid not, Miss Brent, but I'm intrigued. Why would a young woman travel so far from home alone?"

"I grew anxious for adventure." She smiled hoping he understood. "And I am here to see a friend."

"Ah, as a bride to be, perhaps?"

She lowered her eyes with a flush of her cheeks. "I'm unsure, Reverend. Do you know where I can board a coach heading west?"

"West? Not too far into the wilderness I hope."

"I am not sure. It is a place called Laurel Hill."

He wiggled his head with a small laugh. "You must think me very ill-traveled. I haven't heard of Laurel Hill, nor have I been far into the frontier. Some of my acquaintances say it is a very fine part of the country."

Rebecah set her valise down.

"You will find they have comfortable rooms here." Reverend Filmore rang the silver bell on the innkeeper's desk. She noticed how clean and white his hands were. There were no sign of labor. The lace trim of his cuffs were faded to a soft yellow and worn along the edges. He was not a man of means.

A thin man in a buff coat stepped out from the back. "You need something, Reverend?"

"The lady is in need of a room." Filmore made a gesture in her direction. "She has come a long way."

"She'll have to sign the register." The innkeeper turned the ledger toward her and handed her the quill. She dipped it into the ink and signed her name.

"The lady needs passage west," Filmore said. "Will you see to it?"

"The coach will be coming in tomorrow morning. My wife will bring up a tray of food and get anything else you need, miss. A weary journey causes a person to steer clear of crowded dining rooms."

Rebecah welcomed the hospitality. Then the old feeling of dread stole up inside. She was on her way to John Nash—and the dangers he faced. She thanked Reverend Filmore for his kindness, as the innkeeper came around the desk and picked up her bag.

A horn blared, and a man poked his head inside the door. "Coach headed for Baltimore coming in. News from Boston and Philadelphia."

Filmore turned to Rebecah with a gracious bow. "My transport, dear lady. I do not know what path you are on, but I wish you Godspeed." He put on his hat and left.

Rebecah hoped with all her heart, her path would be an easy one and her journey to John Nash swift.

After having supper in her room, and a good washing, she settled beneath a bedcover stuffed with goose down. It was quiet out on the street. Already this land had brought strange sights to her eyes—the slaves she could not forget, the patriotic verve that permeated the air. She lay there thinking what more would she see—Indians—men in buckskins—women is homespun garb—vast mountains and wide rivers?

The moon climbed high and shone through the curtains over the window. Pale blue light painted the walls. She watched the shadows play across the ceiling. Her heart trembled that the man she loved was so close, that she would see him soon. She prayed he would not reject her and closed her eyes to fall asleep, listening to ship bells clang in the harbor.

The next day before the noon hour, a note was sent up with the maid. A coachman named George Mac waited outside.

CHAPTER 2

Ruts in the road rocked and jolted the coach as it lumbered west. Towering elms shadowed the ground where dry leaves blew and whirled against the coach wheels.

Being the only passenger, Rebecah had room to stretch her limbs. In some ways she regretted being alone. She had no one to talk with. The time would have passed quicker with at least one additional passenger. Maybe a bit of conversation would have helped the flutter of nerves in her stomach.

Hours later, looking out the window, she gazed at the sky and smelled the hint of rain in the air. George Mac slowed the horses. They stopped to rest at a trading post. A porch stretched across the front and beside it stood the owner's log cabin. Oak barrels were stacked out front. A brass horn hung from a nail in a post. Sunlight sparkled against it like a shooting star.

There were several men lounging around that day smoking their clay pipes and talking. When Rebecah alighted, the men stood and pulled off their hats. A boy ran forward and tugged on her dress. He had bright blue eyes and freckled cheeks. His long blond curls and round face reminded her of Hugh. She missed him, wondered if she would ever see him again, hoped he was well. But how well could a young boy be away from his family?

A terrier heeled beside the lad. Rebecah looked at the pup, and imagined Hugh had to be missing Jess.

The boy thrust his hand up to her. In it was a single wild daisy, the edges of the pedals tinted brown.

"For me?" Rebecah said.

The boy nodded.

"My thanks, kind sir."

A man in a worn overcoat, brown leather breeches, and tricorn hat, placed his hand on the lad's shoulder. "My son, ma'am. He's had only his mother to give flowers to."

"He's a kind, boy. And very handsome."

The man agreed with a smile. "My name is Davies, the proprietor of this place. The men here are curious."

She glanced at the gathered group. "Over me?"

"You ride the coach heading west."

"Is that unusual?"

"It's been sometime since we've seen it come through. The Indians out in the frontier are on the warpath, and most folks are coming away, not going."

A chill raced through her. What kind of danger was she heading toward?

The man seemed to notice her worry. "Don't worry, miss. Your coachmen go armed. You must have a good reason for traveling that way."

Emerging from the door, a woman stood with her hands over her hips. Her skin was browned by the sun. Creases hugged near her eyes. The boy skipped up the steps and took hold of her soiled apron. His dog followed, his tail swishing.

The woman scowled. "Leave off the talk of Indians, my husband. No need to make the lady fear. Give her ease and let her be. And the rest of you—you may be men of the backwoods, but that don't make ye forget to use your manners."

The mistress of the trading post, showed Rebecah inside to the cool shade of the room. A few men lingered in the doorway.

"We men," said one, "are loyal to our *Glorious Cause*. Up that way, we hear powder and shot and parts for muskets are going to be made. You know what for?"

Another leaned on a birchwood cane and nudged the farmer in the ribs. "Don't go wagging your tongue to a British lass."

Rebecah heard Davies whisper behind her. "She could be a spy. You want Redcoats to come down on the frontier like bats out of hell, do you?"

She sighed and turned to face them. "I may be English, gentlemen, but I'm no spy. A gentleman sympathetic to your *Glorious Cause* sent me to visit his son who lives near." She pulled off her gloves, revealing hands clean and soft.

"Pay no mind to the men, miss." Davie's wife stepped beside her. "They haven't had this much excitement in quite a while."

After a brief stay, it was time to resume the journey. The horses were rested, the coachmen refreshed. Rebecah's skirts whispered along the rough-hewn floor as she walked to the door. The men stepped aside, hats in hand. She turned, one hand upon the jamb and smiled to the woman.

"Thank you for your hospitality."

The woman nodded, her hand over her son's shoulder, as the locals gathered on the porch.

After Rebecah boarded, the coachmen climbed into their seats. With a snap of the reins, the horses moved on, and the coach rolled away leaving a cloud of brown fog behind.

Rolling fields banked each side of the road. It turned and entered the forests, thick and lush, dark and cool. Trees entwined overhead. Sunlight spotted the brown earth with ovals of light. Each passing moment, each turn of the coach wheels, brought her closer to the man she loved. And he had no idea she was on her way to him.

She had been brave thus far. But now she felt she was losing her courage. There was the chance he no longer loved her. For all she knew he could have married. Nevertheless, she would keep her promise to Sir Rodney, deliver the gold, and inform Nash his father had been arrested. If he rejected her, she would return to Annapolis and return to England.

But what if war broke out? She could be trapped. No family. No friends. She'd have to find work and wait the whole thing out.

She bit her lip, stared at the sky.

Does he still care?

Her heart leaped at the thought.

Jack is a good man, and a good man would never send a lady away who has traveled across the ocean and through the frontier to him. He may not want me at first, but I'll find a way to make him want me in the end—if he is free.

The breeze strengthened. Forests murmured with the whisper of wind. The sky grew dark as slate. She watched the whirl of clouds. Thunder pealed. The wind calmed.

The trees stood motionless. An eerie hush fell over the land. Rebecah fell back against the seat. She remembered what Jack had told her about the wilderness storms, how fierce they were.

The coach rattled on. Thirty and five miles left to cover before the spires of Fredericktown broke upon the skyline— thirty and five miles of wind, storm, and shaking trees. She wished they had stayed longer at the trading post, at least until the storm passed and the sky broke open again with the sun. The rain would have sounded differently beating upon the logs. She could have sat and talked with the woman and her boy, listened to the men's tales.

But now they were miles away, and the storm swallowed the light of day.

282

Lightning crossed the sky. Thunder shook the land. Rebecah sat stunned. Her hands gripped the side of the door. Lightning struck a tree. She screamed and covered her ears. The horses strained. The horses whinnied. The coach pitched to one side and veered off the road. It creaked and moaned, slid down an embankment, and landed in a ditch.

CHAPTER 3

Nash placed another log on the fire. His men huddled for shelter in a cave. Cleft into a granite outcropping, it was high in the mountains, hidden by enormous trees. Damp and crusted, it smelled of earth, mold, and years.

Clarke snored with his hat over his eyes, embracing his well-oiled musket. Black Hawk sharpened his knife. The preacher read from his well-used Bible, the size of which fit in his palm.

As the storm raged outside, loneliness for Rebecah seized Nash and he stared with a searching heart at the flames. He could not shake the thoughts, nor purge the feelings. He loved her. But it was over and she was unattainable.

Maldowney came beside him. The fire played over his face and heightened his red hair and beard. "You miss the lass, don't you?"

"Yes, but I need to forget."

"Maybe if you married..."

Nash shrugged. "I'll remain unwrung."

"Life is too short to pine away for a lost love."

"Or be bound to a second choice."

The rain lessened. The thunder rumbled no more. Sunbeams shot through the clouds and Nash watched them from the entrance of the cave.

"The storm has passed. Let's head back to town."

He stepped away from the fire out into the coolness. The elms and evergreens sagged with rain. Mist streamed down upon the land and bathed the flora in white veils. Ribbons of fog lay in the glades, and a hungry hawk flew above the treetops.

From where he stood, Nash looked down into the valley. The air smelled sweet and he was reminded of the way her hair smelled. It had been so fresh and clean, and felt like silk when he ran his fingers through it.

Leaning against a pine, he cradled his musket. The breeze rustled his hair. And as much as he tried not to, he thought about Rebecah with a wounded heart. Was she with Lanley, in his house, in his bed, with his ring upon her finger? Then the memory of her rejection, her believing he sentenced her father to an untimely death pressed on his mind.

He turned and rested his forehead against the rough bark, balled his fist and struck the tree. A moment later, the men emerged from the cave. They took the old trail down the mountain into the gorge. His heart pounded as he kept pace with the others, and he ignored the pain in his leg. He had not brought Meteor this time, thinking the exertion would do him good. Now he regretted it.

Rounding a bend, they came upon an Indian village nestled amid trees. Nash stepped up to Black Hawk. "Go ahead of us. Speak to the elders."

As soon as Black Hawk's moccasins touched inside the village, old men came out to meet him. Between them a council fire smoked and hissed. Black Hawk raised his hands and spoke, and Nash stood several yards behind him.

"I am Black Hawk, son of Running Fox, chief of my village to the north among the Nations. My fathers have no reason to fear. We come in peace. Tell me, fathers, why do you mourn?"

An aged chief moved through the people and stood before Black Hawk. His face was wrinkled in ashy seams.

"My eyes saw General Braddock fall in battle," he said in an oratory discourse. "My eyes saw the young Washington, tall and lean upon a great horse, dodge French bullets and escape the Indian arrow. Now, my eyes are old and I am weary of war. You are a warrior. Are you among those who kill all in their path for pleasure?"

Black Hawk frowned. "I am with the rangers as their scout." He turned and pointed at Nash. "This man waits to speak to you."

The chief raised his face to the sky. "The time of peace is past, my son. The moon is red with blood and the sun with smoke. Enemies are on every side. Who can my people trust?"

"You can trust Logan's friend. He is my brother. Hear his words. Tell him what has happened to your people."

The old chief nodded. "We will meet with him. I had a dream two nights ago. A white man came to our village. Upon him lay a wolf's skin. The head of the wolf was upon his head. Its teeth were large. Its eyes were black and angry. He was sent to hunt the bear. Perhaps your brother is that man."

"Black Hawk, tell the chief we will not harm his people." Nash spoke softly, so not to cause alarm. "Tell him the women and children have no reason to fear us. I give him my solemn oath."

The chief pulled his blanket further over his shoulders. His eyes showed signs of cataracts and peered at Nash through the smoke. "I understand the white man's tongue."

The chief sat, motioned for the others to do likewise. "Many moons ago white missionaries came up the river. I believed their words. I began to think white men were good. But when the crazy fox came, he proved to me there is evil in the heart of every race."

Something lurched inside Nash, for he wondered if it were LaRoux the old man spoke of. "Tell me what he has done to your people."

"He has shot arrows into our hearts that will last forever."

"Where are your young men?"

"Many have joined Logan."

"And the rest?"

"The women mourn for their husbands, the children for their fathers." The old chief hung his head. "They fought the crazy fox and died."

"Who is this crazy fox?"

"He is a man both white and Indian. His hair is black as the crow. But his eyes are not Indian eyes."

Nash twisted his mouth. "LaRoux."

Two women helped the old man rise and he walked on. The sun filtered through the trees and bathed the forest in a veil of eerie light. Blue jays darted ahead and made wild calls that echoed through the forest.

They came to a clearing, a circle of grass beneath a lodge made of deerskin. The bodies of the fallen lay side by side. Steams of blood crept through the blankets beneath them. Women knelt and wept.

Nash walked over to look at the dead. He stood silent a moment, his emotions troubled and growing. Then he turned away. From the campfire, he scooped up ash, rubbed it onto his face as a sign of mutual mourning. Maldowney and Black Hawk followed Nash's lead. But Andrew Clarke stood at a cool distance. He watched them with anger brimming in his eyes and his hand grasping hard his musket.

CHAPTER 4

Sunlight touched Rebecah's face. She opened her eyes, pulled herself up, and stretched out her legs. They were stiff, and her body ached all over. A raindrop sparkled with sunshine, dangled in the window casement. She watched it lengthen and fall like a diamond, splash upon her dress. It made a dark round stain.

She tried to open the door. But it was jammed. The horses whinnied and the coach rocked as they pawed the ground. She called for help. No answer. She shook the brass handle and pushed.

Then a hand with nails blackened along the rims, thrust through the window. A face appeared, and she shrank back.

Yanking the door open, he reached for her. "Take my hand and I'll pull you out. It is useless for you to sit there."

She looked at him guarded. "Where is the coachman?"

"Out here. He is unharmed." He shook his hand at her. "Come, take it."

"But...who are you?"

"My name is Jean LaRoux. Give me your hand."

Though reluctant to accept his help, she grasped his hand and he lifted her out. There were two other men standing in the road, their hair long to their shoulders, their faces tanned and beardless, their eyes dark like their

288

comrade's. He wore dirty buckskins and a string of beads around his throat. She thought perhaps he were a backwoodsman or trapper.

The soles of Rebecah's shoes touched the ground and the man let her go. She turned and saw George Mac standing stark still, his back up against a tree, a musket aimed at his chest.

"Mr. Mac!"

LaRoux grabbed her arm and held her back.

"Leave the lady alone," Mac dared to shout.

LaRoux nodded to one of his men, and Mac was struck across the face. Rebecah gasped and hurried forward. Somehow, she wanted to help him, wipe the blood from his lip, and stay close to him. LaRoux swung her around.

"Where is the other?" he charged. "Tell me!"

He meant Mr. Stone. She glanced at the woods and back down the road. He was nowhere in sight. "I don't know what you mean."

"The *footman* I think you call him."

She set her mouth and looked away.

LaRoux shrugged. "It doesn't matter." His hand eased off her arm. "Tell me your name."

Rebecah gave no reply.

"Where do you come from?"

Still she did not reply. LaRoux leaned forward. "You will not answer?"

"I won't."

He seized her hair. She let out a cry. He twisted the locks between his fingers and came within inches of her face. "Are you saving this hair for a man?"

"Let go of me, you blackguard." Her teeth clenched. "Let go or I'll—"

A musket ball whizzed past LaRoux's head and smacked the tree beside him. Rebecah screamed and ducked. She looked up, saw George Mac wrestle the musket from his captor's hand and take aim. He cocked the hammer back, and LaRoux's men sprinted away.

Grunting in defeat, LaRoux held up his hands, spun around and made for the woods. Mac fired but missed his mark.

Jebediah Stone ran forward. "Mr. Stone!" Rebecah cried as he came out of hiding.

"Laud, I wish I had hit that rascal. Are you alright?"

"A little bruised...and shaken." She gave him a weak smile, forcing back tears. She wiped her eyes, her hand trembling. "Are you hurt?"

"Not a scratch on me. I was tossed off the coach, as you can see by my torn and muddy clothing, but not a bone broken. What about you?"

"If it hadn't been for your quick thinking and keen shot, Mr. Stone, I fear what would have happened. And you Mr. Mac, you were so brave. Thank you both."

Stone tipped his hat. Mac smiled. He lumbered into the ditch and grabbed hold of the horses. "We best get this coach out of this gully and hurry away. Those scoundrels might change their minds and head back."

"Right," said Stone.

Soon the coach was back on the road with Rebecah safely inside. The men climbed to their seats, and the horses pulled forward down the muddy path into the valley.

CHAPTER 5

John Nash stood in front of the Courthouse window watching passersbys move along the street. His face was shaved, his hair clean and tied in a broad black ribbon, his coat and breeches fresh, and his boots polished.

It was a hot day, and all the windows stood open, the breeze wafting inside. People nodded and tipped their hats to one another. Smiles were on their faces, but not his. He wished he could shake off the sick feeling in his stomach. He was a brave man able to bear much, a courageous man. But bravery and courage were not enough to remove the gruesome pictures in his mind of burning homesteads, butchered settlers, and of the fallen warriors.

A blood red sunset sparkled in the windows across the way. The clock struck and at the last stroke, Clarke walked in.

"Word's come. The forts are filling up with refugees from the frontier, and the militia under Cresap has left to scout the Monongahela."

"I'm not surprised people are fleeing." Nash turned sideways in the window and leaned against the frame.

While he spoke, a postrider rode into town. Dust whirled beneath his mount's hooves as he passed out handbills marked with skull and crossbones, mourning wreaths and liberty caps.

"News from Boston!" He slid off his lathered horse.

Interested, Nash leaned through the window to listen.

"By the bones of George Calvert it was no easy ride, people. Storms rolling to the south every day, storms so fierce my horse bolted off the road into the woods and stood frozen with fear. I couldn't make him budge for the life of me. I would've been here four days ago, if it hadn't been for the weather. Roads were muddy. Where's the tavern? I'm hungry and thirsty."

He headed off in the direction pointed out to him. The townsmen talked among themselves. Some gathered in front of the window.

"Says here the Port is closed by order of the Crown," one man said.

"Aye, and to enforce the law, it says reinforcements of new regiments were sent in May backed by the Royal Navy in the harbor." An old man shook his gray head in utter dismay. "Those poor folk up in Boston. May God have mercy."

"The citizens are forced to suffer," said another, "until every pence and duty is paid up for the soggy tea rotting at the bottom of the harbor. What's King George mean to do, starve every last one of them?"

The old man scratched his beard. "And look here. Says Quebec Act. What's that? What we need another *Act* for? Says boundaries for Quebec are to extend far south into the Allegheny Territory."

Fists were raised in angry protest. "They can't do that," a farmer said. "We have grants out there, treaties with the Indians. What about the settlers?"

Nash saw Mr. Boyd, the town clerk, step from his house across the street. It was a red brick building of two stories, with narrow mullioned windows and a double chimney. He shut the door behind him and tugged on the cast iron latch. He then squashed on his hat, and for a moment stood watching the crowd across the street.

"What goes on, gentlemen?" he said, approaching with a steady stride. "What's that you have there?"

292

"Postrider from Baltimore, Mr. Boyd. News from Boston. They've closed the harbor and are starving the people."

"Let me see that." Boyd began reading. "May God have pity on the good people of Boston. How much does the Crown think we shall tolerate?"

"We won't," Nash said from the open window. "Good day, Mr. Boyd. Come inside. We men have things to discuss."

A long, polished mahogany table stood in the center of the meeting room. The floor was bare, the walls empty. Seated was Mr. Thomas Johnson who had come up from Annapolis. Mr. Boyd, looking grave due to the news from Boston, took a seat next to him. The chairman John Hanson and a number of prominent citizens set their hats down and took their places.

These were troubling times. The day had brought worry and anxiety over the future. Hanson held a handbill in his left hand. Dread covered his face.

"Before you begin, Jack, we need to hear this."

Thomas Johnson leaned back in his chair. "Read it to us, sir."

Hanson read the news aloud, then slapped it on the table. "Does the King intend on starving every town that stands against him?"

Johnson leaned on the table. "You men know I only arrived home last night. I heard this while in Annapolis. Tensions are running high."

"What can be done for the people of Boston?" said Nash.

"Philadelphia has promised full support," Johnson said. "Charleston, Wilmington, and Baltimore have joined in giving them aid. New York guarantees a ten-year supply of food. Certainly there will be some kind of resolution."

"That is comforting to hear." Hanson wiped his face with a handkerchief and stuffed it back into his pocket. "Would it not be simpler if Boston paid what the Crown demands?"

Nash stood against the wall, his good leg bent with the sole of his boot against the whitewashed timbers.

"It would, Mr. Hanson. But try to suggest it to the Bostonians. They're taking a stand against the oppressors."

"You speak the truth, Jack," Johnson said. "Tell us—is our county secure?"

"Our town is too large for the Indians to make war here."

He pulled away from the wall, walked over to the table and sat down. "The Indians have proven themselves to be merciless and tireless. Our settlers are scattered, and that put them at a disadvantage. By the time we saw smoke rising over the trees or over some hill, and made our way to them, they were dead and their cabins burned to the ground."

"These are sad events indeed," said Johnson. "You saw as you came into town the large amount of refugees we have?"

"I did."

"The good people of Fredericktown have opened their hearts as well as their homes and churches. In speaking to some of the men, they mean to move their families east once they've rested."

Nash stood. "I must be getting back to Laurel Hill, gentlemen. I'm not too far from town, and beyond the war parties."

"Well, I say we recess, gentlemen," Hanson said. "But before we do, let us bow our heads in prayer for our country."

After a brief but moving prayer, the men gathered up their hats and stepped out of the courthouse. Mr. Boyd and Nash walked out together.

"Why not come and stay a few days at Richfield, Jack? And you too, Mr. Boyd." said Tom Johnson, stopping them before climbing into his carriage. "I would enjoy your company."

Mr. Boyd raised his brows and thought a moment. "Well, I suppose my daughter can do without me for a while. I haven't been to Richfield in a very long time."

"Excellent. You can ride out with me."

"Gladly. But there's Theresa at the door. A moment and I'll return."

While Mr. Boyd crossed the way to inform his daughter he would be away, Johnson squashed on his hat. "Jack? Will you come? Can you resist my table?"

Nash smiled. "I cannot, sir."

"You know my cook is heralded the best in the county, don't you?"

"I do. I haven't had home cooking by female hands in ages."

The memory of his stepmother's feast at Standforth flashed in his mind. He took up the reins of his horse and climbed into the saddle.

"I accept your invitation, Mr. Johnson. Thank you."

With a click of his tongue, he turned Meteor into the street and galloped ahead of the carriage unaware the coach carrying Rebecah turned onto the track that led straight to Market Street.

CHAPTER 6

Fredericktown, Maryland

Though a bit battered, the coach rumbled across the bridge spanning the Monocacy River and rolled over the broad dirt road leading into town. Log homes came into view, and then brick row houses with yards crowded with hollyhock and larkspur. A black dog ran alongside the coach and barked. The horses were slowed, and Rebecah put her head out the window and shoed him away, for fear he'd be caught beneath the wheels.

Her heart pounded. Nash had no idea she was coming. She wondered what he would do and say. She pushed back the glad tears forming in her eyes, and then smoothed her dress with nervous fingers. There wasn't anything she could do about her torn sleeve. The pin she attached to it would have to do.

The horses came to a halt. Some townspeople gathered around, speaking to the driver and to Stone, handing them the bills, asking questions.

"Battered and bruised, gentlemen," said Mac. "We ran off the road in the storm. But we're here in one piece, praise be. Me and Stone, and the lady we bring, were held up by a band of ruffians. But we took shots at them and they ran like frightened rabbits into the woods. We'll tell you more over a pint of ale after we see to the horses."

296

Eyebrows were raised at the mention of such surly fellows, of Stone's marksmanship, and the mysterious lady they had risked life and limb for.

"She's a young lass and pretty as a picture. Brave a lady as ever I saw. English," she heard Stone say.

Rebecah shut her eyes, wishing he had not mentioned she was British. She might be unwelcomed. And why did he lead them on to think she was pretty? To her she was nothing of the kind. Her hair was an unruly mass of curls, her eyes too large for her liking, and her nose too small. But in reality, Rebecah was winsome to look at, able to set men's hearts at a gallop.

"British!" a man spat. Rebecah's heart sank.

"Take it easy," Mac said. "Most of our mothers were British. Besides women don't care about politics."

Mac opened the coach door, lowered the step, and held out his hand. She asked, "Is it safe to do so?"

"Of course it is, miss."

Men stared at the pretty foot that stepped out. The slipper that concealed it was beige satin with a strap; the stocking, with an inch showing, was opaque white. The brim of her hat dipped over one eye and shaded her face. She could see it in their faces, how their prejudice melted like wax to flame.

"Good, sirs. Do you have an inn where I may find lodging?"

The men drew off their hats. An old man stepped forward. "Mrs. Cottonwood takes lodgers. That's her house at the end of the street."

Rebecah looked at the red brick house with the English style garden in the front. She lifted her bag in one hand and her skirts with the other. Offers were made to help, but instead she handed her valise to a boy. As she strolled away, she heard them talking behind her.

"Who is she?"

"Don't know, but she's mighty pretty."

"Did you hear her voice? Like an angel."

A young woman stood on the street corner. A basket filled with peaches hung from her arm. "Miss! Wait. I wish to speak to you."

Rebecah stopped as the girl hurried to her.

"My name is Theresa Boyd. My father is the town clerk. We have a large house, and I heard you ask about lodging. Mrs. Cottonwood hasn't any space left since taking in so many refugees from the frontier."

"Refugees?"

"Yes, because of the Indians. But not to worry, we are safe here. We have a spare room with a nice view."

Rebecah felt touched by Theresa's kind offer, as well as relieved. If there were no rooms in the town, she would have had to rely on the charity of the church.

"But you don't know me."

"Perhaps in England, people are more wary of strangers. But in Fredericktown, we believe in helping our neighbors, strangers or not. Billy Wallens, bring the lady's valise."

The boy grinned from ear to ear when Theresa handed him an enormous, bright yellow peach as payment. The valise was light, and he carried it ahead of them without effort.

Rebecah looked at her gown. "I'm afraid I have made a poor impression, Miss Boyd. I shall be glad nonetheless, to be out of this gown. It's ruined."

Theresa gazed at it. "It looks perfect to me. I shall clean it for you, and stitch up that sleeve. Your journey was difficult?"

"Some of it, yes. I'll tell you about it later," Rebecah said, as they walked beneath a wisteria. "My name is Rebecah Brent by the way."

"Yes, I know who you are." Theresa smiled at Rebecah's bewildered look. "Captain Nash..."

"Captain?"

"He's Captain Nash now, appointed to lead the rangers. He told me about you. Well, he didn't actually tell me, he was wounded and . . ."

"Wounded? He is alright?"

"Don't be alarmed. He survived his wound, although he walks with a slight limp—barely noticeable."

Theresa paused, a cautious but anxious look on her face.

"Is there something else you wish to tell me, Miss Boyd?"

"Yes…He spoke your name in his sleep."

Rebecah's heart leaped. "Did he?"

"Yes and with great feeling, Miss Brent. I offered to write to you for him. But he evaded all conversation dealing with matters of his heart. He is wretched inside. He did not say why."

"I know the reason." Hopeless grief grew in her heart again. "I need to see him. Is there anyone who could take me to Laurel Hill?"

Theresa's eyes lit up. "I can. My papa has a carriage, and I'm an excellent driver. He allows me to use it whenever I want."

"May I speak to him?"

"I'm afraid he has gone to Richfield Plantation and won't be back for a few days."

"Is Laurel Hill far?"

"Not too far. Come inside and refresh yourself while I hitch the horses."

Rebecah stopped walking. She had never imagined a woman hitching horses. "You can do that on your own?"

"Certainly I can."

They entered the cool foyer. Rebecah was shown to a room kept for guests—and wounded friends. She washed her face and hands, brushed out her hair. All the while, butterflies danced in her stomach. Her hands trembled, and the thrill of seeing the man she loved again gave her joy she had not felt in a very long time.

* * *

Theresa snapped the reins and the horses went faster. Rebecah held her breath and gripped the edge of the seat. As they came to a bend in the road, Theresa slowed the carriage. A stone house came into view. Sunlight sparkled in the windows, and an oak bowed its branches over a broad porch.

"We are here." Theresa drew the horses to a stop. "Are you ready?"

Staring at the door, Rebecah swallowed. "I don't know what I'm going to say or do. He may be glad to see me, but then he may shut the door in my face."

"Why would he do that? He's a gentleman."

"You're right." She adjusted the ribbon of her hat. "I should not give into my nerves."

Lifting her skirts, she climbed down and walked up the steps. Her hands felt moist and her stomach jittery. With Theresa standing beside her, she swallowed and rapped upon the door.

Any moment he would answer. She would see his face and he hers. She would smile and so would he. He would be happy to see her. She stood back, bit her lip between her teeth and waited.

The door opened and a black man appeared.

"Is Mr. John Nash at home? I wish to see him, please."

"Oh, Lord." Joab's eyes widened and he smiled.

"Will you tell him Miss Rebecah Brent and Miss Boyd is here to see him? I have come a long way, you see, and…

"Captain John ain't here, Miss Rebecah."

She sucked in a breath. "Oh…Where can I find him?"

"He's gone to Richfield Manor and won't be back for a few days."

"Just like Papa." Theresa shook her head. "He said nothing of Captain Nash going with him, Joab."

"Is it far?" Rebecah asked.

"Too far to travel today," Theresa said.

"Yes, and I mustn't intrude upon his host." She gave Joab a kind smile. "Do you know when he may come home?"

"He did not say." Joab opened the door wider. "Come on inside and I'll bring you ladies something cool to drink. Mighty warm today despite the rain."

Rebecah stepped over the threshold. There was something grand in that action, something satisfying. At last, she stood in his house. She was speechless, stunned. She took in a deep breath, as if to take in everything that was a part of him.

The walls were whitewashed and the fireplace made of mountain stone. Cedar logs stacked beside it filled the room with their scent. On the wall, hung muskets, flintlock pistols, and a powder horn. There were no curtains over the windows. Shutters hung alongside them. The polished walnut floor was bare and clean, and the furnishings few.

Joab handed the ladies mugs of cold apple cider.

"I was stacking firewood next to the kitchen hearth when I heard your knock, Miss Rebecah. Before opening the door, I peered through the window. To my surprise, I saw a pair of young ladies climb out of Mr. Boyd's carriage. I know it were his cause I recognize his horse Perty."

A horse outside neighed, and footsteps crossed the porch. A breath escaped Rebecah's lips and she felt the blood drain from her face.

Jack! Her heart raced.

Joab opened the door and a shadow spread over the floor.

"We've come to call, Joab."

Theresa leaned toward Rebecah. "It's Mrs. Cottonwood. Her timing is awful. You aren't going to like her, Rebecah."

"She's the lady with the lodging in town?"

"Yes. And I bet she's brought her daughter Drusilla with her."

Mrs. Cottonwood stepped inside in her old-fashioned rust-colored dress, with her hair piled up under a large hat. Behind her stood a dark-haired beauty—but still a child.

"I see others have arrived before us. Good day, Miss Boyd."

Theresa inclined her head. Rebecah wondered why she had ignored her.

"Drusilla and I have brought a picnic. Roast chicken and apple pie." She showed Joab the basket. "We shall save some for you of course."

She craned her plump neck. "Well, where is he?"

He raised his hand for her to stop her cackling. "He ain't at home, Mrs. Cottonwood."

"Not at home?" Mrs. Cottonwood drawled. "He must be since he has other guests."

"Sorry, but he ain't here. It's gonna rain again. So you best hurry home."

"Mama!" Drusilla stamped her foot.

Mrs. Cottonwood frowned. "There's no rain coming, Joab, just going. Look what you've done. You've upset my poor girl."

Joab screwed up his face. "Beg your pardon, Miss Drusilla."

Mrs. Cottonwood put her arm around her daughter's shoulders, and narrowed her eyes. She looked Rebecah up and down, shifted her eyes to Theresa.

"I know you Miss Boyd. But who's this?"

Rebecah stood and curtseyed short. "I'm Rebecah Brent, madam. It is a pleasure to meet you and your daughter."

Mrs. Cottonwood's button eyes bore down on her. The prominent round cheeks and wide mouth gave the town gossip the look of an autumn pumpkin.

"Brent you say?"

"Yes."

"This is my daughter Drusilla." Mrs. Cottonwood pulled Drusilla forward. "John Nash is very fond of her."

Drusilla blushed, and Rebecah felt a stab. She looked at Drusilla and wondered how fond Nash was of her. What did she mean to him? Had he pledged his love to her?

No, it cannot be true.

Mrs. Cottonwood raised her brows. "So you're the traveler that was held up. I heard the whole story. It's the talk of the town." She bustled over to her like a fat hen. "You must've been scared out of your wits, Miss Brent. He did not ravish you, did he?"

"Brave Mr. Stone chased them off," Rebecah said. "I'm fine. Thank you for your concern."

"Fortunate for you, the coachman knew what to do." Mrs. Cottonwood sighed. "Oh, we poor women these days. Life is such a danger. And for you to travel across the sea and land to get here."

"Mama!" Drusilla cried, having been forgotten. Mrs. Cottonwood told her to be quiet.

"We must be going. Thank you, Joab." Rebecah walked to the door with Theresa. She turned to Mrs. Cottonwood. "Would you do me a favor, Mrs. Cottonwood?"

"I shall try."

"If you should see Captain Nash, please do not mention you saw me. It is a surprise."

Mrs. Cottonwood wrinkled her nose. "Why should I tell him anything, my dear? You think me a gossip?"

"Well, no, of course not. I only meant…"

"I think he will know soon enough you are here, if he does not know already. He may be glad for your visit, but I assure you, he is more interested in Drusilla."

With her head erect, Mrs. Cottonwood took her daughter by the hand and marched out the door. Their carriage pulled away, and Rebecah felt things might not go as well as she hoped.

CHAPTER 7

South of town people gathered on a hill destined to become barracks for Hessian prisoners. Morning had come, and the day was warm and sunny, the sky blue.

Nash leaned against the trunk of an oak loading his brace of pistols. He wore buckskins, fringed along the sleeves, and leggings.

Out on the grass, townsfolk sat on blankets and chairs brought from the nearby homes. Tables under the trees were bountiful with food and drink. Pastries tempted children's hands. The ladies did not hesitate to fill a plate or offer samples of their baking.

Nash watched Clarke take his turn at the tomahawk throw. He swung, missed the bull's eye by an inch. Behind Nash, Black Hawk stood grave and quiet in deerskin and beaded moccasins.

"It's your turn, Black Hawk. Let the people see real marksmanship."

Black Hawk raised his hand. "No, this is for white men." The eagle feathers in his hair swayed in the breeze. Billy Wallens counted them aloud.

Nash laughed and shook his head. "It's for all of us to try. No doubt you will win. Go on. Show us."

Black Hawk took a tomahawk from one of the men. The crowd grew silent. Boys ran to the front to see an Indian's skill. With one powerful sweep of his arm, Black

Hawk threw the tomahawk, sinking it dead center. People cheered and boys stared with wonder.

The bull's eye was the size of a gold piece made from a piece of tin, set on an A-frame piece of clapboard. Black Hawk showed no emotion as he turned around to see his competitors' reactions.

"It is now your chance, my brother. I will catch you another fat turkey if you match my mark."

"You doubt I could match it, Black Hawk? Well, we'll see."

Nash stepped forward, and locked eyes on the target ahead. He lifted his arm and hurled the tomahawk. It whirled through the air. With a thud, it sunk deep beside Black Hawk's.

The target tipped over on its side and the crowd roared.

* * *

Not far from the field at the Boyd House, Rebecah met Mr. Boyd in the sitting room. By the stunned look on his face, Rebecah knew she was not what he expected after his daughter informed him, upon his arrival home, they had a guest. When he heard her story, he stood and guided her to a chair.

"You were brave to come all this way in such perilous times."

"My reasons were stronger ones, Mr. Boyd."

"Jack has no idea of your arrival?"

"None, sir."

He raised his brows. "I'm astonished."

She gave him a quick smile and lowered her eyes. "Many people are. But surely it has been done before."

"The world is rife with love stories of this nature. But I'll not pry by asking you why you did not warn him."

"Thank you, sir."

"This should be quite a surprise for him. I wish I could see his face."

Theresa drew up beside Rebecah. "Papa, we must protect Rebecah from gossips like Mrs. Cottonwood. She arrived after we did at Laurel Hill with her daughter. You know how set she is on Drusilla marrying Captain Nash."

"I can assure you, he has no interest whatsoever in wedding that girl. He told me himself."

No interest whatsoever. Relief filled Rebecah. He was still free.

"Now I must be off to my office. I shall join you ladies later. You will find Captain Nash on the hill, Miss Brent."

Theresa grabbed Rebecah by the hand and drew her out into the hallway. She tied the ribbon of her hat at least five times, and smoothed the ringlets in her hair through her fingers more than she could count. Her dress was what she had worn to Laurel Hill, and the color enhanced the rose in her cheeks. Yet for the light coming through the windows, sparkling in her eyes, the worry in them she could not banish.

Her heart pounded waiting to leave. Oh, to see him after so long, to hear his voice and feel his touch. She dreamed through a restless night, tossing and turning in her sleep, wondering if she should have sent him word at Richfield that she had come.

Perhaps he did know. What if he had returned to Laurel Hill that morning and Joab told him? If it were true, why hadn't he come for her?

She wrung her hands, rehearsed what she would say. The words stumbled from her lips and nothing seemed to fit.

Walking down the street, Rebecah looked up at the church spires. The Evangelical Reformed Church towered in majestic brick, its spire shooting upward to a sharp point, gray and black against the sky. Beyond it, the spire of Saint John the Evangelist shone stark white in the sunlight, topped with a gold cross. Their presence inspired hope. Yet Rebecah could not fight off the growing anxiety of their meeting again. The mixed emotions were bittersweet.

As she hastened on with Theresa's arm linked in hers, she remembered how he stood there, his stare darkening, as he denounced her promise. Many months ago in England, she had made two pledges. At the first, her heart belonged to him alone. But when circumstances turned, she vowed never to see him again. The latter was said in the throes of heartache and anger, and for that, she was sorry.

Feeling her pulse race, she stopped.

"What is it, Rebecah?" Theresa said.

"I cannot go on. I do not think I should go to him this way, without any warning. He'll be angry, I know it." She laid her hand on Theresa's sleeve. "Let me go back. You can tell him."

Theresa smiled. "There is no need for you to be afraid. Besides, the festival is ahead of us. We've been spotted."

She thought she would die on her feet knowing there was no turning back. Up the hill they went, Theresa smiling and whirling in her girlish manner, Rebecah following her at a slower pace. A large crowd of people gathered near a pair of twin oaks. Rebecah saw men with tomahawks and muskets, dressed in belted hunting shirts and moccasins. Powder horns were strapped over their shoulders, and fox and raccoon-skin caps were on their heads.

Joab drew up beside them on a white mule. He slipped off the bare back, and pulled off his hat. "Miss Rebecah."

"Hello, Joab. Have you spoken to Captain Nash? Did you tell him I came to Laurel Hill?"

"No, ma'am. He didn't come home, but come here straight from Richfield. There he is."

Before Rebecah could do anything, Joab was gone in a flash. She watched him make his way through the crowd.

She bit her lip until it hurt, squeezed her hands together. He stepped up to a man. She could not see his face.

He turned.

Their eyes met and held.

CHAPTER 8

People vanished the moment Nash laid eyes on her. Her face, her coral lips, her jade eyes, intent upon him, reached out and seized. Tears entered her eyes, beading upon her dark lashes, and drew him forward.

"Rebecah," he breathed out.

When he reached her, she lifted her eyes to his. His arms ached to embrace her.

Nash glanced at Theresa. "Miss Boyd."

She gave him a quick curtsey. "Good day, Captain Nash. Aren't you surprised?"

"I am." He swallowed hard.

"Miss Brent is the bravest woman I've ever met," Theresa declared. "She came all the way from England and overland all by herself."

"Will you excuse us?"

He took Rebecah by the arm and moved her through the crowd. People watched as they went by.

"Where are you taking me?"

"Some place where we can speak in private."

A smokehouse stood a few yards away. He pushed open the door, drew her inside, and shut it. She stood in the center of the floor, hands clasped.

"Is it possible?"

"You are… angry?"

"I'm stunned."

"I should have written first."

"It may have helped ease the shock."

"I'm sorry. I can explain."

"I hope you can…Why are you trembling?"

"I'm a little cold."

"In more than one way, last I knew."

She lowered her eyes. "I deserved that, I suppose."

"Why are you here— Lady Lanley is it? Has he come with you or did you run away from the over-dressed fool?"

She looked at him. "I did not marry him."

Nash kicked a loose stone on the dirt floor and it hit the wall. "You swore to wed Lanley."

"Yes, I've not forgotten what I said and did."

"Nor have I. What are you doing here?"

Her eyes softened. "Your father…"

Alarm shot through him. "Has something happened?"

"He was arrested for aiding privateers. Laban Huet was hung at Standforth. Sir Rodney has begged you do not return. Your name came into the charges. He wishes you to stay away."

He frowned. "A son cannot stand by and do nothing."

"That's true. But give yourself time to think."

Nash shook with grief. He turned away and placed his hands on a table in the corner. "You saw him before you left?"

"I visited him, yes, in prison."

Nash's eyes were pained and urgent. "How was he?"

"He was bearing up, and he is treated well. David is seeking a reprieve. I've no doubt he will be successful."

"And my stepmother?"

"You know her. She is the strongest of women."

He sat on a barrel, hands clasped over his knees. "So, you came all this way to give me bad news—you that hate me?"

"Hate you?"

"What should I call your feelings toward me?"

"I never have hated you. I repented for ending the love we felt." She hung her head. "I repented many times over…"

He gazed at her with her hair falling about her shoulders, with miniature curls framing her face, the silk of her bodice, her breast rising and falling.

"Before I left England," she went on, "I wrote to the surgeon who attended my father. He assured me you did not cause the wound that killed him. Must I go on? It is complicated and grieves me."

"Certainly go on," he said. "I think I should know."

She drew in a long breath and paced. "My father arrived in England a month before coming home. He stayed in Portsmouth with a woman. Another man challenged him, a wealthy man who had her for a mistress. There was a duel, you see, and that is how my father came by his wound, and ultimately his death."

Nash reached out to touch her, but dropped his hand to his side. "Why didn't he tell you? Why would he have concealed the truth?"

She lowered her head, emotion stirring. "He was ashamed I suppose. Forgive me for the hard words I spoke, of my rejection and suspicions of you."

"You could have believed me from the start. Why didn't you?"

She looked up at him with moist eyes. "I was afraid."

"But you found out the truth, sailed across the ocean and overland to find me hoping I would forget everything that happened between us and take you back?"

* * *

It hurt. But what could she expect?

312

*His heart has changed toward me. This is my reward—
to reap what I had sown.*

It crushed her, and she turned away to wipe the tears
from off her face.

"I understand. You needn't say anything more. At least
let me give you something from your father to help your
cause," she said, changing the flow of their conversation.
"I've kept it hidden beneath my gown."

She turned away, pulled up her skirt and untied the
money pouch. Shoving down her gown, she then turned
and handed it to him.

"There are several hundred pounds there. Your father
hopes it will help."

Nash took it from her hand. Their fingers touched.
"Yes, it will. It was brave of you."

"There are letters inside."

He opened the bag and drew them out.

Rebecah moved to the door. "I have done what Sir
Rodney asked me to do. So I'll go."

Nash looked at her. "Where are you staying?"

"Mr. Boyd and his daughter were kind enough to give
me lodging."

"They're good people."

"Yes, they are." She looked at his leg. "Does it hurt
much?"

An inkling of an angry smile curved his mouth. "Not
much."

She hesitated, gripping her hands, wishing he would
tell her what had happened, wishing he would have a
change of heart.

Embrace me. Tell me you still love me.

"I'm glad it wasn't more serious. If you…"

"It's nothing."

She looked away, his cold abruptness pricking her.
"Goodbye, Jack."

Pulling open the door, she left. The sky was deep now,
and the shadows heavy like her heart. She hurried across a

field toward the spires, down the hill that lead back to the Boyd house.

She pressed a fist against her heart, her hopes dashed, the road ahead promising to be an unpredictable one.

CHAPTER 9

After reading his father's letter, having been told everything, Nash sat with his hands over his eyes pleading with the Almighty. The King's law was firm—harsh and lacking compassion. Even children were hung in the squares of English town's for stealing bread. How much more heinous did Sir Rodney's crime seem in comparison?

Food smuggled aboard a privateer for the Bostonians. How could a man be condemned for sending aid to the starving?

He thought a thousand thoughts with his back against the wall. At least his father had not met the same fate as Laban Huet. As much as his father railed against the injustice, judges took no action to bring charges against Captain Donely. He was the son of a powerful aristocratic family, many of which were favorites of the King.

Poor Mrs. Huet and the children. Nash thought about the day he met them on the road on the way to church.

Dear Mother. He had some comfort in knowing she was staying with the Hartcourts through this ordeal. At least she was not alone. Still, anguish raked over his soul. He wanted to go to them. Defend them both. Get them out of England.

If I had stayed longer, perhaps I could have saved him. How my emotions ruled me! And he slammed his fist into his thigh.

He looked up at the ceiling, at the slim shaft of light bleeding from it. Then he drew out another letter—this one from David, urging him to be rational and stay in America. It would be grief enough if Lady Margaret were to lose his father, but oh how double the pain would be if she were to lose him as well.

David wrote:

I'm confident I shall clear Sir Rodney. There is no solid proof to keep him in prison, or to sentence him. I shall see to it your dear stepmother is cared for through this trouble. But for you, Sir Samuel's bitterness is overwhelming, and he will stop at nothing to destroy you if you should return.

He is outraged that Rebecah has come to you. Revolutionaries on every quarter are being arrested, thrown in prison and some have hung.

When this is all over, I promise to set your parents aboard ship and get them to America. Perhaps my dear wife and I shall accompany them.

Next, he opened Lady Margaret's letter. She warned him to stay away, to *think of Rebecah* and keep her with him.

Do not fear for us, my son. God shall send us all the aid we need. David and Lavinia are looking after me. Your father is treated kindly. Soon this trial, and your revolution, shall be over and we shall leave home and build a new life with you and Rebecah in America.

Rebecah. How beautiful she looked standing there in the shade with her large-brimmed hat darkening the color of her eyes. Yes, he loved her, and he sat there brooding over all that had happened. He knew he had to swallow his pride.

* * *

Slander and gossip ran deeper than truth that year of 1774. Certain people refused to bridle their wagging tongues in Fredericktown, and when Nash stepped forth from the smokehouse and made his way back, a group of women huddled together. They made slight, deliberate gestures, and spoke between themselves.

Mrs. Matilda Cottonwood, Mrs. Roberta Smith, Mrs. Lettice Tinburgen, the spinster Derwood, and the Widow Watson kept an eye on him. Nash knew they were talking about him and the lady. One corner of his mouth curved into a grin that said he did not care what they thought. Ignoring their stares he moved on, walking under the shady trees looking for Rebecah.

Mrs. Cottonwood called out to him. He turned at the scratchy sound of her voice. Her face looked flushed like a strawberry. Her narrow gray eyes blinked as if a gnat flew before them. "May we speak to you, Captain Nash?"

"If it's about the dance, tell Drusilla I will not be there. I have business to attend to. There are other single men in this town."

She puckered her lips and mustered her breath. "It's no place of mine to meddle in other peoples' affairs…"

Nash leaned toward her. "Then I suggest, ma'am, you do not."

"But I must just this once," she said, shutting her eyes. "It's for the good of our community."

"I don't understand. Excuse me." He went to leave, but she stepped in front of him like a jackrabbit. The other women hovered around, and Nash frowned.

"What is on your minds, ladies?"

"Well, there's talk," said Mrs. Smith, drawing up her shoulders.

Mrs. Cottonwood took a step in front of her. "The lady who you met with, Captain, everyone knows she was at Laurel Hill when Drusilla and I rode out there to see you. How long is this woman to stay at Laurel Hill, and without a chaperone?"

"Is it against the law for a woman to visit my house?"

"No, but we hope she is not staying with you."

"Indeed, where would the lady sleep? No other place but your own bed," Mrs. Smith whispered.

"The Captain is a gentleman, Mrs. Smith," said the Widow Watson. "You'd take the floor now wouldn't you, Captain? Or you'd tie yourself up in a bundle bag."

"That courtship custom may be acceptable to some," said Mrs. Smith, "but it gives way to temptation. Is the lady staying with you?"

"Madams, I was unaware she visited my house in the first place," he said. "There's no breech in morals here. That is what you're insinuating, is it not?"

"But I saw her with my own eyes," Mrs. Cottonwood said.

"No doubt you did," he replied.

"She's from England, we hear," said the Widow Watson.

"That's right." Nash smiled at the old woman. She was the least annoying of the group—eighty and two, her shoulders hunched over, her statue small as a twelve-year-old child. And she had a playful glint in her aged eyes as well as in her laugh.

"An English lass, was I when I first come here to Mary's land, Captain Jack," she said. "Eighteen was I— eighteen and pretty as a spring rose. I had me beaus too, I did. Then I married Benjamin Watson. That girl, she's pretty too. You should marry her."

318

The slim spinster Derwood stepped forward. "She's the lady the whole town is talking about. Her coach was held up, you know. No one knows what happened. One can only imagine."

"I had not heard about that, ma'am," he said.

"She must be terribly in love with you, Captain Jack, to have left home and faced such troubles to find you," said the widow. "More reason to wed her."

"Don't tell him that," Mrs. Cottonwood said. "She's probably a British sympathizer—or a hussy."

Again Nash frowned. "She's not, I can assure you."

"Then *what* is she to you?" said Mrs. Cottonwood.

He knew his response would set their heads spinning. He leaned closer. "Miss Rebecah Brent is the woman I love," he whispered.

The widow cackled joyously. The other ladies gasped. Mrs. Cottonwood's mouth fell open. "Love her? What about my poor Drusilla?"

Nash bowed and walked on. He thought of going to the Boyds' to inquire after Rebecah, and the dangers she had faced to reach him. A pit grew in his stomach, for he had treated her badly.

With an uneasy tread, he mounted his horse. When he opened the door to his house, all was silent and dark. He ascended the stairs and went to his room, slamming the door. He stared at the empty bed, the cold white sheets, the light coming through the window. Why couldn't he have been more understanding? He should have shown her gratitude for enduring a long journey to bring him news of his father, letters, and money for the Patriots.

He sat in a chair, still clothed and booted, his hand covering his mouth, hours passing, until night fell and stars lightened the sky.

CHAPTER 10

At sunrise, Nash saddled Meteor, rode up the mountain, and followed the ridgeline to an outcropping where he could see down into the valley. The spires of the churches pierced a clear blue sky. He dismounted and sat on the ledge, where he could talk to God, mull over recent events, reasoned what to do.

Still agonizing over his father, he thought of Rebecah. His eyes traveled north from one spire to another, to where the Boyd house stood. He pictured her there…or had she found a way to leave on this morn?

The thought of her going caused his heart to ache. He regretted how he had treated her. He should have pulled her into his arms and kissed her. He should have said how much he loved her, how happy he was she had come to him.

He got up knowing he had to talk to her before it was too late. He rode along the creek, paused to let the horse drink, when Robert Maldowney came trekking along the bank toward him.

"I was up at the house and Joab said you were away from home. I had a notion I'd find you here."

Nash looked out at the water.

"Are you troubled?" Maldowney asked. "Is there anything I can do?"

"It would do me good to hear you say God has listened."

"Aye, he hears, and he looks on the heart."

"But never upon a man's reason?"

"In times of battle a man must use his reason in order to survive. In times of danger, storm, and dearth the mind takes over where the heart leaves. But in times of love, that is a time when a man's soul is put to the test."

Nash pinched is brows. "You're right of course."

"I know about your lady. She's come a long way."

"And brought with her sad news of my father." He went on to explain, his emotions mounting. "So you see I must go back to England. I'll take her with me, if she doesn't leave beforehand."

"That would be unwise," Maldowney said. "You would be implicated and thrown into prison."

His friend spoke no truer words, for Nash had known the business his father had been taking part in, a business that both worried him and caused him to admire his father more than ever. "I would trade places with my father. No greater love, remember?"

"Aye, I know. But if you went back, what could you do for him if arrested yourself?"

With a heavy sigh, Nash looked up at the trees and shook his head. "I know you're right. But I'm angry with the truth."

"Trust in the Lord. Your friend, David, sounds like he is a wise man and shrewd when it comes to the law. You say there is no firm evidence against your father. It may be he has already been freed and you'll have word of it in no time."

"Indeed that could be true. David is the best lawyer in Plymouth. The idea my father could have been released by now comforts me."

"Let us hope you will receive that news soon, my friend. And that the lady and you will be reconciled—at least in friendship if not in love."

"Thank you, Robert. But I do love her." Nash put his fist against his heart. "It burns in me like a fire. I've tried to change my feelings for her. I cannot. And then she shows up, looking as beautiful as the first day I saw her. That fire grew. Yet I showed myself bitter and resentful toward her."

Maldowney reached up and gripped Nash's hand. "She will forgive you."

* * *

Carne's barn stood on a rise of ground above Carroll Creek. Wispy willows shaded the water. Mallards skirted along the surface. A gristmill's wheel turned, while the townspeople who strolled by, listened to the peaceful shower of water tumbling down the spokes.

One of the largest barns in the county, with a rough-hewn pine floor and stables in the rear for cattle and horses, Carne's barn did not lack for room as a gathering place. Lanterns affixed to the posts lit the interior in golden light.

The barn was full of people—farmers, laborers, tradesmen, and refugees from the wilderness. Having seen to his horse, Nash walked inside. He weaved his way through the crowd. He had hopes of seeing Rebecah.

Mrs. Cottonwood and her daughters were present. He caught Drusilla's gaze. She blushed and with a shy smile lowered her eyes. Her mother prodded her into the crowd by poking her hard with her finger, causing the poor girl to bump into Nash.

"Good evening," Drusilla said.

He thought her mother's behavior disgraceful. How embarrassed this child was, and how her head had been filled with dreams of marrying him.

322

"Evening, Miss Drusilla. I'm surprised you're not dancing with someone."

She looked up at him young and coy. "I was hoping you would ask me."

"Well, at the moment, I'm looking for someone. Besides, my injury prevents me from being a good partner tonight."

"May I ask who you're looking for?"

"No one you know, Drusilla."

"Oh, but I think I do. Is it that English lady that came to your house? Mother and I…"

A young lad was passing by. He was the same height and age as the girl, fair-haired and anxious. Nash grabbed him by the shoulder.

"Tom! This fair young lady needs a dancing partner. Dance with her, will you?"

"You bet!" With a broad smile, he took Drusilla's hands and whirled her into the mix. A tune started up and the men hurried to select their partners.

Nash looked through the crowd. An ivory cheek. Coral lips. A turned head.

Rebecah stood beside Theresa Boyd, looking as though she wished she were somewhere else.

* * *

"Disgraceful."

Rebecah glanced over her shoulder. Mrs. Cottonwood sat a few yards away with her flock of matrons. A deep frown creased her face.

"I cannot approve of such forward behavior. Visiting his house unaccompanied by a chaperon is a sign of moral turpitude. Lud, to think what would have transpired if Captain Nash had been at home. Girls brought up in the frontier have stronger morals than that. Take my girls, for example. Each one deserves to marry a rich landowner, and shall, even if it's solely based on their good character."

Theresa leaned in. "Did you hear that?"

"I did." Rebecah sighed. "It doesn't matter. I'll be gone soon."

"Of course it matters. Come with me." She looped her arm through Rebecah's and turned.

"Ladies, may I present my friend Rebecah Brent? Rebecah, this is Mrs. Smith, Mrs. Tinburgen, the Mistress Derwood, and Mrs. Watson. You've met Mrs. Cottonwood. They have lived in Fredericktown since before I was born. If there's anything you want to know these are the ladies to ask."

Rebecah curtsied, lifted her eyes to see the affront Theresa had caused. Each woman frowned, except for the Widow Watson. She smiled.

"I'm sure I could have learned a great deal from them, Theresa. But my stay here is short."

"Oh, is it?" Mrs. Cottonwood craned her neck. "Well, that is news indeed."

"Yes, Miss Rebecah is returning home, ladies." Theresa drew Rebecah closer. "It's such a shame. But then one must determine just what *home* means."

Theresa tossed her head and hurried Rebecah away. The women were left with their mouths gaping.

"Old biddies," Theresa said. "Not the widow though. She's nice to everyone."

* * *

He lost sight of her. His heart sunk. Had she gone? He went toward the entrance and would have gone out to find her, but a round of laughter caused him to halt. Clarke and others were having the time of their lives. Between them,

Nash saw Rebecah smile. But her eyes spoke differently. How well he knew them, for he had spent many an hour looking into them. Tonight they were forlorn, lost— because of him.

He went toward her. Another man grabbed her hands, whirled her around, and when he let go, she bumped into Nash.

"Are you alright?" he asked.

She went to leave, but he swung his arm around her waist and pulled her into a concealed corner.

"You mean to run away from me again?"

"I don't belong here, remember? You said it was a mistake."

He looked into her eyes. "I was wrong. I'm sorry." He stepped closer. "Rebecah…"

"Mr. Clarke has agreed to take me to Annapolis since there is no telling when the coach is due back. We leave tomorrow. If there's a letter you wish me to take home, I shall."

"I don't want you to take anything back. I want you to…"

"Jack!" Clarke bounded up to them. "You cannot keep the lady to yourself. She has a line of men waiting to dance with her."

Clarke turned to Rebecah with a bow. "Ma'am, our captain is no dancing man. No offense meant. Will you dance this reel with me? Come on." He took her by the hand and pulled her away. Into the commotion they went.

Jealousy seized Nash, and he fought to contain it. He saw her laugh as Clarke spun her around. She had not looked back, and he hated how it made him feel. Clarke had a belly full of ale. It made him a poor partner, for he stumbled and dipped like an infatuated schoolboy.

Nash stiffened his jaw and glared.

* * *

Rebecah stood where Clarke had left her. She looked over at Nash and met his eyes.

Did he not know how much she yearned for him? Did he not realize she struggled over what to do, desperate that he had not come to her?

She weaved her way out of the crowd. Hurrying into the night, she went down the hill toward the creek where the moon shone bright across the water. She stood on the mossy bank where the cool darkness hid her. She wept silently, wiping her eyes and looking up at the spangled sky.

Why hadn't things gone smooth? She had found love and her world had fallen apart. Alone in a strange country without family or the protection of a husband, beset by loneliness, she regretted her journey.

Hearing someone behind her, she gasped. She turned and saw Nash standing in the moonlight with his hat in hand. Silence seized them both, and they stood motionless staring at one another. A moment and he stepped forward, his breath hurried, his look determined, desperate.

"You followed me," she said.

He stepped closer. "I could tell you were upset and I became worried."

"There was no need to have troubled yourself."

"You should not go wandering in places you don't know. Just beyond those trees, the bank is steep. If you go any farther, you could fall in."

She tossed her head and a curl fell over her eyes. "I knew where I was," she said, pushing it back.

"The creek is known to have copperheads from time to time. Do you know what they are?"

"Some kind of animal, I imagine."

"They're snakes, Rebecah."

She stared at him a moment, a shiver passing over her. "Thank you for telling me. I shall be sure to avoid it."

He came to her. She saw heartache in his eyes.

"I never meant to hurt you," he whispered.

"Nor I you. Doesn't my coming to you prove it?"

"It tells me you still love me."

"You loved me—once."

"I still do. I adore you."

He touched her cheek. His arm went around her waist and pulled her close. "Don't leave," he said. "Instead— marry me."

CHAPTER 11

Near the Potomac, a German settler, his wife and children, finished breakfast. Still the scent of fried eggs and bacon lingered in the rough-hewn cabin. Jonas Muller downed the last of his black coffee, set it on the table, and kissed his lady's cheek.

"I'll be hunting today, Karien. Dar is lots of deer and turkey in da woods dis season."

"Easy for you, *meine liebe*," she replied. "I've got to clean da mattresses today. Cold weather will be here soon and we don't want weevils."

"If I try, Karien, you'll only tell me I'm doing it wrong."

"Dat is true. You go on. I've got work to do."

Jonas grabbed his musket, looped his powder horn over his shoulder, and headed out the cabin door.

"Don't forget to wear a cap, *liebe*." Karien snatched it from the hook on the wall and tossed it to her husband. "The wind is keen this morning."

Jonas squashed it tight upon his head, winked at Karien and strode out into the sunlight.

Their son, age two, sat on the floor playing with his sister Adele. Adele's head bounced from side to side and it made Gustav smile. Stretching her limbs, Adele stood and handed him a wooden block. A stool sat beneath the window and she climbed it.

"Papa will bring home a fat turkey, Adele," Karien told the child.

"Mama, I see someone in the woods."

Karien looked up from working her bread dough and wiped her hands along her muslin apron. A knot of fear formed in the pit of her stomach.

"Come down from da window, Adele." She helped her daughter back to the floor. "Mama will have a look."

Karien gazed into the world outside her window. The towering elms beyond showered the grass with golden leaves. The sky above was blue as a robin's egg. The stream beside the cabin moved like a serpent down the hillside. She scanned the treeline. She gasped and sprang away.

"Oh my *kinder*!" she cried. "Save them, God!"

She gathered little Gustav into her arms and grabbed Adele's hand. She moved the bed aside, took the knife her husband kept underneath it and shoved the blade between the floorboards until they gave way to the hiding place Jonas had made in anticipation of Indian attacks. With trembling hands, Karien put the boards aside and then reached for her children. Adele looked at her with frightened eyes. Gustav sucked his fingers.

"Down, Adele. Go down and stay. Keep your brother close."

Karien reached inside the pocket of her dress and handed the children a bit of sugarcane, hoping it would keep them quiet.

"Let us play a game of hide and seek. You're not to come out until Papa finds you." She put her finger against her lips. "So be as quiet as mice."

Adele's large blue eyes filled. "Mama?"

"Do what Mama says, Adele. Don't make a sound."

Karien helped Adele down, then Gustav. "Mama is going to put da boards back now. We've done this before, remember? Be quiet until Papa finds you."

329

With the floor covered Karien slid the bed back in place. She pulled a musket off the wall. Then she barred the door. Through the window, she saw Indians creep toward the house. Muskets were in their hands, war paint on their faces. Their hair blew back in the breeze. Their copper bodies glistened in the sunlight. They screamed the war cry, and Karien felt her blood run cold.

"Jonas? Jonas where are you?"

As she spoke the last word, she saw her husband running toward the cabin. He stopped, knelt, and fired his musket, felling one Indian. Another ran toward him and swung his tomahawk. He fell back, and Karien saw blood pour out onto his hunting jacket.

She wanted to cry out, scream his name. But for the children's sake, she threw her hand across her mouth and pushed the words back. Terror beat through her heart. Fear seized every fiber of her body. They were at the door, ramming against it. What power did she have to stand against this pack of wolves? She was a woman, a mother, a wife who saw her husband killed.

Tears pooled in her eyes as the door broke in. She stood back and raised the musket. She fired. She gasped. Fear surged through her, for her life, for her children when she saw she had missed. She uttered a prayer and they seized her arms. Her heart stopped with terror. Indians were near the bed, stepping over the floor above the heads of her babes. She fought back like a mother bear, sunk her teeth into the Indian's arm that held her. He knocked her down, gathered up the length of Karien's golden hair in his fist. She struggled and wept—knowing what was to come.

The Indian blazed his knife, ran it through her skin. Blood poured down her face. With her children's names upon her lips, Karien Muller fell back and died.

* * *

Nash drew rein and looked down the hillside. An Indian emerged from the cabin, his chest smeared with war paint. With one quick thrust, he raised the golden trophy in his grasp and yelped. Nash's blood curdled. Beads of sweat gathered on his forehead and his hands shook.

The warrior bounded down the cabin step, joined the others. With cries of victory, they were gone, with sacks of goods, with scalps upon their belts.

A chill raced through Nash as silence descended. His eyes remained fixed on the cabin door. It moved slightly in the breeze. He looked away toward the barn, saw a man upon the ground, his hand outstretched.

Nash's men gathered round, and without a word, he nudged Meteor forward and walked him down the hill. The others followed, their muskets poised, their long knives in their fists.

Inside the hapless cabin, the dusky haze of the sun streamed through the loopholes in the windows. Bread dough lay in a wooden bowl, and there upon the floor lay the body of a woman, her face and dress splattered with blood, her eyes open, searching for the meaning of her death. The golden hair, that had been her glory, was no more.

Sorrowful at the sight, Robert Maldowney knelt beside her and picked up her hand. "Poor lass." He closed her eyes with the palm of his hand. "Andrew and I will bury them. I'll speak a word over their graves."

"Prayer in life would have done them more good. What does it matter now?"

Angry, Nash picked up the red and white patchwork from off the bed. With care, her body was laid within it. Beneath Nash's boots came a whimper. He looked down, heard it again. He moved the bed and lifted the floorboards. Two sweet but frightened faces stared up at him, eyes glistening with tears.

"Don't be afraid, little ones." He crouched and spoke softly. "Give me your hands and I'll pull you up."

First, he pulled out the boy. The girl threw her slim white arms around his neck and squeezed. Her warm face nuzzled his neck. He felt her tears. She refused to let go, so he held her close and whispered what words he could find to comfort her. A moment and she grew quiet. Still her face lay nestled against him.

He lifted the boy into his other arm and took great care the children did not see the blood of their mother upon the floor. Outside the sky rolled with slate clouds. He turned aside at the sound of earth being turned.

Thou art the helper of the fatherless.

With sadness, he recalled the portion of Hosea, while a nagging feeling crept into his chest. He put the children on his horse's back, and looked at the everlasting hills, knowing God had put the children into his hands. But for how long?

CHAPTER 12

"You're working too hard, Mrs." Joab picked up a spade and shoved dirt over a row of chrysanthemums.

Rebecah smiled, leaned back on her knees, and wiped her hands across her apron. "It's well worth it. Next autumn these will be a glorious orange. Do you like gardening, Joab?"

"Don't know. I haven't done it much."

"Tell me a flower you like, and I shall be sure we plant it."

"I like them yellow flowers I seen growing up on the hills when the warm weather come."

"Ah, I think you mean daffodils." Rebecah patted the earth beneath the plant in front of her. "Show me where you saw them and we will dig out some bulbs, and plant them in the fall."

"Mr. John never paid much mind to flowers and such."

"Well, now that I'm mistress of Laurel Hill, we shall build a grand garden."

A whistle came down the hills. With a thrill, Rebecah looked up. She knew that sound, for whenever he was coming home, he'd use it.

She stood and shook the dirt from her skirts. Jack walked down the knoll leading Meteor, his musket over his shoulder. His injured leg had improved under her hand. Nightly she soothed it with a salve made of camphor and herbs.

And who was this in the saddle? A child with long blonde curls, hands firm upon the pommel. And there, a small boy in Maldowney's arms?

"Look, he has children with him."

She yanked off her garden gloves, snatched up her skirts and ran up the hillside. Her heart pounded as her boots sunk into the cool grass. Were they harmed, sick, or hungry? What horrible fate had they met out in the wilderness?

She looked up to see her husband's face. A mix of happiness to see her and concern shadowed it. Oh, how brave he had rescued them.

He put his arm around her and kissed her cheek.

Rebecah looked into the girl's sweet face. It was the face of an angel, shining in a halo of golden locks. But the expression in her eyes told her of fear and sadness that no child should ever bear.

"Hello. I am Captain Nash's wife Rebecah."

"Like the lady in da Bible?" the girl said.

"That's right. What are your names?"

"Adele. He is Gustav my brother. I call him Gus."

"I am glad you have come to our house." Rebecah reached up and helped Adele from the saddle. She did not wish to be put down, and locked her arms around Rebecah.

"Would you and Gus like something to eat—sweet cake and milk?"

Adele nodded, then nuzzled against Rebecah's neck.

She turned to Nash. "They look so hungry and frightened. What happened?"

Nash twisted his horse's reins around his fist and pulled. "I'll tell you after the children are asleep."

* * *

Darkness came quickly that day. The wind strengthened over the hills, shook the trees. Leaves fell and covered the ground.

Nash stood at his window eyeing the outdoors. He wondered if warriors would come this far down the Potomac toward the Monocacy. He turned away, looked over at his wife. She looked beautiful in the glow of the fire, with Gus on her lap and Adele cuddle up in the crook of her arm.

Maldowney let out a burst of laughter and went on telling his Scottish tale of an old man and a lame dog to the children.

"And so, the old man picked up the wee pup, set him on the chair next to him at the table on a velvet cushion, and gave him an ox bone on a silver plate."

Adele's eyes widened and she giggled. Gus yawned.

"It's time we tuck you in bed, children" Rebecah said.

Their hands and faces washed, the children were clothed in fresh linen shirts. As soon as they were wrapped inside the quilts, Gus fell to sleep. Adele whimpered. Rebecah soothed her by humming a lullaby.

Nash leaned against the doorway and waited. She kissed him, held the sleeves of his shirt.

"They're alone in the world, Jack."

"As far as we know. I'll ride into town tomorrow and make inquiry—see if they have any relatives."

He put his arm around her and they soberly walked to their room. Rebecah shut the door and leaned her back against it. "Will you miss sleeping under the open sky?"

He laughed short. "I put up with the raw earth under my back and the moon shining in my face long enough." He gathered her into his arms. "And I was lonely for you."

He tipped her face up to meet his, kissed her long and soft. Taking her to their bed, he fell back with her against the pillows.

* * *

In an orchard north of Laurel Hill, apples fell from the trees and lay brown and shriveled in the grass beneath the sunshine. Yellow jackets hovered, dipped, and landed to taste the sweet fermented juices. That morning the river ran swift and cool, reflecting the blue sky. Bass surfaced to catch jeweled dragonflies. The elms along the bank were a blaze of gold. Wreathed in morning mist, the leaves turned in the whispering breeze. The sky rose red along the rim of the mountains when dawn broke.

Above the scarlet light, clouds were thick and slate-gray. They overtook the sunlight and it began to rain. Nash dressed in work clothes, in leather breeches, homespun shirt, and boots. He wore his hair back, tied with a leather cord his ponytail hanging past the nap of his neck. In his hand, he held a letter. Although his heart was ripping apart, he had done with crying. To him it was what a man did privately.

Dawn came colder and it felt like winter would come earlier this year. His father was gone—dead of an infectious fever and a jaundice condition.

He saw his stepmother's hand must have been trembling in her grief as she penned it. These were not her usual fluid lines, but scribbled discernible words broken and ragged. At one point, the quill had dripped the ink. What he was to do he did not know, for grief blinded clear thought and enhanced regret.

Lady Margaret would remain in England with Lavinia and David for the time being. Standforth had been confiscated by the Crown. Lady Margaret was able to keep her choice horses and move them to the Harcourt's stable. She had her own money to live on, a sum of at least five hundred pounds a year.

You need not worry over me, Jack. Tend your land and prosper. Rejoice with the wife of your youth, raise a family, and be at peace with God.

Nash stared at the letter, drew in quick gasps of air. His heart felt heavy as stone as he placed his hand over his eyes and wept.

Rebecah's hand closed over his. "What is it, my love?"

He handed her the letter. Tears filled her eyes. "Oh, no."

"He's gone, Rebecah…"

"I'm sorry. Do you want to be alone?"

"No, stay with me."

She curled up beside him in front of the fire. Rain tapped upon roof and wall.

"I cannot bring him back. I don't know what I'd have done if I had to bear this alone."

She touched his cheek. He turned his lips to her hand and kissed it.

"Are you cold?"

"A little." And she drew closer against him.

"Here."

He wrapped a quilt around her shoulders. Then he put another log on the fire. It crackled and the flames grew and warmed her.

"You will never forget him. But in time the pain will lessen."

"I've seen death at its worst, but when it's someone you love, someone close to you, it hurts like a knife turning in the heart."

"I know this kind of pain, Jack."

He nodded. "Your father."

"Yes."

He took her into his arms. "I cannot lose you, Rebecah. God help me if I ever do."

She put her finger to his lips to quiet him. "Do not think such things."

"It's the thought someday I may not hear your voice and have you here beside me. I pray God takes me first."

"You mustn't dwell on that. It is true that as time passes, people pass with it. But we will never be apart."

"You're not afraid?"

"Yes, I'm afraid. When I saw you coming out of the woods yesterday, my heart rejoiced. I had fears I might not see you again. But we are together now."

He pulled her closer, his cheek against hers. "I love you, Rebecah. I will until the day I die."

CHAPTER 13

Rebecah wore her best day dress and gray cloak. Their wagon rolled along the notched road, and with a sad gaze, Rebecah looked out across the fields at a group of men and women walking from the slave quarters of a plantation toward a crude whitewashed church on the opposite side of the road. Nash pulled to a halt.

Rebecah's eyes could not leave the scene as the slaves crossed the road in front of them. Her heart ached to see the thin overworked bodies. Yet it was evident within those weary vessels, vivacious souls swelled with the joy of the Lord and the hope of eternal freedom. It shined in their eyes, in their smiles as they passed by. The men pulled off their hats and nodded to the Nash's with the women strolling along in their calico dresses singing.

"Oh, but I love their singing." Rebecah sighed.

"Those are happy songs," said Joab.

"Indeed they are, Joab. But there is more behind the words and melody that make them happy. In spite of their bondage, the slaves sing with joy."

Nash shifted the reins in his hands.

"I'm glad you believe slavery to be wrong, Jack," Rebecah said.

He smiled from one corner of his mouth. "My darling, it is unfortunate not everyone in this world loves their neighbor."

"That is true. Greed and prejudice drives men to enslave others."

"Well, let us pray the minds of our leaders will trouble them so deep on the subject, all people will be free in our new country."

"Look at that overseer standing over there watching them as they go to church. The vulture. Put him in shackles and sell him off. I bet he wouldn't like it."

"If the authorities get wind those men and women are made to work on Sunday, their owner will be fined."

She looked startled and angry. "Do they work them on Sunday, Jack? You've seen this? Then you must say something." She grabbed his sleeve. "Look! The overseer is abusing that poor woman."

Without thinking, she climbed down, hurried forward, and called to the overseer. Nash handed the reins over to Joab and told the children to be still until he got back. He then went after his headstrong wife.

On the edge of a fallowed field, a slave sat with heaving breath after the overseer had released her. She stared up at him with large frightened eyes. She was an elder woman, with long ebony tresses streaked gray. Her body looked thin as a reed under her clothing, and likely to break with the first hard wind. Her dress was torn at the sleeve and worn, once having been fine now a castoff from the master's household.

Rebecah stopped in front of the overseer and he dragged off his hat. "Morning, ma'am." His teeth were black with rot and his face leathery.

"I saw how you were treating this unfortunate woman. Must you handle her so roughly?"

He shifted on his feet. "Well, I don't mean…"

"Does your master approve?"

"I see you're English, ma'am…"

"That matters not. What you are doing is wrong."

"You don't know our ways well enough to judge, meaning no disrespect since you are obviously English. Sometimes I have to use a heavy hand."

Rebecah turned to the woman. "Is there anything I can do to help? Are you sick?"

The slave shook her head. "I'll be right as rain, mistress."

The overseer slapped his riding crop in his hand. "Ain't proper for you to speak to the lady," he said with an angry look. The woman shrunk back.

Rebecah dared to lay her hand on the woman's boney shoulder. "Could she not rest awhile under the trees in the shade and have some water?"

The overseer was aghast at her audacious behavior. "No, she can't. And I'll be glad if you get back to your wagon and not poke your nose in my business." He nudged the slave woman. "Go on, Maddie. Get to your churching with the others."

Maddie ambled away with her hands clenched at her breast. Rebecah watched her. Nash put his hand on his wife's shoulder and spoke to the overseer.

"It would be wise to have a doctor look at these people from time to time."

"My employer does his best. Tell you something though. He intends to sell, including that one, if you want her."

"I do not own slaves."

"You got one there," the overseer said, pointing his crop at Joab.

"He's a freeman," Nash told him.

"That so? Well, you could use a serving woman for your lady. Maddie won't cost much."

"I'll consider it."

"You do that." The overseer tipped his hat. "Enjoy your Sunday."

He strode off smacking his crop against his thigh.

Rebecah bore her stare into him, until Nash drew her away.

* * *

Fredericktown was full of people. Horses, wagons, and carriages lined the streets. Townsfolk were attired in their Sunday best. On Church Street the Nash's were met outside All Saints Church by a cluster of people. They were in time for the service. Joab brought the children inside, and was sent up to the balcony. Slaves, freed blacks, and orphans sat in low wooden benches.

The interior of the sanctuary was aglow with candles. Hymns were sung, and a baptism preformed, followed by the sermon of Jesus and the fishes and loaves. The church was quiet, and Rebecah felt the eyes of certain people glancing over at her from time to time. She moved closer to her husband, slipped her arm through his.

Soon the parishioners were sent home. Nash introduced her to those lingering behind. Congratulations and handshakes were plentiful.

One of the deacons wives approach Rebecah and introduced herself. Mrs. Jacob Finch was her name, a well-liked and well-respected woman in her late sixties.

"We gave up English cloth long ago, Mrs. Nash. But I must say your gown is quite lovely, a beautiful color as I've ever seen."

Rebecah felt her cheeks redden. "How was I to know, Mrs. Finch? I hope I've not offended anyone."

"No offense. You see, we have not seen cloth like that in a long time. It is truly a treat. We hold a spinning school in the church each Saturday afternoon in order to make our own cloth," the gray-haired woman said. "It's homespun, but we wear it as a symbol."

"A symbol?"

"Yes, of our determination to be independent. It is a way of fighting for our rights. Some people call it *freedom cloth*."

"Do slaves also spin and weave it as well?" Rebecah asked innocently.

With a smile of sincerity, she leaned closer and whispered, "I'm afraid not. We must pray to God the slaves have their freedom cloth someday."

Rebecah nodded. "I hope so, Mrs. Finch."

"Your husband holds the same opinion?"

"Yes, and if you will excuse me, I must join him."

While she walked away, the younger women looked on with noticeable glances of envy. Nash was a handsome man, and no longer available. Rebecah's attire was nothing they had ever owned.

Outside on the cobbled sidewalk he said to Rebecah, "Boyd tells me Adele and Gus have a bachelor uncle in Annapolis. Apparently, he is a rich man. No doubt he'll see his duty and want the children home with him."

Rebecah's heart sunk. "I don't want them to go, but I shall accept whatever is right for them. Perhaps this gentleman would see how well they do and will allow them to stay with us."

Nash tipped his tricorn hat to passing ladies. "Boyd thinks the uncle may not want the children to live with him. He may separate Adele and Gus by sending them away to school."

Rebecah looked at him grieved. "Why? That would be cruel."

"Some people favor their social standing above their own family."

"If that is the case, we must do what we can to convince him to leave the children with us."

Through the church doors stepped Theresa, dressed in a sage-colored dress and brimmed hat. She made her way through the people to the Nash's. Nash turned and helped her down the last step.

"Come to the house for supper. Our cook has made a fine roast."

"We'd be glad to. I've business with your father at his office. I'll join you both later." He kissed his wife's hand and headed off.

Gus stretched his fingers out to Rebecah, tossed his arms around her neck and squeezed. She kissed his cheek, and he put his chubby hands against her face. He was hers—hers to love and care for, as was Adele, even if it were only for a while.

Joab moved the wagon on, and she watched it until they turned onto Market Street and were out of view. She sighed and Theresa looped her arm through hers. Together they strolled toward the Boyd house.

By virtue of her beauty and sprightliness, that she was English born and married to one of Frederick County's most prominent men, people stared as she walked by. The men tipped their hats and smiled. Mrs. Cottonwood and her clutch of daughters, walked passed her with heads held high.

"They dislike me, Theresa."

"Pay no mind to them," Theresa replied.

"Is it because I'm English? Is that why they hate me?"

Theresa sighed. "People are quick to judge the English these days. However I believe it's because you married Captain Nash."

She passed a bush and pulled off a leaf. "But they don't know me."

"They're jealous. Can you blame them? He's ever so handsome, and owns one of the prettiest tracks of land in Maryland. You must have stolen his heart at first sight."

"I admit he stole mine."

While they walked along Rebecah unfolded the story of their romance. But soon a booming voice drowned out the words. Standing on a wooden bench, clenching his fists and beating them in the air, stood a darkly clad man.

"Jezebels are among us!" he cried.

The veins on his neck and forehead stood out so clear and blue they looked ready to burst.

"Jezebels, I say, and heed my warning. They come from England. They come from France. They come to defile your beliefs in liberty. They come to defile your menfolk with their charms and rob them of their fortunes. These are she-wolves in ewes' clothing."

Theresa took Rebecah by the arm. "Let us move on, Rebecah. He speaks senseless prattle."

But Rebecah hesitated.

"King George has his men to debate and politicize and enslave us beneath his rule." Spittle oozed and foamed in the corners of the man's mouth. "The Queen has her minions as well to weave their snares."

"I agree with him concerning the King. But he accuses the Queen too harshly," Rebecah whispered.

"It's to stir up the people," Theresa told her. "He wants trouble. Let's move on."

"These deceivers come to our county from gentry stock. We mustn't allow them to undermine our determination, or to worm their way into our society, a society we mean to build upon the sweat of our brows and the blood of our patriots."

He bellowed fire and brimstone, his smutty cravat loose about a sinewy neck. His piercing eyes latched onto Rebecah. He pointed a bony finger straight at her.

"Yes, you're right, Theresa." And she moved on with Theresa beside her.

"See there," the man shouted. "One is among you." Heads turned. Rebecah's breath caught.

Nash rounded the corner with Mr. Boyd.

"Here, sir!" he shouted back. He moved with Mr. Boyd through the crowd. "You dare accuse that lady? Who are you?"

"The name is Pike." The slanderer dropped his hand and drew back his shoulders. "And I do dare to accuse any woman who is of the Devil."

345

Before the words were out of Pike's mouth, Nash grabbed him by the breast of his coat. No one in the crowd interfered, but stood in rapture of what was to happen next.

"Say it to my face again, Pike, and you will regret it!" Nash warned.

"I've no quarrel with you."

"The woman you slander is my wife. You'll apologize and leave our town."

"There's no crime in what I say. I pity you for the situation you've gotten into. From what I hear, she married you within days of her arrival, in a barn, not a church, beneath a full moon."

Nash stared at him. "We were bound in marriage by a man of God, beneath God's heaven."

Boyd stepped forward, as did the other men of the town. "Your sheep's clothing is ease to detect," Boyd said. "The good people of this town will not tolerate you. Though most of us are loyal to *The Cause*, we will not have you slander our women. I suggest you do as Captain Nash demands."

Nash released his grip. Pike smoothed the front of his coat. "Signs of enchantment and witchcraft."

The next thing Pike felt was Nash's fist square across his jaw. He stumbled back and fell into the street. "I shall yield to your assault. It's obvious you've no ears to hear. But the truth shall be revealed, and I hope not a moment too late."

With a lift of his head, Pike dusted off his coat, and turned himself out into the crowd. People scoffed and told him to hurry on his way. Words like *mocker, blasphemer,* and *crazed lunatic* were spoken as he passed by.

A tear ran down Rebecah's cheek. She brushed it away thinking it were silly for her to be so hurt. She looked across the street to see her husband coming toward her. His steps were deliberate, his look grave and concerned.

"The man's a fool!" Nash said, anger still burning in his eyes.

"Indeed he is. I don't think he'll be back." Boyd drew up alongside the Nashs. "Now let us get to our supper before it grows cold. Our cook has an apple pie waiting."

CHAPTER 14

Not once had Rebecah mentioned the odd speaker and his flaming accusations. Her husband's hand in hers was enough to ease her. Everything they had been through brought them closer together. And new challenges faced them.

Lord Dunmore had dissolved the House of Burgesses in Virginia for voting aid to Boston, inflaming every patriot from the Carolinas to Maine. Dare he support the starvation of men, women, and children? Dare he condone to cut them off and hold them hostage? To force the people of Boston to suffer was unthinkable, and the governor of Maryland held his tongue against Dunmore.

A Continental Congress was called. The Intolerable Acts were denounced. Boycotts on English goods defied the Empire. The Americans violated the law by making more wool rather than depend on English cloth. America struggled and clawed toward liberty.

Yet love was still in the world to bind up the wounds, to heal broken hearts, and to comfort the distressed. John Wesley still preached in Britain, and the Gospel was spreading in America. Amid the confusion of politics, a tidal wave of hope and courage swept over the country.

The sun burned bright, the sky a clear azure blue, as the Nashs' coach rolled over the sunlit road leading to Annapolis. The birds were singing in the trees oblivious to the woes of man.

Rebecah laid her head on her husband's shoulder and closed her eyes. She listened to the wheels turn, to the breeze pass through the trees.

They came to a stop, the horses shaking their heads and snorting. The footman jumped down and opened the door, and held out his hand to the lady. Rebecah climbed down, brushing the folds of her dress with her hands. Nash followed and tipped the driver.

The house belonging to Lucius Heinz was two stories tall made of red brick. This fortress, surrounded by a black iron fence six feet high, had every window blocked by heavy draperies. Rebecah saw a hand pull one back in the window closest to the door. They had been seen.

Nash opened the gate and she passed through it. Together they walked toward the door. The lawn had no trees, nor a garden.

The door opened and a servant escorted them into the sitting room. Rebecah sat in an overstuffed chair. With his hand on her shoulder, Nash waited with her. A cold and lonely atmosphere permeated the house. A gaudy porcelain clock on the mantle ticked on, its feet tipped in gold. Cherubs clung to the sides decked in laurel leaves. The clock struck a high-pitched chime on the hour. At that precise moment, as if planned, Heinz entered the room.

Beneath his wig laid a shock of gray hair that had once been as gold as his late sister's. His face was gaunt with heavy lines, his mouth drawn tight. With a courteous smile, he bowed first to Rebecah, then Nash, and turned to his servant.

"Bring my visitors coffee, Ulysses." His voice held a hint of an accent. "And a few cakes." Easing into a chair, Heinz opened a wooden box that lay on the table. "Do you

349

smoke, Mr. Nash? I've some excellent Maryland tobacco if you would like some."

"I never took up the habit," said Nash. "Thank you just the same. May I introduce my wife Rebecah?"

Heinz lit his long-stemmed pipe and blew out the smoke. He gazed at her. "I'm charmed, Mrs. Nash."

"We've come to discuss the children—your niece and nephew."

"They are well?"

"Very well indeed considering their loss."

"I'm deeply grieved for my sister and her husband. Karien was a treasure and he not deserving of her. Did you know them?"

"I'm afraid I never had the honor."

"I'm not surprised. They were determined to live apart from society." Heinz ran his hand over his spaniel's ears. "I warned them, but they would not listen."

The servant entered with a tray and set it in front of Heinz. Coffee was poured and handed out. Rebecah held the Blue Willow cup and sauce and looked at the black liquid. She could not get used to the taste no matter how much she tried. She glanced at the tray. No cream or sugar to flavor it? Obviously, Heinz had bland tastes. His courtesy to his guests left much to be desired.

"I've thought long and hard." Heinz paused, sipped his coffee. "It is too dangerous for the children to stay in the frontier. My duty is to see that Adele grows up taught in the graces of womanhood, and that she marries well. I'll not have her marry a backwoodsmen or farmer."

Nash stiffened at the remark. "A backwoodsman usually takes a wife of his kind, sir. As for farmers, we've some of the most prosperous in Maryland."

"But so few. And I doubt my nephew would ever wish for such a hard life. He will need educating."

"The children need a mother," Rebecah interrupted. "I've grown to love them."

"I understand your attachment, Mrs. Nash. It's natural you should have grown to love them. What woman would not feel that way?"

"We want them to stay with us. Our house is very fine, surrounded by acres of rich forests and fields, and we are close to town. We offer a good life for them. We will instruct both children in the Faith and provide for their schooling. You can see them often."

"I'm grateful for what you've provided. But I must insist they come to me. I'm within my rights."

Nash moved from around the chair and faced Heinz. "Yes, you have your rights. But is this the best for the children? Please, reconsider."

At that moment, Rebecah thought about her cousin Hugh Brent. He was sent away to school too. She never forgot the way he gripped her hand when he left Endfield, the fear and tears in his eyes. They loved each other, and for him to be parted from his family at such a young age was hard.

Heinz shook his head. "I cannot understand why you would want the burden. You should have children of your own."

Troubled by his comment, Rebecah looked at him. "Adele and Gustav are no burden. They are a blessing."

"We would be good parents, Mr. Heinz, and you would always be their uncle and welcomed at Laurel Hill," Nash said.

Heinz knit his brows. "I must do my duty."

"Yes, and duty requires doing what is best for you sister's children."

"I'll think on it a little longer. But for now, my decision stands."

Heartbroken, Rebecah rose from her chair. Ulysses saw them to the door. She was silent, stared out the coach window.

The driver cracked his whip above the horses' heads and they pulled away from the bleak house with its humdrum lawn. And as the last amber light of day faded, so did Rebecah's hopes of being a mother to Adele and Gus.

CHAPTER 15

Upon arrival at the Blue Heron Inn, the innkeeper handed Nash a note. Although he anticipated being alone with his wife in their room upstairs, and wanted to refuse, he could not decline this particular invitation. Certain Sons of Liberty were gathered in the dining room. He explained to Rebecah. Leaving him for the conversation of men, she went upstairs to dress for dinner. She would join him later.

The patriots sat at a long table near the fire in the great hearth. Cedar and pine scented the room. All faces serious, they smoked their clay pipes and drank from pewter tankards frothed with ale. Present were Mr. Thomas Stone, Samuel Chase, and William Paca, joined by four others who were officers of alarm companies. Some were gentlemen bred, owning large tracks of land. Others were simple men, sober beyond their years, committed to the *Glorious Cause*, understanding what it could cost them.

"Good evening, gentlemen." Nash smiled with a slight bow of his head. The men echoed his greeting.

"God save our country," said Samuel Chase, his way of greeting those loyal to freedom. "How is our sister in the wilderness?"

"Anxious and watchful," Nash replied.

"Our threat in the east is but from one side—the British. We hear terrible stories of Indian massacres in the frontier."

"It's true. But it will not deter the supply of the ammunitions from Frederick County. I can give you my word on it."

Chase settled back in his chair. "That is a relief."

Paca leaned forward. "Tensions are mounting in every town and village. Here in Annapolis neighbors are no longer speaking, merchants suspected of being Tory sympathizers are losing business, while patriots meet in secret."

Mr. Stone drew on his pipe. "The governor's carriage was shot at last week outside town. He was not in it."

Out in the frontier, Nash knew the seriousness of the Indian wars, but he had not realized what was happening in the towns to the east.

"I heard Sir William is holding talks with Brent and Red Jacket. Is this true?"

"Aye, it's a fact. The winds of revolution are blowing swifter now, and Americans will have to take sides one way or the other, and I've no doubt the British will win the Indian Nations over to their side if they haven't already. Boston is besieged, and more troops will be on their way. The Sons of Liberty will be ready for them."

Paca tapped his hand on the table. "It's all in God's hands."

A young man leaned forward. His expression was grave, and his hands hugged the pewter tankard he drank from. "We must act soon, or we may end up besieged like Boston. It's reported people are starving and young children have died. I've a sister in Boston and I grieve for her suffering."

Paca patted the young lad's shoulder. "All in Boston are near and dear to our hearts, Danny. We're doing all we can to help and to assure the same does not happen in our city."

Nash narrowed his eyes. "How I would like to be among the men demanding an account from the King for this atrocity."

As the hour passed, the men listened soberly to Nash's accounts of what he had experienced in the frontier. When he had concluded, he pondered the past year, from his journey to England, his painful love affair with Rebecah, his return home to Frederick County, to the thick of a horrific Indian uprising. Then she appeared, the love of his life. What hardships were to come with the Indians and the British, he could not predict. Only he vowed a thousand times over in his heart he would protect her with his very life.

* * *

Upstairs Rebecah twisted the ringlets falling over her shoulders. She changed into a gown of dark teal silk with rosettes along the bodice. While she pulled on a pair of white silk stockings, she thought about the children. At least Mr. Heinz had not been angry they had not brought the children with them. He certainly would have kept Adele and Gus. There was time for him to reconsider, and she prayed his heart would yield.

A knock came at the door and the maid entered. "Captain Nash told me to bring this up to you, ma'am."

Opening the box, Rebecah moved aside the cotton packing and sighed. She stared at the gift within it, picked it up between her fingers.

"Oh, Jack," she whispered.

Holding it against her throat, she turned to look in the mirror. The necklace sparkled in the candlelight. A pearl dangled like a teardrop from the center. His gesture melted her. She smiled and put it on, then turned out the door to go downstairs.

A servant approached her at the foot of the staircase and offered to escort her to the dining room. The room was aglow with candles. Nash looked handsome in his dark blue coat and black boots. When his eyes caught sight of her, a smile swept over his face and he stood.

"My wife Rebecah, gentlemen," he said. His eyes were warm.

The gentleman stood and greeted her. Nash introduced them one by one, and she curtseyed.

"Well, sir," said Paca. "With more faces like your good lady's, we shall win this revolution. Your wife is bound to inspire any man to fight for our freedom."

"Thank you, gentlemen," Nash said. "Now, I hate to leave you, but I promised my wife a fine meal alone. If there's anything more, you know how to find me—in the morning if you please."

He took her hand and led her to a table in a darkened corner of the dining room. He ordered wine, broiled fish and crab, seared beef and vegetables, baked rolls. The fire in the hearth crackled. People filled the room.

Rebecah touched the necklace and smiled. "Thank you, Jack. It is lovely. The prettiest thing anyone has ever given me."

He seemed distracted. She realized a lot of things were on his mind. She was not put off in the least, but saw his mood as a challenge and determined she would get his thoughts off politics and on her.

"People are staring," she whispered. "Is it my gown, you think? Perhaps I should have worn something else."

Nash looked at her. "Your gown is lovely."

"Do you like me in it?"

He touched her fingertips with his and let out a breath. "Yes, I adore every inch of you. I can prove it."

Her face flushed and she held her finger up to her coral lips. "Someone may hear you. You're bold to say such things in a public place."

"Have you another place in mind where I may speak of love?" he said with a slow smile. His meaning was understood and she laughed. "I do see what you mean though, for it is crowded in here."

"Yes, suffocating."

He leaned forward, his eyes fixed upon hers. "*You* leave me breathless."

"Is it true Governor Eden comes here to dine?" she asked, tasting the succulent crab. "On my word, this is good."

Nash sipped his wine. "I don't know. Taste the rockfish. You will like it."

She pierced it with her fork. "You dislike the Governor?"

Nash set down his wineglass and jabbed the beef with his knife. "The man is a bootlicker to King George. One day we will send him packing on a boat to England. Tom Johnson will be the first governor of a free Maryland."

"Mr. Johnson is a good man. But all of this is long in coming…if you win your revolution." She felt a sudden tremor of dread. What would happen to them if *the Glorious Cause* failed?

"The odds look slim, but we will win, God willing."

"But what if the Americans lose?" she said, keeping her voice low.

"We won't."

"I am worried. Can't war be avoided?"

"Try not to worry."

"I cannot help it. Men will die, women will be made widows, and children orphaned. The Sons of Liberty might hang. I've heard of the King's Chief Justice, that he holds no quarter to rebel's, and that is what you men will be branded."

"Yes, and proud of it."

"I am afraid—to lose you." She could not eat a morsel more and sent her fork down.

He picked up her hand and squeezed it. "Change the subject."

Still she looked at him anxious, picked up her fork and moved the food around on her plate. "Fine, I will talk of something else."

"For instance?"

"I cannot talk about the children right now for it would make me sadder than I already am. I've been thinking about Maddie."

He looked curious. "Maddie?"

"Yes, you remember Maddie, the woman at the plantation we passed on the way to town. You know the one the overseer mistreated."

"Yes, I remember. What is it you're thinking?"

Her eyes brightened, for she saw he was interested. Nothing would do her better than to help the bondwoman.

"I could use help with the house and with the children...I mean our children if God should so bless us."

"Are those the only reasons?"

"Could we not do for her what you did for Joab? Could we not give her a better life?"

"Yes. If this is what you want, I'll look into it as soon as we get back."

* * *

Nash had not slept well during the night. He drifted in and out, his thoughts yanking him back awake. His mind was troubled and he thought of many things; his father's dismal passing in a cold prison broke his heart, and his stepmother now left a widow, weighed upon his conscience. He'd written to her, pleading she leave England and come to Laurel Hill. Then there was the dawning revolution.

He sat in the armchair beside the fire and watched Rebecah while she slept. Her breathing was even. Her hair flowed over her shoulders and down her linen chemise. The necklace he gave her hung around her throat.

The instinct to protect and guard raced through his veins. Weary, he put his hands up to his face and rubbed his eyes. Hers fluttered open and gazed at him.

"When we get home, there will be apples in the orchard."

He dropped his hands on his lap and beheld her with longing. "You're so beautiful."

"My eyes are too large and my mouth too broad."

"I adore your eyes," he told her, leaning over. "And your mouth…Well, you know how much I enjoy kissing it." He brushed his lips over hers.

"I'm glad," Rebecah sighed. She ran her fingers through his hair.

"War will come. Hard times are ahead."

"I know."

"I must do my duty."

She lowered her eyes. "I know that too."

"The thought of being separated from you…"

She touched his cheek and hushed him. "You're the bravest man I know. Just promise me, when you go, you will come back to me."

She threw her arms around his neck. He drew her close, and they kissed over and over, and decided to forgo breakfast.

CHAPTER 16

Beneath a vivid blue sky, people were filling the street. Nash and Rebecah stepped out of the inn hoping to make it to the Postmaster's before their coach arrived. A boy had gone ahead of them fifteen minutes before with their bags.

A cart, drawn by two white oxen came to a halt and the driver could not move the animals on due to the crowd. Unable to go out they turned back inside with startled faces.

Nash stopped a man nearing the inn's door. "Excuse me, sir, but why is the street so crowded today?"

The man pressed his lips hard. "*The Peggy Stewart*, that's why. It's brought a cargo full of tea. I hope it sinks to the bottom of the bay."

The man poked his head inside the inn and repeated the words with a shout. Everywhere men rose to their feet and headed out the door.

Nash put his arm around his wife and kept her from being pushed by the mob. Once safe, they headed toward the Postmaster's. But as they turned a corner, they were drawn into the crowd, and it became difficult to stay together as they were pushed and pulled along. Had the whole town gone mad? Nash held Rebecah's hand. He felt her fingers slip away from his. He turned back and looked across the people.

"Rebecah!"

The noise drowned his words to a whisper. Turning in a full circle, Rebecah stretched her hands out to him. With his body, he shielded her against the press. She turned into his arms.

The crowd parted for the Committee to pass through. As expected some men's faces were scarlet with anger, while a few beckoned with their hands for the people to calm themselves.

"The matter will be dealt with in accordance with the law. Be calm, gentlemen."

"Remember Boston! Don't fail Boston!"

The crowd followed the Committee to Stewart's house. A curtain moved in a lower window and someone demanded that Stewart come outside.

The Committee advanced to the door and a man hammered upon it with his fist. A moment and it opened.

Stewart pleaded with the people to be kind and reasonable. His wife was sick, and the riot outside their house would inflame her illness. He feared violence could be done to his family, and so he swore to do whatever the people asked of him.

"You swore by signing the agreement you would abide by our boycott," a man in leather breeches shouted. "You've breached that vow!"

"Yes, you've broken the law, you Tory rogue!"

"No Tory am I," cried Stewart.

"Then burn your ship or be hanged in front of your door."

In the faces of these threats, Stewart stepped forward. Rebecah buried her face against Nash's coat when she heard the threat made Stewart's life.

"They cannot hang him, Jack," she said. "Can they?"

"In cases like this, men lose their heads, Rebecah. The whole town is against him. He has broken the law and shown disloyalty."

With her beside him, he plodded his way to a steppingstone. He pulled Rebecah up next to him. It was clear by the look on Stewart's face he repented of his deed.

"Burn your ship, Stewart," someone shouted. "Burn *The Peggy Stewart* and all the tea with her!"

With no other way out, and to spare his family, Stewart agreed and offered a public apology. He begged to be allowed to land the remaining cargo. A few levelheaded citizens agreed, but the mob leaders shouted loudest.

"Run the *Peg* aground then," Stewart ordered, "and she shall be set afire."

By the strain in his face, his heart was breaking for his beautiful vessel. Stewart torched his ship along jointly with his co-owners. The flames spread upon the decks and twisted like blazing vines up the rigging and masts. The sails caught, cinders floated like black snow through the breeze.

The Peggy Stewart burned in a cloud of pitchy vapor. Smoke poured out of every crack and opening, black serpents amid spouts of orange flame.

Nash held Rebecah close, and lifting her in his arms, he carried her through the crowd. Soon they boarded their coach and rode out of Annapolis a little shaken by the event they beheld, out to the high road leading westward toward the everlasting mountains.

CHAPTER 17

Winter, 1774

Out in the frontier the fields turned golden-brown. The season arrived with thick slate skies, the air brisk and breezy. Flocks of crows speckled the bare trees. Geese flew south and mallards found refuge in the grassy banks of creeks and rivers.

Rebecah placed a fork on the table beside a pewter plate and thought how they would explain things to Adele if word came from Heinz the children were to come to him. Weeks had gone by, and she hoped he had decided to allow them to remain at Laurel Hill.

But what if this was a forlorn hope? It would break her heart to lose them. They had already suffered the loss of their parents.

How can he believe it best to add to their loss by taking them away from us?

Being sent to a man Adele did not know, to a gloomy house, and then to a school for girls, would be a frightening prospect for one so young. And Gus, being only two, would not understand. How would Heinz care for him, love him? Hire a nursemaid to keep him quiet in an upstairs room until he was old enough to send away?

Don't let him take them from us, Lord.

Slamming a spoon on the table, Rebecah questioned why Karien and Gustav had to die—why in such a horrible way. Why did the children come to her and Jack, to love and care for, only to have them taken away?

Why, God? I need an answer.

She heard a coach pull up outside. She drew aside the curtain and watched it halt. A stout woman stepped out dressed in a heavy wool cloak and white cap.

Rebecah dropped the curtain and headed to the door, hearing her husband's deliberate footsteps climbing the steps. She knew then whoever this person was, Jack was not happy she had arrived.

She's come for the children.

She went to the children and gathered them into her arms. Holding them tight, she whispered to them how much she loved them. "I always will."

"Joab!" Nash stormed inside. The door slammed against the wall. Behind him stood the woman.

Joab rushed into the room.

"Joab," said Nash softer. "Bring this woman a mug of warm cider."

"Patterson is my name," she said with a proud lift of her double chin. "Never mind the cider. I must be on my way. My employer's instructions, you see."

She handed him a letter and he broke open the zeal. Dreading its contents, Rebecah watched him. His jaw tightened, and in his eyes, she saw the disappointment rise. Then he handed it to her.

Dear Mr. and Mrs. Nash,

I've spoken with my priest, and he has counseled me in what I believe to be the most honorable path in which I should take on behalf of my sister's children. My heart and mind have been convicted. I mean to take the children to the homeland of their parents. My intention is to quit the Colonies and return home where I am the most prosperous. I have a large house outside of Hamburg in the country.

My family connections have the highest of reputations. It is important the children be with me, their uncle, their grandparents and other relations who have never seen them. I can assure you they shall be well provided for and loved, and I shall employ a governess for Adele and a nurse for Gustav.

You have my thanks for the care you have provided my niece and nephew. I shall in the future write so you may know how well they are.

Your Servant,
Heinz

Patterson arched one brow and fixed her eyes on Adele and Gus. She dismissed Rebecah completely.

"These are the children?"

Adele hid her face. Rebecah kept her close. "You will be gentle with them, madam."

"Of course I will. You are Mrs. Nash, I presume."

"Yes." Rebecah stood, but kept the children at her side. "We have a visitor, children. Say hello to Mrs. Patterson." She knelt in front of them.

Peeking up at Patterson, Adele frowned. "I don't want to."

"Mrs. Patterson has been sent by your uncle."

Patterson stepped forward. Her shadow fell over Gus and he began to whimper.

"They don't need to acknowledge me, Mrs. Nash. I hope you prepared them to leave."

"We did not know you would be coming for them. Mr. Heinz promised to send us word first."

Patterson leaned down. "Little girl, you and your brother will have fine clothes, new toys and books, and you will go to school. I also have sweets inside the coach for our journey. Now you'd like that surely."

"I don't want to go. I want to stay here."

"Perhaps you can visit sometime."

"I want my mama."

Rebecah embraced her. "Your mama is in Heaven, dear."

"Oh," Adele stammered. She pressed her lips into a pout. "Must we go?"

"For now, my darling."

"Can we come back?"

"Captain Nash and I will always welcome you and Gus. Someday you can visit us."

The coachman knocked at the door. Rebecah fought back tears.

"We mustn't forget your new doll, Adele. She shall have a wonderful time riding in a coach. There will be so much to see."

"Like what?"

"Oh, deer and foxes. Come, let's go pack."

She took Rebecah's hand.

Upstairs Adele picked up her doll from off the bed; her slim arms, white and soft as lilies, went around Rebecah's neck. She wept and Rebecah drew her close.

"I don't want you and Gus to go, Adele. You know that don't you?"

Adele nodded.

"Your uncle is you guardian. He is in charge now, and it would be right to obey him."

"Why is he my guardian?"

"Because he is your mama's brother."

"I want Mama and Papa."

"I know." Rebecah brought Adele forward and brushed away her tears. "I'm an orphan just like you and Gus. I was frightened too. But it turned out alright."

She felt a shadow fall behind her and turned to see Nash in the doorway with Gus in his arms. "Patterson wants to leave."

366

Outside clouds were building to the north and Rebecah feared it would rain. The roads would get muddy. The coachman turned up his collar against the wind and wound tighter the reins to steady the horses. Nash squatted down to Adele. She threw her arms around him, squeezed hard, and rubbed her cheek against his. Patterson tried to pull her away. Adele struggled. She broke free and rushed to Rebecah.

"Come, child." Patterson huffed and looked discouraged by the Adele's aversion. "The day wears on. Mrs. Nash, do something!"

Joab shoved his hands in his pockets. "Lord. Lord."

Adele weakened under Nash's touch. He picked her up and carried her to the coach. Patterson opened the door and he put her inside next to Gus.

He turned to Patterson. "You must take good care the children while on the journey."

"I'm a nursemaid. I know what to do."

"You must keep them warm, keep their shoes dry, and see to it they are well fed."

"I will, certainly."

"And you must stay out of any taverns along the way. If anything were to happen, I'll hold you responsible."

"I resent your insinuation that I am ignorant of the dangers of travel. The children will be safe with me, and the coachmen go armed, sir."

"I hope so. As much as I'd like to change things, I cannot."

Patterson climbed inside and shut the coach door. "I'm only obeying orders."

"Perhaps I should ride with you as far as the Monocacy."

"There's no need."

The driver shook the reins and the horses moved forward, turning the coach out onto the road. Nash put his arms around Rebecah. With her face wet with tears, she raised her hand to say farewell. For as long as she lived, she would never forget that day, a day not unlike the time her uncle sent her cousin Hugh away. It would never happen to any of her children.

The coach rumbled down the lane and disappeared from view. But not before a tiny hand waved out the window and a slave in a faded calico dress stepped off the roadside to let it pass.

CHAPTER 18

Rebecah finished the last few stitches in the shirt she was making her husband. She heard a horse neigh, and going to the window, she looked out to see a rider hand down a message to Maddie, turn his mount and ride off.

"The man said it were urgent, Miss Rebecah," Maddie said as she hurried into the sitting room.

"It's from Mr. Boyd." Rebecah tore the letter open. "Fever has stricken several families. The Cottonwoods are down with it. The three youngest have come through and are living in the servant's quarters. The Smiths, the Carnes, several of the Johnson slaves, and a few refugees are afflicted. Now his daughter is ill and he is distracted with worry."

Maddie clicked her tongue. "Poor Miss Theresa. I wonder what the doctor is doing to help."

"Mr. Boyd says the doctor has given up hope of saving her."

Rebecah felt panicked. This could not happen to one so young, one in love with life—her friend.

"I must go to them."

"Snow is coming."

"I have no fear of snow," Rebecah said.

Maddie took a step forward. "I'm coming with you. I'm a good nurse and you'll need my help."

"You're sure?"

"I've nursed plenty of sick folk in my time. I know what to do—know more than most doctors 'bout fevers and childbearing."

"I would be grateful if you came with me. Fetch your cloak. Joab can saddle my horse. But we will have to ride together."

"Not to worry. My old bones can take it." And off Maddie went, calling for Joab as she passed out into the hallway.

Joab came through the doorway with a load of firewood in his arms. "What's Maddie squawking about?"

"Maddie and I are going into town to inquire after Miss Theresa. We may be there quite a while. I know the cold aches your joints. But would you go out and saddle my mare?"

"You don't need me to come with you?" He set the firewood down.

"Not this time."

* * *

Granite clouds swept over the horizon. The wind blew against Rebecah's face, blowing back the hood of her gray cloak. She edged the mare to the post outside the Boyd's house. A black sheet hung over the door to warn visitors that sickness lay within.

Ice sickles hung from the porch. A dusting of snow on the roof stirred with the wind and fell like powder. Maddie alighted from the horse first, and then Rebecah. After she knocked several times, the door opened enough for Hilda to peer out.

"We're here to see Miss Theresa, Hilda."

Hilda put her hand up and shook her head. "I know ya came a long way, Mrs. Nash, but she's too sick for me to let you in da house."

Nonetheless, Rebecah ignored her and stepped inside. Maddie followed. Mr. Boyd came out of his study and met her. He looked as though he had not slept in days.

Rebecah drew off her cloak. "Maddie and I are here to help. Surely you would not send us back out into the cold."

He stared at her a moment, his face drawn and haggard. "No, Mrs. Nash, I wouldn't. How kind of you and Maddie to come. I fear for my child. She is near death's door."

"We will change that." She pulled off her gloves and put them on a chair. "We will go up now, Mr. Boyd."

Inside Theresa's room, red coals seethed and a gentle fire burned in the fireplace. Every breath was a struggle, hoarse, raw, and painful. Memories of Endfield Manor came back to Rebecah—the struggle to save Lady Kathryn and Lavinia, how she and March nursed them both, one dying, the other left to live to grieve the loss of a mother. This fever, however, was of a different plague, and Rebecah was requisite to rely on her intuition and Maddie's experience.

Hilda wrung her hands and stood at the foot of the bed. "She shakes all over with da chill."

Maddie pushed up her sleeves, dipped a cloth into the bowl of water beside the bed, and threw back the covers. She dapped Theresa's face, ran the cloth along her arms and legs.

Rebecah stared at Theresa. It worried her how deep the flush on her cheeks was, how heavy the beads of perspiration on her face, her chemise soaked through. "Mr. Boyd has reason to worry, Maddie. She is seriously ill, isn't she?"

Maddie shook her head. "This is a strong fever. But don't fear. I know what to do."

From the pocket of her apron, Maddie removed a packet and handed it to Hilda. "Make tea out of this for Miss Theresa."

"What is it?" Rebecah asked.

371

"Willow bark. I seen it cool a fever many times."

Maddie drew from her apron a jar of ointment and opened the lid. "This is scented with mint, eucalyptus oil, and camphor. It'll break up the congestion."

She turned Theresa over and rubbed the ointment deep into Theresa's back and then her chest. Her strong hands anointed Theresa in long, tender strokes as she hummed a hymn.

With this done, Maddie and Rebecah dressed Theresa in a clean nightshift, and pulled the quilt over the girl. Hilda returned with the tea in a large ceramic mug and handed it to Rebecah. Rebecah spooned a little into Theresa's mouth.

Mr. Boyd stood by watching, his brow of furrow of worry. "I could not stay away. How is she?"

Rebecah looked over at the anxious father. "Her fever has not yet broken. When was Dr. Cole here?"

"Last night." Boyd's eyes never left his daughter's face.

"What did he say?"

"That it is the same condition the other folks have. I've been up all night at her bedside fearing I would lose her. I've been in such despair."

His voice broke off and he started to tremble. Rebecah looked at his tired face, at the uncombed hair, and his gray eyes marked with dark circles. She stood and went to him.

"Mr. Boyd, you're in need of rest."

"How can I, ma'am, when she is my only child?"

"You will do her no good if you fall ill yourself. I promise we will take good care of her while you sleep, and will wake you at the first sign of change."

"It is good of you," he said. "Thank you."

"Hilda," Rebecah waved her over. "Please help Mr. Boyd to bed."

Hilda gently led Mr. Boyd from the room. All night Rebecah and Maddie sat at Theresa's bedside. At dawn her fever broke. An hour later, the church bells began tolling.

"Do you hear the bells, Maddie?"

"It ain't Sunday."

"No. They ring because the town has made it through." Smiling she turned and embraced the old woman. "All is well now."

* * *

Nash rode Meteor down a trail leading to the acres belonging to Laurel Hill. His fields stood barren and windswept. The biting cold caused his leg to ache. He could not help but think of the warrior who had let loose that arrow upon him. Still, he refused to curse him, and instead accepted his lot.

I hope Maddie has more of that liniment of hers. He rubbed his thigh with the palm of his hand.

When he brought Meteor across a serpentine brook, deer sprung across the field. Juncos perched in the branches of the evergreens and tore pine seeds from the cones.

He considered himself fortunate to have not seen a warrior out on patrol this time out. Settlers he and his men met along the way had not seen an Indian in a month, or any of Dunmore's men, who could be as ruthless, and yet there hung a tenseness of danger in the air.

His heart swelled to see the windows of his house shine in the sunlight. He sent out a whistle, the one she knew. He waited. Rebecah did not run out to greet him.

Instead, Joab hurried as fast as his old legs could carry him from the barn. Hatless, he raised his hand and smiled.

"Good to have you home, Mr. John. I've got a pot of stew shimmering."

"Sounds good, my friend. You've been well?"

"I'm fit as a fiddle," said Joab.

Nash dismounted.

Joab ran his hand over Meteor's coat. "My, he needs a brushing down. His coat is thick with muck."

"I'll groom him later. I'm tired."

He led Meteor to the barn and drew off the saddle. Joab filled a bucket with oats.

"Everything alright here?" Nash asked.

Joab patted his right ear. "Yes, I've been here all night, Mr. John."

He wished he could do something about Joab's hearing, and felt sorry for the man. He leaned a little closer. "No, Joab. Is everything alright at home?"

"Yes, but it's been boring without you around."

Nash wondered why. There was plenty of work to do.

After settling Meteor, he went to the house. "Rebecah," he called. He set his pistol on the table and looked around. Her sewing basket sat beside her chair near the fireplace. A quilt she had stitched lay over the back of their settee. Joab had a fire going in the hearth and the room felt warm, but not warm enough without her.

"Where's my wife?" he said turning to Joab.

Joab looked over at Nash as he closed the door. "She went into town to see Miss Boyd."

"Did she say for how long?"

"She didn't say when she'd be back."

Nash frowned. "I see. Well, ask Maddie to fix me a bowl of your stew…and some bread if we have it. I'm starved."

Joab shook his head. "She ain't here either. Miss Rebecah took Maddie with her."

He was not worried. He expected her to visit friends in town and take Maddie along as a companion. She'd gone into town many times before. But disappointment filled him that she had not been home to greet him. His arms longed to hold her, feel her close against him, smell the lavender in her hair. He'd give her another few days, and then ride over to the Boyds' and get her.

CHAPTER 19

"Are you alright, Maddie? Am I moving my horse too fast?" Rebecah said over her shoulder.

"I'm just fine, Miss Rebecah. I'll be glad to get home though."

"Me too. It isn't too far now."

They rode home under a thick gray sky. The wind grew stronger and constant, flushed her face, and passed through her gloves and cloak.

"Miss Rebecah, there's a mighty storm coming," Maddie held tighter. "Maybe we need to turn back."

The temperature plunged as rapid as the wind blew, and the women shivered and wished for home. "We are closer to Laurel Hill. Don't worry. We'll be alright."

Snow began to fall fast, the kind her beloved had warned her about, snow that drove the cold to the marrow and brought a deceptive silence to the land. Spotting a notched tree trunk, she drew up her mare. The initials LH etched into the bark made her draw in a sigh of relief.

"See those letters, Maddie?" She reached out and traced her fingers along them. "They stand for Laurel Hill." Through the veil of snow, Rebecah looked toward a glowing light in the distance. "Look—there's home."

Gray mountain stone stood out against the snow. Smoke curled from the chimney.

Jack, you must be home. Please be there.

Her horse flicked its ears with a snort and stomped its hoofs. Shaking the reins, Rebecah nudged her on. Drifting gray fog fell down the slopes and into the valley, and along with it the howl of a wolf. Maddie moaned. "Lord, have mercy on us. Wolves!"

Rebecah looked up with a start. Starvation drove the wolves, and they barked and bayed. She should have brought a pistol with her.

Fearing them, Maddie pressed her face against Rebecah's back. "Watch over us, Lord Jesus," Rebecah heard her whisper.

The mare trudged down the hill. A shadow bounded forward against the white curtain of snow. The horse reared as a stag with great antlers bounded out of a thicket. The mare twisted and turned. Maddie fell from the horse's back.

"Maddie!"

Rebecah tried to control the mare, but it reared and beat its hoofs. Her hands slipped from the reins. She twisted to ease the fall. She tried to get up, tried to reach, to brace herself. Then as she raised her head, she watched in horror as the mare galloped off, the reins dragging through the snow, its blonde mane whipping in the wind.

"No! Come back!" she shouted.

Maddie got to her feet. "Oh, Miss Rebecah. You hurt bad?"

Rebecah fell back. Her vision blurred. Shaking with cold, she put her hand up to her head and found blood there. The wind blew hard and stung her face. From the thicket, two wolves raced after the stag, leaped through the snow in a blur of gray over the hilltop. But one turned back. Its eyes locked onto the women. It crouched and snarled, stalked forward and growled.

The wind hit Rebecah like a fist to keep her down. Fear seized her, and she gasped. Maddie rushed back, grabbed a branch from the ground and swung it at the beast as it approached.

"Ha! Get away! Get away!"

She smacked the wolf's jaw. It yelped and raced off.

"It's alright, Miss Rebecah. He won't be back."

Against the wind, in each other's arms, the women headed toward Laurel Hill. Maddie hummed and sang as they went forward.

"I'm goin' through the wilderness. Yes, my Lord and me. Cross the river and the valley. My sweet Jesus and me."

Like a fire kindled in her bones, the words to the old spiritual moved Rebecah. She gazed down the hill at the house. Mustering the air in her lungs, she called out. Would he hear her over the din of the wind?

She stumbled forward. Her cloak caught something buried in the snow. She pulled at it and it tore. Tears swelled in her eyes, drifted along her cheeks, turning to ice crystals.

It could not happen. Not now. A cramp—it surged through her belly. She doubled over. Shocked, Maddie drew her close.

"Hold on to me, Miss Rebecah," Maddie cried. "Don't you let go!

* * *

Nash shot up from his chair. A moaning on the wind, he thought he heard her voice calling to him. A horse neighed. He rushed to open the door. *Her mare!*

Fear shook him, froze him in place. Rebecah was nowhere to be seen. But there stood her horse saddled and bridled without a rider, snow encrusted upon its coat and mane, its eyes wide and weary.

Joab drew up beside him. "It's Miss Rebecah's horse. Where is she?"

"I don't know, but I'm going to find her." Nash grabbed his hat and coat, and plunged out into the storm. Thrusting his boot into the stirrup, he mounted the horse. He followed the mare's tracks. A little ways and he stopped, cupped his hands over his mouth and called her name.

Climbing the hill, the snow drifted behind him. When he reached the top, he saw the women. Rebecah was on the ground, Maddie trying to lift her.

He dug his heels into the mare's ribs and the horse plunged through the mounting snow. Vaulting from the saddle, he gathered Rebecah into his arms. Snow caked her lashes. Her lips were blue.

"We were thrown. A stag came running, and then…there were wolves…," Maddie said swallowing hard. "I smacked one of them good, Mr. John. But poor Miss Rebecah."

"You're very brave, Maddie."

"Miss Rebecah, she's not good at all."

"We must hurry. You ride. I'll carry her."

"I tried to lift her, Mr. John…"

"It's alright, Maddie."

His heart trembled, fearing the cold had gone straight through her, fearing he might lose the love of his life.

He held her tight against him, trudged through the blinding sleet toward the house where the glow of the hearth fire reddened the windows.

Inside their room, a flood of firelight poured over the walls. The air had an icy scent, and the fire added the smell of cedar.

Nash crawled in beside Rebecah to warm her body, pulling her up against him and wrapping his arms around her beneath the blankets. It was around seven in the morning when he rose and changed his clothes. He stood at the window, looked at the snow-covered land.

"Jack?" Her quiet voice stirred him and he turned.

"Lay still, my love," he said, moving beside her. His fingers caressed her hair, and he leaned over to kiss her forehead.

"You found me. Oh, my love, you found me and Maddie." Easing against him, her eyes glowed. Part of him was angry for what she had done. The other could not blame her compassionate impulses.

She touched his face. "Are you cross with me?"

He traced her nose. "I should be."

"I would not blame you if you were."

"I could have lost you. You could have died out there." It was his greatest fear—losing her.

With a cry, she placed her arms around his neck. "I had to go when word came that Theresa was sick."

"I know, my love."

"And when her fever broke, and she was out of danger, Maddie and I had to come home." She moaned and drew up her knees. "Something is wrong. Oh, it hurts."

He laid her back. "Where?" He ran his hands over her, desperate to understand, to know what to do.

"Oh, Jack. Find Maddie."

He rushed to the door and opened it. "Maddie! Come quick. Miss Rebecah needs you."

Maddie's footsteps could be heard rushing up the staircase. When she entered the room, she moved Nash back and he listened to her speak gently to Rebecah.

"What can I do," he said, his body stiff with worry.

"Nothing you can do. Mr. John."

He stared at his wife as she curled up in pain.

Maddie put her hand on his arm. "You don't know, do you?"

He shook his head. "Know what?"

"Miss Rebecah is losing a child."

A heavy breath passed through his lips. "I…did not know. Why didn't you tell me, my darling?" And he sunk to his knees, picked up her hand, and pressed it to his lips.

"You've got to let me help her," Maddie said. "I know what to do. Have Joab boil some water and bring it up here."

He stood, watched Maddie draw back the covers. On Rebecah's white shift was blood. "Rebecah?" He grabbed Maddie's arm. "She's dying!"

"You go on now, Mr. John. Do as I asked."

"Yes," he murmured, turning out the door, his hands flexing in and out, beads of sweat forming on his brow. It was bad enough knowing they would lose their first child. But the thought he might lose her too caused his heart to beat like a hammer.

Please, God. Let her live.

He ran down the stairs, found Joab in the kitchen, gave him instructions, and returned to the staircase. Before he climbed it, he glanced out the frosted glass by the front door, saw a blur of the mountains beyond his fields white and blue with snow.

One retreat into those dark, sweet shadows with her, he thought. *Just one!* What care did he have for governors or kings, warriors or Redcoats now? All that mattered was the woman he loved.

* * *

Rebecah's eyes fluttered open. She turned her head, and through their window, she watched the snow tumble off the evergreen boughs on the hill. She ran her hand along her belly, knowing what had happened. A feeling of emptiness filled her. A part of her was gone. It was unexpected. She did not want this. It had been too early to tell him. What had she done wrong?

"Rest easy, Miss Rebecah," Maddie said.

"My babe?"

"Yes…gone, Miss Rebecah."

"Why, Maddie?"

"Not your fault. Blame it on that mangy wolf. He scared your horse and you were thrown. That's all it took."

Downstairs the door opened and shut. Footsteps tread the stairs. Maddie stood from the rocking chair at the bedside and opened the door.

Nash came in and moved aside to allow a man older than he to enter. Rebecah kept her eyes on Nash. His face was flushed from the cold, his eyes full of sadness.

"Rebecah, my love," he said. "This is Dr. Pierce. He's come to inquire after you."

"You must forgive me," the doctor smiled, "for not having brought Dr. Cole. He is indisposed with several of the townspeople."

He drew off his heavy coat and handed it to Joab. "I arrived yesterday. Dr. Cole sent for me. The epidemic was too much for one man. How are you feeling Mrs. Nash?"

How could she hide the grief in her eyes? "I do not know." She looked at Maddie and held her hand out to her, clasped it.

Dr. Pierce turned to Nash. "I need a moment with your wife. Her servant may stay in the room."

Outside the door, in the sunlit hallway, she knew he leaned against the wall, waiting, praying for her. Pierce timed her pulse, felt her forehead, and looked at her eyes. After gaining her permission, he drew back the bedcovers to examine her. He spoke kindly and asked her questions.

"You will need bed rest for several days to regain your strength. This happens to the majority of women. It was early in your pregnancy."

"It does not take the heartache away, Dr. Pierce."

"Indeed not. But you're able to have more children."

She turned into Maddie's arms. How warm they felt surrounding her like a mother cradling her child.

"Hush now." Maddie stroked her hair. "You cannot undo what has been done. Your little one is in Heaven, and one day you'll see him."

No words could end the pain squeezing her heart.

"A boy." And she turned her face to the wall and wept.

CHAPTER 20

Winter hurried on and soon a golden spring came. Dogwoods bloomed along with mountain laurel. Corn poked through the rich soil and grew tall into summer.

The year 1775 had thus far been a bittersweet one for John and Rebecah Nash. The loss of a child was one eternally in their hearts. Both had wondered what color their son's eyes would have been. What would it have felt like to have held their own? And then, Gus and Adele were gone far across the ocean to Germany, the likelihood of ever seeing them again was slim.

Letters arrived from England that had taken months to reach them. Lavinia wrote the family was well and missing them. Samuel Brent was the exception, and little was said of him. Lady Margaret had grown weak with the passing of her beloved, yet she kept busy with Mr. Wesley's ministry. Lavinia birthed a baby boy, named after his father. Dorene's child was thriving, a girl, but Dorene lacked maternal feelings and hired a nurse to care for the babe. Lanley was disappointed it had not been a son.

It was a shining morning, the leaves on the trees a soft green moving in the breeze. Rebecah and Maddie were washing clothes in the brook that ran at the bottom of the hill between the mountain and the house. With a sigh, Rebecah lifted her face to feel the warmth of the sunshine and the sweet caress of the breeze. Her heart hoped her beloved would come home soon, for she missed him terribly when he was gone for the woods.

She looked with longing at the path he had taken up the mountain, at the quivering leaves on the trees above it, at the shadows.

As much as she tried, Rebecah could not waylay her concerns. It pressed upon her, and the stories that she had heard coming in from the west and from Fort Frederick were enough to cause a restless mind. Then there was news coming in from Boston and Philadelphia. A declaration of independence was on the horizon, and fierce debates raged. In spite of the peace and solitude of the valley, her mind could not rest.

Maddie knelt next to Rebecah. They rubbed lye soap into the clothes making a great lather.

"You miss Mr. John?"

"I do, Maddie," she answered, wringing the chemise in her hands. "Did you know I've never washed clothes in my life until I came here? I was spoiled."

Maddie chuckled. "Your hands are too pretty and fine to do washing."

Rebecah smiled and sat on the grassy bank. Done with the wash, she slipped off her shoes and hiked up her skirts above her calves. She dipped her feet into the cool water.

"I'll carry the washing up to the house," said Maddie, lifting the basket. "Now, don't you go catchin' cold."

Rebecah shook out her hair until it fell over her shoulders and laughed regardless the heaviness in her heart. "You sound like Margery."

"Who is she?" Maddie swatted a stonefly away from her face.

"My servant back home. She practically raised me. She watched well over me as you do."

Maddie chuckled and swished her shoulders. "Praise be. Now I've work to do, instead of sittin' here talkin' the day away."

Rebecah stretched out her hand. "Maddie, I'm glad I am with child again."

Maddie smiled. "Oh, I is happy too. Children are a blessing from the Lord, and you are coming through your time well."

Rebecah ran her hand over her belly. "It won't be too long before he is born." This made thoughts of Indians and war fade. Joy filled her.

"How you know it's a boy? Could be a little girl."

Rebecah swished her feet back and forth in the stream, while Maddie glanced up at the hills.

"We best get back. No telling who might be up there in the forest, and I ain't leavin' you here by yourself."

Rebecah gathered up her shoes, and as they neared the house, a carriage pulled by a gray mare arrived.

"I felt bored at home," Theresa said, drawing to a stop. "May I stay a few days?"

Rebecah kissed her friend's cheek. "Of course you can. Your visit is a welcomed relief. Come inside."

She had no idea at that moment British soldiers were fleeing across the Potomac after a bloody confrontation.

* * *

No word had reached Rebecah, but she knew in her heart her beloved would return soon. At least she hoped and prayed, while feeling panic rising in her that she refused to show the others. As the sun was settling over the mountains, she lit a candle and set it in the window casement. If he were to come home during the night, he would see the light and it would lead him home to her arms.

They supped at seven. She moved the roasted sweet potatoes around on her plate and chatted with Theresa. They cleared the dishes, and Maddie set to work washing.

Joab went out to get more water from the well. Rebecah set to repairing one of her dresses. A rip ran down the side seam. It should have been cast out long ago, but such things were kept longer in the frontier.

Theresa read by candlelight near the hearth.

"I'm glad you have acquired some books at Laurel Hill, Rebecah."

"They are precious indeed. What have you chosen?"

Theresa turned to the spine and read, "Robinson Crusoe."

"Yes, it is one of my favorites."

"He was a man tested like many here in the frontier."

"Indeed that is true. He was in solitude until he met Friday, and he grew closer to God, not through hearing sermons or attending church, but in his loneliness with only a Bible to read."

Theresa sighed. "I can only imagine such a life. He was very ingenious in the ways of survival. Oh, and the natives. Just reading about them gave me the shivers."

Rapid footsteps approached, and Joab ran inside the room. Looking panicked, he stood before Rebecah trying to catch his breath.

"Joab, what is it?" A chill raced through her seeing the fear in his eyes. "What is wrong?"

"Redcoats coming—four on foot—two on horseback."

Theresa rushed to the window and drew back. "He's right."

Rebecah hurried beside her friend. Two officers on horseback rode side by side. The one horse a dapple-gray that hung its head low as it ambled forward. The other steed was taller than its companion, chestnut brown with a flowing mane and a high step.

The men on foot marched with an effort. Their uniforms were dirty and ragged, the white wool breeches smeared with dirt, the coats dingy russet.

Rebecah unbolted the door and went out on the porch. The riders drew rein. The officer to the left drew off his hat and inclined his head in gentlemanly fashion, while the other stared at her with guile.

"Madam," said the officer, bowing in the saddle. "Captain Taylor at your service."

"Welcome to Laurel Hill, Captain." She could have choked on the word *welcome*. "I am Mrs. Rebecah Nash. May I present Miss Theresa Boyd?"

"It is an honor, ladies. I can see Miss Boyd is no doubt born to the Colonies. But to find an English lady here in the wilderness is indeed a surprise."

"No more than to see you upon it, sir." She pinched her brows a moment, wondering how he could tell the difference between her and Theresa. Theresa had not said a word. "Are you far from your regiment, Captain?"

"Yes, we are far indeed, madam. My men and I have been traveling for days."

"You are lost?"

"I've no cause to explain how we came to be in this part of Maryland. The exploits of military affairs would bore you," Taylor said. "We are quite weary, and shall need food and lodging, at least for the night."

"Our barn and stable is adequate, Captain. We've oats and hay for your horses." She knew they'd take them whether she offered them or not.

He looked over at it, shifting in the saddle, then at the officer mounted beside him.

"Search the grounds," he ordered.

"Is that necessary?" she said, watching the armed soldiers pass her. "Your men will find nothing except hay and livestock."

"Where is your husband, Mrs. Nash?"

"He is away on business, but shall return soon."

"He has left you here unguarded?"

"Not at all. Joab is an excellent shot." She glanced at Joab. He stood near her, musket in hand.

Taylor laughed. "One old man is not enough to hold off a war party, madam."

388

"The warring tribes are to the west, Captain. We've nothing to fear here."

"I hope you're right, Mrs. Nash, especially seeing you are carrying a child. But I must warn you, we encountered a band of warriors on the other side of the Potomac. Eight of my men were killed. And we heard in Virginia, that several settler families in the frontier have suffered at the hands of savages. They're closer than you might believe."

Of course his news caused dread to rise within her. If it were true, her beloved would be returning any time now to protect her. He would know just how close they were.

Taylor dismounted and proceeded up the stairs booted and spurred. "Fortunate for you we are here. I'll post a guard. But I shall not impose upon your privacy. We are gentlemen, madam. The barn shall suit us."

"How long do you intend to stay, Captain?"

"We will be gone in the morning. To stay longer would be unwise."

"Indeed. Unwise and unjust."

* * *

That night the stars stood out bright as winter frost, innumerable as the sands of the sea against a coal sky. The breeze whispered and stirred through moonlit trees. The air smelled sweet with the aroma of wild grape and ripening blackberries. A man could taste it upon the tongue as he took in a lung-full of air.

By day, the sun had heated the ground. It felt warm to the touch beneath Nash's blanket. The river murmured below the clefts, a peaceful cadence in a strange world.

He looked up at the stars, his musket in the crook of his arm. A meteor arched across the sky and vanished, a second one followed.

He wished the world were different. He thought of his father, and the arrows of grief returned.

He thought of his beloved. Rebecah was waiting. He should have been home days ago. She must be worried. At sunrise, he would head back. Perhaps this would be the last time he would patrol so far.

Perhaps it was time to remain on his own land, with her beside him.

CHAPTER 21

Captain Taylor and his men were now within the barn snoring away after dining on Laurel Hill's venison. The sentry Taylor posted outside the house stood armed beneath the sycamore.

Rebecah's eyes fluttered open after a dream left her heart beating and her soul longing for Nash. She turned her head, reached out and touched the cold pillow beside her. She gathered it into her arms.

Where is he? Why has he not come home?

Days had come and gone, long, lonely days. Missing him, yearning to see him, to hear his voice, to be held by him was a hard thing to carry, and the worry was even worse.

She looked out the window where the moon was shining. Was he looking up at that orb the same moment as she? She felt him, as if he were there with her.

"God," she whispered. "Keep Jack safe. Bring my beloved home to me."

An hour before dawn she could sleep no longer, and so she rose and dressed in brown homespun, the bodice laced with faded blue ribbons. At the mirror, she lit a candle and combed out her hair. She would let it hang free today, for he liked it such. Soon the sun would rise, and perhaps then she would see him coming down the mountain path toward home.

391

She slipped on her boots. Lacing them, her hair fell over her shoulders. She went downstairs and opened the door. The sentry turned, tipped his hat, and returned to his watch.

She scanned the dark line of trees, the gentle slope of the mountain. The sun peeked above the horizon, the light a thread of magenta. She put her head against the post and waited. She must be the first thing he sees.

The call of a woodland bird hung on the breeze, low and ominous in its murmuring. The sound startled her. Shadows moved among the trees. The sentry brought down his musket. He pulled back the hammer and it clicked. Captain Taylor appeared in the doorway of the barn tucking in his shirt.

A form leaped from the trees and ran toward the house, doubling over, disappearing into the darkness. Another moved and sunk to the ground.

The sentry turned and warned her to retreat inside. Taylor, with his flintlock pistol in hand, rushed forward with his men, and shouted to her when he saw her terrified face. She ran back through the door. Joab and Maddie were in the kitchen.

"What is it Mrs.?" said Joab, placing the firebrand back in its place.

"Indians! Lock every window and door."

Joab threw the bolt over the kitchen door. Maddie lifted her hands away from the bread dough. "Lord, have mercy on us."

"Maddie, hurry and wake Miss Theresa."

A musket hung above the fireplace. Joab had it down in a flash, and with hurried fingers swung the powder horn and shot pouch over his shoulder.

"Jack. Oh, Jack," Rebecah whispered. She looked out the window beside the front door. The warriors were smeared with war paint. Beaded belts held their tomahawks, shot and powder pouches.

One man in particular stood out among them. He was their leader, a man of no nation or origin, a man who warred by his own rules, and commanded with bewitching power. He was called murderer and thief, and Rebecah had encountered him once before.

Jean LaRoux raised his musket over his head.

Rebecah threw her hands against her ears to drown out his bloodcurdling cry. She retreated from the window. She could not block the sounds, the blasts of flintlock and musket, the cries and war whoops.

Dim light came through the loopholes in the shutters. She rallied, pulled another musket from the wall and poured gunpowder into the barrel.

Joab turned to Rebecah. "Mrs. I see dead Redcoats out there, and the rest are running away."

"Cowards," Rebecah said, thrusting in the ramrod.

"They're abandoning us. No one will be here to help us." Theresa stood in the center of the room with Maddie beside her. There were no tears in her eyes, no tremble in her voice. Only she stared at the door locked in fear as footsteps pounded up the steps, onto the porch.

Joab shouted over his shoulder against the noise. "I'll hold them off as long as I can, but you women get out through the back. Run into the woods and stay low."

The thuds against the door chilled the blood.

"I can't leave you, Joab."

"I'm right behind you, Mrs. You got to get out now."

Again and again, the Indians rammed their shoulders against the door.

"Run! Run!"

Maddie and Theresa reached out and holding each other, they ran to the back of the house and cautiously went out in the misty air coming down the hills. Rebecah's heart pounded. Pulsing fear trembled through her. They tried to reach the cover of the trees, tried to escape what could mean their capture or even death.

393

But the Indians were upon them, pulling at them, dragging them, throwing banded arms around them.

"Be still or die!" shouted LaRoux, yanking Rebecah by the hair.

LaRoux swung her around, trying to control her, but she fought back like a wildcat. She bit his hand and he threw her down. Her hair fell over her eyes. She looked up. He stared at her, his legs spread-eagle across her body.

Rebecah would rather fight and die, than be taken into the wilderness by this horrid creature. And so, she turned upon him, beating at him with her hands. She kicked and shouted. She twisted against him. Maddie and Theresa tried to reach her, but were prevented. Tearful they urged her to stop for fear LaRoux would kill her. Indeed LaRoux would have when he forced her on her knees and jerked her head back by her hair. She cried out. He pulled his knife and laid the blade against her throat.

"Kill me," she whispered. "I'd rather die than go with you." Then she remembered she carried a life and regretted what she had said.

"Ah, I know your face," he said. "You were the woman in the coach. Perhaps I should kill the others instead." He grabbed her chin, moved her face close to his. His breath was hot and foul.

Rebecah winched and tears pooled in her eyes. He stared at them, for they looked like crystal with sunlight striking them. She was beautiful even now, but he did not let it soften him.

"No," she whimpered. "Please, do not hurt them. Let them go."

LaRoux laughed and pulled her up. "You will come with me."

"Please. I'm with child."

An Indian stood behind them, and LaRoux pushed her back against him. "Bring her," he ordered. He then turned and walked ahead.

The Indian held her up and spoke in his native tongue. She moved on with him following her. She glanced back at the house.

Joab. Was he alive?

Shaken and frightened the women walked past the dead. They had been scalped. Rebecah hid her eyes from the gruesome scene of blood and torn flesh. Theresa threw her hands over her eyes, cried. She called for her father and shook within the cruel hands that held her.

Rebecah turned to her.

"Theresa—"

Theresa looked at Rebecah with such misery and helplessness that her breath escaped her. Maddie's face was one of horror and sorrow.

"Maddie," and she threw out her arms to her.

The trees swallowed them in the misty darkness. Rebecah's face was wet with tears, her heart pounding as the world spun. Trembling, for the dark, for the shadowy hemlocks encompassing her, for the hands that pushed her forward, she laid her face against Maddie's shoulder.

"Jack. Jack, my love," she whispered against a rising wind.

CHAPTER 22

Nash stopped at the edge of a cliff overlooking the Potomac. Deep pools swirled below and great fish moved like shadows within them. Reflecting the trees and the twilight sky, the river murmured like a cooing mother giving life to all upon her banks.

An eagle cried, wheeled like windblown thistle above the jagged rocks imbedded deep into the river. The breeze lifted it higher until it reached the top of a tall pine.

Normally to see such a magnificent bird would have caused Nash to smile. But not today, not after he had discovered his wife and two others had been taken by renegades.

He stalked down the narrow path to lower ground where the murmur of the river grew louder. He and his men had spread out, and seeing the position of the sun, he headed back to join Clarke and then the others further downstream.

For a week now, he ate the dried venison in his pouch, drank from the river and streams, and slept restless in the woods. He followed the old hunting paths. Here he found broken twigs on bushes and a woman's ribbon. He snatched it in his hand, smelled lavender and rosewater upon it.

Rebecah! He knew then she was alive.

He had seen crouching on a limestone cliff a mountain cat with its ears flattened and its jaws snarling with hunger. He had seen a solitary bear on the hillside prowl through the woods, halt, and pant, with its hair on end.

All these he expected, but what he saw now evoked a deeper instinct of caution. He crouched and examined tracks. He waited, listened to the sounds of the woods and wind, discerning anything different. A moment more and he stood, the tassels of his sleeves flitting in the breeze.

Sinking back, he fixed his eyes upon a man coming in his direction. Sweat beaded on his forehead and soaked his hair. A green-eyed horsefly whirled before his face, fierce for the taste of salt and blood. Nash flinched, but dare not move.

The Indian paused. Then he bent and drank from a stream of water flowing down the limestone wall. He wore no war paint. But his dusky, half-naked body glistened with oil. He stood there, dressed in his beaded leggings and moccasins, clout and sporran, like some regal prince of the wilderness. His face umber. His eyes black as coal.

Narrowing his eyes, Nash looked through the trees. Another warrior crept among them. A moment more and another brave moved up the edge of the mountain slope, so close that Nash could make out the scar on his right cheek.

This was enough evidence for him, and so he remained still until they moved on. He started at a run up the mountain slope, plunging through rhododendron and wild grape vines. Meteor lifted his head, flicked his ears. Nash pulled up onto his back and dug in his heels.

The sun sunk deeper. The last remnants of rays drove deep into the water and the fathomless forest. Faster Nash went along the leafy trail. He smelled pine and rotting leaves. Another odor hung in the air, the putrid scent of death and blood. He drew rein. Before him hung scalps, eagle feathers, and other ornaments meant to strike fear into the heart. His blood ran cold. A chill ran up his spine. He saw something hunched against a tree.

Clarke was dead. Blood covered his face and dripped down his neck into his buckskins.

Anger rose and Nash choked under its force. Then he smelled the scent of savage men, unmistakable as the scents of bear and elk, fox and wolf. There was no time to grieve or bury his friend.

He moved off the path and dismounted. A bullet smacked the trunk of a pine, splintered the wood beside him. He turned to meet the attackers. Angry Bear was on Nash before he could fire. One sinewy fist slammed into his face, while a knife caught the last glimmer of sunlight across its blade.

Nash raised his musket and blocked the blow. Angry Bear threw his body against him, and they tumbled together down the slope.

Nash's head struck a rock and the world went dark.

* * *

Awakening to the smell of charred flesh and the angry speech of those not his own people, fear seized Nash. His heart quickened to strike against his chest. His temples throbbed. The taste of blood and earth were in his mouth.

Before he lifted his head from the ground, he uttered, "Preserve me from men of violence. Help me now in my time of trouble."

The words slipped from his lips slurred and whispered. His head ached. Scratches from woodland bushes were upon his face and hands, caked with dirt and sweat. He had been dragged through thorny briars and sharp twigs on the way to the Indian encampment.

His bruised mouth bled and the blood caked in a corner of his lips. He tasted it, and spit out the tainted saliva into the dust. He pushed himself up on his knees. A word was shouted fierce and bitter. Laughter followed. Warriors moved around him.

His vision cleared and what he saw before him caused his stomach to heave. He gasped at the gruesome sight—a blackened corpse. Flesh peeled away, revealed bone and sinew, the faceless head hanging against a hollow breast, now fodder for crows and buzzards.

Who this unfortunate soul had been, Nash did not know. He could have been anyone—a settler, soldier, or trapper. A gust of wind whipped through the trees, stirred the embers at the foot of the pyre.

"You'll die as this one did." An Indian crouched beside him. "You'll die for the death of Logan's people."

It was Angry Bear who spoke. He now carried Nash's musket, pouch and powder horn. A fresh scalp hung from his belt, no doubt the scalp of the unfortunate human being dead against the charred post—or, *dear Lord*, Andrew Clarke's.

He stood to face him, his muscles stiff with rage. The bitter wind howled in his ears, and clouds above him blocked the sun.

Clenching his teeth, Angry Bear struck him in the ribs. The fierce blow knocked him to his knees. He remained there a moment with his breath heaving. Angry Bear pulled his knife. Nash believed the warrior would have plunged it into his heart. But it would have been too quick a death. The stake was slower.

He hoped he could have broken free and wrestled the warrior's knife from his hand. But other hands held him fast. They tied him to the post. He strained to get free. His sweaty hair hung over his eyes. The shadow of death approached him, and in the horror and gloom, he saw it leering.

The Indians' awful cries were deafening. They piled sticks and branches around his feet, stuffed dry moss into the spaces. Terror shocked Nash out of his senses. He cried out to God, and called Rebecah's name in a coarse murmur, for his throat closed and choked.

Angry Bear stepped up to him, a splinter of lit wood in his hand. He passed it before Nash. Nash drew back. Then Angry Bear touched it to flesh. Nash clenched his teeth and let out a muffled cry. He panted for air, forced back the sting of tears forming in his eyes.

A voice called out. As one the Indians turned. Out of the forest a chief came forward, his half-naked body glistening with bear fat, his beaded leggings gartered above his knees with scarlet cloth, his hair dressed with eagle feathers.

With his face painted for war, he looked fierce and aged from his turmoil. An entourage of braves followed him. Raising his face proudly, he stepped up to Angry Bear and took the flaming stick from his hand. His eyes turned to Nash.

Would he remember their friendship? Would Logan show mercy on his brother who never did him or his people any harm?

CHAPTER 23

The women huddled in each other's arms. LaRoux sat across from them eating a piece of meat his men had roasted over the fire. His face looked hard, creased, and his black eyes cold as onyx.

Rebecah watched him through the gray haze, wondering what he planned to do. Theresa's head nodded against her shoulder. She was thankful the girl slept, that her tears had dried for now. Maddie too.

Terrified, her emotions ran as high as the mountain that loomed before her. Yet for the child she carried, Theresa and Maddie, she knew she must bury her emotions and guard her tongue. She must clear her head and use God-given wisdom and courage as her guides.

LaRoux glanced over at her.

"What is it you intend to do with us?" she asked.

He threw a gnawed bone into the fire. "Much of that will be up to you. We go to a village west of here. Life among the Indians isn't so bad."

"Then you mean to trade us to the Shawnee."

LaRoux crawled forward and crouched in front of her. "When we first met, it was not a good thing?"

"No."

"You will find it was. I intend to keep you for myself."

Rebecah stared back at him, panic growing within, as he stood and walked away. Theresa moved in her arms and awoke with a fright.

"Hush, my dear." Rebecah caressed Theresa's hair. "It is well. Go back to sleep."

Rebecah felt her shudder. She watched LaRoux stand and walk away. He blended with the darkness as if it were a part of him. And she thought how true that was.

"Are you frightened, Rebecah?" Theresa whispered.

"Try to sleep."

"Are you weeping?"

"I am, though I'm trying not to."

"We shall help each other, you, Maddie, and me."

"At least we have each other."

"Oh, my poor father. How shall he bear it?"

"My husband and his men will look for us." Her heart throbbed and her hands shook. "We must try to find home again. We must believe and trust that it shall be so. As we travel we must leave signs for the men so they can find us—cloth from our dresses, ribbons, broken twigs on the bushes, anything to give them a sign."

Theresa looked over at LaRoux, his back to them and his figure cut in blackness against the shadows of the hemlocks, etched by grim moonlight.

"I pray he pays for the evil he has done," she said.

Rebecah pulled her closer and looked at LaRoux, but with different eyes. "What matters is escape and rescue. Leave LaRoux's fate to God."

* * *

Dawn rose. Rebecah opened her eyes. A broken night of restless sleep had ended, and reality came flying back at her.

LaRoux pulled her up, separated her from the other women. Hands stretched out to her, but she could not reach them. The Indian who had been kind to her followed, then the women and the rest of LaRoux's ragtag band of scoundrels.

Rebecah stumbled over a root. The Indian helped her up. She asked his name. Grey Wolf it was. He could speak not much more English than that. His speech was Delaware, and from time to time he motioned with his hands for her to understand. There upon a limb, a red bird. Here a stream to drink from. What had brought him into LaRoux's band of men she did not know. She found it bewildering he was with them.

They entered a mountain pass where the river roared over rocks and black cliffs loomed. Theresa and Rebecah were strong enough to make the difficult trek, but Maddie struggled. Rebecah moved back to her and looped her arm around Maddie's waist.

"Here, let me help you."

Maddie held onto Rebecah. Roots and stones barred the way. With each step, Maddie heaved her breath. She was testing LaRoux's patience, which was a perilous thing to do. Rebecah tightened her hold.

"Maddie, you mustn't weep. We will make it. Once we reach the bottom it will come easier."

LaRoux turned his fierce eyes. He waited as they drew closer. "She is too weak." His lips curled into a snarl. His dirty hands were upon Maddie and he yanked her away. Rebecah and Theresa cried out, shrieking and clinging to Maddie as he dragged her from them.

Grey Wolf looked on.

"You would leave her here to die," cried Rebecah. "You mustn't."

LaRoux thrust Maddie on the ground. "Would you rather I kill her now?"

Rebecah rushed forward. "Let her alone."

"She stays behind," spat LaRoux. "She is too slow."

"I'll not take another step without her."

LaRoux put his hands on his hips and laughed. Rebecah burned with anger. She had tried to be diplomatic for the good of the women and herself. However, with LaRoux's cruelty, those reins of constraint slipped through her hands.

"How I wish I had that knife of yours," she said, her eyes aflame. "For if I did, I would plunge it into your heartless chest before you laid another hand on us."

His smug smile faded. He grabbed her wrist and squeezed.

"You're a woman. You are weak. What you wish to do cannot be done. For what you speak is it not a sin in the eyes of your god?"

"What is in my heart, you'll never know."

He threw her off. Grey Wolf stood behind her and caught Rebecah. LaRoux grunted and turned to go. "Mother," said Grey Wolf, "needs dark-faced woman."

LaRoux paused and watched as Grey Wolf helped Maddie to her feet. He lifted the old woman into his arms and carried her as if she were a feather.

Rebecah wondered if LaRoux were losing the allegiance of Grey Wolf. He would have no man turn on him. She had no doubt at the first sign of betrayal he would try to kill Grey Wolf.

She glanced back. It was the farthest she had been from home. Her Maryland, her home, her beloved—they were behind her now and how her heart throbbed.

The wind murmured and it began to drizzle. She clasped her empty stomach, where hunger was now a common thing. She longed to comfort the child within her womb. *Let my child survive, dear God.*

A few miles upriver, they made camp for the night. Exhausted, their feet sore and their bodies aching, the women huddled together against the trunk of a beech tree.

Grey Wolf walked into the forest. A moment later the crack of a musket echoed through the woodland. The sound startled the women, all looking up hoping it meant rescue. Instead, it meant they would eat that night. He brought them meat, of what kind they did not know.

Grey Wolf glanced over at Rebecah, and in the glare of firelight and smoke, she saw pity in his eyes. Could it be possible he felt compassion for three unfortunate women, one carrying a child, the other young and frightened, the last a poor black woman who had endured hardship and despair all her life only to think she now faced the remainder of her days a slave to Indians? Rebecah could not tell, yet she hoped his heart convicted him.

* * *

At the break of dawn, the women were given water, but no food. Her stomach growling, Rebecah quickly gathered the nuts that lay on the ground. Before LaRoux could catch her, she handed some to Maddie and Theresa, and shoved the rest into the pocket of her tattered dress.

On they traveled along the Potomac's north branch, the mountains shadowing the water in lush splendor. Another river they met, the Savage, as it tumbled and spilled into the Potomac. They crossed to the other side, walked through great forests, rested beside gurgling streams with rocky waterfalls, where the trees were enormous.

Over a crest, they came to an Indian village. The women looked down at the lodges, the campfires, the children romping in the grass, the Indian women cooking over a fire. Rebecah wanted to die then and there. Then she felt her baby move and set her hand across the tiny imprint of a foot. Tears sprang into her eyes.

Maddie put her arm around her. "It'll be alright. At least we are together."

Theresa laid her head on Maddie's shoulder and together the women, clinging to each other, made their way toward the village.

I must be strong. I mustn't let them see me cry.

CHAPTER 24

"I have found their trail," Black Hawk said, as he walked through the fog of the forest. He studied the prints along the ground, the disturbed leaves and broken twigs. He moved to the right, paused a few yards off from the others.

"They traveled west along the ridge."

"Nash and Clarke, you think? Or the women?" asked Maldowney.

"Both. Many signs here." He hovered his hand over the path. He bounded ahead and the men followed. Black Hawk froze and raised his hand to halt. He turned.

"Turn away if you cannot look upon the face of a dead man."

"Who is it?" asked Dr. Pierce.

"It is Mr. Clarke."

Maldowney moved ahead. Dr. Pierce and Mr. Boyd followed a few yards back. And that is when they saw the body of Andrew Clark, his bloody head hanging low upon his breast, his hands clenched at his sides.

"Ah, poor Mr. Clarke." Mr. Boyd looked away.

Robert Maldowney sunk to his knees beside the lifeless heap of misery. Black Hawk crouched beside him.

"Warriors have done this. My brother fought them here." Black Hawk pointed with his hand northward. "If they had killed him, he too would be here dead."

"Then Nash has been taken prisoner?" Maldowney said.

Black Hawk nodded. "They will kill him."

Maldowney straightened out Andrew Clark's limbs and crossed his hands over his chest. After he spoke a prayer, they left him lying in the forest with the leaves of past autumns to cover him.

* * *

Logan listened to Angry Bear's discourse. He'd captured a white man, triumphed taking the scalp of another. Logan raised his hand. Angry Bear acquiesced.

When Logan turned, Nash raised his bruised face. He looked over at the war chief through the strands of sweaty hair hanging over his eyes. His breath heaved. Sweat beaded upon his forehead and trickled down his face, mingling with the blood upon his lips.

He could not attempt to approach him, for he was still bound hand and foot, but free from the threat of being burned alive—at least for now. Logan loved him once as a son, even now spared him. But would he give in to Angry Bear's demands?

His body was weak from hunger and torture, and yet he stood before the sachem. The old man walked around Nash, paused and made a mystic gesture with his hand. Over his chest hung a gruesome deerskin thong of bones and painted red figures. The scalplocks of his enemies hung from his belt. His face, painted white, appeared ghost-like. He shook a rattle of turtle shell and weaved around Nash.

Nash did not move when Angry Bear leaned near.

"He has powerful medicine," Angry Bear said with a curled lip. "The words he speaks, he speaks to all white men."

"I don't fear his magic," Nash said. "God, who made earth and sky and sea, guards me against his evil words."

Around Nash crowded warriors. From the woods they came, from the rocky crags overlooking the river. They crouched on the ground around Nash. Most were young men edgy for battle. There were twenty-three of them, including Angry Bear, twenty-three lithe braves, stripped to their belts, oiled with the fat of the bear, their hair dressed in eagle feathers, painted for war.

Angry Bear fisted Nash's musket. A fresh scalp hung from his beaded belt, no doubt the scalp of a man who had once been Nash's friend. Clarke had fought beside Nash, drank ale with him, broke bread at his table, laughed with him, debated him. The gruesome sight caused his soul to lurch. Grief and rage dug its talons deep.

When he thought of Rebecah and her plight, and what might lie ahead for her, his heart groaned.

Sunlight fell upon Chief Logan, and it bothered Nash to see how old he now appeared. He had gone from peacemaker to war chief in the prime of his life. Cruelty shone in his eyes, not the warm and wise look that Nash had known before.

Logan motioned to Nash to speak.

"Many moons ago we smoked the peace pipe in your lodge, you gave me the honor of an Indian name, you welcomed me with open arms."

"I did those things. You are still a son to me."

Nash sighed. "I am thankful you still love me as your own, and since I have taken a wife, she is also part of your family. I seek her among the tribes. "

Logan's impassive stare etched with interest. "You have taken a wife?"

"Yes."

"Why do you seek her among the tribes?"

"She and two other women were taken. You know the pain of losing those you love. Hear my cause and let me go free to find her. She carries my child. Let the peace that we've had between us remain strong."

Logan's troubled eyes peered at Nash through the smoke. He turned to the men around him. "The white man seeks his wife among our people. How many of our women have been taken? How many children murdered and left for the wolves and vultures?"

"There have been many," Nash said. "Must my wife and unborn child be counted among them? If you let me live, I will find her, and I will speak of the mercy of Logan and of his wisdom."

"I have heard of three women taken from the valley near the great river by a man not of the Nations, not of the English."

Stunned, Nash stared at Logan. *LaRoux!* Although he knew, he asked, "Who is this man?"

"Jean LaRoux—your enemy and mine."

"Then let me hunt him down. Let me save her and the others."

Logan swung his hand forward. "Let him go."

Angry Bear stood. With ruthless eyes, he drew his tomahawk and threw down a challenge. "Let us see how brave this man is you call a son. Let him prove he is a better warrior than I."

Angry Bear let out a loud cry, raised the tomahawk above his head. He ran toward Nash. Nash caught him by his wrist. Locked together, the two men struggled against each other with barred teeth. Nash wrestled Angry Bear to the ground, pressed his arm toward the hot coals. The tomahawk fell from Angry Bear's hand when the blistering heat touched his flesh.

The warriors cheered them on, and Logan watched in silence. With his knee against Angry Bear's chest, Nash grabbed the tomahawk and raised it. He could have buried the blade into Angry Bear's skull, but instead he struck it into the ground an inch from Angry Bear's temple.

"I'm no murderer," Nash shouted at the stunned warrior. "You wanted my death and you killed my friend. I have spared yours. You're indebted to me the remainder of your life."

Angry Bear drew himself up, squaring his shoulders. He nodded, acknowledging his defeat. Nash turned to Logan. Logan held his arm out to Nash.

"My soul is grieved for your family, my brother," Nash said, taking hold of the chief's arm, looking into Logan's eyes.

"I know your words are true and from your heart." Logan swept his hand toward the forest. "Go and find her."

And so, Nash went into the forest, his musket, powder horn, and shot restored to him, his eyes fixed west toward the everlasting mountains in search of the woman he loved and the man he meant to kill.

Chapter 25

Though Jean LaRoux had led this band of renegades through the frontier to rob, steal, and murder, he was not their leader in Grey Wolf's village. His face was new to them, but word of him had reached their ears many moons ago, before the flowers of the woods had bloomed and the locusts twilled in the heat of day.

Grey Wolf was chief, and he welcomed Rebecah and Theresa into his lodge, to dwell with his wives, Open Flower and White Fawn. Theresa was terrified of him, but Rebecah showed no fear and much respect. Grey Wolf did not wish them as wives for he laughed he had enough and plenty of children to feed. They were the slaves of his wives, and work they did from before the sun rose to long into the night.

The day they were brought to the village was a frightening one. The people gathered around a fire. The women sang and then were silent. It was a time of testing to see which among the women were the strongest. Thrust into the dirt beside the fire, their arms went around each other, until they were yanked apart.

Rebecah sat upon her knees. Her hopes of being treated with kindness were dashed by what she witnessed, and what was to come. She stared in horror as Theresa was dragged closer to the fire, her hands and feet bound with strips of leather cords. Listening to Theresa weep, she shook with fear for her friend's life.

She dug her hands into the dust. Her eyes remained fixed upon Theresa. The panic in the young girl's eyes was unbearable to see. Rebecah pleaded with Grey Wolf, but his face never turned to hers. She looked back at Theresa and stretched out her hand.

"Be strong," she said. "They will not kill you. Be strong."

A whimper escaped Theresa's lips. All color drained from her face. "Do not come near," she managed to say through her tears. "Look away."

Four braves and a squaw surrounded Theresa. The braves held her down. The squaw bent over and scratched Theresa's limbs with a stick covered in thorns. Theresa cried. Thin trickles of blood ran along her legs into the dirt.

Her heart pounding, Rebecah struggled to stand, being great with child. Her mind raced and reeled. She called out to Grey Wolf. LaRoux stood beside him with his arms folded.

"You must stop this! She is but a girl," she pleaded. "She has done no harm to any of you."

Grey Wolf lifted his head and made a motion with his hands to the people.

When it was over, Rebecah and Maddie washed Theresa's wounds and applied the healing salve an Indian woman had supplied them. Maddie cradled her in her arms and hummed.

From that first day, every bone in Rebecah's body ached. She worked in the garden and washed clothing in the stream. She stood in the morning light at the edge of the water, her hand against the small of her back. LaRoux sat on a rock watching her.

"You should not be a slave. It would be wise to have a husband."

"I have a husband."

"After the child comes, I may want you."

"Then I pray God takes me before that time."

LaRoux plunged his knife into the ground. "And if God does not?"

She paused and pushed back her hair. LaRoux stood. He lifted her up by her arms. Pressing her against him, she trembled. His fierce eyes searched hers.

"I would have had you that day on the road if it had not been for the man in the trees."

Enraged, she shook herself free from his grip. She went to lift her basket to go but he yanked her back.

"You would have warmed to me, Rebecah. I would not have needed to force you after the first kiss." Then he pressed his lips hard against hers. Disgusted, she shoved him back and he laughed. "It is too much for you?"

She wiped her mouth. "You disgust me."

LaRoux took a step forward. "I am weary of this game," he shouted.

She hurried away with tearful eyes. Sunlight poured through the trees and warmed her face. But her hands, oh how cold they felt, and the sick feeling from that forced kiss would never leave her.

Jack. Oh, Jack, my love. Find me.

Beside Grey Wolf's lodge a kettle hung on crossed sticks simmering over a fire. Open Flower and White Fawn sat on the ground beside it and smiled to Rebecah. Neither looked as poetic as their names. Their white deerskin clothing was striking and they kept their hair in a single braid, but life in the wild had marred their faces.

"Good day, English woman," Open Flower said.

"Good day," she said and paused.

White Fawn made a graceful gesture with her hand. "Come, sit with us."

"I've much work to do."

"Mother has worked enough. You must rest now."

Rebecah nodded in assent. "I'll go and rest, but inside the lodge."

Maddie was tending a child who had fallen and scraped his knees. She had become a medicine woman, and her skills kept her from being traded to another village.

"I shall go mad if I must stay her another day," Rebecah said, and explained what LaRoux had done.

"You must tell Gray Wolf," said Theresa. "Perhaps he will send LaRoux out of the village."

"Gray Wolf would not understand."

Maddie shook her head. "No matter where I go, there's trouble. But we'll cross over Jordan in the good Lord's time."

Rebecah looked at the old woman with wide eyes. "What are you saying, dear Maddie? Are we to die in this place?"

"We'll live. You'll see."

"But LaRoux—"

"Now don't you worry about LaRoux. He'll not last long, an evil man like that. You got to think about your babe."

"Yes." Rebecah ran her hands over her belly. The babe moved from her touch. "My time is soon, and I'm frightened. You will help me, won't you?"

Maddie closed her hand over Rebecah's. "I've birthed lots of babies, Miss Rebecah, and you is a strong woman. It'll be fine."

Theresa handed Rebecah a wooden bowl filled with water. How different she looked. The sun had turned her skin tawny and bleached her blonde hair almost white. Rebecah too had changed. Her creamy skin was darker now, her hair sun-streaked with gold.

"I've been thinking," she said, taking the water from Theresa with a grateful nod. "We should try to escape while the men are gone. I heard Grey Wolf speak of it. God have mercy on those they may meet."

Theresa sat beside her. "I've been hoping we all would go. But Maddie is old, Rebecah. She may not make it."

Maddie cackled. "I'm old but strong." She scooted the child out the opening. "I got to go with you, to bring Miss Rebecah and her baby through the birthin'."

"And what about you, Rebecah?" Theresa said. "Perhaps we should wait until after the child has come. It would be too difficult for you to travel."

"My child is safer in my womb, then in this village."

"But there's no telling how long it will take us. What if you have the child on the way? Oh, Rebecah, you're certain?"

"More certain than anything. We must try."

Theresa bit her lower lip. "It will be dangerous."

"I know. But I'm willing to take that risk."

"We'll make it if we trust that God will show us the way, and not fear our going," said Maddie.

Theresa laid he head across her drawn knees. "I miss home. I miss my father."

Rebecah grasped her friend's hand. "I know, for I ache sore for my husband. All this time I've believed he is searching for us. If we try to follow the river, we may meet up with him. There is no other thing for us to do but to go home."

The three women put their arms around each other. Tears slipped from their eyes when they recited a Psalm together.

The Lord is my shepherd I shall not want...He leadeth me beside still waters. . . ."

CHAPTER 26

Nash searched the old hunting trails for any imprint of moccasin or boot. He looked for signs, but found none save what animals had left. Above the Potomac were the oldest trails used long before the white man stepped foot there or whose eye had seen the ridge of mountains.

The heat was high, and the leaves on the trees curled. Locusts and cicadas whirled in the forests. By dusk, the river reflected the colors of the setting sun. The horizon filled with thunderheads. Deep rumbling rolled and in the distance, he saw lightning streak across the sky.

In a clearing stood Fort Frederick. A sentry standing on the wall saw Nash walking toward the gate. "Who goes there?"

"John Nash of the Catoctin Rangers. God bless our country and hang King George!"

A moment later, the heavy door opened. A troop of patriots greeted him as he ducked through the opening.

"I'm searching for my wife." He addressed the corporal in charge. "She and two other women were taken captive by the Indians."

"There are others looking for them as well." The corporal turned, his bayonet catching the glow of sunset. He motioned for Nash to follow him toward the barracks. From out of a doorway came Robert Maldowney. He

417

threw up his arms and shouted to his comrades when he saw Nash.

"From the mouth of the lion! Praise be to God, Jack. They slew you not."

He ran forward, threw his arms around Nash and hugged him. Nash asked about the women, and Maldowney shook his head.

"Thank the Lord, there's Mr. John." Joab approached him with tears in his eyes. "I'm so sorry, Mr. John. I tried…"

Nash laid his hand on Joab's shoulder. "Not another word. I know you would have laid your life down for them. I don't blame you for what happened."

Mr. Boyd and Dr. Pierce rushed out in urgency.

"We gave you up for dead," said Boyd. "Thank God you're alive. Any news on the women? Is there anything you can tell us?"

"My pains have been rewarded like yours."

"Come, we must talk," said Mr. Boyd.

"We are all anxious to hear of the journey that led Captain Nash back to us, Mr. Boyd," Dr. Pierce interrupted. "But he must have food and rest."

Nash halted his steps and looked to the well-meaning doctor. "Dr. Pierce. It's good to see you."

"And you. It appears you've been through a terrible ordeal. Where is your horse?"

"He now carries Chief Logan on his back as a gift for saving my life."

On the barracks porch sat Black Hawk. He looked up at Nash as he approached. Nash smiled at him. "Black Hawk, my heart cannot say how glad I am to see you."

"You fought bravely, I can tell."

"But with fear racing through my veins."

Inside the barracks, room was made for Nash with much excitement. Ale brimmed over his pewter cup and the helping of venison stew steamed from a wooden bowl.

Resting there to eat and drink, Nash looked at his comrades in arms. There was Robert Maldowney, preacher and protector, a giant of a man in buckskins, with a shock of red hair and a tartan baldric over his shoulder. Beside him sat Mr. Boyd, a man unaccustomed to the wilderness and its hardships. It showed in his face, that and the anxiety for his daughter. His hands rested on the table, fingertips touching fingertips, his pensive gray eyes never leaving Nash's face.

Nash would not have recognized the good doctor if it had not been for the fact he recalled his identity. A serene man, in a hunting shirt, leggings and cap, had cast off the finer black attire of a physician for the fashion of the backwoodsman. Joab sat beside him, his hair a little grayer.

And then there was Black Hawk. Nash knew a change had come over him. Had Theresa Boyd's capture brought on the melancholy showing in his face? He had shaved the sides of his head, and his tuft of hair was fastened with feathers. Upon his face, he wore war paint. No doubt, this was a sign he had declared a personal war upon her captor.

"We found Clarke in the woods dead," said Maldowney. "A brave man and a loyal friend lost to all those who knew him."

Nash's heart was sore because of Clarke. He looked into his mug of ale as the others spoke about him. Each man spoke in turn, then Nash. He told them about his capture, Logan, and Angry Bear.

"My word, Nash. You came so close to them killing you," said Boyd. "What you must have suffered."

"It's nothing compared to losing my wife to LaRoux."

Maldowney patted Nash's shoulder. "Don't worry, my friend. We will not rest until we find her and the others."

They huddled around the table and laid out their plans. They would travel over the Allegheny west. Black Hawk would scout ahead, and they would search every village, every settlement no matter how long it would take.

Black Hawk stood. "If the women escape, they will travel toward the east, over the mountains along the great river. We must watch for them in the forests, listen for their voices on the wind, wait for the sounds of the jays calling. The deer will roam ahead of them. These are the signs we must wait for."

Nash's heart quivered. It was agony to think of her struggling through the wilderness in search of home. How could she and his unborn child survive? It made his search for her even more desperate.

* * *

Dawn rose with the heat of summer. Nash dashed cold water on his face as the others stirred awake. Wiping his jaw with a towel, he went to the window and looked out. The light from the campfire outside the barracks danced in eerie yellow shadows against the stone walls of the fortress.

Atop the parapet stood a sentry, his musket poised in his hand, his eyes fastened on the woods. Then came the alert, the call to arms. Men rushed out, pulling on boots and strapping on powder horns and pouches.

Climbing the parapet, Nash looked over the side. Within the trees, Indians advanced. The men fired and showered the woods with bullets. The parapet filled with smoke and the smell of sulfur. A second rank of men fired as a flood of warriors rushed toward the fort. Several fell under the volley. Tree limbs snapped and bark splintered from the hail of bullets. The crack of muskets echoed across the clearing. The quivering flames of torches weakened against the smoke.

"Handle. Cartridge. Prime!" shouted the officer in charge. Captain Sparks who was destined to be among the Maryland musketmen under Colonel Cresap's command in the coming year looked glorious among his men, dressed in a dark navy coat, white breeches, and jack boots. His men were few in number, but were holding their own.

"May God help us!" he said, standing beside Nash. "Look at the number of savages."

"We outnumber them three to one. They'll not get over the wall as long as we are alert." Nash took aim, fired, and the bullet made its mark. He reloaded his musket and fired again. An arrow whizzed past his head and struck the man behind him in the shoulder.

The Indians fell back into the thick of the forest. Nash crouched on the parapet with his back to the wall, pushing the ramrod through the barrel of his musket. Maldowney panted up to him with a fist full of arrows.

Sparks grabbed the arrows and handed them to Nash. "You know the Indians better than any man among us, having lived out here in this God forsaken wilderness. What arrows are these? Can you read what tribe they belong to?"

"These are Cayuga war arrows, and this is a Shawnee hunting shaft. I can tell by the markings." Nash ran his fingers through the quills.

"I thought those tribes were in the north to make war," said Sparks astonished.

"Apparently a few have stayed behind," said Nash. "I'm not surprised."

Then the scene darkened. Through the haze, a sorry figure ran toward the fort. In ragged buckskins, a man tripped and fell over a stone, then struggled to get up. Once on his feet, he hastened on. The warriors yelled and shot arrows at the fleeing form, hitting the ground near the poor wretch's feet.

"The poor soul," groaned Maldowney. "No doubt a prisoner they've let free to torment us. God help him."

"I know that man!" shouted a fellow soldier.

"Aye, 'tis Adam Lee, the trapper," yelled another, over the din.

Limping and crying out, Adam Lee rushed toward the gate. Sparks ordered the men to fire into the line of Indians, hoping somehow to save the hapless man.

Again, Adam Lee stumbled and struggled to pull himself up. But this time an arrow penetrated his arm. He cried out and tried to move forward. Another arrow sunk into his leg and he fell upon his right knee. He crawled forward, crying out for help.

"In the name of God, open the gate and get that man." Nash started down the ladder.

Sparks yanked him back.

"Do you want that flood of vipers to come into the fort? If that gate is opened, they will kill any man who rushes out."

"We cannot let them murder that man in cold blood." Nash jerked his arm away. "I won't stand here and watch."

"It's too late."

"It isn't. Let me go out and get him."

"They've killed him. Don't you see the trap?"

Nash pressed his lips. He rushed back to the edge of the parapet and saw Adam Lee on the ground. An Indian ran over and pulled out his hunting knife. The Indian grabbed Lee's hair. With a triumphant yell, the Indian retreated to the line of trees, shaking the blood-soaked scalp at the fort. The soldiers and frontiersmen shot at him in one barrage. They cursed the warrior to hell and back, some shooting while others reloaded.

Nash fixed his eyes on the warrior. He raised his musket and took aim. He cocked the hammer. He squeezed the trigger and fired. His bullet struck a tree and missed. The Indians embarked across the Potomac into

Virginia and were gone. Outside the fortress walls, the grassy plane was strewn with a half dozen dead warriors and one poor frontier settler. Not a man inside the fort was killed, but six were wounded.

The sun rose higher drenching the land. Black Hawk met Nash and the others at the gate of the fort. Sunlight touched upon his bronze armbands, and the feathers in his hair waved in the breeze.

And so an hour later, they left Fort Frederick in search of the women they loved, and the man who had stolen them away.

CHAPTER 27

Rebecah lay awake listening to the tree frogs and the crickets. A hoot owl in the forest called. The three were a strange mixture. The sounds were soothing. But the owl's incessant screech seemed ominous in its measure. It was not superstition that attacked her. But the idea of how wild and dangerous the frontier was. The darts of doubt pricked. Fear stabbed. Her soul moaned. All she knew to do was to obey what stirred in her mind and entreat Heaven for herself and the others.

Strengthened, she rose and woke Theresa. Maddie was wide-awake shoving things into a buckskin bag. They had been saving and hiding dried venison, suet, nuts, and maize cakes for days.

Rebecah slipped on her moccasins and drew up the laces. She went to the opening and peered out. The village was asleep. The fire in the center smoldered with red coals. She turned to the others and whispered, "Come. Do not make a sound."

The moon sprayed the forest in a soft misty glow that would light the way. Stars stood out against the black sky. The breeze blew warm against the women's faces and the pines scented the air.

Holding each other's hands, they slipped into the forest, entering it with hearts beating, fearful of discovery as they began their long journey home.

424

They hurried as fast as they could through the dense forests, crossing streams and climbing steep hills. They rested when too tired to go on, and when dawn rose, they stood on a crest and looked out at the vast mountain range before them.

So far to go. She then wondered if they would make it home, or perish somewhere in the mountains. Maddie's hand grasped hers. Theresa put her arm around her shoulder.

"Look at that," Maddie sighed. "Ain't God wondrous?" She pointed to a silver thread in the distance. "There is the river."

The wind brushed Rebecah's face and she drew in a deep breath. "The river will lead us home."

They walked on, pushed until nightfall. Too dark to go on, they huddled together in a grove of hemlock until sunrise.

As the hours came and went, the sun moved across the sky to the zenith. Rebecah felt the first grips of birth pains in the late afternoon, mild at first, then growing more intense.

Jack will find us. He'll come through the woods and run to me, lift me in his arms and take me home.

Maddie knelt beside her. "I had five babies in my young days. All sold to other masters by the time they were six years old. But I ain't gonna cry over that now, Miss Rebecah. I'm gonna help you birth yours."

"I'm afraid, Maddie."

"The Lord made you a strong woman." She checked the baby. "You'll do alright. Your baby's head is down."

"That is good?" Rebecah panted.

"Very good. But you mustn't cry out. For all your might, you got to be as quiet as you can."

Rebecah's hands clung to Maddie and Theresa like a vice. She drew up her legs and bore down. She thought how awful it was to be giving birth in the wilds. She thought how any moment the child would slide forth, and she'd carry the babe nestled against her breast through the woods, across streams, over the mountains, with the hopes that her milk would be enough, that her strength would return.

She pushed again, and thought her teeth would shatter with clenching them.

"You're doing fine. I see the head now," said Maddie. "Push again, Miss Rebecah."

Bearing down, Rebecah bent forward, her hands bracing her knees. A moment later urgency was replaced with joy.

"You have a baby girl, Miss Rebecah." Maddie's voice rang with joyous laughter along with Theresa's as she wrapped the child in torn cloth from her petticoat.

Rebecah reached for her newborn. "Is she alright?"

Maddie laid the bundle in the bend of Rebecah's arm. Tears fell from her eyes as she gazed at the black eyes, the sweet bow mouth, and the tiny fingers. "Indeed she is."

"But her cry is so weak." Tears sprang into Rebecah's eyes.

"Now don't you worry, she's beautiful. She looks like you."

With her heart swelling, Rebecah looked down into the sweet face, moved aside the cloth from her baby's cheek and smiled. "I shall call her Abigail."

"The prettiest babe I ever did see."

"I think so too, Maddie. Ah, her hands are so tiny."

"And you did so well. You'll have your strength back in no time."

"I couldn't have done it without your help. Thank you."

"No need for thanks. Just promise me you'll let me watch this babe grow, let me help take care of her."

"You will be Aunt Maddie to her and stay at Laurel Hill forever. Oh, but she is pretty. Poor child—to be born in the wilderness."

Theresa touched Rebecah's shoulder. "It was better to have had her here than in the village. One of Grey Wolf's wives could have claimed your baby."

"You're right, Theresa. She is mine, and no one can take her from me."

Theresa sighed. "This was the most amazing thing I've ever seen. I'll never forget this day for as long as I shall live."

"We shall guard her well and bring her home," Rebecah said. "Jack and I have a little girl. Now I know we shall make it back."

She rested the remainder of the day, but at sunrise, the women rose from their beds of moss and leaves and made their way along the woodland path toward the east.

Rebecah carried the infant near her breast. She envisioned each step brought her closer to home. She looked up through the trees to the blue sky. Her stomach ached with hunger, but her heart was full.

They stopped beside a stream and drank. Kneeling upon the mossy brink, Rebecah cupped her hand and dripped it into the water. The water tasted sweet and cold.

Theresa knelt beside her. "Are you tired, Rebecah? We can stop if you want to."

"A little farther I think." The babe lifted a fist and cooed. "There is still much daylight left."

"Do you think they will follow us?"

"I don't think so. We've gone quite a distance."

"I'm glad. I feared our captors more than the dangers of the wild, especially LaRoux."

"So did I. Now we mustn't fear, for he is far from us and we will never see him again. We must hasten on, and make as many miles behind us as we can."

"We are close to the river," Theresa said, as they walked on. She paused and lifted her hand. "Look there— a break in the forest and a field before us."

The three women emerged out of the pine grove to a dell of grass and purple thistles. Goldfinches fluttered from the stems to the downy heads. Bumblebees darted here and there, and hovered. A meadowlark sang, and a great hill rose beyond the field, destitute of trees.

Through the field they went, their attire catching the course caresses of the thistles and tall grass. They climbed the hill and reached the summit. Breathless the three women stood silent, looking at the wide vista of row upon row of mountains. The wind fanned their faces. It smelled of pine and wildflowers.

"Have we missed the trail?" Theresa said.

"I hope not." Rebecah raised her hand above her eyes.

"The mountains look as if they go on forever."

Rebecah turned to her friend. "Come, we must cross them."

Theresa moaned. "I'm weary."

"We all are. But we cannot give up."

Rebecah grabbed Theresa's hand, and together with Maddie, they plunged into the heart of the mountain range toward the river with hope in their hearts.

CHAPTER 28

By mid-morning, the sky grew heavy with clouds, the forest dark and brooding. The birds hushed. Anxious and frightened, Rebecah stared at the ominous sky. A storm was coming.

Her babe whimpered and she held her closer. The sucking calmed the infant. She loved her tiny Abby beyond what mortal words could describe, and the desire to protect her was as strong as a mother lion's. Where could they go for shelter? She searched the surroundings for a cave, an overhang of rocks, anything that would provide protection from the elements. She turned to Maddie and Theresa, her hair floating away from her face.

"We must find a safe place before the storm comes," she called over the howl of the wind. "We haven't much time."

The others nodded and moved ahead at an arm's length.

Thunder rolled in the distance, like a giant wave of the sea moving to shore, then crashing upon the world. The forest was thick here, laced with heavy vines that hung from the elms. The sky grew pitch. Rebecah shivered. The thunder was fierce, the lightning blinding.

They were blessed and did not doubt they were watched over. They found in the broken limestone a cave large enough for them all.

429

"Here!" said Theresa, who first saw it. "We shall be safe enough here."

Maddie poked her head inside, and went in with the sturdy walking stick she carried. "No snakes or animals," she called back. "Though if there were animals, we could've eaten them."

"I think I could eat anything at this point." Theresa helped Rebecah sit next to Maddie, and dropped beside them. Three friends, three sisters they had become with their arms around one another.

The cave had dry twigs and moss. Outside were cones and bark. Maddie and Theresa gathered as much as they could. Maddie set to rubbing one stick against another. It took some time, but soon the moss was smoking. The cave glowed with firelight, and their shivering bodies grew warm. The storm rushed through the forest.

"Theresa, take my knife." Rebecah pulled it from the sheath attached to her calve. "Fasten it to Maddie's stick and make a spear."

"Seeing game is one thing," Theresa said. "Killing it is another. I have never hunted before. I don't know how."

"We are hungry. One of us must find something."

Theresa blinked back her tears. "I'll try."

From her dress, Theresa tore strips of cloth and bound the knife to the end of the stick. It was light, sharp, and strong.

Rebecah was starving, and her baby needed her milk. Maddie was growing weak from a lack of food, and the arduous journey. Theresa's eyes were glazed with hunger.

Rebecah took pity on the poor girl. "Here, you take Abigail. I can do this."

"You're sure?"

"Keep Abigail close, and if she begins to cry lend her your finger."

With the weapon in hand, she stepped from the mouth of the cave. She walked under the trees, her feet sinking into layers of leaves. Her mind tossed with her condition and plight. She was dirtier than she had ever been in her life. Her mouth parched, and the lips her husband relished to kiss were cracked. The skin he once caressed no longer felt silky, her hair a mass of tangles. The need to cry overtook her, yet she pushed it back, deep, down, hidden.

She had to remain strong. She could not give in.

The desire to laugh rose. She closed her eyes and envisioned herself a year ago, dressed in soft linen and lace, her body perfumed and her hair shimmering. She was at Endfield dancing with the handsome colonist that pursued her. She remembered how she looked the day she stepped from the coach in Fredericktown. Oh, how the men's eyes followed her.

The wind pushed her back and she said aloud, "Look at me now. Look at me, God." A tear escaped and riveted down her cheek.

Deer crashed through the forest, leapt over fallen trees, disappeared into the brush. She heard an animal cry. Her hand tightened upon the spear. She raised her arm. The rabbit was two yards from where she stood, caught in a tangle of bramble. She stepped slowly, silently. A lump grew in her throat. She had never killed a thing in her life. But it had to be done. She swallowed and before the rabbit could catch her eye, she drove the knife into its side.

Soon the meat simmered over the fire. Rebecah felt strength returning.

"We will make it now," said Maddie in a soft whisper.

Theresa laid her head in Maddie's lap. Maddie's hand smoothed Theresa's hair, like a mother would do.

Rebecah watched the old black woman close her eyes and settle back. She then realized Maddie had hardly eaten a morsel and feared she was dying.

CHAPTER 29

Standing alone on the edge of a cliff made of black shale, Nash watched the sun set in the west over the mountains. Magenta light shone through the trees and faded as a sky of cobalt blue descended.

The breeze strengthened, and he smelled the scent of rain and evergreen. His blue eyes lifted, and he watched a flock of geese fly toward the river. His heart was sick for his beloved. The wilderness was so vast. How could he find her?

Feeling his chest tighten with anxiety, his pain deepened. He sunk to his knees. His soul cried out for help. What could he, a mere man, do to find the lost in these formidable mountains? There was only one who knew, and he begged his God for guidance, for aid, for wisdom.

"Show us the way, Lord."

A hand fell over his shoulder and he turned to see Black Hawk. "Do not worry, my brother."

"We've lost the trail, haven't we?"

"I shall find it again. I will watch the birds and the animals in the forest. They will show which path to follow."

He stood beside Nash with his arms folded over his chest. The tassels of his leggings blew in the light breeze.

"You make it sound so easy, and for you I'm sure it is."

"An Indian knows these things."

Nash paused and watched an eagle bank across the sky. "What we need is a miracle." He kicked a stone over the edge.

"Mr. Boyd looked not so good," Black Hawk said.

"I'm glad Pierce took him back to the fort. For if his daughter is dead in the forest, and he was to find her…if I found Rebecah…"

"My brother mustn't think too hard."

Nash got up and brushed the side of his buckskins. Maldowney drew up beside him.

"Which way now?" he asked.

"West toward that range along the river."

He searched the westward ridge. Venus stood out above the mountains, and the moon rose above it. Black Hawk opened his arms toward the heavens. Nash took a step back, and looked on with his heart breaking for his wife.

Black Hawk sang in a clear golden voice that echoed across the deep ravines and recesses of the mountains.

Lord of Heaven and of Earth, show us the path!
Ehu! Ehu! Ehu!
Master of Heaven and of Life, give us strength!
Ehu! Ehu! Ehu!

Upward Nash gazed, and what he saw took his breath away. The lone eagle he had seen before flew across the face of a great cloud etched in the last silver light of sunset. Its outstretched wings caught the wind and it flew higher. Swooping down it screeched, and something powerful rushed into his soul. He felt her near, smelled her perfume on the breeze, felt the strands of her hair brush over his cheek. He heard her voice faintly, and even fainter that of a babe's cry. He had to find them even if it meant laying his life down, hoping Jean LaRoux would fall into his hands.

* * *

They passed through thick forests along an old Indian hunting trail. The trail was narrow and indiscernible, having been forgotten through the ages. All that day they traveled along it. When night fell, they slept in a grove of hemlocks with inches thick pine needles to cushion the hard ground.

By noon the following day, now closer to the headwaters of the Potomac, to the branch of the Savage, Black Hawk discovered a sign. Nash hurried forward when Black Hawk raised his hand. A piece of blue cloth fluttered from a wild rosebush. Nash pulled it off and closed his hand over it.

They proceeded a mile or more, close to the ridge with the river below. They were to cross it, when Nash caught sight of something moving along the other side. He hurried to the edge of the ridge and lay on his belly. The others followed his lead.

"There's the rogue," he said in a low voice.

Maldowney pushed back his red shock of hair into his hat. "May the Lord render swift judgment upon his soul if it cannot be saved."

"Yes, and allow me to be His instrument."

"Do you see the women?" Maldowney asked.

"No." Nash set his teeth. "I'll kill the cursed blackguard."

Nash pushed his musket butt hard against his shoulder and squeezed the trigger. LaRoux's hand gripped his arm and he stumbled forward. He rolled part way down the hillside, and then scurried like a frightened rabbit back into the brush.

With no time to lose, Nash ran after him. He wanted to find LaRoux and kill him. A flesh wound was not enough.

He thrashed across the river to the other side and climbed the bank. In the forest, Nash looked through the trees, up the ridge. No sign. Just then, an Indian sprang from behind a tree. Nash dodged the attack and swung his musket.

The Indian, a youth, fell backward. He threw his hands over his head and began to chant, shaking and with his eyes rolling back.

"Black Hawk!" shouted Nash. "Either tell me what this savage means, or…"

"He prays his death song," Black Hawk answered. "He is crazy in the head."

"Tell him I won't kill him."

Black Hawk spoke to the boy and the boy, ceasing his song, gazed up at him. Nash pulled him to his feet.

"Ask him where the women LaRoux captured are."

Black Hawk spoke calmly. The boy listened, and the wild emotions that had been driving him settled.

Black Hawk asked him, "What name have your fathers given you."

"Soaring Eagle."

"Where is your village?"

"West, upriver."

"Why were you running, little brother?"

The boy swallowed and his expression turned to grief. "Beyond those trees my father lies dead. He is Grey Wolf, a great warrior. LaRoux led him from the trail of peace, from joining our brothers in war. LaRoux is angry the woman he wanted slipped away with two others. When we returned to the village, we left with LaRoux to find them. Then my father wanted to turn back, and so LaRoux tried to kill him."

Black Hawk turned to Nash and in English said, "They are alive. And they escaped. We are close to them, my brother."

435

CHAPTER 30

Mist rose from the dark hollows of the mountains. Along an Indian hunting path that had been long forgotten and overtaken with moss and dead leaves, the women emerged hungry and tired. Rebecah walked ahead of the others. Her boots were worn through and her clothing torn from branches and thorns. But the steady walking, the fresh water and air, the sustaining roots and blackberries had strengthened her.

Abby, as she was called, thrived at her breast and was a peaceful child. Yet Rebecah knew they needed more to eat, else her milk would cease and her baby die.

Weariness lay in Maddie's eyes. Now thin as a reed, she labored with each step. Theresa now looked a wild thing, her face gaunt and dirty, her hair hanging in a mass of twists.

They passed along a wooded foothill. Below, between two precipitous mountains lay a glade hidden by great trees of pine, walnut, and oak, where sunlight filtered through the breaks like silver stems.

"What is it?" asked Theresa in a quiet voice.

"I see smoke rising above that line of trees," said Rebecah. "It's faint and a distance away, but it means someone is there."

"We must avoid it," said Theresa alarmed. "It could be an Indian camp."

"No, for they set fires in the late evening. It could be Jack."

Rebecah slowed her steps. Theresa and Maddie stood beside her sighing with relief to see a cabin. She felt this too. But as she looked at the flowers of the field, thinking how much more lovely they were arrayed than any silken-dressed ladies at a ball, the reality touched her that she and her friends were no longer alone.

Arm in arm the women emerged from the woods. A shorthaired dog on the porch perked up its ears, stood, and bayed. Rebecah's babe cried.

From the cabin door, a woman put her hand above her eyes.

"There's a woman. Oh, she will help us."

The woman dropped her hand. She shouted for her man who, upon hearing his wife's panicked voice, came running around the corner with musket in hand.

Holding Maddie between them, Rebecah and Theresa moved on hoping this secluded couple would not turn them away. Maddie collapsed in their arms. The baby continued to cry, and would not be comforted. The dog ran ahead of its master and barked.

"Please," Rebecah said with heaving breath. "We were captured by Indians and have escaped. Please, give us shelter until we can go on."

"Come up to the cabin," said the woman. "You've no reason to fear here. Dear Lord, you've an infant with you."

"My daughter Abigail."

"Have you milk to give her?"

"I do. Though I believe not for much longer."

"'Tis easily remedied. We have food aplenty here, and I've a child I'm nursing. What a miracle that you and your wee one survived."

The woman's husband put up his hand, and the women halted in their steps. Rebecah's heart sunk. The man's stature did not trouble her; it was the look in his eyes. He was bearded, and wore the buckskins so prevalent to the backwoodsman. In his appearance, as well as his lady's, he had not starved, nor had he feasted. His face was lined by a hard life. The gray eyes showed suspicion and caution.

"How do I know you haven't been followed? If you have, the Indians will be coming down upon us. I cannot risk it."

He turned away. His wife called him back in an alarming tone. "Are you the man I married? Or are you some cold-hearted creature I do not know?"

Turning his head, he looked at her.

Wide-eyed, Rebecah stood forward. "You mean to turn us away? We are three women in distress, and I with an infant."

"Only a bounder would dare!" Theresa began, but Rebecah put her hand on Theresa's shoulder to calm her. The man frowned.

Abigail continued to cry and Rebecah cradled her. "If you will not take us in, at least give us food and water."

"I would not deny you that," he said.

"But you would deny us protection."

"I have to think of my family."

"That is honorable indeed. Nevertheless, as a man and a Christian, is it not also in your power to help us? For I'm certain we haven't been followed. We've traveled over these mountains for days without seeing another human being. If indeed you fear reprisal, then give us something to carry and we will be on our way, though we are tired and our Maddie is ill."

The man paused and looked at her with a steady yet contemplating light in his eyes. By it, the certainty he was not a cold man by nature could be seen. He lifted his eyes and looked toward the woods. There was no movement within it, no Indian slipping through the brush.

"I believe you," he said. "I've seen one Indian in these parts, and that was six months back. He was an old fellow either lost or looking for a place to die."

"Then we are beyond their reach?" Theresa asked.

"Aye, that may be. Come inside. My Liddy will give you something to eat."

Hours later, after eating a feast of venison stew, the women were hopeful. Next to Liddy was her own babe's cradle, and she rocked him as she talked with Rebecah.

"It is quiet in this place." Rebecah laid Abby in a basket the woman had provided, and folded a blanket over her. "I imagine it is a good life, but there is danger living so far from a settlement or town. Why did you come so far?"

"To get away from those who wished to keep us apart," Liddy said. "It was the only way for us to be happy."

"Your family did not agree with your choice of a husband?"

"They were against it. We could have gone north, but they would have followed us. My father is an unforgiving man and would have gone to any length to keep me from the man I wanted."

"I have loved like you."

Liddy turned her eyes to Rebecah. "Then you know what it's like to suffer for love's sake?"

"Indeed I have known it well, yet the joys of love I have known to be greater."

"I believe there are many women like us in the world."

"More than we may know."

"But I think some of them to be cowards, for they forfeit true love for money and a life of comfort."

"You are brave indeed, Liddy."

"I was a lady once." Her son whimpered and she lifted him from the cradle. "My family has lived in Baltimore for more than a hundred years. The house is a large manor, and the plantation is prosperous. My father raises horses, and has not lacked a single day of his life. My

439

mother is kind but cared not for my happiness in love. She cared not for her own, so why should she have wished anything else for me? She sat silent while my father commanded me to marry where I did not love."

"Why did they reject your choice?"

"My father supports the King. William has revolutionary ideas."

"Ah, my husband faced the same problem while in England. That is where we met. How did you get away?"

"William came to my window during the dead of night. He pulled me out and we stood together beneath the stars in each other's arms. How could we be parted? So we escaped and came here…Tell me your story. It must've been frightening to have been taken by the savages."

Rebecah told her all that had happened, from the day of her father's death to her leaving England to come to the man she loved. She then said, "I fear for my husband."

CHAPTER 31

Morning sunlight drenched the trees of the forest. A night passed beneath a roof, refreshed by food and drink, and a warm blanket. Theresa cared for the woman who once nursed her back to health. Maddie was resigned to whatever was God's will.

"I'll stay or go," she said. "It don't matter to me. I'm old and weary and destined for Heaven."

Standing outside on the porch, Rebecah looked toward the river. She wondered if she should risk a washing. The grime on her body irritated her, and she felt ill from it.

She looked back inside the cabin and told Liddy, "I wish to go down to the water's edge and bathe."

"It's what I do on warm days," Liddy said. "The water will do you good if you find the right pool. You go on. There are plenty of us here to watch your Abby for a while."

She followed a narrow path. Birds stirred in the trees. Dragonflies rested upon wet stones, and a single cabbage moth fluttered over the dying flower of a pink lady slipper.

She listened to the breeze and the gurgle of water moving over the rocks. She glanced up, hearing the caw of a kingfisher. He stood upon a branch, blue-gray in the light, a minnow in the claw of his foot. He whipped it up to his beak and swallowed it, and rising from the branch, flew away.

Awed, she drew off her dress and careworn shoes, and stepped into the water. She scrubbed her limbs, bent over letting the water rush through her hair, through her tattered chemise. Tears came up into her eyes and she began to weep. She splashed the water over her face, and stood there trembling. The torments she had been through surfaced and overflowed.

She walked up the bank and sat beneath a willow.

"God," she whispered, "I will go on believing he is searching for me. Until I reach home, I'll go on believing. But you must make me strong in my faith, gird me up so I do not stumble."

Suddenly her skin prickled. Something near. Something dark and dangerous. A shadow fell over her as she lay in the grass. It blocked out the sunlight that touched her eyelids. It forced away the warmth of the sun on her skin. She gasped. Her eyes flew open and she saw a man standing over her, the thrums of his buckskins quivering in the breeze.

Scrambling away, her feet pushing against the earth, her hands reached for something to protect her. Rebecah tried to cry out, but could not.

As she moved back the man followed, taking deliberate steps until the trunk of a tree prevented Rebecah from going on. She twisted to the right and tried to stand, but he held her wrist.

Then he spoke to her. "Did you think I would not search for you? Did you think I would not find you and take you back to where you belong?"

Rebecah struggled against the man who held her wrists. With swift cruelty, he clasped his dirty hand over her mouth before she could cry out. In horror, her eyes fixed upon his dark ones, and filled up.

Even though her heart was pounding, Rebecah worked her mind, and knew her choices were few. Either struggle and risk LaRoux's knife, or submit and live. If she were to alarm the others, they could fall prey to him. She could not bear to think of her precious infant dead because of her. The Monroes had shown a great deal of kindness. They too had a child. Then there was Maddie and Theresa. No, she would not resist him. She would do whatever he demanded in order to save the lives of the others.

LaRoux ran his eyes over her. "You've had your child?"

She nodded.

"Then you know what will happen to it if you cry out." He removed his hand from her mouth.

"Yes, I know what cruelty you would show, even to a child."

"You will not speak again, but come with me. They will all die if you do not. It would not be hard to do. There's but one man and I watched him go into the woods to hunt."

He touched her hair, brought a damp curl over her shoulder. Then he brought it to his lips and kissed the silken strands. His touch frightened her, repulsed her.

A strange light shone in LaRoux's eyes, a light that said he believed himself triumphant, that he had gained what he desired, and soon would conqueror her. Rebecah looked away and stood back. LaRoux put out his hand and motioned for her to come. It was then she noticed the blood on his jacket.

LaRoux laughed. "Ah, you see my wound? It's but a graze. Do you wish to know how I came by it?"

"Why should I?"

"You will want to know the name of the man who did this."

"It is unfortunate he missed his mark."

"You're sorry he did not kill me?" He drew close and grabbed her by the arm. His mouth curved into a cruel sneer. "I tell you this. I will kill him if we meet again. You will watch him cry like a woman and beg for his life. You will watch Nash die."

Her heart slammed. *Jack!*

When he took her by the arm to lead her away, she looked back at the peaceful dwelling on the knoll, and wondered if she would ever see the ones she loved—her child and husband—again.

CHAPTER 32

The three men hurried on without speaking, keeping their eyes keen and their hearing sharp. They had no time to cover the footprints they made, but made every effort to conceal their going, by mounting great rocks and making over them, rushing over leafy turf, and avoiding the slim, protruding branches of the younger trees so not to break them.

Black Hawk discovered a fresh trail. Moccasin tracks and boot tracks were evident. Several yards ahead, Nash looked out across a glade. What he saw made his blood run cold.

From the shadows of the trees emerged warriors. Fringed scalplocks hung from their leather leggings. Feathers in their hair were those belonging to the eagle and hawk. Hatchets at their belts glinted in the sunlight. Quivers strapped on their backs were full of arrows.

Nash moved back with bravery rising in his heart. Through the black war paint that crossed the Indian's eyes, Nash recognized Angry Bear.

For a moment, he watched the picturesque warrior. He studied the direction of the Indian's eyes, how he planted his feet firm and apart. The warrior's face appeared chiseled with that granite warlike expression that thrives in the heart of the vengeful.

Angry Bear's eyes fixed upon the grove of trees. He held up his hand to his warriors and waited. His eyes narrowed like those of a panther.

"For though I walk through the valley of the shadow of death, I will fear no evil, for thou art with me." Maldowney whispered the verse and drew in a breath.

"We're outnumbered," said Nash.

"I'll go out to them, and when I do, you must hurry from here," Black Hawk said.

Nash yanked him back. "Are you out of your mind, my brother? They will kill you."

Black Hawk hurried out from the trees. Instead of raising his tomahawk and crying out the war whoop, Angry Bear lifted his face and hand.

Nash's nerves were as taut as a bowman's string. Having kept his musket aimed at Angry Bear for several minutes, he blinked his eyes to stay focused. If the Indian warrior raised his weapon to strike Black Hawk, Nash was prepared to cut him down. He was ready to face the consequences, for the sake of his Indian brother's life. But it appeared the two men were speaking to one another with mutual respect, and it baffled Nash. He watched Black Hawk stretch his arm over Angry Bear's, and they laid hands on each other's shoulder.

"A truce you suppose?" Maldowney said.

"It looks that way. But I won't trust it."

Black Hawk turned and walked back to where Nash and Maldowney waited.

"My brother, you must speak with Angry Bear. He has not made war on you, and has sworn his life is yours for sparing his. You must come and listen to him."

"You're quick to trust the man. I've seen the hate in his eyes, and it causes me to doubt any pledge he might make. And what about Robert? Are we to risk his life as well?"

"He will not break what he has sworn—and he has word of your woman."

Maldowney laid his hand on Nash's shoulder. "If it's true he brings word of Rebecah and the women, then you must hear him out. But be vigilant. Black Hawk and I will stand with you. Won't we Black Hawk?"

The Indian nodded.

For a minute, Nash made no answer. Then, rallying all the courage he had, he moved out from the trees and walked toward Angry Bear. Angry Bear drew an arrow through his hands and snapped it in half. He held out the pieces. Nash took the broken arrow in his fist.

"I gave my word I would not take your life. I have given you the broken arrow as a sign there is no war between us."

"There are those of us who wish to live in peace. I desire it, Angry Bear."

"I have heard of your woman. I will tell you this because I too have a woman."

"What do you know of my wife?"

"Two women are in a cabin not far from here that escaped those who took them captive."

Only two? "How do you know this?"

With his expression impassive, the warrior pointed to a mountain that loomed over the valley. "Over this ridge we met LaRoux's men. It is them that say LaRoux has taken a white woman and left her friends. They have broken their pack with him and gone back to their people. You must follow this path along the river. It will take you to the cabin—to the others. There is an infant there they said is the woman's."

His heart slamming in his chest, Nash fixed his eyes on Angry Bear. "We will go to this place. Swear to me, you will not harm those who live there."

Angry Bear squared his shoulders and nodded.

"For this I owe you a debt, Angry Bear." He held out his hand. Angry Bear raised his arm from his side and took hold of it.

CHAPTER 33

Rebecah pressed her back into the large boulder behind her, deluding herself that somehow it would keep her safe from the unimaginable danger she was in.

LaRoux sat around a campfire tearing pieces of the rabbit he had killed and roasted, between his teeth. He stared at her and tossed the bones into the brush.

"Come with me," he said, standing over her.

"I'm weary of walking."

"Get up. There's a brook at the bottom of the hill. I'll take you there to drink and to wash."

She must obey him, or else he would force her. The hill was easy to descend, and below it, the stream flowed through the forest floor of dead leaves. Rebecah got on her knees, cupped her hand and drank. She washed her face and dried it with her ragged sleeve.

She turned to go back up the hill, but as she moved, LaRoux grasped her wrist from behind. The strength by which he held her was gentle, yet with the unyielding hold of an iron shackle.

Looking back, she caught sight of a band of bronze encircling his forearm. Sunlight hit it. Its similarity to the one Black Hawk wore was striking. Below it, she saw the place where her husband's bullet had grazed him. She tried to pull free, but could not match his strength.

"Let your gaze be for me."

She frowned. "I'll have none of you."

"You must decide to either have me or be the wife of an Indian."

"I'll never be persuaded any other way, for I know you for what you are."

"And what am I?" he said drawing closer.

"A thief and a murderer. A kidnapper."

"I'll not deny it. But there are worse sins."

"You have taken me away from my child."

"You'll forget. You'll have others."

"I shall not forget. Do you expect me to love you when you've taken me from my baby and brought so much pain to my life?"

LaRoux released her hand. "You *will* forget."

Rebecah shook her head. "There is one thing you cannot take from me, Monsieur LaRoux—my memories. I wonder. What was it that made you the kind of man you are? Why do you hate so much?"

His face twitched. She had hit a nerve.

"Hate keeps me alive. Hate causes my blood to rush through my veins. Hate triumphs over my enemies."

For a moment, she felt sorry for him. How sad it was for a man to live his life prone to hate and opposed to love.

"Hate brings a man to an early grave, alone, friendless, without another human being to mourn his passing. Is that what you want?"

An angry fire rose in his eyes and he flung her back. "I will tell you what I want. It is you, Rebecah. But I will wait for you to come to me. I know you will—eventually."

"Long ago you gave me cause to fear you," she said. "Now you wish me to hate you even more?"

"I'm not fond of that idea."

"Let me go."

"No, you will go with me beyond the mountains where no one will find us."

"I will not go with you!"

 "You've no choice."

"I do. Drive your knife into my heart. I will not go from this place."

LaRoux drew out his knife and threw it down. Then he crushed her to him and kissed her lips. She would not yield. He pushed her back toward the campfire. She could smell the meat upon the spit, the rancid smoke rising from it.

"Sit," he said, motioning with his hand for her to take some meat.

"I know better than to eat anything offered to me by my captor."

"Very well, go hungry," LaRoux told her. "Soon you will learn to depend on me."

Unable to take any more, she turned away with her hands over her face. She hurried to the rock and fell upon her knees under it. Tears streamed down her cheeks. She dashed them away, and drew herself up.

She must run—run for her life—run for Abigail, for Jack her beloved—even if it meant her life.

Her hair fell free about her shoulders, and she shoved it back from off her face. It felt heavy and dirty. She stood. The ground was soft, but peppered with pine needles and cones, stones and bits of wood. She stepped back, grimaced with pain. The soles of her feet were bruised and bleeding. Not long ago she wore satin slippers and silk stockings. Now she wore rags and there were holes in her shoes. Her legs were bare and dirty, her dress in tatters.

She reached up, touched skin that had once looked like ivory. Now it was burnished by the sun. Each strand of her hair lacked the silken luster Nash loved. Her hands were chaffed.

She wondered if she were ever to hold her babe in her arms again. And would she feel her husband's arms around her? Oh, his arms. The moon climbed the sky and she closed her eyes from the world around her and thought how warm and protected she felt in them.

Starvation got the best of her, and baring the pain gripping her stomach, she took some meat from LaRoux and ate it. Darkness set it, and with it despair and loneliness. Nothing would abate it, not even the soft, fragrant glow of the fire that warmed her.

She stared at the red coals. LaRoux said, "When we reach a village, I'll see to it you have new clothes to wear. Will that please you?"

She did not answer.

"Take off your shoes."

She glanced up at him. As his eyes bore down upon her, she slipped them off. He took them. "I will give them back later. You won't dare try to leave without them."

His hand fastened upon her arm and pulled her up. When he leaned close, she scurried back. Through the firelight, his face was burnt umber and ablaze with want. Fear surged through her.

"It would be easier if you were to give yourself freely," LaRoux said.

"Don't you believe in God?"

"What a strange question."

"You should fear Him. What you are about to do…what you want to do…"

He grabbed her and pulled her against him. She pushed back, beat him with her fists. He pushed her to the ground. She hit him with the full force of her knee. He rolled over onto his side in agony, and she struggled onto her hands and knees. He reached for her as she crawled away, swearing he would kill her if she did not come back. Her heart pounded against her chest and she gasped for breath. He lunged at her. She picked up a handful of dirt and flung it into his face. He fell back blinded.

Time not sparing, Rebecah got to her feet and ran. Sobbing, her hands stretched out into the darkness, her feet stumbled over roots and twigs, stinging with pain.

LaRoux shouted behind her, swearing he would catch up to her and then she would see who her master was.

It was a hill she climbed. The pine needles were like thorns beneath her feet to slip her up and cause her to fall, and cut into her soles. She dug at the earth with her hands, pulling herself up the hill, kicking her feet out behind her until she reached a great outcropping of rock and crawled through cast off leaves and branches until she reached the top and swung herself over.

The ridge of blackened stone escalated into a great precipice overlooking the river. She hurried across the rocks, slips of lichen and moss, tuffs of coarse weeds growing between the cracks.

She raised her hand to her heart, felt it beat some warning to stay true to her flight. She must go on, lose herself in the depths of the forest.

Stars studded the sky and the moon shot its beams through the sycamores. Rebecah could see ahead a short distance. She bit her lip as she moved on, for each stepped seemed more painful than the one before. She looked to the right, then to the left, trying to know which way to go.

So this is what it has come to. This is how it will end. Jack will never find me, for I am to die here in this wilderness.

Before her lay a natural path made by deer. It cut straight through the grove of evergreen.

"Hide me, Jesus, in thy name."

Would he send angels to take her from the world, to rescue her from her miserable flight? Would she not see them stretching out their arms to lift her away?

She crept forward at the top of a cliff overlooking the Potomac. Laying on the rock, she watched it move below in the growing moonlight. How it swirled over the rocks, how the trees shadowed it along the banks.

Sick, hungry, and shattered, she breathed out. "I am a child of the wilderness at last. How quiet it is, how still."

Peering over the edge of the precipice, she saw a shadow fall along the bank, and then movement in the trees.

LaRoux!

Scrambling back, she got to her feet, and hurried into the woods, plunging through brambles of wild rose and grape, stumbling over roots that ensnared her ankles. Her bruised and bleeding feet slowed her, and she tried to endure the pain as she hurried.

She stood still when she heard him shout her name. "Rebecah! I will find you."

She turned full circle, looking for anything that could protect her. What could a stick or rock do now? Desperation filled her. The darkness overwhelmed her. Her mind flooded with crazed fear like a cornered creature.

She turned to the right. A fallen sycamore.

She ran toward it, fell into the leaves, tucked her body beneath it. She gathered leaves around her, pulled down the branches.

Winded, she drew her arms over her head and her knees to her chest. Suddenly the woods were silent. Not a sound, not even wind.

She felt him near, closer and closer. She heard the crunch of a leaf, the snap of a twig. Then she heard his heavy pant, and held her breath.

LaRoux was within yards of where she lay.

Help me, God. Do not let him find me.

She shut her eyes tight, trembled.

Wait. Don't move. Stay still.

Slowly she exhaled. Her heart pounded. For an hour, she did not move, frozen with fear. Looking through the branches she watched the moon and realized death had passed her where she lay. But how far death had gone, she knew not, and wondered if he might not turn back and find her.

A quickening of the heart jarred her. With an aching she remembered why she had left England and come to this wild, unforgiving place. A little smile crept over her mouth.

My beloved. Oh, how she loved him. She crossed the ocean and traveled to the frontier to see him again, to love him again, to be his wife forever and ever. They had a daughter. They were a family.

She pressed her body tighter within her hiding place, imagined her beloved's arms about her. Her body shook with the want to cry. Her hand covered her mouth, the other her eyes to wipe away the tears.

CHAPTER 34

"Two white men and an Indian approaches!"

Mrs. Monroe hiked her skirts above her ankles as she dashed from the back of the cabin to where her husband worked cutting firewood. He dropped his axe and grabbed his musket. Nash, Maldowney, and Black Hawk halted when he raised it and cocked the hammer.

"My name is John Nash. We are looking for my wife, and two others."

Monroe lowered his weapon. "You got an Indian with you, sir, and…"

Nash walked toward him. "Black Hawk is my blood brother. This is Robert Maldowney, a man of the Gospel."

"Come inside." Monroe showed them the way. Mrs. Monroe gasped when Black Hawk ducked his head through the door. Her husband assured her all was well.

Theresa sprang up from a chair. "Captain Nash!" She threw her arms around him. "Oh, poor Rebecah. She has been taken, sir—down by the river. I've been praying…"

"Do not worry, Theresa." He looked into her face and touched her cheek. "I will find her."

Maddie smiled. "The Lord will direct your path to Miss Rebecah. He has got to, sir, cause look here who needs her mama." In her arms, she held a baby and drew back the blanket from the child's face. "Here's your child, your little girl."

Nash's heart leaped and he hurried over to Maddie, looked down into the sweet face of his daughter. Immediately she seized his heart. He handed his musket to Maldowney and took her into his arms.

"My girl," he said, tripping over his words.

"Miss Rebecah named her Abigail. Had her in the woods while we escaped. Ain't she beautiful?"

"As beautiful as a spring day. Look Black Hawk. Look Robert. I've a daughter."

Black Hawk, impassive as ever, raised his brows. Maldowney stepped up to have a look. "A fitting name for her, Jack. *Abigail* means a father's joy."

"And so she is." Nash kissed the little head, and then turned to Monroe. "Sir, I know my wife was taken. Will you show me the place? I and my brother will follow that trail and find her."

Monroe nodded. "It's just down the hill at the riverbank."

"I have one other request. Do you have a horse?"

Monroe shifted on his feet. "I do."

"Will you lend it to my friend here, so that he may ride to Fort Frederick? Miss Boyd's father and intended are there. He will bring them back with mounts and supplies."

"A good plan, sir. For the women are too worn out to travel by foot. My horse is in the barn."

"I will saddle him and be on my way," Maldowney said, and went out.

Nash turned to Theresa, saw a mix of concern and hope in her eyes. "I will pray, sir, God will make your feet as hinds' feet, that you are swift to find Rebecah and bring her back to all of us."

* * *

Standing above the river on a precipice of rock, they could hear deer crashing through the forest. Black Hawk drew out his long knife. Nash's finger looped inside the trigger of his musket and his thumb pulled back the hammer. He looked down at the river. The muscles in his arms contracted when he saw a lone figure pass between the trees and disappear.

He glanced at Black Hawk. "LaRoux?" he said, speaking low.

Black Hawk nodded. "A man, yes."

Together they moved ahead, silent and with stealth. "Look," said Black Hawk. Looped over a branch he found a strip of linen. He pulled it free. "She's left a sign."

Nash looked back at the precipice thinking how she had to have stood there. She was near. He wanted to call out to her, but if it were LaRoux he risked endangering her.

Stay where you are, Rebecah. I'm coming.

With his musket in hand and his heart pounding, he sprinted ahead. He knew LaRoux too was searching for her, and he prayed he would find her before his enemy.

* * *

Rebecah feared if she were to stay curled under the fallen tree that she would give into the desire to close her eyes for good and never wake again. She lived, but she had become a gaunt being, hardly able to go on. And her mind was weak along with her body. If help did not come soon, she knew she would not be long for this world.

She crawled forward, knowing it were a danger. Yet, the darkness hid her from LaRoux. Perhaps he had gone far ahead of her by now.

Moaning and biting her lip, she crawled out. Sunlight poured through the trees. Her body stiff from not moving, she stood trembling with the realization she had come close to the edge of a great cliff. Rough pines jutted through its face. She looked at the gorge below. Ribbons of mist moved in the lowlands. She turned east toward home.

"Rebecah!"

Startled she shrunk back. She breathed heavy and looked at the ground wide-eyed and frightened. Then she ran in the opposite direction of the voice, stumbled, and fell. Clambering up, she struggled on.

Sudden as the wind, startled deer bounded past her and scattered into the forest. Then she saw a face she hoped never to see again. LaRoux had climbed the hillside. He stood there in the gray light very close. His dark eyes contracted with a sudden burst of sunlight.

Rebecah knew if she were to run, he would stop her. Trapped, she struggled not knowing what to do. Her eyes glanced to the left where the rock fell away into a cliff-side. She inched her way toward it.

LaRoux's eyes were fixed upon her. He held out his hand to her. "That would be a foolish way to end your life."

"Would it?" Her voice trembled, her hands shook. The wind blew her hair back from off her face and shoulders. She moved forward and stood at the edge. Her battered feet felt the sharpness of the rock.

Below her were elms and oaks, sycamore and spruce. Her eyes filled with blinding tears. She did not wish to die, but what was left for her now?

Her tired body shivered. Tears slipped from the corners of her eyes. She closed them and being prepared for either LaRoux or the cliff, she heard her beloved's voice whisper on the wind.

"Move away, my beloved. Move back."

Could it be true? Her eyes shot open and she looked down. Coming up the rocks was Nash with his musket and powder horn strapped over his shoulder, and Black Hawk moving to the right of him. She froze with the feeling of elation, wondering if her mind deceived her.

Digging his knee into a crack in the cliff, Nash pulled himself up beyond LaRoux's view. He stood. His back was to the vast emptiness, and the wind shoved against him. At last, he faced LaRoux, who turned at Nash with a wild and fierce look. Like lightning, his knife flashed in his hand, and he passed it in front of him.

Nash pulled his musket forward and took aim. "Rebecah," he said. "Move away from his reach."

* * *

LaRoux sneered. He paced the rock, passing his knife between his hands.

"To shoot me like a dog would be murder," LaRoux said. "Put down your musket and draw your knife to make this an even fight."

"You're in no position to speak of murder, LaRoux" said Nash. "You've done the foul deed enough."

"Shoot then. Or cross my path."

Nash lowered his musket and yanked his knife from its leather sheath.

"Know this white man. If I kill you, I will have your wife, and when I'm done with her, I will wear her beautiful hair upon my belt."

Then he leaped forward and plunged his knife into Nash's shoulder. Down they went together near the edge of the cliff. Nash kicked LaRoux off, pressing his hand against the wound, blood oozing between his fingers. He rolled away from the dangerous edge and got to his feet.

LaRoux sprung, caught him by the wrist and throat. In turn, Nash held back the murderous hand that held the knife, and strove to free himself from another blow.

Locked together, they struggled backward and forward along the rocky precipice, the glare of the sun striking upon their buckskins.

LaRoux's eyes were fierce and hungry for blood. He pushed Nash back and struck his fist against his wounded shoulder. Shearing pain shot through him. His blade dropped from his hand. He heard the clanging sound it made as it fell down the rocks.

At that moment, Black Hawk climbed the edge of the cliff and stood forward, his face stern and concentrated.

"Black Hawk. Have you come to glut your revenge?" said LaRoux.

Black Hawk replied by drawing out his knife and staring hard at his enemy.

Nash noticed the copper bands around each man's arm. "What revenge does he speak of, Black Hawk? Tell me, for I will not let him have your blood this day!"

Black Hawk took a step forward. "We are of the same mother. Yet his blood is not that of my honorable father. For his evil he crushed the heart of many."

"Because of you I was cast out," shouted LaRoux. "For it, watch your friend die. Then I will have your life too."

LaRoux raised his knife. Black Hawk dove between the two men, and the knife plunged into his chest. The blood poured out from his body, pooled onto the stones. He staggered forward, grasped LaRoux by the arm. In the struggle, they fell together over the precipice. Nash's heart slammed against his chest. He gasped over and over, heaved for air.

"Black Hawk!" *No, my brother. Not you.*

With the horror of it, he staggered to the edge and fell to his knees. Below LaRoux lay dead, his neck broken, his body twisted. Nearby Black Hawk's body lay between two pines.

Tears blurred Nash's vision. He balled his fists and struck the ground. "No! No!"

Was it so wrong for a man to weep at such an hour? Was it wrong for his heart to plow into the depth of harrowing grief at the sight of his friend lying broken and lifeless? Was it wrong for him to press his fists against his eyes and cry out? Black Hawk, his brother, his friend. Black Hawk who had tended him when wounded. Black Hawk who had loved him as a brother. Black Hawk who had traveled with him through the wilderness and had laid his life down was gone.

Rebecah knelt beside him, wrapped her arms around his waist, and cried. He turned to her, touched her face, her hands, and crushed her to him in a long desired embrace. Together they wept. Together they grieved.

For a long time they were silent. Then he pulled her up. She fell against his arm and he held her fast. He kissed the hand that she had laid across his chest, then her cheeks and her lips. He brushed her hair back from off her face, and wiped away her tears.

Nash buried Black Hawk where he had fallen, and he and Rebecah spoke a prayer over that lonely place.

* * *

When they reached the cabin, they smelled venison roasting on Mrs. Monroe's spit. There was Maddie sitting on the porch with her hand waving. In her arms, she held Abby, whose tiny hand rose too.

Nash carried Rebecah in his arms across the span of meadow grass. "Abby waits for us, my love," he said. Then he paused. Beyond the bank of trees came riders. "Look, it's Robert. He has Joab, Mr. Boyd, and Dr. Pierce with him.

Theresa came out onto the porch. When she saw her father, she ran toward them. Pierce hurried to her, lifted her hands to his lips, and then took her to her father who wept tears.

"Oh, Jack," Rebecah sighed. "There is joy this day regardless of our grief. I believe he loves her."

Sorrow was felt by all at the loss of Black Hawk. Theresa knew he had loved her, and so she went and stood a ways off from the others beside the stream to think of him. Nash's heart was broken and bleeding, but the presence of his wife and newborn daughter overshadowed the grief.

Together with the Monroe's they sat together inside the cabin with a good fire, eating good food. Rebecah washed Nash's wound and bandaged it. They spoke of their ordeals. But John and Rebecah Nash did not speak, for they felt that precious solemnity of happiness as they sat together, Rebecah cradling their baby in her arms and Nash gazing at the sweet face belonging to his daughter.

At sunrise, they journeyed with the others into the woods as one, down a path leading to a great valley and home.

EPILOGUE

Rebecah stood by the window. Snow fell through the haze of moonlight, the land soft blue, covered in frost.

Nash's hand caressed her forearm. She leaned back against his chest. His arms went around her and pulled her close. Together they looked out at the fields and the everlasting mountains beyond them. His cheek lay against hers until their lips touched.

Her eyes looked into his, moist with happy tears. Happiness and love had slain sorrow. She did not speak. Her look told him everything. The war with Britain would reach the wilderness, and he would leave her for a time. She knew. She understood.

Joab would die at Laurel Hill. Maddie would follow months later and be laid to rest beside him. Theresa would marry Dr. Pierce and have six children. Robert Maldowney traveled on into the wilderness to preach the Gospel. And by the time Great Britain and America were at peace, Lady Margaret came to live at Laurel Hill. The Harcourts sailed with her to America, and David set up a law practice, Lavinia a welcoming home to all that stood on Court Street.

Abby would grow up to marry a lawyer, live in town, have a houseful of children, support her husband's practice, and become an accomplished portrait painter.

As for John and Rebecah Nash, for the rest of their lives they would bear the burdens of the other. For, dear reader, a three-fold cord, whether made of scarlet thread or brown jute, is not easily broken.

AUTHOR'S NOTE

Outside my back door, I can view the rolling Catoctin Mountains. I've tried to imagine what life was like in the days when they loomed over what was referred to as the Wilderness. Fredericktown was a Maryland frontier village in the 1700s, nestled in a peaceful valley. Through these novels, I have endeavored to paint with words images of a time long ago.

The story of Chief Logan's family is based on historical events though there are conflicting accounts of what actually happened, as well as the massacres at some of the homesteads, and the sinking of the Peggy Stewart. John Wesley's sermon is from an account in his diary.

There are other characters who lived and breathed in the time of the American Revolution mentioned in this book that I have fictionalized.

Archibald Boyd ~ Fredericktown's town clerk.

Logan ~ Indian chief and peacemaker.

Mellana ~ Chief Logan's wife.

Koonay ~ Chief Logan's sister.

Shikellimus ~ Chief Logan's father.

Thomas Johnson ~ Frederick County lawyer, delegate to the Continental Congress, Brigadier General during the Revolution, supplier of ammunitions from the Catoctin Furnace, and first governor of a free Maryland.

John Hanson ~ Deputy Surveyor, sheriff, county treasurer and Chairman for the Committee of Observation in Frederick County, Maryland. One of Maryland's leading Patriots.

Thomas Stone ~ Maryland delegate to the Continental Congress and signer of the Declaration of Independence.

Samuel Chase ~ Maryland representative to the Continental Congress and signer of the Declaration of Independence.

William Paca ~ Annapolis lawyer, along with Chase co-founded the Ann Arundel chapter of the *Sons of Liberty,* signer of the Declaration of Independence.

Anthony Stewart ~ Co-owner of the ship the *Peggy Stewart*, burned in the second American Tea Part in Annapolis Harbor.

Michael Cresap ~ Maryland frontiersman.

Jacob Greathouse ~ Believed by many sources to be the leader in the massacre of Logan's family.

John Wesley ~ English preacher and evangelist.

OTHER NOVELS BY RITA GERLACH

The Rebel's Pledge

Surrender the Wind

And

THE DAUGHTERS OF THE POTOMAC SERIES

Before the Scarlet Dawn

Beside Two Rivers

Beyond the Valley

Rita Gerlach's website

www.ritagerlach.blogspot.com

Made in the USA
San Bernardino, CA
17 May 2014